THE
POSY RING

BOOK ONE OF
THE ANNALS OF FLOWERFIELD

Catherine Czerkawska

Saraband

Published by Saraband,
Suite 202, 98 Woodlands Road,
Glasgow, G3 6HB,

and

Digital World Centre, 1 Lowry Plaza
The Quays, Salford, M50 3UB
www.saraband.net

ISBN: 9781912235063
ISBNe: 9781912235070

10 9 8 7 6 5 4 3 2 1

Printed and bound in Great Britain by Clays Ltd, St Ives plc.

Praise for Catherine Czerkawska's writing:

'A powerful story about love and obligation…a persuasive novel, very well written.' JOHN BURNSIDE

'Moving, poetic and quietly provocative.' *INDEPENDENT*

'Clear-eyed, succinct…a much more substantial piece of work than its slim page count suggests.' ROSEMARY GORING, *NATIONAL*

'Take any aspect of the novelist's art and you'll find it exemplified here to perfection.' BILL KIRTON, BOOKSQUAWK

'Heart-warming, realistic and page-turning.' LORRAINE KELLY

'Beautiful – lyrical and sensual by turns.' HILARY ELY

'Blisteringly eloquent.' Joyce Macmillan, *SCOTSMAN*

'A romance of Scotland's great Romantic. There is a pastoral beauty… their courtship is drawn gorgeously. *The Jewel* finally gives voice to Jeany Armour, the girl who sang as sweetly as the nightingale, who was muse, mother, wife and lover to Scotland's national poet. This is her song.' *SUNDAY MAIL*

'Uplifting…does much to put right the wrongs of historians. The characters come to life beautifully on the page…Serves as a superbly researched biography of a deeply admirable woman who until now has been…unjustly neglected.' UNDISCOVERED SCOTLAND

'Beguiling and enchanting…Czerkawska is an excellent storyteller… Full of suspense…and lush sensuality, so you can almost feel the grass brushing against your skin, and smell the honeysuckle in summer evenings.' *SCOTTISH REVIEW*

'A beautiful historical novel.' EDINBURGH CITY OF LITERATURE

'Czerkawska tells her tale in a restrained, elegant prose that only adds to its poignancy.' *SUNDAY TIMES* (SEASON'S BEST HISTORICAL FICTION)

'A compelling read, … … … of history, nature and romance.' …

Also by Catherine Czerkawska

This is for my late and much missed mum,
Kathleen Czerkawski,
who loved vintage long before it became fashionable.

GARVE
EILEAN GARBH

N

Lighthouse
Remains of Clachan
Allt na Breac
Tobermore Well
Loch an Tarbh
Standing Stones
Dun Tarbh
Dunfaire Broch
Dunstrone Broch
Fish Farm
Glen Laogh
Ardbeg Clachan
Walled Garden
Sgurran Fithich (Raven's Peak)
Auchenblae
Portree Bay
Deserted Village
Celtic Cross
Clootie Tree
Viking Remains
Meall Each and Dun
Dunblae
Eilean a Cleirich
Dundarrach
Scoull Village
Glen Each
Currich Farm
Scoull Bay
Port na Currich
Loch Dubh
Scoull Hotel
Port Manus
Ardachy house and gallery
Boathouse
Kilmory
Ailech
Distillery
Drumellen
Carraig
Caladh Village
Auchenairney Farm
St-Columba's Kirk
Keill Bay
Ealachan House
Keill Village
Manse
Primary School
Eilean Colm
Port a' Ghille
Kilcolm
Hotel
Knockbaird
Hilltop Town
Lighthouse
Dunshee
Kilcolm Bay
Brigid's Well

AUCHENBLAE
SEEN FROM THE BAY

PROLOGUE

The islands of Scotland are home to a fair mixture of dark-eyed, dark-haired folk and it is popularly supposed that they are descendants of survivors of the Armada debacle, sailors who came ashore in Scotland, either voluntarily seeking sanctuary or unwillingly as victims of storm and shipwreck. We should, however, remember that the native Celts are as likely as not to be dark, although there are red-headed Scots and fair-haired Vikings here in plenty.

Tales of the Armada and Spanish treasure may have been exaggerated by subsequent generations, although there is certainly some evidence of the wreck of a Spanish galleon in Tobermory Bay. Those Spaniards who were unfortunate enough to founder off the coast of Ireland might, had they survived, have told a tale of the wholesale slaughter of those who surrendered, albeit at the hands of government troops rather than the natives, who may have been more disposed to be sympathetic. The fate of those who landed in Scotland was a little different.

It must be borne in mind that the great Spanish expedition followed on from the execution of the Scottish queen by her cousin Elizabeth. If the politics of the time were complicated in England, they were doubly so in Scotland, with something of a divide between Highland and Lowland allegiances. Even that division, like all such history, is far from clear, being open to misinterpretation and prejudice.

Without knowing the personal tales of the survivors who reached these small Scottish islands in comparative safety, we can only guess at the nature of their lives thereafter. Some were returned to Spain and of those, a great number perished on the voyage. A few remained. Their stories seem to be lost in the mists of time and even official records may have been deliberately falsified for the safety of all concerned. The Spaniards were, after all, the enemy.

From *Island Tales*, Rev. Bartholomew Scobie
Edinburgh 1900

ONE

Daisy glimpses the house as the ferry nears the island, a brief, tantalising hint of grey stones that seem to have become a part of the hillside, embedded in it, as objects become embedded in ancient trees. She was on the island only once before, and she's hardly even sure that she recognises the house, not until she's on the lane, peering in through the rusting wrought-iron gates on the landward side. Memory plays tricks but she knows that she must have seen it three times, all those years ago.

Thrice. Like a charm.

Her father wouldn't willingly have pointed it out to her on the way to the island. She's sure of that now. So the first sight must have been as they climbed the hill, when they had been intent on the task in hand. She had seen it briefly, in passing, but there had been no time to stand and stare. All the same, it comes back to her with a peculiar intensity as soon as she sets foot in the narrow lane that leads to nowhere but the hill. She can feel her father's hand in hers, his fingers calloused from the fiddle, and the smooth band of his wedding ring. He smells of Imperial Leather soap and some mysterious, indefinable herbal scent, and he has tied his mane of dark hair back into a ponytail. She remembers the perfume of flowers and wanting to pick them. She was always picking wild flowers in those days and always disappointed that their blooms drooped so quickly in their jam jars of water. She had tried to pull away from him, drawn to campion and vetch, but he had said, 'No,

3

Daisy. Maybe later. But let's do what we've come to do first, eh?'

He had it stored away inside his T-shirt, the wish.

'Next to my heart!' he had said, with a grin that was no grin at all, folding up the white silk with the words written on it. She had copied it out laboriously, sitting at the folding table in the warm van. In marker pen so that it would fade slowly. That was the way the magic worked. As the words faded, so your wish might come true.

'It's worth a try,' her father had said, with a little grimace. 'Anything's worth a try.'

She was worrying about the scarf that belonged to her mother, a white silk scarf, a precious possession. But her father said it didn't matter and scarves were replaceable.

Now, she remembers the lane with its profusion of flowers and this house, glimpsed only in passing back then, behind its wrought-iron gates. She had badly wanted to stop and look at it, momentarily entranced by some quality of mystery. She was a great one for stories, a great reader, even then. 'Daisy always has her nose in her book,' her mother would say. The house, glimpsed so briefly in passing, looked as though it belonged in a story. She had wanted to stop and gaze at it, drinking it all in, but her father had pulled her onwards.

She had sensed a kind of panic in his voice.

'No. No, Daisy, we can't stop *here*.'

'Why not? It's an interesting house.'

'Because somebody might see us.'

'Who? There's nobody here. It looks empty.'

'It isn't empty, Daisy. It isn't an empty house. I think somebody lives in it.'

Even then, even as a child, she had thought he seemed both certain and nervous. As though he knew who lived there. As though he didn't want to be seen by whoever might be looking out of those windows. It had been raining that long-ago morning, the kind of torrential Scottish rain that people call 'stair rods' after a dry spring, but the sun had come out and the air in the lane was hot and humid and sweet-smelling. The lane was full of flowers: late bluebells, early meadowsweet and, above them, a riot of creamy honeysuckle and wild roses, pink, white and every shade in between. And birdsong. The birds were singing their hearts out after the rain. They had disturbed them as they walked, and she could hear the beat and flutter of their wings among the leaves.

'No. No, Daisy, we can't stop *here*.'

'Why not? It's a lovely house.' But his fear had been infectious, and they had hurried on.

*

Today, she has parked the blue Polo in a muddy clearing, hardly a lay-by at all, uncertain about parking at the house and unsure about being able to turn around at the other end of the lane. She feels a throb of anticipation, and there it is. The house again, just as she has remembered it without really remembering its exact whereabouts: a huddle of stone walls half hidden at the end of a green lane, beyond rusted iron gates. A faded wooden sign, to the right of the gate, has the single painted word: Auchenblae, just visible, although another winter will probably obliterate it completely. The house feels undisturbed, sunk deep in time. Dreaming. She puts her hand into the pocket of her jacket and brings out the heavy bunch of keys that the solicitor has given her. They feel too ancient, too large and unwieldy to be the keys to any real house. She imagines herself walking along the soft, mossy driveway. But she is in two minds. Should she climb the hill or explore the house? Which should she do first? Does she want to climb the hill at all? Why is she so reluctant? Why is she hesitating?

She dredges up the memories of that previous time.

It had been hard to breathe beneath the stunted island trees. Airless. And besides, she had been holding her breath. Now, she has no very clear memory of the climb. Her memories of the walk are just a jumble of green leaves, the track winding on and on through willow and birch, rising beneath their feet. She had grown tired in the airless lane. The hill had seemed steep, but probably wasn't. Just that she was smaller back then. Maybe he had carried her for a little while, giving her a piggy-back. It was what he had done so often, her tall father, carrying her easily.

'Gee up,' she would have said, clinging to his ponytail. 'Gee up, horsey!'

Viola Neilson. That was her grandmother's name, the grandmother she had never met, never known. Jessica May. That was her mother's name. Jessica May Neilson, born in 1960 when Viola was forty and still unmarried. A nine days' wonder, surely, on this island. A scandal. But Viola was alone in the world with inherited money and a house and she wanted the child. She could and did make her own arrangements. Sweet Jessica May. Daisy remembers her mother's warmth, her gentleness, the flowery scent of her, as though she had somehow absorbed the scent of her own name. Sweet May. Thinking about it now, she can see that Jessica May must have inherited Viola's determination at least. Perhaps the mildness had been deceptive after all, or reserved only for her husband and her small daughter.

Home for Daisy at that time was the van. Warm and cluttered. If it had been shabby and a little less than clean, she didn't remember. Children seldom notice such things unless they impinge on their comfort. And the van was comfortable, with cushions, throws, the scent of patchouli and ylang-ylang. Joss sticks. Candles. Nineteen-year-old Jessica May Neilson had met Rob Graham when he was playing the fiddle at a folk festival on the island. Bravely, she had stood up and sung with him at an open mic session in one of the pubs. It must have been love at first sight. A *coup de foudre*, the French call it. Irresistible. Soul mates right from the start. But Daisy had never been able to talk to her mother about it. Jessica had died too soon, much too young, so she had only her father's word for it, and Rob's account had been patchy at best. 'She had a voice like a skylark. She sang and the sun came out. She was magic.'

Daisy had used her imagination – and the few surviving photographs – to fill in the rest, to fill in the gaps in her knowledge of the pretty woman, long red hair blowing in the wind, smiling indulgently at Rob. But there is so much she doesn't know. So much still to find out. And perhaps the key is here, now. Along with this bunch of ridiculously heavy iron keys that weighs down her pocket.

When Rob left the village with his fiddle, his *bodhrán* and his suspect cigarettes, he took lovely Jessica May with him in his painted van. She left without a backward glance. She left her mother, she left her home, she left the village. She would sing and Rob would play, 'Gypsy rover came over the hill, down to the valley shady.' It was their song. 'He whistled and sang till the green woods rang, and he won the heart of a lady.'

They were married long before Daisy was born. Her mother had emphasised that. 'We were married a whole year before you were born, Daisy Daisy.' Her father still does that: the affectionate doubling of her name like the old song about the bicycle made for two. Not that it would have made any difference to Daisy whether they were married or not, but it seemed to make a difference to Jessica May. They had travelled about and Jessica May had home-schooled Daisy for a while.

'I always thought,' said Rob, many years later, 'that they would meet again, make up the quarrel. Viola didn't approve of me, the little she knew of me, which wasn't much. She presented your mother with an ultimatum. Bad move. They were so alike. But Viola would have loved you. I'm sure of it. I never thought it would go on that long. I tried to persuade your mum to do something about it, but she liked to do things her own way. At first she didn't want to contact home and then she didn't feel she could. Too much water under the bridge. She was afraid, I think. Afraid of rocking the boat. Afraid of upsetting things.'

When Daisy was eight, Jessica May had fallen ill, fading away as though somebody had enchanted her. Daisy remembers her mother growing thinner and frailer. Somebody had taken her warm, vibrant mother and left this strange attenuated creature in her place. A changeling. At the end, it was as though all that was left in the van was love. Love and pain. And then there was nothing, because her mother had been taken to hospital where everything was clean, white and impersonal. Hard-edged. Nothing like the van with its sprawled cushions, its crocheted throws.

It was then that they had copied out the words of the wish, writing them carefully on white silk, sailing to the island, labouring up the track that led to the Clootie Tree at the top of the fairy hill: Dunblae.

'Do you think it'll work?' she had asked and her father had said, 'It'll do no harm to try.'

At the top of the hill, she remembers, the atmosphere changed. The track was a friendly place, breathless with heat, loud with birds. But the top of the hill was a different matter entirely. Even then, as a child, she had been aware of a certain foreboding. Later, she learned the word 'numinous' and knew that it described the hill. But it was more than numinous. It was other-worldly in no good way. For the first time ever, she had been afraid of a place, rather than afraid of a person or an event. The place itself frightened her. The tree – bending with the prevailing wind, clinging onto life amid the rocks – frightened her. If her father had not been there to reassure her, she would have taken to her heels and run back down the track, back to the van that was and always had been their sanctuary. The tree was a gaunt and ancient hawthorn and it was festooned with rags, the clooties that gave it its name. They fluttered from its many hoary branches, bizarre washing hung on lines. Wishing rags. Although she had no words to describe it at the time, the visit had stayed with her. As an adult, she realised that it was the intensity of the emotion that had unnerved her. Each piece of cloth was imbued with an individual sorrow, a sense of longing,

8

like their own for Jessica May to be well again. She could feel it. The panic and desperation were almost tangible. The desire for the restoration of some balance. Some hope for the future.

'Where is it?' her father asked.

She pulled the silk scarf from her backpack.

'Here it is.'

He was tall enough to tie it onto the tree, pushing other pieces of rag aside to make room for it.

'What now?' she asked. 'What do we do, Dad?'

For the first time ever, he seemed to be at a loss. 'I don't know, hen.'

'Should we say a prayer?' Ever since her mother had fallen ill, the van had been in one place, a permanent campsite. And Daisy had been going to a proper school, a small primary school where they sometimes went to church, where the priest sometimes visited, where they said prayers.

'I don't know any prayers.'

So Daisy said one. 'Our Father who art in heaven...'

'I didn't know you knew that.' He stroked her hair.

'We say it at school.'

'I don't think it's the right prayer for a place like this,' he said uneasily. 'Do you, Daisy?'

'What do you think we should say then?'

'Your mother would know. But I'm afraid I don't.'

'I know another one. "Hail Queen of Heaven." But it's a song, really. A hymn.'

'Say that one then. Or sing it. Can you sing it?'

'I think so.' She stood with her hands steepled, palms together, as they did in school, and she sang, 'Hail, queen of heaven, the ocean star, guide of the wanderer here below, thrown on life's surge, we claim thy care, save us from peril and from woe. Mother of Christ, star of the sea, pray for the wanderer, pray for me.' She repeated the last two lines and he joined in. He could always pick up a tune in no time.

9

He nodded. 'Yes. That's better. That makes sense. Pray for the wanderer. That's us.'

At last, they turned away and retraced their steps down the hill. She had expected more. She had expected magic. A miracle. The heavens opening. A chorus of angels at least. She couldn't help feeling disappointed, although she pretended that she believed in it. At the bend in the track they turned around one last time. She saw their pathetic flag of white silk, already blending with the other rags suspended there. So many wishes. Then they were walking downhill, slipping quietly past the house, past Auchenblae. He pulled her along, not letting her linger there.

'Come on,' he said. 'Hurry. Hurry.'

Once again, she had wanted to stop, fascinated by the obvious age of the house, like a mini castle, she thought. Even then, even though she was a little girl, it had seemed quite magical. Now it seems smaller, at least from this side, although she can tell that there is more of it on the sea rather than the landward side. But her father wouldn't stop. The van was tucked away in a lay-by. They climbed in and drove off, drove straight onto the ferry and away. He didn't even wait to make tea. 'We'll stop later,' he said.

He had reluctantly pointed the house out to her one last time, her third sight of it, when they were safely on the ferry, and then only in response to her excited questions. They were leaving it far behind, his relief palpable, the house and the hill and then the whole island of Garve dissolving into the mist. She had expected a miracle, but none came. Her mother lingered for a few more weeks only. The wish lasted longer than Jessica May.

She has never been back since. In fact, she had almost forgotten about it until the unexpected arrival of the official letter. Daisy hesitates between the lane and the house, still convulsively clutching the keys in her pocket. There had been nothing random about her father's knowledge of the house, the hill and the tree. He knew all about it, because he had been here before. *And how*, she thinks.

TWO

When the solicitor's letter came, she had been doubtful at first, wondering if it was a hoax. She had called her father. He was playing at some festival down south. It's what he does. One of the grand old men of folk. That's what they call him, although he doesn't think of himself as particularly old and he isn't. Perhaps it's just that he seems to have been performing, playing the fiddle, for years.

'I'm a baby boomer,' he says, grinning. 'We don't get old.'

The young fans like him, give him the kind of respect that would have amused him when he was a young musician himself. Now he tolerates it. He has always been a kindly man. His music matters more to him than almost anything else. Except for Jessica May. Except for his daughter. After his wife died, he had sold the van, moved to Glasgow for a while, rented a flat so that Daisy could go to school. He had taken whatever work he could find and he had been reasonably successful. When the landlord decided to sell the tiny West End flat, he had managed to buy it so that Daisy would always have somewhere to call home. There had been gigs in pubs, session music, private tutoring. One year – a good year – he had played for a television advertisement and as well as the mortgage, that had bought Daisy new clothes, a bike, a school skiing trip. He played the fiddle, people said, as though he had sold his soul to the devil. Perhaps he had. He still does. But everyone knows the devil has all the best tunes.

She had read the letter aloud to him over the phone. There was a long silence. He sighed.

'Auchenblae,' he said. 'It means Flowerfield, I think. In Gaelic.'

'Yes. The house. My grandmother died and, Dad, she left the house to me. Viola's left everything to me. I had no idea. No idea it was hers. You never said a word. Never told me where Mum used to live. Gone away, you said. Lost touch. Why didn't you tell me, Dad? I could have found her. Could have visited her. Could have got to know her.' She could hear the resentment in her voice and tried to moderate it. He had never been less than caring where she was concerned. He must have had his reasons.

'I didn't know she was still alive. I didn't see how she could be, really. She must have been a great age.'

'She was. But that day. That day when we walked up the hill. That day when we made the wish. She would have been alive then. Viola. She would have been there then.'

'Maybe. Probably. Yes.'

'You wouldn't let me stop. You never told me you even knew the place. Why?'

'To tell you the truth, I was afraid, Daisy. I was afraid.'

'Of what, for goodness sake?'

'Of losing you.'

'How could you have lost me?'

'Your mother was so ill. But she wouldn't give in. I thought, if Viola knew, she would have wanted you. And back then, she might have got you. Your mother was dying, Daisy. I knew that. They wouldn't have left you with me. Not if Viola had stepped in.'

'I don't see what difference that would have made. She was only my grandmother. You were my dad. Nobody could have kept us apart.'

'I think they could have. I was a bit of a mess. After your mother died. And even before.'

'You weren't.'

'Oh, I was. I was, you know. But I'm glad I never let you see it.

Glad you never knew. She might have got you. You didn't know her. I never knew her well. Jess wouldn't have it. But Viola was a strong-minded woman. Like your mother. Once she set her heart on something, nothing would stop her. And that was *just* like your mother. I was so frightened of losing you. I'd lost your mother. I couldn't lose you as well.'

Daisy paused. She could barely take it in. 'So why did we go back at all? Why did we risk it?'

'Desperation. I'd have tried anything. I remembered the hill and the Clootie Tree. Your mother talked about it. She asked me if I would go. How could I refuse?'

'The wish,' she said, after a while. 'Did you ever think the wish would work?'

'No. Not really. I knew it wouldn't work. Except...' He hesitated.

'What?'

'Because I knew it wouldn't work, because I knew how ill your mother really was, I kind of made another wish. A different one. It was a supplementary wish, if you like. I thought I might be allowed one more. In the circumstances. One for luck. That's the way magic works, isn't it? Tricky.'

'What kind of wish?' She was intrigued now, in spite of her shock, her anger. Besides, she loved him. Could never stop loving him.

'Not for myself. Or for your mother. Just for you.'

'And did it work? Did that one come true?'

'You tell me. Are you happy? Happy enough, anyway?'

'Of course I'm happy. You made sure of that.'

He had too. He had given her as much security as his wandering soul could manage. He had given her unstinting love and support. An education. Self-respect. What more could she ask?

'Sometimes these things take time,' he said.

The phone crackled a little. He would be somewhere in a sea of mud, with his new van and his old fiddle. There would be a

13

new woman too. There always was. He was still an attractive man. Although in that respect, he had waited until Daisy grew up, waited until she had gone to university. She could hear music in the background. The thin sounds of a whistle. A *bodhrán*. A woman singing.

'Sometimes they take years.'

'What do?'

'Spells,' he said. 'Wishes. Sometimes they take years to come true.'

*

Today, she has come to see the house.

'Let's reconnoitre,' her father would say. He still does. 'Let's reconnoitre,' or 'Let's make camp.' She feels she ought to reconnoitre first. Perhaps make camp later.

It is earlier in the year than on that previous visit, but she's pleased to find that the lane is already full of flowers, full of the yellow and blue and pale green of spring: violets, primroses, a few early bluebells. She drove here between hedges of dazzling golden gorse, so bright that she wished she had thought to bring sunglasses. Whin, they call it here. The birds are singing their hearts out after the rain. She can hear the beat and flutter of their wings among the leaves.

She feels a throb of anticipation, and there it is. The house again, just as she remembers it: stone walls in a big rectangle, two and a half storeys from this side, with a mossy roof, a sturdy square tower at one end, three or more storeys high with a crumbling battlement at the top, two rows of casement windows in the main building reflecting the light like so many mirrors, all half hidden at the end of a green lane, beyond rusted iron gates. It seems largely unchanged, forlorn in the manner of all empty houses, but especially old houses. Even in spring, the garden seems to be making determined efforts to smother the building. Lord knows what it will be like in summer. It occurs to her that all this is now her responsibility. It is up to her to reject or to accept the responsibility of doing something about it. *With what?* says the sensible part of her mind. There will be very little money left once inheritance tax is paid. Just the house and its contents. The magnitude of it all overwhelms her. It seems unreal. *What am I doing here?* she thinks. There is a stillness about this house, a quietness about it that the birdsong, the low drone of insects, only serve to intensify.

The hill can wait. The sad old tree, with its burden of other people's wishes, other people's desperation, can wait too. For now, the house is calling to her. She can hear its siren song. The answers to a hundred questions. She pushes open the rusted gate that flakes under her fingers, sets foot on the soft green path and walks towards the door. The place feels undisturbed, sunk deep in time. Dreaming. She senses that she is about to wake it. How will that feel? Maybe she should have brought a friend with her. People offered. Not her father, though. He had pleaded work. A gig, he said. She sensed his disapproval, although he would never admit it, never discourage her from doing something she felt passionately about. She had turned all of them down, thinking that this ought to be a private moment. Now she's not so sure.

She takes the bundle of keys out of her pocket. Almost hidden between the old iron keys is an ordinary Yale, incongruous among the rest, but that's the one they've told her to use. There is no crime to speak of on the island and the house is well off the beaten track. There had never been any trouble 'of that sort' for Viola. Or so the lawyer had said, mysteriously. She had found herself wondering what other sort of trouble there might have been, but she didn't ask. She remembers the solicitor, Mr McDowall, in his Glasgow office, a room so crammed with books and deed boxes and yellowing pieces of paper that she wonders how he ever manages to find anything at all in a place so Dickensian – such a throwback. The only other time she had ever been in a lawyer's office was with her father, years earlier, when he had bought the Glasgow flat and had been asked to sign the documents. That had been quite devoid of books or papers – a sleek office furnished in pale wood. Nothing at all like this.

Mr McDowall caught her bemused glance, chuckled, a laugh so dry that it sounded like the rustle of parchment. 'We don't subscribe to the paperless office here, Ms Graham. Never have. Never will now, I suppose. Once I'm gone, all this will go too, but not until then.'

The other keys are a miscellaneous and anonymous bunch, long and short, fat and thin, including a heavy key with a brown label, upon which is written 'back door' in a thin hand. She wondered if this was Viola's handwriting or even some long-ago housekeeper. Some were for internal rooms, some even for pieces of furniture.

'These are the keys of your castle,' said the lawyer. 'I'm told these old keys have a value. What would people do with them, I wonder? Other than sell them as scrap metal.'

'They're quite decorative. People do buy them.'

'Oh yes. It's what you do, isn't it, Ms Graham? Dealing.'

She nodded. That word always sounded faintly suspicious, as though she were doing her deals with bags of white powder in the city's less salubrious alleyways. 'Antiques and collectables. Yes.'

'Do you have a shop?'

'Nothing so grand, I'm afraid. No. I do fairs and markets. And online. I'm small fry, really.'

'Well, Auchenblae will be the ideal place for you. I expect you'll have fun exploring.' Mr McDowall angled his varifocals so that he could gaze at her through the right part of the lens.

'Maybe.' She looked doubtfully at the keys. 'But I have no idea what's there. Do you? Was my grandmother a collector?'

'You might be pleasantly surprised. Although I must admit it's more than a year since I was there myself. And I suspect she was more of a hoarder than a collector. I don't know whether there's very much value in the contents, except as an undisturbed record of a Scottish house with a very long history.'

'How long has it been standing empty?'

'Most of the winter. Although I think very little has been done to it for many years. It isn't exactly falling down, but it certainly needs some attention. Miss Neilson had a bad fall in the autumn and was taken to hospital on the mainland. She was well into her nineties, you know. But until that time, she had been quite spritely. Surprisingly so. Her sight wasn't what it had been. She complained of rheumatism. But she was, as they say, as sharp as a tack. A stubborn old lady. She only gave up driving five years ago, I believe. She told me that she knew the time had come when she mistook two dustbins at the end of somebody's driveway for a pair of tourists.'

'She had a sense of humour then?'

'After a fashion. And sometimes at other people's expense. Didn't suffer fools gladly, that's for sure. But she wouldn't give up the house, even though her doctor and such friends as she had on the island told her that it was all too much for her. Told her she should sell up. Make herself comfortable. Doctor MacGregor tried to enlist my help.'

'Maybe she didn't want to leave the island.'

'Oh, she would never have left the island. But there was the possibility of one of the new affordable houses in the village of Keill: warm, dry, cheap and easy to run.'

'She wouldn't move?'

He shook his head. 'It was no more than a few miles away, but I knew better than to interfere. You couldn't ever persuade Viola Neilson to do anything she had set her mind against. Or indeed to refrain from doing something about which she had already made up her mind. A few people rallied round – the way they always do on the island. I don't think they liked her much but they always look after their own, and they considered her to be more or less built in with the stones. As is Auchenblae, of course. Forgive me, Ms Graham, but she wasn't a particularly likeable person.'

Daisy smiled. 'I get that impression.'

'There's a shop in the village of Scoull a couple of miles along the road. They would bring groceries out for her. And a medical centre in Keill, farther south. They would fetch her into the surgery when she needed it. The postman would check up on her in passing, although I doubt if she got much in the way of mail, so he would even make a detour to make sure she was OK.'

'It sounds like a lonely old age.'

'Maybe, but she was used to her own company. I paid her the odd visit. I like to go fishing in that part of the world, so I would – as the Spanish say – kill two bulls with one sword. It was about a year ago that she summoned me for a more formal meeting.'

'Mr McDowall, how come she found out about me? Well, I suppose I mean, how could she not know about me?'

'You didn't know about her.'

'That's true. But my father was very cautious. He had his reasons. I don't know whether they were good reasons or not, but he was very wary of her. I would have thought curiosity might have got the better of her. It seems that she didn't even know about my mother's death. That's tragic.'

'I think she didn't want to know. Your mother and she were very much alike in some ways. Stubborn. Easily offended. Your mother decided to cut all ties, both with the island and with Viola. As far as she was concerned there was no going back. Then, after she died, your father respected her wishes. Even though he could probably have done with some support. A wealthy grandmother might have been a godsend back then.'

'I had a granny. My dad's mum. She lived down in Ayr. She died only a couple of years ago. I loved her to bits. We were fine.'

But she hadn't been a wealthy granny, thought Daisy. She had a sudden pang of longing for her grandma Nancy's living room in the wee council flat not far from the river: the gas fire, the ginger cat, Jimmie, sleeping on the fluffy rug, the television in the corner, the nest of tables pulled out to hold mugs of strong tea, caramel logs, teacakes and shortbread, always set out on the same old plate with daffodils, the sole survivor of some long-lost tea set. When she was younger she had spent weekends there when her father had the occasional gig. Later, she had gone regularly, once a month. She would sleep on the sofa and in the morning her grandma would make toast castles, slices of bread propped up into a tower shape, with battlements cut along the top and scrambled eggs in the middle. It was all gone now, new tenants in the flat, most of the furniture sold or sent to the charity shop, Jimmie rehomed with a kindly neighbour who had shared his care anyway. *Oh God*, she thought. *I wish you were here right now, Grandma. I do want to talk to somebody sensible about all this.*

Mr McDowall seemed to read her thoughts. 'I can understand that this has all come as something of a shock. Especially since you knew nothing about Viola.'

'Dad was afraid. He was very much afraid of losing me.'

'Well, I suppose it could have happened. Viola Neilson was quite an influential woman back then. And of course, time passed and it must have seemed utterly impossible to make any contact at all. She didn't even know that her daughter was dead.'

'And didn't know about me either?'

'Apparently not.'

'You've got to wonder why nobody told her. Over the years, I mean. My dad isn't exactly famous, but there would have been a certain amount of publicity here and there. Well, I know there was.'

'She wasn't much into gossip. She could repel all attempts at small talk. I've been on the receiving end of her sarcasm more than once.'

'So how did she...?'

'How did she find out? It was the winter before last, before she had her fall. Somebody had given her a lift to the doctor's surgery. Some small health problem. She told me she was looking at an old magazine in the waiting room. She said even then it was several years out of date. A well-thumbed copy of *Scottish Field* or *The Scots Magazine*. I don't know which. There was a piece about your father. She must have recognised him.'

'I'm surprised she did. She hardly knew him.'

'That's true. But – more to the point – there was a picture of the two of you together. He was playing at some festival in the Borders.'

'I remember it. There's been something of a revival for him. Back when he met my mum, he was doing rather well. He's still a fine musician. But he sacrificed so much for me. The two of us. Gave up touring. He'd tell me it was all worth it, every last day of it, but...'

'I'm sure it was worth it. Anyway, there was a large full-colour picture of you and your father and ... well ... you are so very like your mother. Even I can see that, now that I've met you. And of course it's many years since I saw your mother.'

She remembered the article and the picture. Her dad had been playing a summer festival in the Borders and she had taken a stall, packing her car with vintage clothes, handbags, costume jewellery for sale. Somebody had interviewed them for a 'father and daughter' piece. She had always meant to contact the magazine and ask them for a copy of the photograph but she had never done it. Her dad had been standing with one arm around her, his fiddle in the other hand, their heads leaning together, and they had been grinning. He had probably said something daft. He often did.

'I don't know if I *am* like my mum. Not that I remember much about her. Well, I remember her, but I find it quite hard to see her in any great detail, in my mind's eye, I mean. But when I see pictures of her, the few photos we have, I suppose I *do* look a bit like her.' The red hair and the freckles, those had come from her mother.

'And of course, as far as Viola was concerned, Jessica May had never grown old.'

'She never did grow old, Mr McDowall.'

'No. Of course not. But Viola didn't know that at the time. She just saw the picture and it must have given her such a shock.'

'It must.'

'She said it was as though all the intervening years had just disappeared, dropped away in a moment. There you were and she thought for a brief moment that you were your mother. She was unusually emotional about it, even when she was telling me.'

'Poor Viola.'

'Which was when she asked me to find out more, to find out whatever I could. Which I did. It was easy, of course. All this kind of thing is easy now, if you can handle the internet. My assistant ferreted it all out in short order. It's just that until then, Viola simply didn't want to know. Even when the facts became clear, she cautioned me against any headlong and impulsive disclosures. Those were her very words. That wasn't what she wanted at all. That wasn't her way. If I had to find a word to describe her attitude, I would say it was almost one of embarrassment.'

'Embarrassment?'

'Yes. It was as though she felt embarrassed that she hadn't known about you. That she hadn't known about your mother either. That the years had gone by and she had been content to remain in such ignorance.'

'We remained ignorant as well. Well, I did. It's extraordinary. I wish I had known. I tried to ask my dad about Mum's family once or twice, but he said she was an only child and there was nobody left. My other granny – dad's mum – I think he kept her in the dark as much as me. He never spoke about Garve if he could help it. We knew Mum was born there, of course, but I remember asking him about it when I was in my teens. That single visit when I was very young and my mum was so ill. There was something on the news about the island and I said, "didn't we visit it?" He said he had been playing at a folk festival there, which is where he met my mum, and that was how he knew about the Clootie Tree where folk left wishes. But he didn't tell me that my grandmother still lived there. He implied that she had died not long after he and Mum were married.'

'If it's any comfort, I think if she had lived longer she might have tried to contact you herself.'

'But there wasn't time?'

'No. There wasn't time. In the autumn, she had a bad fall and it was as though that triggered something in her. She deteriorated very quickly. She was taken to hospital on the mainland. I visited her there and we sorted out her will. There was never any question of mental incapacity. She was still perfectly lucid, perfectly sharp. But physically, she had simply worn out. Once she knew about you, she wanted you to have everything. And here you are. The new owner of *Achadh nam Blàth*.'

'Sorry?'

'That's the name in Gaelic. Field of flowers.'

'Of course. Auchenblae. And here we are.'

THREE

1588

She was the sun in his sky. That was how he thought about her, right from the start. After the cold chaos of the past months, the misery, the pain, sickness and despair, she seemed, however briefly glimpsed at first, as warm as the sun, or like the pale gold of the oranges that grew in the garden his mother had loved so much. It was home that Mateo was pining for, home that the girl brought to his mind: the light springtime days, the pink and white almond blossoms and blue skies of home. He had no notion of that season here, in the miserable North. For all he knew, it would be much like now: cold, wet and inhospitable. When he closed his eyes, he could still see her, could call to mind his first sight of her, as though, in that moment, something of her had been imprinted on whatever lay behind his eyes, the mysterious place where memories, dreams and hopes were stored.

Lilias. The name suited her: tall, pale and straight as a lily.

She was wrapped in a voluminous woollen outer garment – he couldn't say whether it was a cloak or a blanket – that made her look monumental, like a painted statue, like an image of the blessed virgin or a young saint from one of the churches of his island. It was woven in some kind of fine wool, dyed yellow, and it billowed around her in the wind. She looked faintly unreal, as though if he rubbed his eyes, she might disappear. She was standing on a low promontory with the crumbling remains of a circular tower behind her. It was very like the round tower where he and Francisco had hidden for a while in Ireland. It amazed him later that he should have noticed her first, before everything else, noticed – how foolish – that her woollen cloak, if cloak it was, had something of the colour of the rocks in it. The grey rocks of this coast were made vivid with some yellow overlay that he had seen in Ireland too, albeit in different circumstances. There, the yellow had been stained red with the blood of his friends and colleagues, his shipmates, while here, the yellow was pure and unadulterated. As yet. He trusted to nothing. He carried a weapon, a small fighting dagger from Toledo, a gift from his uncle. There had been no gifts from his father. There had been a dagger for Francisco too, but the younger lad had lost his, letting it fall into the water in the midst of all the confusion. Mateo had his weapon carefully concealed about his body, beneath his clothing, but accessible enough if need be. He found its presence reassuring and, so far, he had managed to keep it with him, which was something of a miracle in itself.

He and Francisco staggered ashore on the island of *Garbh* from the vessel that had brought them this far, a single-masted birlinn that had taken them away from the horrors of Ireland, in search of a less ill-fated welcome in Scotland. Hope was a great thing. The voyage, short as it was, had cost them dear and there was almost nothing of value left should they need to bribe their way from here onwards, which was very likely. He was uncomfortably aware that Francisco was relying on him, believed that he had a plan. He had no plan, other than to resolve their immediate need for food and shelter, and find some kind of assurance that they would not be killed on sight. They would just have to trust to luck, which had served them well enough so far. The captain, a cheerful islandman with an abiding dislike of the English, knew these waters well, but he would bring them only so far in these heaving seas, anchoring offshore and sending them ashore in a tiny skin-covered tender that rode the waves efficiently enough. Even so, Mateo had noticed how the two men rowing them had zig-zagged, presumably to avoid a succession of perilous rocks just below the surface.

Even back in Ireland, they had been a scant handful of men, those survivors of the *Santa Maria de la Candelaria*, his ship, or rather his captain's ship. He had been the navigator. Had there not been so much else to appal and terrify him, that alone might have kept him from sleep: wondering how much of the disaster had been his fault. In his calmer moments, of which there were very few, he realised that he could not have foreseen these devastating events. Who could? Well, perhaps Medina Sidonia, their leader, had known. Had foreseen. Had embarked upon the venture with great foreboding, knowing the whole enterprise to be doomed, but in the way of powerful men everywhere, had proceeded with it anyway, for a host of reasons that had little to do with those who would suffer most.

So many young men were dead.

He, Mateo, had done his best with astrolabe and charts, but the *Maria* had broken her back somewhere off the rocky Irish coast, in spite of all they could do to invoke the protection of the Blessed Virgin after whom she was named. His captain, Alejandro, had gone down with the ship, as had so many. It was something of a miracle that he and Francisco had the skill of swimming. Few in La Laguna could swim, but he, Mateo, had spent weeks at his uncle's house beside the sea and from splashing about in the water, he had learned and had taught Francisco, always the lesser of the two lads in terms of daring as well as in years.

The ship had run ashore on the north-west coast of Ireland. By then, many of the surviving sailors and soldiers had been beyond help anyway: lice-, bug- and flea-ridden, sick to death, starving but unable to eat what little food there was, because of the sickness. And terrified. Above all terrified. This was not what they had expected. Not what they had been promised. They had been promised victory and glory and golden spoils. It had struck him even then that there were, in all likelihood, no golden spoils to be had. And certainly not here. Aboard the ship, the rats had been healthier than the men, but ultimately their fates had been similar. A few of the men, Mateo and Francisco included, had stayed with the broken vessel as long as they could and the tide had washed them ashore along with the ship. Many had perished by jumping overboard too soon, but some would perish by waiting too long. There was no right decision. It was all luck, even though he had remembered his uncle's advice. Francisco's father, Santiago, had been a fine seaman in his day.

'Stay with the ship as long as possible,' he had said. 'Leave only when it seems most prudent. When staying would be fatal.'

A big baulk of timber had come to their aid, allowing them to float and paddle. As he and Francisco struggled ashore, and even as he hauled the younger man out of the water by the scruff of his neck, like a drowning dog, he had seen rodents out of the corner of his eye, sure that some of them had swum to shore like themselves and were swarming up and over the rocks.

The men waiting for them on the shore had not concerned themselves with rats. Their prey was different. Who cared about mere rats when the enemy was within their grasp? Even those sailors and soldiers who had managed to swim and crawl ashore had not survived long. There had been such savagery that Mateo could not now bear to think of it. The images would rise unbidden to his mind and he would find himself wringing his hands or digging his nails into his palms until it hurt, in an effort to banish them. They haunted his dreams and he knew that Francisco was similarly afflicted, since he had heard him calling out in his sleep, had reached out more than once to shake him awake. On one occasion, hearing hoofbeats in the distance and fearing lest Francisco's nightmares would give them away, he had put a hand over his cousin's mouth to stifle the screams. The lad had lain so still afterwards that he had a sudden fear that he had smothered his cousin in his panic, but the boy had only fainted and came round a few minutes later in sickness and confusion. Mateo had an inkling that some of the people of Ireland, the ordinary people, leading lives of manifest poverty, would not have been so savage when confronted with needy young men who seemed less monstrous than the tales told of them, but it was clear that mercy was not in their gift, even had they wished to dispense it to the shipwrecked Spaniards.

Instead, those in power had methodically and brutally cleared the country of the enemy, much as a farmer and his men will kill vermin as they flee a barn, running from the dogs sent to roust them out. Those whom the sea had not seen fit to take had been slaughtered on land instead, terrified and pleading for their lives, their pleas ignored or mocked. He had seen a dozen of his companions summarily executed, even as they surrendered, begging for mercy, and only afterwards had the local women emerged to give the bloodied bodies a scarcely decent burial, wrapping them in coarse linen and sliding them into the pits their menfolk had dug for the purpose, intoning prayer the while. He and Francisco would surely have met the same fate if they had been discovered. The widow who had given a handful of survivors shelter in her small byre alongside her single cow was clearly terrified of the consequences for herself, pitying them but almost beside herself with fear. Well, they had left her in peace as soon as possible, leaving her besides a few of the coins they had been able to secrete about their persons, taking only some bread and cheese, walking by night as much as they could, and hiding by day, wherever they could find some shelter from the autumn downpours: ruined stables, ditches behind drystone walls, unguarded haylofts, the remains of a round tower that Francisco said he hated, without knowing why. Mateo scoffed at him, but felt exactly the same unreasonable fear. Mateo thought he knew where they were, at least, on the far north-west coast of this country, and knew that their best hope, nay, their only hope, lay in finding a vessel willing to take them to Scotland, where they might meet with a less ferocious welcome.

There were only five of them by this time, and they looked to Mateo for leadership, as the most senior of the party in authority, if not in years. They had looked to him for direction on board the *Maria* in the same way. He did as much as he could, but the reality was that there was no achievable plan, no respite, no succour. Close to starvation, they had been drinking from brackish pools when they couldn't find springs, eating the nuts and berries of autumn and, when hunger overcame them, the raw shellfish by the seashore that sometimes made them as sick as the sea from which the creatures came. One night, three of their party, sailors from Santa Cruz, simply disappeared. As the light drained out of the sky, they had begun to make their way through a small patch of woodland with stunted, wind-blown trees and an undergrowth of some fiercely spiny shrub that tripped them and tore at them as they passed by. A few glossy but maggoty berries remained on the shoots, and they ate them eagerly, hoping that their sweetness meant that they were edible. To tell the truth, they were so weak with hunger that they hardly cared if the fruits were poison or not, as long as death came quickly.

Somehow, stumbling on through the trees, they had become separated into two groups. When grey daylight came, the other three men were nowhere to be seen. Had they been captured, or simply lost their way? Mateo and Francisco dared not shout. They took shelter amid a tangle of ivy and half-dead honeysuckle, with the stink of some strange fungus in the air, and waited, but there was neither sight nor sound of their companions. Mateo never discovered their fate, but suspected that they too had been caught and summarily killed. It sometimes struck him that the fate of those poor lads had been to his and Francisco's benefit, since it was easier to travel as a twosome, and it was – at last – easier to persuade the Scottish captain of the little merchantman to give passage to two Spaniards rather than five, who might become troublesome, however much the man might believe that his enemy's enemy was his friend. That was an uncomfortable thought, to be sure.

On the voyage to *Eilean Garbh*, his skin itching unbearably, running wick with bugs and lice, and exhausted to the point where even sleep would not come, he thought that, had the *Santa Maria de la Candelaria* survived the journey, they might have been on their way home by now. But the weather had defeated them first and last. He of all people should have known, with his skills at navigation, his seamanship, his learning, that the whole expedition was unwise. Well, reading is one thing and experiencing quite another. It is all very well to consider yourself an islandman born and bred. The seas around his home could be perilous and he had thought himself to be a reasonably experienced sailor, but he had never known anything quite like this: the cold, the ceaseless winds, the endless heaving seas and — let's face it — the inadequacy of the *Santa Maria* when faced with the conditions they had encountered.

The men had been frightened, demoralised, homesick as well as seasick. The weather and the rocks of this inhospitable country had dealt them blow after blow, driving them straight into the arms of the waiting enemy. He had never been seasick before. Had considered himself impervious to the sickness that had afflicted so many of the soldiers in particular, early in their voyage. The sailors had laughed at them just at first, confident in their own abilities. And yet most of them had succumbed eventually. He too had been sick, over and over again. He had even been sick aboard the relative safety of the birlinn that brought them from Ireland to *Eilean Garbh*, retching constantly, with nothing but a little blood and spit, his stomach heaving.

With the autumn day already darkening, they were decanted from the tender, with no great gentleness, pushed onto the white sand, and left alone there. The boat immediately pulled away again, the oarsmen fighting with wind and waves, back to the single-masted oak vessel that had brought them here. The captain and his crew were obviously relieved to be rid of their human cargo. As though to welcome them with a volley of shot, a heavy shower of rain drove into their faces from the west. At that moment, walking unsteadily on the pale sand, glad to be on land if nothing else, Mateo looked up, shivering, his teeth chattering, and saw the young woman standing some distance away, watching the incomers. She was tall, swathed in golden wool, and although she had pulled the garment over her head against the driving rain, her hair had escaped from it and was blowing around her shoulders. Red hair. He saw that she had red hair against the yellow wool, the whole unfurling like a strange flag in the wind. It might have reminded him yet again of the blood on the rocks of Ireland, but instead it made him think of sunshine and the golden orange groves of home.

Even as he gazed up at her, he saw that she was no phantom. She had been joined by a small figure, similarly swathed in wool, brown wool this time: a child perhaps, who tugged at her to attract her attention. She glanced down, pulled the garment more closely around herself, took the child's hand and began to walk away, quite briskly, as though alarmed but not panicked, disappearing over a little ridge of land. His gaze swivelled round and he saw that there was a house above them: a low, grey stone building with a dark thatched roof and chimneys, and a large stone and slate tower at one end. The Captain, McAllister, had promised to set them ashore close to a McNeill stronghold: 'a friend to the Catholic cause and no friend to the English,' was what he had said. Mateo did not entirely trust this judgement. He trusted nobody these days. But when he looked at Francisco's poor, pale face in the failing light, he didn't know what else to do. They must just climb up to the house, if they were able, and throw themselves on the uncertain mercy of McNeill of *Garbh*.

FOUR

The green track that constitutes a driveway to Auchenblae ends
in a space, an area covered in rudimentary tarmac. Whoever laid
it hasn't made a very good job of it. Moss covers it and small self-
seeded willows and elders are poking through, but there will be
plenty of space to park her car. Daisy will have to make a list of
things to do before she can put the house on the market. The house
and contents have been valued and the inheritance tax paid out of
the estate. Given the remoteness of Auchenblae and its general
lack of modernisation, the value isn't as high as it might be. There
will be a little money left over, or so Mr McDowall has told her.
But not much. Certainly not enough for a major renovation of a
house this size. Or even a small renovation. If she sells it immediately, she'll avoid capital gains tax. This is what everyone expects
her to do. In any case, the thought of so much money makes her
dizzy. She could sell it at a knockdown price, and still have more
money than she could make in a lifetime of dealing in collectables.

Daisy is a great one for lists. She has even been known to add
tasks already done to her lists, just for the joy of crossing them
off. Her fingers are itching to get started on a new 'Things to Do'
list. But for now, she'll explore the house. Then she can go back
to the hotel in the village of Scoull and take stock. She has booked
a couple of nights there, unsure as to how habitable Auchenblae
might be. Looking at the rather grim face of this building, she's
glad she did, glad she followed the lawyer's advice.

'Perhaps you ought to assess what you're getting into first,' he had said.

To her right, as she stands facing the house, there's a long, low outhouse at right angles to the main building. Her first thought is that this may have been a stable, but it doesn't look big enough. There's a chimney at one end, leaning precariously. Perhaps there had been a boiler room, perhaps this had once been the gardeners' domain. There must have been gardeners at one time. This modest building is separated from the main house by a broad pathway, already becoming choked with weeds, that leads from the hard standing in front, through a stone archway, and round the side of the house. She can hear the sea, faintly, and the cries of seabirds. This side of the house is sheltered from the worst of the weather, but she thinks the other side, facing the south-east, might get its fair share of wind and rain, especially in the winter. It's not as exposed as the west coast, but stormy, all the same.

She surveys the house. The door, with a couple of uneven steps in front, is made of wood and very sturdy: oak probably. There's an old bell pull to one side and a tarnished brass knocker with a fierce green man, glaring at her like Marley's ghost. There's a small heraldic panel over the door but the stone carving is so worn that she can't say what it once represented. She spots the Yale lock – incongruously modern – and, beneath it, a heavier cast-iron lock that one of the other keys probably fits, although she has been told that nobody ever uses it. The frontage to the right of the door has an oriel window (she dredges the word up from somewhere, wondering how she knows it) – a small projecting bay with rather pretty stonework and glass that undulates and bubbles with age, but the other windows on this side of the main house are small pane casements, two rows of them with skylights in the slate roof suggesting another set of attic rooms. To the side looms a chunky stone tower, four-square and solid. It looks grim and unused, its windows blank and uncurtained, a parapet wall, a chimney stack and a low slate-roofed structure on top.

'Hell's teeth, Mr McDowall was right. It *is* a castle,' she says aloud. 'I didn't realise it really was a castle.'

Just how old is this place? She knows that the Victorians were fond of building mock tower houses, adding them to eighteenth-century Scottish country houses to give them a spurious authenticity. But this doesn't look like a nineteenth-century addition. It looks as though it has stood here forever. She feels a sudden fluttering in her stomach, but isn't sure whether it's nerves or excitement. The key, a small and rather tarnished Yale, fits into the lock, but won't turn. Not at first. Daisy remembers that there is a can of oil in the car, and thinks that she's going to have to go and fetch it, but quite suddenly the key bites and slides round. The door swings open with a ridiculous, horror-film creaking that makes her smile. Not just any old castle then. Dracula's castle. In miniature.

She goes through the door, and finds herself wiping her feet on a muddy coir doormat that sits slightly askew on the uneven flagstones. She's in a small hallway, a porch really, but built into the house rather than out from it, with double glass-paned doors straight ahead of her. There's a pottery umbrella stand, with a selection of faded golfing umbrellas and a couple of slender silk parasols sprouting from the top of it. She hauls this over, contents and all, to prop open the outer door, unwilling to cut off her escape route all of a sudden. Escape from what, she can't say. Woodlice scurry from beneath it, dazed by the sudden exposure to daylight, but when she looks again they have all disappeared. Where have they gone? She almost trips over a pair of muddy green wellies and realises, with a pang of regret, that they must have belonged to her grandmother. And here they are, just where Viola left them.

The inner doors don't appear to be locked. She turns the knob and the right-hand panel swings open much more smoothly than the outer door. She props it back on its hinges and it stays open, reassuringly. She steps straight into a large room. She had been expecting a hallway of some sort, but this is more of a hall in the old-fashioned sense of a huge room: broad and long and high-ceilinged. You could hold a dance here if you wanted. Good for parties. There is an open stone fireplace on the end wall to the right, choked with years of ash. There is a battered Chesterfield, piled with faded cushions, a low oak table with heaps of books and well-thumbed magazines in front of it. Just behind her, the oriel window that she saw from outside has a window seat covered in dusty red velvet and there are matching, equally dusty curtains. She imagines Viola sitting there, watching the wrought-iron gates to the world outside. Well, the postman and the doctor had called sometimes, and the occasional neighbour; Mr McDowall too from time to time. Daisy has the disturbing thought that none of these would have been the person Viola wanted to see. Viola had only wanted to see Jessica, and Jessica had never come back.

The room is impressive, with a stripped wood floor, worn rugs softening the broad planks. It fills the whole depths of the house between the landward and the seaward side. There are tall windows directly opposite, flooding the place with light, even through an accumulation of interior dust and exterior salt. To her left, as she stands facing the back of the house, trying to take it all in, she sees a stair with a wooden banister and turned balustrade, rising towards the upper floors, disappearing into the relative gloom. There is a big exterior door on the seaward side as well, although it looks as though it hasn't been opened for some time. Might it, at one point, have been the actual front door, a way into the house from the sea? She wonders if there is a path up to the house from the bay below, since it stands some way above the shore. Perhaps people came more often by boat. Maybe the way she has just come in was the back door, at one time. So many questions. So many layers of history in one changed and changing building. She feels inadequate, in need of an architectural historian, but doesn't think such a person exists on the island. Perhaps she can find one in Glasgow. She has already looked online, but can find very little about the house. It seems to have largely escaped scrutiny, although surely it must be listed. She'll have to ask Mr McDowall.

The low door to the right, beyond the fireplace, is half open, and she can see sunlight filtering in. Venturing inside, she finds a large and chilly lavatory with chipped black and white tiles on the floor, a wash-hand basin, a washing machine with a willow basket balanced on the top. There's a row of pegs with a couple of waxed jackets hanging from them, spotted with mould, and a dangerous-looking electric heater on the wall. Cobwebs. Lots of cobwebs. A large spider lurks in one corner. She's not fond of spiders, but doesn't like to kill them either. One wall of this room is taken up by a bank of built-in cupboards. She opens one of the doors to find toiletries, toilet paper, bleach. Another has neat piles of what look like thin towels. A third has intriguing boxes and baskets, with objects wrapped in newspaper. She manages to restrain herself from investigating these. It could take all day.

She moves back into the middle of the large room and stands facing the sea. There is a passageway to her left, behind the staircase, where she can glimpse more oak doors. The kitchen lies that way. Beyond that, there must surely be a way into the tower, unless you can access it only from the outside. There's too much to take in all at once. The walls in here are plastered and painted magnolia, although there are wooden panels on either side of the fireplace. Between the windows are shelves, crammed with books. Ancient leather bindings rub shoulders haphazardly with modern paperbacks. There's a decent television, and an elderly transistor radio. The whole place is warmer than she expected, perhaps because of the morning sunshine filtering in. She wonders just how watertight the house is, although it smells dry enough right now: a scent of dust, old paper, the faintest tang of wood smoke and soot from the fireplace. Underlying everything is some indefinable floral scent, pot-pourri perhaps. And now, the scent of greenery is filtering in from outside, freshening the air.

She can't help herself. Impulsively, she shouts, 'Hello! Is any-body there?' although what she would do if there was a response, she hasn't the foggiest idea. Run for her life, she thinks, smiling. Her voice echoes back to her from the high ceiling, from the rooms upstairs, from the passageway to the left.

'There, there, there...' it says, soothingly.

It strikes her that the house, even in its abandoned state, is friendly and civilised enough. 'Lived in,' her grandma Nancy would have said. There is nothing threatening in the atmosphere of the place. She has helped with the odd house clearance, doing vacation work for an auction house. She knows what it's like to set foot in a house and find it utterly repellent. It happened only once or twice, but she can still recall the feeling. One in particular – a grim sandstone apartment on the south side of the city – had been so full of unhappiness that she had found it hard to breathe, never mind empty drawers and cupboards or pack boxes. Eventually the regular removal lads had sent her out to buy sandwiches and cakes from a nearby café and after that had encouraged her to lurk in the back of the van, stacking boxes for them. On the way back to the auction house the foreman had remarked how the woman who once lived there had become a virtual prisoner, ill and neglected by her husband. It had gone on for years.

'Bit weird how you picked up on that, Daisy,' he had said, looking sidelong at her.

Auchenblae is different. It feels manageable, in spite of its obvious age, as though somebody – Viola perhaps – has just stepped out, gone walking in the gardens and might be back to reclaim her wellies or her coat or one of her umbrellas. It isn't unpleasant or threatening, but it is still faintly disturbing.

She rummages in her shoulder bag. Mr McDowall had given her a floor plan of the house and now it seems quite simple. This is the biggest room in the house. The kitchen and something labelled as a scullery are along the passageway to the left. Upstairs there are five bedrooms and a family bathroom, and beyond that, up a narrow stair, are four small attic rooms, a box room, another lavatory, all once the province of the servants, no doubt. How

Viola must have rattled about this place — and that, she thinks, is without even considering the tower.

Leaving the front door open, she goes past the stairs, along the passageway and finds herself in a big square kitchen that looks out towards the seaward side of the house. It has an ancient deal table, marked and scratched and scrubbed. There is a Victorian range on the inner wall, with ovens and a fire, a clothes airer suspended on a pulley just above it, cast-iron pots and some stainless-steel pans stacked on a shelf under the table. There's a typically Scottish dresser on the opposite wall, with a row of spice drawers along the top instead of a plate rack (*worth something*, she thinks, mechanically) and an ordinary electric cooker, which is presumably what Viola used. Everything is covered in a fine film of dust. Her movement through the room disturbs it and it dances in the long lines of light filtering through the window. Back towards the front of the house, a doorway from the kitchen leads into a narrow scullery that smells oddly of potatoes, a dark room with sinks, dish drainers, even a dishwasher. Viola had clearly allowed herself some modern conveniences. In the far corner of the main kitchen, there's an archway with a door that looks considerably older than the rest. There is a lock with a big key. She turns it with some difficulty, tugs it open, and finds a turnpike stair spiralling both up into light and down into comparative darkness. She can just make out a narrow window in the outer wall, high above her.

The tower.

'I won't go there just yet,' she tells herself, aloud. Her voice seems to ring out, disturbing the dust even more. She hauls the door shut, hearing the crash and bang of it echoing through the tower, and goes back into the friendly kitchen, unwilling to give in to nerves, but uneasy all the same.

It is a fine spring day and she wants to explore the gardens, but, methodical as ever, she knows she ought to find out about the bedrooms first. She has only one more night booked at the hotel. Mr and Mrs Cameron, who own the place, have been understandably curious about Daisy and her inheritance, but they have been discreet and welcoming. Everything about it is good, especially the food, but it isn't cheap and she doesn't want to spend too much money. She needs to know if it's feasible to move in here, assess the house and make some decisions about its future. She's committed to an antiques market outside Glasgow in a week's time, so she can stay on the island for a few days if she wants to. There'll be plenty of time for the gardens this afternoon. She has left teabags, milk and biscuits in her car. There's a fridge that some considerate visitor, Mr McDowall or his representative perhaps, has switched off and left clean and empty. She sniffs cautiously at it before closing the door and switching it on, but it smells fresh enough. It powers up with a little shudder, but seems to be running smoothly. She sees an electric kettle that looks fairly new. She could make herself a cup of tea. Do a bit more exploring before going back to the hotel.

She leaves the kitchen and ventures upstairs. After the warmth of the downstairs rooms, it feels chilly up here. On this floor, there's a corridor running the length of the house, wood-floored with a narrow and somewhat threadbare runner down the middle, windows facing the landward side of the house, looking out on the driveway and the green hill beyond. There are five rooms off this corridor, all looking out towards the sea. The first, its door standing wide open, is a big bedroom with an en-suite bathroom tucked away in one corner. The bathroom has a Victorian cast-iron bath with ball and claw feet, and a lavatory with a polished wooden seat and an old-fashioned chain running down from a water tank set high on the wall. The porcelain pan is a riot of blue flowers. The bedroom itself is crammed with brown furniture, large walnut wardrobes, a monumental double bed (more like a mausoleum, she thinks) with a green silk eiderdown that smells of mothballs, tables on either side piled high with books, old brown medicine bottles, even a carafe of water and a crystal glass. There are lamps, rugs, a dressing table with a large oval mirror on a wooden stand, costume jewellery festooned over it, cosmetics, old and rather lovely scent bottles, some still full of dark, half-evaporated perfume: Guerlain, Lanvin, Chanel. There's a high-backed oak chair and a blanket chest, both decorated with crude carvings, both much older than the other furniture. When she opens the chest, it seems to be full of shoes. It smells of leather and sweat with an underlying hint of beeswax. This must have been her grandmother's room.

Briefly, she opens the wardrobe doors, wonders if Viola had ever thrown an item of clothing away. It's a vintage paradise: coats, dresses, scarves, gloves and handbags. A pathetic fox fur leers out at her, staring head and bushy tail. The room smells of camphor and feathers and is peculiarly airless. The heavy brocade curtains in here have been pulled half shut. She pushes them back, letting in the light, tries to open the window, but it's much too stiff. The hasp has been painted shut. *I couldn't sleep in here*, she thinks. *I just couldn't*. She closes the door behind her and, like Goldilocks, investigates the other rooms. Will one of them be just right?

Three of these smaller bedrooms have old-fashioned but conventional furniture – two singles and one three-quarter bed, oak chests of drawers, Edwardian wardrobes. They look as if nobody has slept in them for years. One has a whole wall of bookshelves, filled with the same odd mixture of precious old books and secondhand paperbacks that she saw downstairs. At the far end of the corridor is a bathroom, with – she's relieved to see – a newish lavatory and an ordinary-sized bath. Next to this is perhaps the best bedroom of the lot. Or the most immediately habitable. There's a three-quarter bed, not made up, but with a clean mattress protected by a blanket, two feather pillows, pine furniture, a wooden floor with a couple of sheepskin rugs. The curtains here have been pulled back and the room is warm and stuffy. It gives her the strangest feeling, as though she herself can remember being here, being in this room, lying on the bed reading in the afternoon, listening to music, making plans. But she has never been here before.

It's quite unlike the rest of the house and at first she wonders why, but then she realises that there is a definite feeling of the 1960s and 70s about it. There's a picture of Queen tacked onto the wall alongside a vividly coloured poster for *Grease*, Danny combing his hair, Sandy sitting sweetly at his feet. There's a portable Dansette record player and a heap of vinyl discs: Queen, Blondie, Aerosmith and then more folky stuff: the Incredible String Band, Planxty, The Dubliners, Joni Mitchell. The books are an odd jumble of Enid Blyton, *The Wind in the Willows* and *Watership Down*, with more grown-up paperback novels: *The Bell Jar*, *Rebecca*, Stephen King's *Carrie*, a slim copy of *Jonathan Livingston Seagull*, *The Lord of the Rings*.

This was my mother's room, she thinks, suddenly. *When she was a girl. This is the room she left to go off with my dad. She just abandoned everything and never looked behind her. This is the place she could never come back to.*

She is overwhelmed by some indefinable emotion: is it sadness, resentment, curiosity? A mixture of all three, perhaps. She sits down on the bed, her head spinning with the strangeness of it all, that she should be here, alone, in her mother's bedroom. That her mother lived in this room when she was younger than Daisy is now. That she, Daisy, never knew, never has known anything about it.

'What will I do?' she asks, sending the words out into the empty house. 'What on earth am I supposed to do with this place? With all this stuff? Mum? Grandma?'

'I've no idea,' says a voice from downstairs, faintly amused, echoing along the corridor. 'What do you want to do with it?'

FIVE

She remains seated on the bed for a moment or two, rigid with apprehension, her heart pounding. She can actually hear it beating in her ears. Then she thinks that ghosts tend not to appear in broad daylight and shout up the stairs, even in houses as old and strange as this one. But who is he? Where has he sprung from? And what on earth is he doing in her house? For a moment she feels panic-stricken, wondering how she can evade this stranger, find a way out in case he's blocking the doorway. Briefly she contemplates heading for the attic. Maybe there's a back stair, one for the servants to use. Then she thinks, *This is Garve. This is the island. There's no crime to speak of here. Maybe the odd bit of pilfering or poaching.* The voice is fairly young, Scottish, amused. The amusement is reassuring.

She gets up, walks along the corridor, cautiously peers down the stairs.

'Hello?' she says, as she had done earlier. 'Who's there? What do you want?'

She descends until she can see him more clearly. He has come in through the door she left open at the landward side of the house, and is standing just inside as though reluctant to intrude too far, rocking back and forth on his heels, peering up at her, hands in the pockets of his jeans.

'I'm so sorry if I startled you. But the door was open and I thought the bell pull might come off in my hand, so I just...' He shrugs, helplessly, smiling, used to charming and disarming people. She comes down the stairs in a little rush and halts in front of him.

'Can I help you?' she asks, with a certain brisk formality. There's something faintly familiar about him, but she can't work out what it is. And she's still disturbed by his presence, by his uninvited entry into her space.

He holds out his hand and she automatically shakes it. She can't help herself. 'Calum,' he says. 'Everyone calls me Cal. Cal Galbraith. I asked for you at the hotel and Mrs Cameron told me you'd be here.'

The island, of course. Garve. She supposes everyone must know all about everyone else's business. It must be both comforting and irritating to live here. He's gazing around. She can see the conflict in him between civility and curiosity. He needs to reassure her, to be polite, to chat to her. But he can't help himself. The urge to look at this room, to explore, to stare at things, is almost overwhelming. Well, she can understand that. She can see that his fingers are itching to handle things, to pick them up, to touch them. He restrains himself with an obvious effort and focuses on her.

'Ah,' she says. 'Mrs Cameron. Yes – she's been very interested in me. Everyone keeps asking me what I'm going to do with all this.'

'That's what you were asking yourself when I came in.'

'Well, I was asking somebody, anyway.'

'You're Viola's granddaughter?'

'I am. But I never knew her. Did you? Do you belong to the island?'

He doesn't sound as though he belongs to the island. Not wholly. There's only the faintest Hebridean lurking beneath a very definite and much harder west of Scotland accent.

'After a fashion,' he says. 'My mother was born here on Garve. She was a McGugan and it seems to have been an island name.' He puts an almost comic emphasis on the name. 'The family moved to Glasgow when she was a wee girl. My father has some kind of island connection too, although his branch of the Galbraiths moved away years ago. He certainly painted here, back when they were first married. He's an artist,' he adds, by way of explanation. 'You may even have heard of him. William Galbraith.' She nods. William Galbraith is quite a well-known name in Glasgow, but he quickly moves on. 'I spent most of my childhood holidays here on Garve.'

'Did you?' she says, feeling the need to take control, ask questions.

'We all did, back then: me, my sister and my mum. And to answer your question, no. I met your grandmother a few times but I wouldn't say I ever knew her. Hardly anyone did. Not well, anyway. She was a bit of an anchorite.'

She admires his choice of word. She can see Viola as a female hermit with the community bringing her food and fuel. 'And you'd be too young to know my mother?'

He nods, sticking his hands in his pockets again. He seems congenitally unable to keep still for any length of time. He's tall and spare and dark, in blue jeans and a loose white linen shirt, creased and crumpled. The energy sparks and crackles off him like electricity. She has the sudden random and bizarre thought that he could handle himself well in a fight. Like a terrier, he would never, ever give up. His brown hair flops over his forehead and his eyes are brown too, beneath dark brows, but full of good humour at the moment. All in all, she thinks he's nice-looking. But then, as her father never tires of telling her, looks aren't everything. Handsome is as handsome does, he would say, quoting her grandma Nancy.

'Yeah, well, I think your mother might have left by the time I was born. Or I'd be too young to remember. I'm thirty-six.' He pulls a face as though the realisation of his great age horrifies him. 'Mrs Cameron at the hotel would have known her, though,' he says, after a moment or two. 'You should ask her. Eyes and ears of Garve, she is.'

She finds herself again wondering what he wants. And where she has seen him before. Spoken to him even. Something about him is familiar. Not in the hotel, surely. She was only in the bar for a short while last night and if she had seen him, she would remember.

'Have you ever been here before?' he asks.

'No. Not in the house. We passed it once, my father and I, but he never told me anything about my grandmother. Or this place. It's all come as a complete surprise.'

'Wow!' He looks genuinely concerned. 'Poor you!'

'Everyone keeps telling me how lucky I am. How excited I must be.'

Inexplicably, she has a desire to burst into tears, bury her face in the dusty cushions of the Chesterfield and howl until she runs out of steam.

Maybe he has seen her lip trembling. He smiles at her, reassuringly. 'Well, maybe you are lucky, but it's one hell of a responsibility, isn't it?'

'Yes,' she says, taking a deep breath. 'It is. I have decisions to make. But ... why are you here?' She wonders if that sounds very blunt, but he must have a reason, other than rampant curiosity.

He looks sheepish, screws up his face, scratches his neck in what she will realise is a characteristic gesture when he needs time to think. 'Well,' he says at last, 'I'll admit it's partly nosiness. Everyone is nosy about this place, let's face it. Only a few people have ever been granted admittance. But, mostly, because they told me you were here on your own. Christ, that sounds creepy. I mean, I wondered if you could do with some help.'

The answer fazes her. It's true, after all, she could do with some help. But why would he offer? And yet, from what she has seen of Mrs Cameron, who is a thoroughly nice woman, the islanders must think he's OK, must think it's fine to send him to Auchenblae when she's there on her own. Mrs Cameron had been very solicitous over breakfast, pausing by her table to chat, offering to accompany her, offering to send her husband instead. 'A young lass like yourself in that grim old place? I'll be worried about you all day long.'

As though reading her mind, he says, 'Mrs Cameron will vouch for my good intentions. She's known me since I was just a baby. We have a kind of holiday house here. Nothing like this house. A but 'n' ben really. But she knows all about me, knows where all the skeletons are buried.'

'Are there many? Skeletons, I mean?'

'A few. The stuff I got up to in my teens. The stolen apples, the odd fish poached and I don't mean cooked in the hotel kitchens. The odd scrap too.' He is suppressing laughter again. 'But she knows I mean well. And I just wondered if you wanted some help.'

'What sort of help?'

'Any sort of help you want! I'm here a lot. On the island, I mean. We have a family business in Glasgow but I come here all the time. Whenever I can really. I can lift heavy things. It's a useful skill.'

'I'm not so bad at lifting heavy things myself,' she says, buying time, thinking of all the boxes she has hauled in and out of the back of her car. It's amazing just what you can get into the back of a Polo with the seats folded down, although occasionally she has given in and hired a van for the day.

He wanders over to the windows facing the sea. 'What a beautiful situation this place is in!' he remarks.

'I know. It's amazing.'

'Is that the back door, or the front door?'

'I don't know. I took that, where I came in, to be the front door, but now I'm not so sure.'

'Can we open it?'

'I was just going to do it. I was investigating the bedrooms. I'm booked into the hotel for another night, but after that, I was wondering if I should stay here till the end of the week.'

He pulls a face. 'And will you?'

'Maybe. I found my mum's old bedroom. I could sleep in that. It's OK up there. Not damp. I haven't been up as far as the attics. I might leave that for another day.'

'What about the tower?'

Now it's her turn to pull a face. 'Not yet.'

'Will we open this door then?' He's there, suiting the action to the words. 'Do you have the key?'

'I have keys galore,' she says. 'These are the keys of the castle.'

It is one of her dad's favourite tongue-twisters. 'These are the keys of the castle, and the castle belongs to Theophilus Thistle. Theophilus Thistle is a thistle sifter by trade...' She remembers them chanting it together: her dad, her grandma Nancy, herself, all joining in.

'Wow. You certainly do have keys.'

There is a heavy bolt on the back door. He slides it across and the noise of it echoes around the room. She's sorting through the bunch of keys, finding the substantial labelled key that she had hooked onto the rest for safekeeping. It fits. She turns it in the lock and it opens with a satisfying click.

'Well,' he says, grinning, 'you'll be very secure from the sea side of this house. No pirates or Spanish sailors are going to make it through this door, anyway!'

SIX

1588

Mateo paused on the shore, waiting, as always, for Francisco to catch up, and gazed at the house. It seemed grim and forbidding, although he noticed two or three small and expensively glazed upper windows with their lower wooden shutters firmly closed against the weather. So there was a modicum of wealth here. It struck him that the young woman did not have the air of a peasant. There had been a certain confidence about the way she stood still, watching them for a while, the decisive way she strode off towards the house. She would have gone to raise the alarm, even though she hadn't looked as if the sight of them had worried her very much. But then, he thought, with a wry smile, who would be thrown into any kind of panic by such warriors as they had become? Two more wretched, beaten souls it would be hard to imagine. No threat to anyone. Inadvertently, he found his hand reaching for the spot where the dagger still lay concealed at his breast, beneath the filthy linen shirt, the padded doublet and the battered jerkin, stiff with salt, noxious with the smell of damp leather and sweat. He found himself patting the spot gently. Perhaps some threat after all, if the need arose. He would not go quietly. But perhaps the need would not arise. He hoped not.

Mateo wondered, not for the first time, if he would be able to make himself understood sufficiently to explain their situation.

He had managed it with McAllister, but he knew enough to realise that seasoned sailors often spoke foreign tongues. He himself spoke fluent English, better than Francisco certainly, whose skills all lay with music and painting. Scots was difficult but not beyond him. That being the case, he thought in passing, why were they here? Why in the name of God had he allowed his soft-hearted cousin to accompany him in such an enterprise? He had had some inkling of what lay ahead, but Francisco? None at all. He should not be here. They had been persuaded by Mateo's father, who thought that Francisco needed 'toughening up'.

'It will make a man of him,' he had said.

Instead, it had very nearly killed them both, and might yet prove fatal.

While Mateo was still very young, his father had engaged a tutor for him, a religious man of some learning who, displaced from the only life he had known in the monastery where he had lived for some twenty years, had fled England in 1540. He had then travelled bravely but perilously through France and Spain over many years, a pilgrim, and ultimately washed up like a piece of holy flotsam, like the sacred statue of the virgin herself, on the Guimar coast of Tenerife at Candelaria. The man had taught him Latin and Greek, English, a little French and more besides; something of philosophy and much more of his own great love: mathematics. He had inspired the same joy of numbers in Mateo. Following on from that, there had been the rudiments of navigation too, which Mateo had learned as much from a fascination with the underlying principles as from any great love of the sea. He had sailed between the islands many times with his uncle and his father, to La Gomera, where they had property, and to La Palma, where they had family. It had given him, he thought now, a false sense of his own capabilities. His father had taught him all he knew of warfare and fighting, not sparing him at all. He still had the scars to prove it. But he had been too inexperienced to know how little he really knew. What had seemed like an adventure in prospect had become a nightmare in reality. He wondered all the time if he had been responsible for persuading Francisco, who admired him enormously, to join in too. For all that his father had wished it, Mateo had exerted no real pressure, but he feared that his own restlessness may have infected his younger cousin. Francisco – Paco, they called him at home – had always followed him. And it would be true to say that Mateo had not actively deterred him. Had it been because he selfishly wanted company? A friend? Because he himself had not really wanted to go at all? The responsibility of that weighed heavily on him now, as it had done for the whole unhappy voyage.

In Ireland they had scarcely interacted with anyone, afraid of the inevitable consequences. The widow who had afforded them the convenience of her byre for a little while had spoken a mixture of Irish and the odd English word. It had struck him that it was much easier to make yourself understood when a tongue was foreign to both parties to the conversation. At last, when it became clear that only Mateo and Francisco were left alive, and when Mateo feared that his cousin might pre-empt the swords or nooses of the soldiers and die of fever or starvation or even terror, they had sought shelter from a night of driving rain in a remote graveyard. Did the rain never cease here? He remembered the white limestone slabs peeping through the turf, as though some massive skeleton were buried there, and the smaller human bones scattered on the surface of the graves, where the soil was too thin to cover them properly.

The building at the centre of the burial ground was small, plain and very strange, built of the same flat grey-white stones that littered the landscape, corbelled to form a roof. They took shelter inside, bedding down on the earth floor in front of a rudimentary altar consisting of a slab of limestone on two upright rocks. Well away from this altar was what looked as though it might have been a fireplace of some kind, although the smoke would only find its way out as best it could, there being no chimney. Looking at Francisco, shivering with the cold, Mateo thought he might have risked a fire, but having neither fuel nor flint, nor even a dry stick or two, the question did not arise. The place seemed more pagan than Christian, but it was the only shelter they could find in this remote and hostile landscape.

Surprisingly, they slept, and at the first light of day, were awoken by the unexpected arrival of a young man, riding on an elderly donkey. They had thought the place long abandoned. As though to avoid any antagonism from two ragged strangers, however travel worn and weary, the man immediately confessed himself to be a priest, Father Brendan, although his dark woollen hood and cloak were anonymous enough. He seemed more afraid of them than they were of him, but they communicated in a mixture of fractured English and Latin. It struck Mateo – and almost made him smile – that the gestures for a lack of aggression, for innocence, a spreading of open, weaponless hands, the act of backing away, a shrugging of shoulders, an ingratiating smile, were the same, even between such foreigners as they were. Like dogs intent on avoiding a fight, they understood this much, at least.

Peaceful intent established and the need to speak in English likewise, the priest told them that there was to be a burial in the graveyard the following day.

'I have to make some preparations. A gravedigger will follow later, although the graves here are very shallow. The place is no longer really suitable for a good Christian burial, but an old woman of my parish has died, her husband is buried here and it was her dying wish to lie alongside him. Who am I to deny her? Besides, it will be easier to hold a Catholic requiem here, well away from prying eyes and ears.'

Mateo explained their situation as best he could, without going into too many of the dreadful details. He gave their names, Mateo and Francisco de Tegueste. The priest thought they were brothers, and he was tempted to agree, but then he remembered the word cousin. Father Brendan was clearly struggling with his own conscience. The tradition of his country and culture demanded a measure of hospitality to strangers, but how far should that hospitality extend when those strangers were most certainly the enemy, about whom so many dreadful tales had been told? Mateo had heard some of them himself, repeated and enlarged upon when he was aboard the *Santa Maria de la Candelaria*. Word had been put about that the Spanish carried whole torture chambers aboard their ships, specifically for the purpose of tormenting captured populations. That they murdered babies, raped women, branded the survivors in terrible ways. Tortures and mutilations on a previously unknown scale had been rumoured. Well, having witnessed what had happened in Ireland, it seemed to Mateo that both sides in this war were equally capable of hideous extremes of cruelty and depravity. But some of the tales had bordered on madness: that the Armada contained ships laden with pox-ridden whores, sent to infect fine upstanding Englishmen with deadly diseases. Some vessels were even said to be filled with wet nurses to suckle the hundreds of war-orphaned children. Any women at all would have been acceptable, wet nurses or whores alike, said some of the sailors, ruefully, but in the same breath they always acknowledged that there was little space even for the men themselves, never mind demanding mothers. People would believe the most incredible tales, and consequently their fear and hatred of any deemed 'foreign' grew, measure for measure.

It was clear that the priest had heard some of these stories himself, but could not reconcile them with the two half-drowned, starving rats taking shelter in his oratory. At last, he took bread from the panniers on his donkey's back and a leather flask of ale, and encouraged them to eat and drink. They accepted gratefully, and watched while he made such meagre preparations as he deemed fit for his funeral service, sweeping away the white dust and accumulated dirt, the dead insects, the droppings of birds, mice and other small creatures, from the rudimentary altar, placing a couple of candles and a wooden cross there. Mateo offered to help, but he shook his head firmly. He found the grave that was to be redug, and left a marker there in the shape of a twisted hazel staff. Then he covered candles and cross with a shabby piece of linen, remounted his equally shabby donkey and beckoned to them to follow him.

'I dare not give you any real shelter,' he said, addressing his remarks to Mateo, who was managing to keep up with the very slow pace of the elderly beast, while Francisco followed in their wake, along a narrow track that wound away from the oratory and, if Mateo was not mistaken, towards the sea. This, the priest explained, was all that remained of an old 'coffin road' from a time many years ago when the oratory and the burial ground had been more used than now.

'It was once the cell of a blessed anchorite,' he said. 'Perhaps you don't know what that is? A holy woman. Her name was Niamh. People would come here and bring her food, drink, fuel, offerings of various kinds, and, in return, she would pray for the souls of the departed who were buried here.'

Mateo thought that it must have been a lonely and chilly exist-ence, but a peaceful one. A peaceful existence seemed greatly to be desired at this moment, however lonely and chilly.

'It would be more than my life was worth,' Brendan contin-ued, 'if it were discovered that I had harboured *Spaniards*.' He emphasised the word, as one might say 'vermin'. 'And the people of my parish have great need of me in these uncertain times. It is only because these remote lands are still under the sway of the great Gaelic chiefs that I have any measure of freedom to practise my religion, but even that seems to be under threat daily. It's the only reason that such oratories as that one' – he gestured back the way they had come – 'are still in use from time to time. Nobody ventures out here who does not already know about it. But I have been asking the Good Lord what I am to do with you. *For* you.' He corrected himself.

'And has the Good Lord answered you?' asked Mateo, solemnly. 'We seem to be going towards the sea again.'

'We are. My village is some miles farther on. But you say you came ashore on the west coast, and now we are heading more northerly as you can see by the position of the sun.'

Such as it is, thought Mateo, glancing at the pale circle in the sky, so shrouded in cloud that it might easily have been mistaken for the moon.

'It seems to me,' the man continued, 'that you might meet with a more favourable reception in Scotland. There are many over there, especially in the west, who are no friends to Queen Elizabeth.'

'No indeed.'

The Queen of Scotland had been executed by her cousin only the previous year. Long anticipated, the act – when news of it arrived – had nevertheless seemed extraordinarily brutal and unscrupulous. But kings and queens have their reasons and no doubt the shrewd Queen of England had hers. As to Mary of Scotland, Mateo knew only that she had once been very beautiful, a vain but soft-hearted and impulsive woman, who had been greatly wronged, cheated of her kingdom. His father had heard as much when news of these events travelled south. Mateo thought that he would never take anything at face value again, never believe anything but his own eyes. All the same, he had some stirring of interest at the thought of washing up on a Scottish shore. It had always seemed so utterly remote and unreal.

The priest drew his patient beast to a halt. 'We're very close to the coast of Scotland here, sir. I've never ventured forth from this island myself, but if you stand upon any high hill in these parts and look north-west on a clear day, you will see Scotland. I suspect that the sea holds few fears for you.'

'Then you might suspect wrong, Father Brendan.' Mateo permitted himself an anxious glance back at Francisco, who had barely been keeping up with them. 'Paco?' he called. Francisco smiled, and embarked on a shambling trot. It broke Mateo's heart to see him. 'No, no,' he said. 'Take your time.' He turned back to the priest. 'As you can see, Father, my young cousin is all but broken in body and spirit. He's barely seventeen years old. The sea has been no friend to us these past months. But yes – I understand that Scotland might be our best hope of freedom. We might stand some small chance of beginning the long journey home from there.'

'Then I may be able to help you. A mile from here, there is a decent enough harbour, with a few cottages, and an inn of sorts. I suggest you don't venture in, but conceal yourselves somewhere and wait while I try to make some arrangements for you.'

'What arrangements?' Mateo asked suspiciously, though he saw no other way for it but to trust the priest.

Father Brendan sighed, as though reading his mind. 'There is a Scotsman I know by the name of McAllister, and he captains a small merchantman. They call it a birlinn or galley in these parts. It is a ship that sails – as often as weather and tide permit – between here and some of the Scottish islands. He's an unmarried man and when he's not at sea, he frequents the inn.'

'But if he's not there?'

'I have a fancy he is. I think I caught sight of him earlier today, as I passed by. He was drinking his ale and gazing at the sea. We exchanged a few words. Pleasantries. But of course, I didn't know what was waiting for me at the oratory. The weather has been uncertain and I think he's waiting only for wind and tide to suit him. These sailors rely on their pagan practices and superstitions when it comes to the sea,' the priest added, regretfully. 'They should be saying prayers to Our Lady! However, McAllister remarked that he would soon be sailing, since he smelled change in the air. The winds would be blowing from the right direction, he said, or some such observation. I don't pretend to know much about the sea. But perhaps you do.'

'I know something.'

'I said that perhaps the sun might shine for old Brigid's funeral, and he grinned at me and said he doubted that. He observed that it would be a rough passage to Scotland, but not impossible. He's a man who is not averse to a risk here and there I fancy. The cargo changes with the seasons. And sometimes it is human cargo, I think. He could be persuaded to set you ashore on one of the more favourable islands. But he is not a generous man. I have to ask you, can you pay him anything? Do you have the wherewithal? For I would give you something if I could, but the truth is that I have little enough even for my own needs and those of my parishioners.'

The priest surveyed them doubtfully, clearly wondering if they had any resources at all and, if so, where they might be concealing them.

Mateo drew a deep breath. 'I have a little money left. I've been saving it, hoarding it about my person, for desperate times.' A few gold coins were stitched into the lining of his filthy undershirt. Along with another keepsake that he would, he thought, sooner die than have to sell. His talisman. His luck. But perhaps the coins would be enough. And if not enough, then the knife might suffice. One way or another. 'Father Brendan, it seems to me that all times have been desperate for us, of late, and now I must spend what little I have left, for surely this is the only way in which I can hope to save my life – and his.' He looked back at Francisco, who had managed to catch up with them, and was now seated on a stone, trying to pretend that all was well with him, when he was clearly exhausted. The priest looked thoughtfully at him, took a small leather flask from inside his cloak, and motioned him to drink. The spirit brought an unaccustomed flush to his cheek and a smile to his lips.

Brendan took the flask and handed it to Mateo in turn. 'Drink. It will put heart into you.'

The spirit was rough and heady and did indeed put heart into him. Into them both. It gave them the strength they needed for a final push. They concealed themselves as best they could in a grove of thin hazels while Father Brendan rode on to see if he could arrange their passage at a price they could afford.

SEVEN

Cal and Daisy step out into an extravaganza of green and blue, gold and pink. The house sits on the sheltered eastern side of the island, but this part of the garden slants south-east and now, approaching mid-day, it is very warm for the time of year. The ground outside the house is already a mass of budding bluebells and campion, interwoven with violets and primroses, almost at the end of their short season. The land slopes gently down to the remnants of a stone terrace above the sea.

'Wow!' she says, inadequately. 'Isn't this beautiful?'

'Do you know, I've only ever seen this from the sea,' Cal says. 'I have a boat and I come along here fishing for mackerel from time to time. But when Viola was around, you somehow didn't trespass on her beach. I don't suppose she would have seen you if you did. But you just didn't. I think we were all a wee bit scared of her.'

'So there is a beach?'

'Down there. It's not huge. If we can find the way down, I can show you. Viola used to keep a rowing boat there as well, I think. Back when she could still get about. Many people here do. My father told me she used to row round to the village, to Scoull along there, for her shopping. Where your hotel is. She always preferred the sea to the road. Look. There's a path.'

'Are there cliffs down there?'

'The cliffs are mostly in the north and south. But it's pretty steep – or looks that way from the sea. It can be a bit treacherous.

There must be one or two other paths down, but this is clearly the main one.'

He is pointing to their left where a track, just visible among the undergrowth, curves down towards the sea. Across to the right there is a block of what may once have been stables and workshops, long and low, with slate roofs.

'You're short of nothing here.'

'Nothing but cash to do anything with it,' she says, drily. 'Enough to pay the taxes. I suppose that's some consolation.'

Behind them, a crumbling wall extends beyond the tower, running parallel to the coastline for a little way.

'What's that? Back there?' Daisy asks. 'I've seen it on a plan but there was so much to take in all at once. There's supposed to be a walled garden.'

'There is, although I've never actually been in it. That could be part of it, attached to the tower and sheltered by it. If you motor or row just a bit further along the shoreline, you can see a wee headland, and there's some sort of stone structure on it. Circular. We'll be able to see it if we head for the shore.'

'Is that Dun Faire on the map?'

'That's it. Nothing to do with the fairies, though. I think it's probably a broch, a small fortress.'

'I know what a broch is.'

'Sorry. There's another one at the other side of the island.'

'Is there? Do you know,' she says, 'there are people who call themselves brochologists.'

'You're joking!'

'They argue about whether various piles of stones really were brochs or not.'

'I'll bet they're mostly guys.'

'They could be.'

'We do like to categorise and label, don't we?'

She remains silent. She is remembering one Christmas when her father, feeling flush after some well-paid gig, had bought her a hand-built doll's house, complete with furniture and furnishings, tiny curtains, a dinner service, pots and pans, and even a family of bendy dolls with porcelain heads, all in Victorian dress. She still has it and loves it, but at the time she was simply overwhelmed by it, by the responsibility of it all. Many of their Christmases had been happy but low budget. That Christmas, she didn't do anything except sit in front of the miniature house, gazing at it for hours on end, afraid to touch it. Her father had been disappointed. 'Don't you like it?' he had asked, but she had just replied, 'I love it, Dad, but I need to get used to it.'

Now, she thinks that she will have to get used to all this, but it's a scary business. Part of her wonders if she should just follow Mr McDowall's advice and sell the whole lot, lock, stock and barrel. Put it on the market and see what happens. She could travel. Buy a more manageable house on the mainland. A bigger flat in Glasgow. Rent or even buy a proper shop. It's a can of worms. A Pandora's box. Once she opens it, all kinds of things will come flooding out and her world will never be the same again. It gives her a feeling of panic.

'Shall we try and get down to the sea?' Cal asks, impatiently. He clearly likes to be on the move.

'Yes. Why not?'

They start to pick their way among primroses and violets, passing the remains of a stone terrace with half-obliterated flagstones, surrounded by a low wall looking out over the sea.

'It's almost like a big rock garden here.' He glances back towards the tower. 'I don't think it's huge, the walled garden, I mean. But it would be sheltered enough to grow apples, pears, plums. Things thrive here if they get a bit of shelter from the wind and the salt. Back at the hotel where you're staying, one of the old owners planted all kinds of shelter belts so that they could grow things. God knows what state your walled garden is in now, though.'

'A secret garden. This place has everything.'

'It's amazing.' He shakes his head, seems to be regarding her thoughtfully. Wanting to say more but not sure how to begin. Instead he says, 'Look back at the eaves of your house. Rows of nests there.'

'Are they house martins?'

'They are. They tart them up a bit every year. It's supposed to be lucky to have them nesting on your property. Filthy but lucky. They're not long back, actually.'

They find themselves on a narrow bluebell-fringed track, heading down towards the sea. Everywhere, threaded among the rocks, there's a mass of green leaves and thorny stems. Some are brambles, only just in bud, but there will be a fine crop of berries later in the year. Others seem to be roses.

'Burnet roses,' he says. 'They're everywhere. Never seen so many. Sorry, I'm doing it again. Lecturing you.'

'Och, don't be daft. I want to know everything about this place and you clearly know more than I do. Is that the white rose of Scotland?'

'The very same. Thorny. Beautiful. You wait. Another month or so and they'll be flowering all over here.'

The track is well worn, almost obliterated, but something has kept it just visible: foxes perhaps. Once it must have been much broader, a proper track from the sea to the house, because there are flat stones thinly covered with a layer of sandy soil. They can hear the steady swish of the sea and the sharp cries of oystercatchers below, the shrill din of house martins behind them. Somewhere nearby is the melodic gurgle of running water, a burn tumbling from the slope behind the house, down towards the seashore.

'Nice, isn't it?' he says, turning to look at her.

'It's more than nice. It's wonderful.'

He grins again. 'And it's all yours.'

'Don't.'

'Why not?'

'I don't know. The responsibility, maybe. It panics me a bit. What am I to do with it all?'

'You can take your time, can't you? You say you've enough to pay the taxes.'

'So I'm told. But with nothing much left over.'

The track ends in a slew of flat grey stones and then they are on the beach. It is sheltered by rocky slopes on either side and to the north, she can see the small promontory he had mentioned earlier, with a stone structure, a mouthful of teeth, on top. From here it doesn't even look man-made. It looks as though it is part of the landscape, the bare bones of the hillock on which it sits.

'Is that what you meant? Dun Faire?'

'That's it. An expedition for another day maybe.'

She's surprised, but also touched by his assumption that there will be another day, another expedition. Well, what would be the harm in it? He seems to be good company.

Behind them the house, seen at this distance, looks even more like a fortress. The tide is quite low and the sea has deposited a line of shells and pebbles here, with a few pieces of seaweed, like question marks along the shoreline. There are tiny bird footprints on the white sand. There's a low wall, and tied up against it with a piece of massive but frayed rope is a tubby wooden boat, the planks sprung, the wood rotting.

'What a pity,' Cal says, striding over to it. 'I do love boats. And this is a really old one.'

'Could you fix it?'

He shakes his head. 'Don't think so, hen. I mean, anything can be fixed, but this would need such a complete overhaul that there wouldn't be much of the original left. It would be like the axe that had seven new handles and seven new blades! My boat's a lot better than this. I can take you out fishing some time, if you want.'

'Does this bay have a name? Other than the name of the house.'

'It's called Portree.'

'I thought that was...'

'On Skye, yes, but it just means the port of the king. Or leader, I suppose is more accurate. Fiercely proud of their own wee sovereign territories.' He grins at the notion.

She sits down on a rock and pushes up a ridge of sand with her trainer. The sea catching the sunlight, row upon row of tiny waves, looks very enticing. She'd like to take her shoes off and paddle, but she's inexplicably shy in his company. Not like her at all. But then he has slipped off his Skechers and he's already in the sea, casually holding out his hand to her. So she leaves her shoes neatly beside the rock and joins him, taking his hand.

'We get jellyfish later in the year,' he says. 'The big ones like swimming lampshades won't harm you, but they're not very nice when they get stranded. You have to watch out for scalder. Long pink trailing things. See if you get those on your skin, you'll definitely know about it.'

They paddle, hand in hand, splashing gently through the water, stopping to look back up at the house from time to time. His fingers feel warm and dry. 'At least this gives me some perspective on it,' she says.

She stubs her toe on something, says 'ouch', releases his hand and reaches down to pick up — what is it? Something heavy and wooden. He takes it from her and examines it, brushing damp sand from it. 'Now that's really something,' he says.

'Why? What is it? Is it something off a boat?'

They are looking at a heavy chunk of oak, roughly circular, about twelve centimetres in diameter, with a deep groove around the top, two big holes through it and a semi-circular opening at the bottom. It has the look of a mask, or a weird face. You could stand it upright and that's exactly what it would look like.

'I think it may be off a ship. It's a block — you know — the rope would have gone around it. It looks very old, though. Probably off a wreck.'

'*Were* there shipwrecks around here?'

'Oh yes.' He gestures out into the Sound. Far away, she can see the distant misty hills of other islands, row upon row of them. Or a single large island. She isn't sure what she's looking at. Closer, and to the south of the bay, probably within rowing distance, is an islet, shaped like a seated beast, with a low hill on the top, a flattened cone. She had seen it more clearly from the hotel.

'It's too shallow out there,' he continues. 'Or it's shallow in parts. There are hidden rocks. All kinds of ships, big and small, were wrecked out there over the years. Divers come out in the summer to see what they can find. There are rumours of treasure, but as far as I know nobody has ever found anything valuable. Interesting yes, but not particularly valuable. Not even anything as recognisable as a wreck. Just bits and pieces.'

'But surely something wooden like this wouldn't survive for so long.'

'Oh it could. In salt water and buried deep in silt it would. Things come ashore in the winter storms from time to time. You should keep it. It kind of belongs here, doesn't it?'

'I suppose it does. Weren't there ships from the Spanish Armada wrecked here?' She tries to dredge up fragments of history. 'Some of them were wrecked off the west coast, weren't they?'

'Well, mostly off Shetland. And Ireland, I think. They were trying to get down to Biscay. There was a galleon wrecked in Tobermory Bay I believe. It got blown up eventually.'

'Blown up?'

'So they say. By an English spy. Elizabeth had only just chopped off Mary Queen of Scots' head so there was a bit of tension going on. But I don't think anything was wrecked here. Although there are stories.'

'What kind of stories?'

'Of Spaniards coming ashore. Deliberately. Because they didn't stand quite such a good chance of getting their own heads chopped off here in Scotland.'

'I see what you mean. Isn't there supposed to be Spanish blood here? And in the far north.'

He wrinkles his nose. 'Well they say so, but Celts could be dark too. Some of them. It's a dangerous bit of coastline right enough. You wouldn't know just how dangerous, when you see it in summer. But it can get a bit hairy in the middle of winter. Or even in autumn. There was a visitor here last year who kept going on about how calm and sheltered the waters were. I kept wanting to tell him, wait till you see it in October or November. The locals have a lot of respect for the waters here. With good reason.'

*

They go back up to the house and take their find with them. They don't hold hands again. From this side, the impressive doorway on the seaward side of Auchenblae makes this look very much like the front of the house. Perhaps it was not only Viola who preferred to travel by sea. The block is still wet and the damp wood looks dark and faintly sinister, even more like a small mask or a Celtic head. She stands it on the windowsill at the seaward side of the house. Cal stays indoors while she fetches her Polo through the wrought-iron gates, parking it by the front door. She sees that he has left his own car, a big and almost new SUV, squeezed into the lay-by behind hers. The windows are tinted, so she can see nothing of what is inside. She brings in her tote bag of milk, teabags, the packet of chocolate biscuits she bought in the village stores this morning. She can hear him banging about in the kitchen and heads down the passage in search of him. He has boiled the kettle, foraged for mugs and even found teaspoons. She puts the milk into the fridge, which is chilling nicely. It looks a bit lonely in there but it's a start. She's going to have to get in some supplies if she decides that she's brave enough to stay here for the rest of the week.

They take their tea and biscuits into the big room and sit on either side of the dining table – more old oak with a patina of great age about it – their chairs tilted so that they can look out of the windows. A significant part of the charm of the house lies in the views of the sea and the distant islands.

'So,' he says when he has eaten several biscuits in quick succession – where does he put them? Grandma Nancy would have said that he needed a few fish suppers inside him – 'doesn't fresh air make you hungry? Anyway, have you made your mind up? Are you going to come and stay here?'

'I'm not sure. I'm going to go back to the hotel and have some lunch and think about it for a bit.'

'Good plan. But if you do decide to stay, you'll need some shopping.'

'I can do that in the village, can't I?'

'There's a Co-op in Keill as well. That's the next village along. You pass my road end to get to it. Where would you sleep?'

She thinks about Viola's room and shudders. 'Probably in my mum's old room. I don't think I can face my grandmother's room. But the bedrooms are clean enough and Mum's room is next to a decent bathroom.'

'Well that's a plus!'

'There's surface dust, just. I can make up the bed. There's a washing machine in the cloakroom along there. I'll see if it works, do some washing. No reason why it shouldn't.'

He looks briefly around. 'There's no central heating. It's warm enough in the day now, but it still gets chilly at nights. There must be a wood store somewhere. Probably out the back there. But you shouldn't use the fireplaces until you've had the chimneys checked out.'

More things for her lists. 'Is there a chimney sweep?'

'People tend to buy the brushes and do it themselves. Otherwise it means bringing somebody over from the mainland. Although most people don't live in such ginormous houses.'

'There are plenty of heaters.'

They had found three or four electric oil radiators, as well as the fireplaces. When they switched on an immersion heater in the kitchen, somewhat to their surprise, they found that the water grew warm quite quickly.

'After all – Viola was living here comfortably enough till last year,' she observes.

'She was. It's OK, isn't it? You could easily stay here for a bit. If you won't find it too lonely. And you really don't need to worry about the island. Viola was safe enough here for years.'

'I'd like to have a look at the attics. Just to see what's in there.'

'I'd like to have a look at the tower,' he says suddenly, draining his tea, pouring himself another mug. 'Can you get into it from this part of the house, or only from the outside?'

She realises that she has been avoiding the tower, avoiding even thinking about it, never mind proposing to investigate it.

'There's a door in the kitchen. I opened it and had a look in. There's a spiral stair, going up and down. I'm sure that's the way in.'

'It looks safe enough from the outside. Viola looked after her property.'

She can't say why the thought of the tower makes her nervous. After all, it and this house are part of the same building. But the tower has begun to loom large in her mind, its mysterious bulk lurking in her thoughts.

'I don't think I want to explore it just yet. Perhaps later in the week.'

He seems to have come to a decision. He drains his mug again, looks at his watch and stands up. 'Listen – I must be off. I have a ferry to catch.'

She can't hide her disappointment, even though she thinks she should. He's much too attractive. 'Are you going away?'

'Only for a night or two. I'll be back late tomorrow or, failing that, lunchtime on Wednesday. I have things to do, people to see. Business, you know.'

'Right.'

'You'll be in the hotel tonight. So that's OK. Why don't you stick to this part of the house for the moment? Make up a bed. Go and get some supplies. Make sure the heaters work. That sort of thing. Give me your mobile number. Here – put it in my phone.' He hands her his iPhone. 'The signal is pretty crap in places, but look – it seems to be working in here. There should be a landline here as well.'

'It's off. The solicitor told me it was one of the things I'd have to do. I haven't contacted them about it yet but I could do it this afternoon.'

'How about I come along the day after tomorrow? Wednesday? We could venture into the tower together. See what's what. I'm sure it'll be OK.' He looks around. 'I suspect some of the furniture in here may well have come from the tower. This table even. That press cupboard over there. Some of the chairs.'

'Yes. I think so.' She's impressed by his knowledge. 'That's what Mr McDowall told me.'

'Have you seen the curiosity cabinet yet?'

'What's that?'

'In your hotel. Well, it isn't really a curiosity cabinet at all but that's what they call it here. I'm surprised you haven't seen it. It's on display in the hotel. Ask them about it. It's a Jacobean embroidered box. Very beautiful. Wish I had it. It came from this house.'

'Really?'

'Way, way back when. I don't think you'd have any claim to it.'

'Oh, I wasn't thinking...'

'No, of course not. It's a McNeill heirloom. Belongs to Donal and Alys McNeill. She makes jewellery, has a gallery down at Ardachy between Scoull and Keill. He helps out in the gallery, does some gardening – he might do a bit of gardening here if you can pay him – takes fishing parties out as well. He's built in with the stones, but she arrived only a few years ago. Anyway, they allow the hotel to display it. Under glass of course. And with an alarm. It must be worth a small fortune.'

'It must.' She has always dreamed of finding something like this, something magical. Well, she thinks, looking round, she's never had a better opportunity than now.

'But Donal has this thing about it belonging on Garve, which of course it does. The old lairds of this place were McNeills at one time and the casket belonged to them. It must have been handed down through the family. I've often wondered about your Viola's name. Neilson. Means the same thing of course. Only anglicised. Anyway – have a look at the casket. It's wonderful.'

'I will.'

'And I'll come back and we'll venture into the tower together, if you like. On Wednesday.'

'OK.'

'Is that a plan?'

'Yes. Yes, it's a plan. I think I'd like that.'

He stands up, pats his pockets, looking for his keys. 'I must go. It's been great. And I'll see you soon.'

'Wait,' she says suddenly. He is already outside the door, but he halts and turns back, looking over his shoulder.

'What?'

'What do you do?' she asks. 'I mean, what *is* your business?'

'Didn't I tell you? It's a family business, really. Antiques, fine art, collectables. Good stuff. We have a pretty big shop. In Glasgow. Byres Road. You might even know it. Island Antiques.'

He smiles at her engagingly, turns and strides away, his car keys jangling, leaving her questions hanging in mid-air. A dealer. No wonder he wants to help her out. No wonder he has been so keen to set foot inside Auchenblae, a house that has its fair share of objects that might or might not be antiques, fine art and collectables.

EIGHT

Later in the day, still feeling angry and indignant with Cal, and almost as angry with herself for being taken in by his friendly exterior, she locks and bolts the big door at the seaward side of Auchenblae, pulls the front door behind her and drives back to her hotel, an elegant Georgian house just outside Scoull village, set a little way back from the sea and surrounded by gardens, vivid with early-flowering rhododendrons and azaleas. She goes into the bar, empty just now in the lull between lunch and dinner, asks for a white wine spritzer, and sits morosely in a corner, drinking and gazing at the optics. The dust in the old house has made her thirsty. When the wine hits her stomach, she realises that she is hungry as well, although it's too early for dinner, a bit late for lunch. She had been too excited at the prospect of seeing the house for the first time to eat much of her 'full Scottish breakfast'.

Mrs Cameron bustles in and sits down at her table. 'Well?' she says. 'How was it?'

'Confusing. It's a big house.'

'Aye, you're right there. And an even bigger garden. But what did you think about it all?'

'Honestly? I don't know whether to be terrified or delighted.'

'That's quite natural, surely?'

'I don't know. Nothing like this has ever happened to me before.'

'Did Cal Galbraith find you? He was asking about you. Said he wondered if you could do with some help so I sent him along.'

'So you *did* send him along to find me? Well thanks very much for that.'

Mrs Cameron's fair, powdery cheeks flush pink. 'Did I do the wrong thing?'

Daisy has the good grace to be embarrassed by her own rudeness. Her father has never been remotely authoritarian. 'Don't tell lies and whatever else you do, try not to be rude,' were just about the only rules he lived by and expected her to obey. But of these, rudeness, discourtesy, was the thing he hated most. If being kind involved telling a few white lies than that was fine too. She finds herself smiling, as always, at the thought of her father and his ultra-simple codes of behaviour. 'No,' she says. 'I'm sorry. You didn't do the wrong thing at all. He seems nice. But you do know he's an antique dealer, don't you? And I kind of wonder whether he might have an ulterior motive. They often do. I mean, I should know.'

Mrs Cameron puts her hand to her mouth. 'Oh!' she says. She flushes an even brighter pink and now Daisy feels worse. *Stop it*, she thinks. *Stop being so sensitive.*

'My dear – it never even occurred to me, but so he is. The family have a wee cottage at Carraig, way beyond Scoull Bay and Ardachy. Cal is the only one who comes these days, but he spends quite a lot of time here and I've known him since he was a lad. I hardly ever think about what he does for a living.'

'No, I'm sorry. I don't suppose you do.'

'He's Cal, that's all. His father used to come here to paint all the time. Pictures, not houses. With his wife. Before the children came along. But I believe his parents are still running the shop in Glasgow and Cal does a lot of the buying. Island Antiques, they call it.'

'He told me. In fact, I know it.'

'He goes here, there and everywhere. Looking for... oh!' She halts again. 'Well I do see what you mean. He has occasionally said he'd do anything to get a look inside Auchenblae.'

Daisy starts to laugh. She can't help herself. *And that clearly includes chatting me up*, she thinks. *Holding hands. Charming me.*

'He's got some cheek,' says Mrs Cameron, laughing as well.

'Now I feel bad. Maybe he *is* just being helpful.'

'Maybe. But I'm not surprised you're suspicious.'

'He's gone to the mainland for a day or two. But he says he's coming back.'

'Oh he's always coming back. Can't keep away from Garve. I think if he didn't have the shop and a house in Glasgow he'd be here all the time. He loves it so much.'

'I pass the shop sometimes, although I've hardly ever been in. I live in Glasgow too, you know. Anyway, it's pretty impressive – one of those gorgeous shops where you just know you won't be able to afford anything. Everything set out as though it's in a house.'

'Like Auchenblae?'

'No. Nothing like Auchenblae. A much grander house altogether.'

'So what will you do, when he comes back?'

'I suppose I'll ask him what he really wants. Thing is, Mrs Cameron, I'm an antique dealer too. After a fashion. Oh – nothing like Cal's shop. I sell online, and at fairs. And I used to pay for a bit of space in a big antique centre. Not very good space, as it turned out. Things kept being pinched. But I know how it all works.' She wonders how she can explain. 'There's such a hierarchy in the antiques world. What happens is – I might buy something at auction. I don't know, say a silver toddy ladle or an old teddy bear. I know I'm going to sell it on, but a lot of the time I'll be selling to another dealer – maybe a specialist. Then he or she will sell the thing on again. Most of the selling is done to other dealers. I often buy from dealers and sell to dealers. And every time, the price goes up. Everyone gets his or her bit of profit.'

'I never realised.'

'But I'm way down at the bottom in the pecking order, just

above the boot sale mob, and Cal, he's right up there with the pricey people, the objects of virtue, so called, the fine art. They sell a lot of stuff with a Scottish provenance, but it's very good stuff. Wemyss ware, Monart glass, Glasgow Boys, Arts and Crafts. I expect they sell on to London dealers as well. But then *they* have huge overheads. And even Byres Road can't be cheap.'

'Oh, I think they own the building.'

'Do they? Well that would make a difference. God, they're not exactly struggling are they?' She thinks of herself, haunting chilly car boot sales at six in the morning, hauling a ton of boxes out of her car, which always seems to have to be parked half a mile away from the entrance to whatever hall the antique or vintage fair is in this month, unpacking and arranging, only to have to do it all again at the end of a long day spent being nice to the public. She thinks of the hideous free-for-all at the end of the fair, when everyone, weary and sometimes disappointed to have barely made the cost of the stall, tries to escape at once. 'It must be nice to have a shop like that,' she concludes, ruefully. 'I miss so many good things at auction because I just can't afford them.'

'William Galbraith, that's Cal's dad, he's very successful as an artist, I believe.'

'Well, I've certainly heard of him and seen some of his pictures, but I don't know very much about him.' It strikes her that she has seen the odd canvas displayed on an easel in the window of the Byres Road shop: gloomy urban landscapes mostly. They are not pictures she would ever want to live with.

'His mum, Fiona, is an art historian. She worked for one of the big auction houses. I think between them they invested wisely and Cal reaped the benefits.'

'Is he an only child?'

'No, no. There's a younger sister, Catriona. She's married, living on the mainland. Hill farming, I believe. Has kids. Three at the last count. But you know, he's a nice man. He had a bit of a reputation as a bad lad when he was young but I think he's managed to live that down. It was mostly mischief anyway. Never sits still for a minute, but I don't think he'd do you a bad turn.'

'I'm sure you're right, but most of the big dealers I know – well, all the dealers really – seem to think that business is business, and their generosity tends to evaporate where a bargain's concerned.'

There's still something nagging at her, the renewed sense that she has seen Cal before. But maybe it's just that she has seen him in the shop, in passing.

'Are you all right, dear?' asks Mrs Cameron.

'Yes. Just a feeling. I keep thinking I've met him before, and I'm sure I have, but I can't quite put my finger on where. Glasgow's a big place, but you do tend to run into people. Maybe I need another spritzer.'

'Have you eaten?'

'Only a couple of biscuits. I'll just have to wait for dinner now, I suppose.'

'Oh I think we can rustle up some sandwiches for you. Would ham and cheese do you?'

'Wonderful.'

Mrs Cameron fetches another white wine spritzer from the bar, and presently the young chef emerges from the kitchen with a round of ham and cheese sandwiches on home-made brown bread, and a bowl of salad on the side.

'You're a saint,' says Daisy. She's suddenly ravenous.

*

Later, fortified by sandwiches and wine, she decides she'll have a shower to wash the dust of Auchenblae out of her hair, then a siesta and then maybe a walk down to the seashore before dinner. Such luxury. On her way back to her room, she suddenly remembers about the curiosity cabinet, the embroidered box that Cal had mentioned, and wonders if it is in the residents' lounge. She had forgotten to ask Mrs Cameron about it but she ventures in, anyway. This room too is quiet, although there is an elderly man sitting in the most comfortable chair, in a patch of sunlight, ostensibly reading a newspaper. She sees that he is fast asleep, his glasses sliding down his nose and the paper balanced precariously on the edge of his knee. He is at the far end of the room, and she catches sight of a display cabinet, just inside the door, well away from the sunlight. She tiptoes into the room, so as not to wake him.

The casket is stunningly beautiful and – she immediately realises – probably worth a fortune. Cal is right about it. She has only ever seen its like in museums. It is a Jacobean box, heavily embroidered in raised work, the colours a little faded, but still good, glowing subtly in this mercifully dark part of the room. It stands on tiny gilded feet and the panels seem to be telling a story. Many of these caskets depicted biblical stories but she isn't sure which one this is. A woman in flowing blue robes stands amid growing things, a profusion of flowers and grasses and ears of corn. Daisy sees that they are the flowers of this island: primroses, violets, foxgloves, wild roses. All seasons in one. There are birds: swans and seagulls and swallows. She recognises a pair of oystercatchers. Down in one corner, there is even a tiny mouse. And there is a house, embroidered in grey silk with mica fragments for windows. With a start of surprise and excitement, she sees that the house has a square tower with a long rectangular building to one side. It fills one whole panel of the casket. Surely it must be Auchenblae?

Various objects are arranged on shelves in the glass cabinet: a shuttle, a lace collar, a fan, a pincushion. There is a hand mirror and a coral teether, a heap of pebbles and shells and swansdown. There is a scrap of yellowed paper with faded handwriting on it but she can't read what is written there. She realises immediately that these must be the contents of the cabinet, even though there are no labels, no interpretations, no notices telling her what she is seeing and how she ought to think about these things. She can think whatever she likes. She notices that they are all women's things, and is excited to realise that this woman must once have lived at Auchenblae, must have sat before its fires, lived her life in its rooms, walked in its garden, and threaded her way down the path to the seashore that she and Cal had walked that very morning. How strange, she thinks. How very strange.

She must have said the words aloud, because the elderly man wakes up with a start and just catches his newspaper in time. It's Mr Cameron, the hotel owner. He smiles over at her. 'Caught in the act,' he says. 'Sleeping on the job. Don't tell Elspeth, will you?'

The hotel is a family business, run by the Camerons, their son, George, and his wife Laura. The older couple have a small apartment at the back of the hotel, while George and Laura live in a bungalow next door. Laura is heavily pregnant with their second child, George is perpetually harassed, and the senior Camerons are helping out.

'We keep hoping to retire, but it never seems to happen,' says Mr Cameron with a sigh. 'I think Elspeth likes it that way.'

'I was just looking at the casket. It's so beautiful. Aren't you lucky to have it?'

'It's only on loan, lass. Donal McNeill is the rightful owner. But I suspect it did come from your house.'

'Yes. So I was told this morning.'

'Were you? Oh – Cal. Aye. Elspeth said he was sniffing about.'

She can see that Mr Cameron is not just as charmed by Cal as Elspeth. Which seems significant. Perhaps Cal is the kind of man women lose their heads over, even older women. He certainly has charisma.

'It was in the McNeill family for years. They've been in that cottage down at Ardachy for about a hundred years, and the wee box was always there, I believe. But I'd lay bets it originally came from your house. They used to call it the "old laird's house" you know.'

'Really?' She's intrigued.

'Aye, lass. And this is the new laird's house, or it was until they turned it into a hotel. Auchenblae was a McNeill stronghold

74

for centuries, but then in the eighteenth and nineteenth centuries there were huge upheavals. The house changed hands several times until it was bought by the Neilsons. Viola's grandfather or great-grandfather maybe. They were industrialists of some sort, seeking an island retreat like so many of those who used to come here. And maybe there was a family connection since the names are similar. McNeill and Neilson. But maybe it's just coincidence.'

'I know so little about all this. I must try and find out more.'

'I don't know the details, but there are people on the island, people born and bred here, who could tell you all about it. You'll need to speak to Donal McNeill for one. He knows a lot of the island history. Viola's father was Hugh Neilson. He was wounded in the Great War but lived for long enough to have a child. They're all buried in the cemetery at Keill, along the coast. Your forebears.'

'I'll have to go and have a look.'

'You will. Do you have plans for the house?'

She sighs. 'I'm not sure. I'll have to think about it.'

'You wouldn't consider living here, on the island?'

'Oh I might consider it, but whether I can afford it is another matter. My grandmother left me the house but not much in the way of ready cash. Not when everything is paid up.'

*

Later, after a deep and dreamless nap that leaves her feeling unreal and vaguely disorientated, she sits in the comfortable armchair, gazing out at the sea, and phones her father. The mobile signal isn't too good and he's in a pub somewhere. She can hear people laughing and talking in the background, the sound of somebody tuning up a fiddle. She can tell immediately that he's excited. She needs advice, reassurance, maybe even wants to ask if he can come and give her some moral support, stay in the house with her for a few days, but he has news for her. His agent has been in touch. There's the possibility of a string of gigs: late spring and summer folk festivals. Nothing major and it isn't going to make his fortune.

He'll be playing for a popular singer. He's too old and too experienced for overnight success. But the star has specifically asked for him – and his fiddle, of course.

'It's nice to be asked,' he says. 'A couple of months. Not so much a tour as a few good gigs. I suspect somebody else dropped out and they could only think of me!'

'Don't put yourself down, Dad! You'll do it of course.'

'Do you think I should?' he asks and she can hear the uncertainty in his voice.

'Of course you must!' She's seized with the feeling that their roles have been suddenly reversed. For years, she has asked for his support, his advice. Come running to him when things didn't go her way. Or when there were choices to be made. Now, he needs reassurance that he's doing the right thing. He is so much in the habit of putting her first that it's hard for him to remember that she's all grown up. For years she has accepted the way he has always prioritised her, but now her conscience is pricking her. It's his turn. He has given up so much for her, so many opportunities. Never once complaining. Never letting her see that he wouldn't rather stay with her. And perhaps that has been the truth. He has always loved her unconditionally. Always put her first. But she can't go on demanding that forever, can she? Or at least not all the time.

'I really think you should go, Dad,' she says.

'Do you? Do you really?'

'Absolutely. In fact, I'll be angry if you don't.'

'But what about the house?'

'I don't have to make any immediate decisions.'

'Is it a wreck?'

'No. It's in surprisingly good condition. I haven't even seen all of it yet.' The tower pops into her mind, the grim, forbidding bulk of it. 'There's a lot of stuff. Furniture. Antiques of all kinds as well as quite a lot of rubbish. And who knows what's going on beneath the surface.'

The light-hearted remark gives her a small frisson. Who knows indeed.

'Are you going to stay there? I mean sleep there?'

'I'll maybe give it a try till the end of the week. This hotel is very nice but it's quite pricey when I have a big house of my own a few miles along the road.'

'That's true. But won't you be lonely?'

'A bit. But there's no crime here to speak of, Dad, and after all, any ghosts will be relatives. So they'll probably be friendly.' Once again that little frisson. *Don't tempt providence*, she thinks.

'Well. If you're sure. I was going to suggest coming up there for a wee while, but now I'll have things to do. It's exciting, though. As long as you'll be OK.'

'I'll be fine. Honestly. I'm coming home at the weekend anyway. I have a fair, remember? Although my stock's a bit low.'

'You could bring some of the stuff from Auchenblae.'

'Maybe I could. But I want to take it slowly. I'm pretty sure I'll come back here next week and try to stay a bit longer. Which is why I want to stay in the house. There's so much to sort out. I need to do it properly. I don't want to let something go and then find out it's really valuable. I need to do my homework.'

'Well, I'll help you this weekend, anyway. Haul a few boxes for you.'

'That would be nice.'

'Keep the villains at bay, eh?'

'Oh yes.'

The dealers who frequent these low-key fairs and boot sales can sometimes be intimidating, especially if you are a young woman manning a stall on your own. They come very early, sometimes even gaining admittance via the back door, or hopping over gates at outdoor sales, and gather around as you are unpacking boxes. They push and shove, handling things, grabbing, snatching, making unreasonably low offers for items. It has happened to her more than once, leaving her feeling intimidated and somehow violated. Now,

77

she has taken to carrying a walking stick or a big golfing umbrella or at least leaving one close at hand, so that she can fend them off if need be. She hasn't had to use it yet and isn't sure that she ever would, but its proximity gives her confidence.

Suddenly, just as she has ended the call and put the phone in her bag, the image of Cal Galbraith pops into her mind and she realises where she has seen him before. Not all that long ago either. How could she have forgotten? Except that she had seen him in a completely different context and back then he was dressed for winter, the encounter brief, albeit striking. She just hadn't made the connection.

It had been in Glasgow, well before Christmas: a grey day with a lazy wind that blew straight through you. Funds were low and she had bought far too much stock at auction, so she had chosen to do a sale that was something between an antique fair and a boot sale. The lower end of her market. Sometimes she has bought things here herself, and has even found bargains from time to time: a shapely Swedish glass vase, a piece of art pottery with a vivid blue and green glaze, a long and lovely shepherd's plaid in black and white wool, buried in a cardboard box beneath a table. 'Just an old tablecloth, hen,' the dealer said, accepting a ten-pound note with alacrity, but she knew better. This was a hundred-year-old survival. Maybe even older.

As a seller, it was very different. The wintry weather and the early rising seemed to have brought out the worst in people. The usually cheerful and friendly Glaswegians seemed surly and uncommunicative. And when the men – it was always scruffy, middle-aged men – crowded around her as she was struggling to unpack her bits and pieces, they felt stifling, faintly menacing and she was aware that her heart was racing.

'For fuck's sake, get a move on, hen!' one of them muttered, grabbing a newspaper-wrapped package before she could stop him. It contained a teapot in the shape of a white rabbit. 'We huvnae got all day! I'll gie ye 50p for this!'

She recognised him as another stallholder. She still sees him in the salerooms she frequents: a big man with a face like a ham, fingers like sausages, his belly protruding, even under his winter jacket. He seldom pays much for anything, but he likes to stand at the back and talk loudly about the 'business' and about the bargains he has found. He also likes to slag off his customers, whom he appears to loathe.

She snatched the pot back from him, almost dropping it. 'Leave that alone!'

'Keep your hair on, hen!'

That was when a man who had been standing at the back of the crowd trying to see what she had already put out edged his way to the front of the group and turned to face his fellow dealers, blocking their view of the stall.

'Patience, gentlemen!' he said.

One of them jeered at him. 'Get the fuck out of the way, pal!'

That was when the newcomer's voice changed suddenly to pure Glasgow. 'Oh aye? Are you planning to make me, *pal*?'

It should have been daft. He wasn't exactly a muscle man. Even though he was wearing a winter jacket and was muffled in a scarf, he was whip thin, tall and spare. All the same, her first thought back then was that he looked dangerous, as though he could handle himself in a fight. Duck and dive like a boxer. There was a sort of controlled aggression about him in this situation. She thought that he would make a far better friend than an enemy, which was just as well, since he seemed to have decided to play the gentleman.

'Ach, away tae fuck back to your ain stall, Jimmy Johnson,' he said quite lazily and with a little grin. She was shocked by his language, which seemed at odds with his smart jacket, his shiny shoes. 'We all ken fine you like to bully folk into giein ye the stuff for nuthin! Especially wee lassies!' He looked around. 'Is that no true?'

Unexpectedly, there were a few nods and murmurs of agreement from the other men.

'You got a stall here the day, Jimmy?' he asked, switching from intimidating to friendly in an instant.

'Aye, I have.' Jimmy seemed reluctant to answer but couldn't help himself.

'And does Big Agnes ken you're harassing wee lassies?'

There were a few sniggers from the crowd. Big Agnes was Jimmy's wife. Daisy sees her in the salerooms to this day. She plonks herself down in the front seat and stays there. It's always Jimmy who does the bidding. Agnes is the keeper of the purse, though. She's a formidable woman as only west of Scotland women can be. When she nips out for a fag, she leaves her hat and gloves on the seat and woe betide the unsuspecting punter who moves them.

One of the spectators said, 'Christ, your coat'll be hingin on a shoogly peg if she finds out, Jimmy.'

The rest of the men guffawed – that loud, ostentatious laughter that only men seem to indulge in.

The bully spread his hands, backed away. 'OK, OK,' he said. 'I was just looking for a bargain.'

'Aren't we all?' The younger man grinned. 'I'll be along later. Have a wee word with Agnes. See what you've got.'

Daisy unwrapped a few more of her items, in a hurry to get it done now while there was a human barrier, however tenuous, between her and the more predatory dealers.

'You?' The bully looked at her saviour with thinly disguised contempt overlying a certain nervousness. There was something about the newcomer that the older man clearly found intimidating. Daisy could understand it, but couldn't quite put her finger on why it should be the case. 'I don't deal in your kind of stuff.'

'Naw. Nae virtuous objects for you, eh, Jimmy?'

Jimmy looked puzzled, as well he might. But Daisy found herself smiling. *Objets de vertu.* Who on earth was her scathing knight in shining armour? She didn't entirely approve of him mocking somebody else's ignorance, but then, Jimmy was asking for it. Did he belong to one of the city auction houses? Well, he didn't sound as though he did. Not posh enough. He sounded as though he belonged to Glasgow, with that hard edge to his voice and his gallus manner – that Glasgow word meaning bold, cheeky, flashy even – although there was something else, something softer and more foreign lurking just below the surface. She was intrigued.

The crowd shuffled off in search of more novelties.

Her saviour stuck his hands in his pockets and turned away.

'Thank you,' she said. 'It was very kind of you to rescue me.'

'Any time! Though I expect you'd have managed. I just couldn't resist the chance to piss him off. He's such an arse though, isn't he? All mouth and nae trousers. I'd best be on my way, hen. He's right. All the good stuff goes early. Just that you don't have to bully folk to get it!'

He gave her a brief wave and headed off into the crowd. That was that. She had thought him attractive and she still does. Briefly, she had even fantasised about him coming back, bringing coffee and doughnuts from one of the stalls that sold supplies to hungry dealers and visitors. But of course he hadn't come back. Why would he, she thought, when she was in shabby winter clothes, her hair scraped back, her skin pallid from the early start and a cold sore just starting on her lip. She had never seen him again until earlier today, at Auchenblae. Cal Galbraith. Antique dealer and unlikely boot sale hero.

NINE

1588

The ship was a single-masted birlinn or galley, built of oak, Mateo judged, although he had seen nothing quite like it before, and wasn't entirely sure that he trusted it to take them safely to another country, no matter how close that country might seem. It looked like a vessel from another age to his eyes. But what choice did they have? The galley was small and turned out to be highly manoeuvrable, with oars as well as sails. Her captain, Alistair McAllister, spoke Gaelic to his crew, but summoned enough of the Scots tongue, with even the odd Spanish word picked up from God knows what encounter, for the benefit of his passengers. He answered Mateo's questions about the vessel, how she was rigged, how she sailed, and this proved reassuring, not least in that Mateo found he could understand him and make himself understood in return. It seemed that McAllister was a competent seaman with a healthy respect for the waters between Ireland and Scotland. Moreover, his crew obeyed him instantly and without demur, which spoke well of his seamanship and his authority.

'Few people on the island of *Garbh* speak anything but Gaelic,' he warned Mateo, 'although Ruaridh McNeill, the laird, can converse easily enough in Scots. His sons and daughters too. The laird's wife, Bláithín McGugan, came from the isle of Islay, but she died some years ago. There's a grown-up, unmarried daughter living at home, and another much younger daughter, Ishbel. It was her birth that caused the death of her mother.'

'And the whole island is his?'

'Aye. He's their chief. There's an older son, Kenneth, away in St Andrews for his education.' McAllister said this with a slight sneer. 'And another son, Malcolm. He's been fostered with the chief of Clan Darroch, on Jura.'

'Fostered?'

'Aye. It's the custom of this country. To send a son into the household of another man. McNeill has never seen fit to marry again, although it was expected. Most men do. Women too for that matter, if they're widowed. But the elder of the two daughters is of an age where she can run the household well enough, and until she finds herself a husband, perhaps McNeill has seen no need to encumber himself with a wife. Ruaridh is one of those men who ca canny!'

'Excuse me?' Mateo didn't understand.

McAllister frowned. 'He trims his sails to the prevailing winds.' He gestured at the rigging.

'Ah. I see,' said Mateo, thinking that this was something he and his shipmates had certainly not done.

'He's a wise man. And of course he's not without resources, having many men at his beck and call, tacksmen and tenants, and enough cattle with decent grazing so that they needn't go hungry.'

All of this McAllister ventured in the course of the voyage, but as they came closer to the island, he fell silent and seemed anxious only to be rid of his illicit cargo. They approached the island from the south-west but it was clear that they were heading for the more sheltered east coast of *Eilean Garbh*, where what McAllister called the 'big house' was situated.

'*Achadh nam Blàth* is its name,' he told them. 'There are other good houses on the island, especially to the south, but none to match this one. It means field of flooers in the Scots tongue. But you will see few signs of any blooms there today.'

Mateo had seen no flowers as they approached the island, although some small trees – most of them leafless now – seemed to be grouped around the house, sheltering it as far as possible from the prevailing winds. Perhaps there had been a deliberate planting. A naked hillock rose above the building to the south with a ragged, wind-ravaged copse atop, but he could not name the trees. On either side of the house, the land – what he could see of it through the encroaching mist – rose and fell, long and hilly, like some mysterious hump-backed animal. He could just make out low houses with thatched roofs, crouched in the shelter of the hills, with a drift of smoke hanging over them and over the big house too. So there might be fires and warmth. He had a sudden sharp pang of sadness that threatened to unman him. He was sick for his home. Longed to be elsewhere, where the sun shone, and the flowers bloomed all year round. What were they doing here? Why had they ever come? He gave himself a shake. This would not do. He and his ability to barter, to persuade, might be all that stood between a humiliating death for himself and Paco. And having come so far, he had best do whatever he could to save them.

'What do you think will happen?' asked Paco, at his elbow. 'It doesn't look like a very hospitable place, cousin.'

'No. It does not. But it's our best hope of escape. And the house seems civilized enough. Or so the captain seems to think.'

'Do you have the letter from the priest? Do you have it safe, Mateo?'

Mateo reached inside his jerkin, not for the first time. The gold was all gone. The fee had been paid before they left. McAllister had insisted on it. While they were lying low in the galley, Father Brendan had come to the harbour bringing a hastily written note on a scrap of thin paper, harvested from the beginning or end of a book. This must have been a great sacrifice, since books were just as scarce as paper in these parts. The priest had sealed it with wax and a signet bearing a crude image of the Blessed Virgin Mary. They would just have to trust to his good will as far as the contents of the note were concerned.

'This is by way of introduction and a brief explanation,' Father Brendan had said when he handed them the note. 'I am not at all certain that McNeill has any skill at reading and writing. So many of these island chieftains see fit to employ a scribe to write for them. But I'm told that the elder of the two lassies may have learned her letters from her mother before she died, so perhaps she fulfils that role. You must just trust to luck. I'll pray for you.'

'I have the letter, safe and sound,' he said to Francisco.

'You don't think he has betrayed us, do you?'

'No.' But Mateo spoke with a confidence he did not quite feel. 'No, I think he's a good man. Although whether his letter will make any difference, I can't say. He spoke nothing but the truth. We have no resources except our own wits. We must trust to luck, and hope that his prayers are answered.'

*

Some little while later, that is precisely what they were doing: trusting to luck and the prayers of an Irish priest. Their unexpected arrival had been noted and almost immediately, a party of burly islandmen, bristling with weapons, came hurrying down to the shore to greet them. They were wrapped in woollen plaids, their dun and grey blending with the landscape. McAllister had given him the right word for the garment that seemed to serve as a cloak, body covering and blanket all in one. For a brief moment, Mateo thought that they were about to be slain, as their companions had been slain on sight, in the west of Ireland. He saw Francisco's face grow even paler if that were possible and found himself reaching for his dagger. But the men only surrounded them and by brusque gestures and a certain amount of jostling, encouraged them to walk towards the house. The Spaniards were in no position to object. The men were not gentle and their speed was too much for the ailing younger lad, who stumbled and fell. One of the men picked him up by the scruff of the neck, none too gently.

'We'll hae tae oxter him!' he said, cryptically, and when Mateo only spread his hands and shrugged, he summoned the assistance of a colleague and, with hands under his elbows, more or less carried him, his feet dragging along the ground. It was humiliating, thought Mateo, but there was no other way his cousin could have finished the journey and he himself was too weak to help.

The contrast between the chilly exterior of the house and the extreme warmth of the interior was marked. A blast of welcome heat came from an enormous fire of peat and spitting, blue-flamed driftwood at one end of a great hall. There were cooking pots and from one of them a savoury smell filtered into the room. The fireplace housed various cooking implements, including a flat black pan, from which an elderly woman was carefully removing cakes with a wooden paddle. The scent of toasted oatmeal was added to whatever was emanating from the pot. In an instant, the sickness evaporated and Mateo realised that he was ravenously hungry.

The sudden access of heat made their heads spin, and Francisco clutched at his arm to steady himself. A tall man with long red hair, shot through with grey, rose to his feet from a heavily carved chair beside the fire and stared at them with mingled hostility and curiosity. He was dressed in a short saffron-dyed linen shirt (*why are they so fond of this colour?* Mateo thought) with a short jacket over it, woollen trews and hose.

'Well, well, well. This is a rare occurrence on *Eilean Garbh*,' he said in Scots, with a peculiarly mirthless grin, like an animal showing its teeth in threat. 'What brings two such ragged strangers, interlowpers, unbidden and uninvited to my island?'

Noting the stress on the word 'my', Mateo managed to summon a bow and brought Francisco with him, only because he was holding him so close. It struck him that he didn't know the customs of this country at all. Any gesture they made might be open to misinterpretation.

'Sir, I'm happy to meet you. Am I right in thinking that you are Ruaridh McNeill, Chief of *Garbh*?'

'You have the advantage of me. You know my name. I don't ken yours.'

'We're cousins: Mateo and Francisco de Tegueste of the town of San Cristobal de la Laguna, on the island of Tenerife.'

'Which is?'

'Far south of here. A great distance. Some call them the Fortunate Isles.'

'Do they indeed? Why so? They don't seem to have been very fortunate for you, lad.'

'The sun shines there all year round. There are flowers and many fruits.' He stopped. 'But you're right. We should not have left. We had a long voyage and many adventures along the way.'

'I imagine so. A long voyage and a very foolish *misadventure*, from what I hear. And what brings you to my island?' His lips twisted in a grimace. 'But I ken fine what brings you here.'

'Sir, we have a letter. May I?' He gestured to the breast of his jerkin, afraid that the man would think he had a weapon concealed there. Which he did. But he would rather not think of using it.

'A letter?' McNeill held out a big, gnarled hand, impatiently. 'Let me see.'

Mateo handed the precious missive over. 'There was a priest. Father Brendan. He helped us. Found us passage to your island with a man called McAllister.'

'Alistair? Aye. I saw his galley. He deposited you upon my shore and hightailed it out of here as fast as his oarsmen could carry him. I ken Alistair McAllister well enough. He wouldn't do you a bad turn, although I'd wager he charged you dear for whatever favour he was persuaded to do for you.'

'We paid him the whole of what we still had in our possession, sir. But we were desperate. And it means we must throw ourselves on your mercy.'

McNeill took the letter, broke the seal, unfolded it and gazed at it in silence for a moment or two. Then he raised his voice.

'Lilias!' he shouted. 'Where are you, lass? I need you.'

He turned his attention back to the pair, and quite suddenly pulled an oak bench across from its place beside the fire. The bench was heavy, but he shifted it as easily as if it had been made of straw.

'Here,' he said. 'Your friend seems on the point of fainting clean away like a lassie. Sit yourself down lad, before you fall down.'

Mateo deposited Francisco on the bench and pushed his head forward. His cousin sank forward, his head on his knees. 'Thank you, sir. I'm afraid he's at the very end of his strength. And we've eaten very little for weeks. Months even.'

'That we may be able to remedy in due course. But don't thank me just yet, son. I haven't made up my mind what to do with you.'

'Father?'

Mateo turned around at the sound. It was the woman they had seen earlier, as they approached the bay below the house. Divested of her wrap, she was revealed to be a tall girl, of perhaps eighteen summers, dressed in a simple worsted gown, kilted up to reveal a golden petticoat – the saffron colour again – beneath. There was some lace at her throat, and she wore a necklace of small freshwater pearls. All of this, perhaps, was in token of her status in this community. The red hair that he had seen blowing in the wind, longer and more vivid than her father's, but familial hair all the same, had been tamed and was pulled back, quite severely, into a long plait. He had never seen hair quite this colour before, and had to stop himself from gazing at it in wonder. A pair of slender, long-nosed dogs, sleek as grey and white seals, sloped into the room behind her, setting up a great barking and growling when they saw the two strangers.

'Hush, Bran, Finn!' she said sharply. 'No use in raising the alarm now, when you were sleeping soundly earlier!'

The dogs slunk off to sit by the fire, eyeing the incomers over their shoulders from time to time and curling their lips to show their contempt.

Wordlessly, McNeill handed her the letter. She took it, glanced across at the men, smiled faintly at them, and began to read.

'You don't know what the priest wrote?' McNeill asked.

Mateo shook his head. 'No, sir. The letter was sealed. But he was kind to us. Kinder than he needed to be and at some risk to his own safety, I fear. I hope he is not betrayed.'

'Aye. There are some who are fearless in fulfilment of their own Christian vows. Not many, these days, I'll allow, but a few. You were lucky to meet him. And what's your story? How came you to be wandering the Irish coast in search of deliverance? And speaking in the English tongue, as well.'

'I was taught by a tutor, an exile. From an English monastery. My father believed in learning.' *And fighting*, he thought. His father had believed in fighting. Manly virtues. There had been nothing indulgent or kindly about him. As he saw it, mind and body alike must be disciplined.

'Aye. And so do I believe in learning, having suffered from the lack of it all my life. I will make sure my sons are not so deficient. Although I would have them learn the arts of war as well. The times are very uncertain.'

'We came with an unwise expedition. You're right. Most of our ship-board friends, our fellow countrymen, are drowned or slain. I'm sure you have had news of it by now.'

'We have. And are in two minds about it: whether we approve or not. My main concern, however, is that I should bring no trouble to this island, which is my own, its people in my care. Do you bring trouble in your wake, Mateo de Tegueste?'

'I hope not. It's not my intention. There are just two of us, and few people who know we're here. Only the priest. And beyond him, McAllister and his crew.'

'Aye, well, they are men who would keep a secret for a thousand years, so we need have no fear of *them* whispering tales into hostile ears.'

He glanced at the young woman again. 'This is my daughter. She also has more learning than her father. Tell me, Lilias, what does the letter say? Does it confirm their story?'

'Aye it does. It's very brief, father. The priest says he writes in haste. He has taken pity on them and found them passage to a safer country.' She scanned the note, frowning a little. 'He isn't certain why, only that they don't seem to be of evil intent' – here she glanced at them – 'and it seems the Christian thing to do. He asks that we shelter them for a time, and make enquiries as to how they might be returned home for they have...' She hesitated, gazed at the letter again, colouring slightly. 'He says they have suffered much.'

Her skin was so pale as to seem translucent, with a dusting of freckles, as though some friendly saint had scattered gold there. That's what he found himself thinking. But she would never be able to hide her emotions, never dissemble, colouring easily and often.

McNeill gazed at them in silence for a moment. Mateo could hear the big piece of driftwood in the fireplace crackling and sparking and settling into its enormous bed of ash. The woman who was tending to the cooking went about her business quietly, humming under her breath. Outside it was almost dark and a wind was rising, wailing about the roofs of the old building and moaning in the chimney, sending little gusts of peat smoke back into the room. He thought how terrible it would be to be cast out again, into the chilly night. They might as well be dead. Francisco would be dead, in no time at all.

McNeill seemed to have made up his mind. 'Well, the former I can do. I can give you shelter, if you're prepared to work for your keep. All stray dogs who take shelter here must do some work, even Bran and Finn here, although they are remiss at times.'

The two dogs raised their heads simultaneously and wagged their tails, obligingly.

'As for the latter, the enquiries as to how you might win home again, I am not entirely sure about that. Sirs, I would much rather keep your presence here a secret until I find out what way the wind is blowing. This is a woefully divided country. But those who unlawfully kill a lawful queen cannot expect very much in the way of regard or respect from the professed subjects of that queen, can they?'

In the gathering gloom, Mateo saw a sudden flash of anger on the man's countenance, but it was as quickly veiled. He knew that it was not directed at himself, or his cousin, and was glad of it. He thought about the Scottish queen, the news of her execution at the behest of her English cousin. Perhaps the priest had been right. Perhaps they might be safer here than anywhere else in these islands.

Francisco raised his head. He spoke to his cousin in Spanish. 'Tell him we'll do anything we can, anything they wish, if only they'll give us food and shelter for a while. I would dearly love to be able to stop running for a while, Mateo.'

McNeill looked enquiringly at Mateo. 'What does he say?'

'My cousin has little English and is not at all well. Misery and sickness have robbed him of his courage, as such things are wont to do. I think they have made a coward of him. Of us both, perhaps.'

To his surprise, Lilias interposed. 'Gentleness is not the same as cowardice. And sickness can turn the bravest of us into mere bairns.'

Her father did not reprove her for the interruption, but only smiled at her. 'My daughter is a soft-hearted creature. But so was her mother and I can't complain about that, having so much regard for her.'

'Francisco says that we will do whatever we can in exchange for food and shelter. And he's right. We will. For as long as you see fit to keep us here.'

'My daughter is also right about your cousin. He seems very sick. There's little strength in him that I can see. He's weaker than my wee Ishbel.'

'But there's strength in me, sir. I can work for two. Until he feels well enough.'

'Well, well, we'll see.' McNeill raised his voice slightly. 'We need some light!' he said and an elderly man immediately hurried up to light several candles secured about the room from a taper thrust into the fire. 'For now,' he continued, 'I think you must wash, and Beathag here,' he gestured at the woman who had been cooking flat cakes and tending to the cooking pots, 'Beathag will find you some clothes. What you are wearing must be exceedingly verminous and your garments are certainly filthy. Even for one like myself who is not just so particular about a wee bit of mud as some in this household.' Here he glanced across at his daughter again, a smile playing about his lips.

It was true. The heat was drying their rags and the smells emanating from them were not pleasant. Mateo thought he had grown used to the stench of unwashed garments and bloodied, fouled bodies, but this was beyond all endurance. He was ashamed.

'These garments must be destroyed,' added McNeill. 'Once you are in a more respectable condition for a *siobhalt* – a civilized – house, we can think about food. And find somewhere for you to sleep.'

Lilias spoke to Beathag in her own tongue. The older woman regarded the pair of them with deep suspicion in her dark eyes, but at the behest of her mistress, came over to them and motioned to them to follow her to a door at the tower end of the great hall.

Lilias smiled at them. It made Mateo realise how seldom he had seen the kindly smile of a woman directed at himself over these past months. Not since they had sailed from home and his aunt had embraced him and bidden him and Francisco farewell. His own mother was long dead. Usually, his father frowned on these displays of affection, but even he had been caught up in the emotion of the moment. Mateo had an almost overwhelming sense of sorrow, a great desire to be comforted. He was too exhausted, too miserable to feel anything for the young woman but a vague thankfulness that she seemed to be regarding them with sympathy rather than the all-pervasive fear, suspicion and hatred that had been their lot over the past months. For the present, that was enough.

'Go with Beathag,' she said. 'She'll show you where you can wash. And she'll find clean clothes for you. But – you have no possessions with you? Nothing at all?'

Impulsively, Mateo reached inside his clothing. 'May I?' he said, still afraid of giving offence. When McNeill nodded, he pulled out his treasured dagger, reversed it and handed it to the chieftain, with another little bow. 'This is our only weapon, sir. I wish to hide nothing from you, so perhaps I could leave it in your safe-keeping until I have need of it again.'

McNeill took the dagger and examined it. He raised his eye-brows. 'Small but beautifully made. Then perhaps you are men of some consequence after all, and not the thieves and vagabonds your appearance would suggest. But I've long learned not to judge men by their outward appearance. Thank you for your confidence in me. You'll find it is not misplaced.'

As they were following Beathag, there was a scurrying of feet and a little girl with the same vivid red hair as Lilias and her father came running into the room. She halted at the sight of the Spaniards.

'Oh!' she exclaimed, nonplussed. 'These are the men we saw on the shore, Lilias. You said they would be coming here and I didn't believe you. I thought they were beggars and might pass us by or go to Beathag for food. Who are they? I don't like strangers!'

'They are visitors, not strangers, Ishbel,' said Lilias.

She held out her hand and the child ran over and took it, swinging from her arm. Mateo thought she must be seven or eight years old. His sister had a little girl of about the same age. This must be the last child, the daughter whose birth had, as McAllister reported, 'caused the death of her mother'.

'They have come a long way and suffered a great deal on the journey,' continued the older girl, 'so we must make them welcome. Isn't that our custom, Ishbel? Isn't that what I have always taught you, and what our mother taught me before you were born?'

McNeill looked indulgently at his two daughters. 'Soft,' he said, in the Scots tongue. 'Soft, daft lassies. My wife, Bláithín, was a great one for welcoming the stranger to our shores, if any ever ventured so far.'

'She was,' said Lilias.

'Me – I'm not so certain about this, but I make up my own mind. There are times when such generosity is folly. Not everyone sets foot on my island without malice in their hearts so you'll forgive me if I'm cautious. But my Bláithín was right in this, at least. It is our custom not to turn the stranger in dire need away from our door, and it is also our custom not to do violence to any who come in peace, once we have offered hospitality. So you need have no fears, sirs, as long as you do not abuse that hospitality. Eat with us, and then sleep without fear of betrayal.

TEN

The following morning, this time suitably fortified with the full Scottish breakfast, including tattie scones, eggs and crispy bacon, Daisy checks out of the hotel.

'We do have a room free if you decide you want to come back, dear,' says Mrs Cameron, kindly. 'Don't feel you have to stay in the house if it doesn't seem...' she hesitates. 'Comfortable. If it's not comfortable for you there. It's a big old house by any standards. Especially if you're not used to country living.'

'I'm sure it'll be fine,' says Daisy, with a confidence she doesn't really feel. 'I live on my own a lot, you know. It's my dad's flat but he's away half the time.'

Still, she thinks, *a tiny city flat isn't quite the same thing as a remote and ancient house.* She certainly won't be reading *The Shining* in bed tonight.

She drives down to the Scoull village shop where she buys some supplies: milk, bread, butter, eggs, more biscuits, a packet of bacon, a few tins, a couple of bottles of wine and a bottle of island malt whisky. She hadn't investigated the Auchenblae cupboards yesterday, so there may be unsuspected stores in there, although she doubts if, latterly anyway, Viola had much of an appetite. She has a feeling she may have need of the odd dram of whisky before the week is out, for purposes of courage and comfort if nothing else.

The house already feels faintly familiar. She senses that just as she will have to get used to being there, the house will have to get used to its latest owner. She has a sense not so much of hostility as anxiety, if such a word can be applied to a building. It is a cloudy day, threatening rain. Elspeth Cameron has told her that sometimes the rain clouds skip right over the island from the west and head for the mainland, but today the forecast is for showers. All the same, she opens the door of Auchenblae on the seaward side and finds a big stone, shaped like a rudimentary figure, with a broad base, a tiny head and a narrow neck. They hadn't noticed it the day before, but it seems to be deliberately left there as a doorstop. She hefts it into position, wondering if it has been shaped, or if it is a natural stone. One more thing to find out about. The wooden block is still perched on the windowsill where she left it, drying out slowly.

She unpacks her shopping and is pleased to see that the fridge seems to be working. She switches on the immersion heater, goes upstairs, and takes a sheet, pillowcases and a duvet cover from the bottom of the pile in the linen press. They smell quite fresh. A clutch of home-made lavender bags fall out as she tugs at them, and they still smell faintly of the herb, as does the bedding. She makes up the bed in what was once her mother's room. There are a couple of hot water bottles in the linen cupboard too. Grandma Nancy would have worried about the damp, so she fills both of them and tucks them under the covers.

Rewarding herself with a big mug of coffee, she takes it into the big living room and switches on the television. *Bargain Hunt* is on. 'You could do a whole series of programmes from this place,' she says aloud to the television. 'Maybe I'll issue an invitation.'

There is a rattle of rain on the windows and the delicious scent of rain-soaked grass drifts in the doorway. A squall has come bowling in from the sea. She leaves the television on, since the voices are comforting, and heads up the stairs, past the bedrooms, to the second stair, darker and narrower, to what was once the servants' quarters. The light is muted up here, since these rooms are tucked into the roof, with sloping walls. Anyone of any height would be forever banging his or her head. Cal certainly would. Small, dusty skylights, one in each room, are the only sources of natural light. She would have to stand on a chair even to open them, let alone look out. There are grim iron bed frames, looking vaguely institutional, although one of the rooms, a little larger than the rest, has a rickety brass double bed. There are chipped washstands, bedside cabinets with broken hinges, a dismal collection of substandard furniture and naked lightbulbs without shades. Perhaps the Neilsons had thought that their servants deserved no better.

As on the floor below, one of the rooms seems to have been used for storage and has several tea chests plus – more intriguingly – a couple of oak blanket boxes with iron hinges. The more accessible of the two seems to be full of old table linen, layer upon layer of it, so densely packed that the leaves of stiff cloth have begun to stick together. The sour smell of hundred-year-old starch emerges from the box. She can see damask tablecloths in fascinating patterns with the blurred and slightly random designs of handwoven linen. There are tea tablecloths and tray cloths with cobwebby lace inserts or crochet edging, heavy white cotton embroidery on white linen. She flattens the cloths down again with some difficulty and fastens the lid. Something else that will need to be examined, catalogued, maybe laundered before selling. So much work. She's again torn between the desire to explore and sort everything and the urge to let somebody else take over and just get rid of it all for her.

At the end of the corridor is a bathroom with a worn tiled floor, very like the one downstairs, but in much worse condition. There's a lavatory with nasty brown stains on the porcelain, a cracked pedestal sink with a cold tap, a small hip bath tucked into one corner. A wobbly cupboard holds a few suspicious brown jars and bottles and a pile of thin towels, frequent laundering having reduced them to a sort of uniform grey. The contrast with the furnishings in the rooms below is striking. Beside the bathroom door, she finds a low door that she thinks is a cupboard, but when she opens it, she sees that it is another staircase, a bare stone spiral, very gloomy and damp. She doesn't venture in, but she thinks it must once have given the staff access to the main bedrooms and the big downstairs room, so that they could carry water and tend fires without intruding on the family too much.

I'm glad I wasn't a servant in the Neilson household, anyway, she thinks. *They weren't exactly pampered, whoever they were.*

She leaves the servants' quarters behind with some relief, and heads back down to the living room. She finds Viola's wellies and shakes them, in case of spiders or even mice. Only a little dried mud falls out. To her surprise, they are a comfortable fit. The rain has stopped and the sun is shining so warmly that it is raising steam from the flagstones at the sea side of the house. Making her way along this side of the house, she discovers that there is an exterior door to the tower after all. It's at the far end of the building, and can't possibly be back-to-back with the one in the kitchen. A private stair? The door looks ancient, its wood bleached by wind and rain, the planks studded with nails. It is firmly closed and possibly locked, but she's certain that the key will be somewhere on the bundle Mr McDowall gave her. All the same, she decides that she'll leave it for another day. When she has company. *When Cal is here*, says the unwise part of her that finds him so attractive.

Beyond the tower, there is another small gate in the exterior wall, already almost obliterated by spring growth. She picks her way along to it, glad of the wellies, avoiding nettles and brambles and low-growing roses, and peers through a narrow iron gateway, into a wilderness of growth, even now in early spring. It will be a jungle later. In search of another, more accessible entrance, she makes her way through the house to where her car is parked and scans the wall beyond the tower on this side. Sure enough, there's a low stone archway with another worn armorial panel above it. Double wooden gates once barred the way, but one of them has fallen inwards. It lies flush with the ground, weeds and grasses springing up between the joints in the wood. Clearly, Viola had paid to keep the house wind and watertight, but the gardens had not been a priority for her. The other half of the gate is still standing, with a cast-iron handle in the shape of a large ring, held in a clenched fist.

She edges through, but the growth on the other side makes it hard to see the full extent of this walled garden. There are three or four moss-covered apple trees in bloom and what must once have been espaliered fruit trees against the walls. She can make out the roof of a summer house against the far wall, and an extensive climbing rose that seems to have scrambled randomly and unchecked over walls, shrubs and trees and is already showing some tiny buds. There are more of the low-growing and ferociously spiny wild roses in here too. Soon it will all look very beautiful, however untamed. There is a vast, red rhododendron with a cascade of blood-red petals, torn off by the recent squall, and camellias in full bloom, just starting to shed their petals too.

Birds are singing, bees are buzzing everywhere and after this morning's rain, there are clouds of midges under the trees. It's early in the year for them, but the damp warmth in here seems to be attracting them. They haven't yet discovered her, but once they do, it will be an uncomfortable business. She retreats, again overwhelmed by a mounting sense of panic at the magnitude of the task in front of her. Perhaps she should offer the whole place to the National Trust. But she immediately dismisses the idea. She needs the money and besides, she suspects that they are always offered far more crumbling mansions than they have resources to deal with them. She thinks the house is wonderful, but it isn't exactly a national treasure. She goes back indoors and makes a list of things to do. When it reaches three closely typed pages on her tablet, she sighs, saves it, shuts the device down, and pours herself a small whisky – for medicinal purposes, she tells herself. Garve whisky. It tastes of seaweed and honey and makes her instantly light-headed.

The door is still open, with the curiously shaped stone leaning against it. She can hear the sea, the oystercatchers patrolling down by the shore, the martins flying about the eaves of the house. She sits on the Chesterfield and puts her feet up. *Tomorrow is another day*, she thinks, just before sleep overtakes her. Unsurprisingly, she dreams about the house and – less predictably – about a ring. In the dream, she has lost a ring and she is hunting for it, searching among the stones and the wild white roses, but it is too small to be easily found, and the undergrowth is much too thick. The spines on the roses hurt her hands. She wakes up with a start and finds that her left hand is indeed hurting. She must have touched something in the garden and now there is a little line of blisters that she has been scratching in her sleep.

Later in the day, she manages to speak to somebody about reinstating the landline. The best mobile signal she can get is upstairs, in her mother's old bedroom, especially if she leans out of the window facing the sea. There must be a mast somewhere, maybe even on a nearby island. She phones her father.

'Are you all right?' he says and she can hear the anxiety in his voice. He is torn between feeling that he should be there, and thinking that she has to stand on her own two feet at last.

'Yes, I'm fine, Dad. It's OK here, honestly.'

'Well, make sure you lock the doors at night.'

This isn't remotely comforting and she tells him so. He laughs.

'I know, hen, but I worry about you. You'll be fine, though. Garve isn't exactly a hotbed of crime. You said so yourself. Better than the city, anyway.'

Eighteen months ago, she had been mugged in Edinburgh. People sometimes laugh when she tells them, but she generally feels safe in the middle of Glasgow where people don't walk on by, but can be relied on to help. She wasn't injured, only shocked and angry. She had been walking from the theatre to stay at a friend's house in Morningside. She had known one or two of the actors and had made the mistake of accepting their invitation for drinks after the show. By the time she was leaving, the taxi queue was monumental and she had decided to walk. When she was passing

Bruntsfield Links, somebody had pushed her hard from behind so that she fell to her knees, snatched her bag and run off before she could so much as scream. The police had found the bag, empty of course, in a bin beside the pathway. She had been unhurt, except for bruised knees, and at least her keys had been in her pocket. But it comes back to her from time to time: the peculiar, random violence of it.

When her father rings off, she thinks once again that it isn't the non-existent criminal element on Garve that worries her. It's the great weight of the past that seems to be lingering in and around this old house.

It will be very hard to get to sleep tonight.

*

Later that evening, after a sandwich eaten in front of the television, and a very large glass of white wine, she calls Mrs Cameron on her mobile and asks her about Viola's grave. It seems that Viola is buried in a graveyard outside a village called Keill, farther along the coast.

'There are old and new cemeteries. But the Neilsons had a family plot, a lair, up there at the old church, which is just a ruin now. So they opened it up for Viola. The priest came over from the mainland and they had an ecumenical service in the new church, St Columba's, and then they went up the hill afterwards. Everyone that was able walked after the coffin.'

'That's nice.'

'It was. Your grandmother couldn't be doing with fuss, but she always came to the island funerals, you know. Anyway, it's quite a bonnie place, the old graveyard. Perhaps you might like to take some flowers.'

'I could take some from the garden.'

'Aye. She'd have liked that. It bothered her that she couldn't keep up with that huge garden, but she certainly didn't want anyone coming in regularly either. She liked to keep herself to herself.'

'I wish I'd known her. I didn't even know she was my grandmother,' she says. 'I mean, I didn't know I had another grandmother. I thought she had died years ago.'

'Well, the funeral was a quiet affair, but enough people from the island came. You know, we do look after our own here.'

'Of course.'

'We sang "Be Thou My Vision".'

The melody comes into her head, plaintive and Irish, played on her father's old fiddle. The words are familiar too. Her parents had sent her to a Catholic primary school while professing not to be very religious themselves, and after her mother's death it had seemed natural for her to go on to a Roman Catholic secondary school with all her friends. Her father certainly wasn't a believer, and she remembers having a conversation with him when she was in her teens and fighting against everything that she was being told at school. As ever, Rob had told her to be aware of other people's feelings, but to follow her heart.

'How could Mum believe any of this rubbish?' she had asked him.

'Your mum was an island girl, Daisy,' he said, mildly.

She can remember it because he so seldom spoke about her mother's background, or where she came from. She knew only that Jessica had been born on the inner Hebridean island of Garve, but Rob had always implied that her grandmother on her mother's side had died soon after he and Jess were married. Other than that, he had managed to avoid talking about her. They had been back to Garve once, when they had climbed the hill and left the silk scarf tied to the tree, but even then, he had been ambiguous about his wife's childhood home, waving vaguely towards the south of the island. The fabrication had taken root, grown strong and tall like the Clootie Tree. When they had done the 'Granny Project' in her first year of secondary school, and they had been told to go home and ask their grannies, if they had them, what life was like when they were young, she had tried to tackle him about it.

'Most folk have two grannies. Why do I only have one? What happened to the other one?'

He had reiterated that her other granny was long gone, and wasn't Grandma Nancy more than enough for anyone? For a while she had been satisfied because she loved Grandma Nancy. Then, when religion became such an issue, she had raised the topic again, this time in a roundabout way.

'Did you send me to a Catholic school because of Mum?'

'In a way. It was what she wanted.'

'And what about you?'

'I don't really believe in much, if the truth be told.'

'I don't either,' she said, mutinously. 'So why do I have to pretend I do?'

He was pottering about the tiny kitchen of their apartment, and she was helping. He had a rota of meals that he was good at cooking: chilli, shepherd's pie, macaroni cheese with added tomatoes for vitamin C, haddock with oven-baked chips and salad. She was becoming more adventurous in her teens and had taken to buying cookery books in charity shops and experimenting. For somebody so good at musical improvisation, so generally impulsive, Rob was a surprisingly cautious cook, reluctant to deviate from any given recipe.

'Don't rock the boat, Daisy,' he said with a sigh, and she could see that he didn't really believe what he was telling her. He had always been a great one for rocking all kinds of boats and she told him so.

'I mean, hang on in there. At school. Don't make a fuss. You're getting a very good education.'

'But what about Mum? What did she believe? Did she actually believe in all this body and blood stuff? And guardian angels? And the blessed Virgin Mary hauled up to heaven by a bunch of angels?'

'We didn't talk about it much. There were things she just wouldn't discuss. If you must know, I think she had her own set of beliefs, and she ignored what didn't suit her. It was the way she was. She was a Celtic Christian, if anything.'

'What do you mean?'

'Her Catholicism was a bit different from the Roman variety. She believed in a little bit of magic. She had a great love for the landscape. Lots of Celtic Christians found their God in the natural world, and weren't averse to the odd Goddess as well,' he added, mysteriously. 'I think Jess liked that idea.' He would do things like this occasionally. Just come out with all this mystical stuff. In her teens she was embarrassed by it, although later on, she loved him for it.

'I don't understand.'

'You'd best look it up,' he said. 'But don't go asking about it at school.'

'Why not?'

'They might not approve. I don't know much about it, but it always seems a bit pagan to me.'

She had asked, though. She had asked one of the Irish nuns, Sister Brigid, who was young and sweet-faced, and who taught them English Literature with wild enthusiasm and a hefty dose of Irish and Scottish poems and stories thrown in whenever she got the chance.

Sister Brigid had waxed lyrical about Celtic Christianity, and Daisy had found that her father was right. The natural world had been very important, as had meditation and setting sail in small boats, and making it remarkably easy for pagan communities to transfer their loyalties to Christ. The impossible, mystical things these holy people believed in seemed somehow more credible to Daisy, even as a girl, than the impossible things she was sometimes asked to believe in by the nuns and by Father McGawn in church. Not that she went very often.

All this comes back to her now, when Mrs Cameron mentions "Be Thou My Vision".

'I know that hymn. Dad used to play it on the fiddle. Still does. He loves the melody, although it makes him sad. It's beautiful. I quite like the idea of God as a hero or as a high tower, even though it's a bit...'

'Pagan. Yes. Be thou my high tower. Gorgeous though. How are you getting on there? At Auchenblae. At Flowerfield.'

'I'm fine. I've been doing a bit of exploring. Cooked myself something to eat. Drunk some wine.'

'Well have another glass before bed. That way, you'll get a good night's sleep. And if you get nervous, just give us a ring.'

'I can't possibly do that. I can't wake you up in the middle of the night.'

'Oh, I'm a light sleeper at the best of times. I'm awake reading more often than not.'

'Even so. It's very kind of you, but I'll be fine, honestly.'

*

When it grows dark, she goes round the ground floor, checking doors and windows, making sure everything is locked, including the door into the tower. She can hear the slight echo on the other side as she turns the key, and she scurries out of the kitchen. She slides the bolt on the door at the sea side of the house, switches off the downstairs lights and is reassured to see that the moon is almost full, a friendly face gazing in at the windows. She takes her phone into the bedroom with her, and the radio from the kitchen, switching it on to hear the familiar strains of "Sailing By" and the shipping forecast, wondering if her grandmother did the same.

She reminds herself that this is a very old house, and that there will be noises as the building cools and settles down for the night. She and her father have always laughed at those haunted house television programmes where people shriek and run away at the slightest sound. Now, it doesn't seem quite so funny. When she switches the radio off, it's the silence that's alarming. In Glasgow, there is continuous external noise, the constant white noise of traffic, fading in the early hours, but still present, the occasional ambulance or fire engine, planes flying overhead, voices in the street outside. Here, the silence seems absolute at first, pressing in on her ears. After a while, she thinks she hears a faint rhythmic drumming sound and then realises that it is her own heartbeat. A breeze blows in from the west and rattles the window panes. She gets up and opens the window. Outside, she hears the high peet, peet, peet of some seabird flying past, a lonely sound. She leaves the window open, aware of the distant and soothing sound of waves on the shore, gets back into bed and dozes.

She is woken by a single distant thud from downstairs. She sits bolt upright, listening. Her rational mind tells her that something has fallen down in one of the rooms. There is something faintly familiar about the noise, but she can't place it. There is no way she can bring herself to go down to investigate, though. Not right now. She pulls the sheet up to her chin and props herself against the pillows, but every nerve is tingling. The house is quiet. She is just closing her eyes when she hears a shuffling and scurrying overhead, as though somebody is partying up in the servants' quarters. She sits upright again and switches on the bedside light. And the radio. The shuffling noise stops, starts again. Her phone buzzes beside the bed, making her jump all over again. She lifts it and sees that it is almost two o'clock, and that there is a text message from Cal.

'If you get this, you're still awake. Are you OK?' it reads.

'Yes I'm still awake,' she replies. 'No I'm not really OK.'

'What's wrong?' he writes, with a sad face.

'Noises.'

A minute or two later, the phone rings and she answers it. She's ridiculously relieved to hear his voice, even though he's miles away.

'Daisy,' he says. 'You've got me worried. If I wasn't in Glasgow, I'd come round.'

'Nice to hear a friendly voice.'

'What can you hear? I mean, in the house?'

'There was a big thump, somewhere downstairs. Sounded like something falling down. And I can hear things up above me. In the servants' quarters. Shuffling and scuffling noises. It sounds like somebody's partying up there.'

He laughs. 'Oh, sweetheart, I know what that will be. I get that

106

in my cottage sometimes. It'll be mice.'

She's briefly astonished by the term of endearment. She has female friends who wouldn't think twice about pulling him up about it. Maybe even punching him on the nose. She can't help smirking. But she quickly realises that it's casual and habitual with him rather than condescending. She's alarmed by the fact that she likes it. Not from anyone else, but from him. Which is worrying.

'Can mice make all that noise?'

'You'd be surprised. Sometimes they sound as if they're wearing tackety boots.'

'Well, I'm not keen on mice, but I'm relieved it's nothing worse.'

'Did you think ghostly McNeill servants were having a ceilidh up there?'

'Kind of,' she says, lamely.

'Listen, I'm coming back to the island tomorrow. I'll fetch some traps. And these plug-in things that do stuff to the wiring. I'll try and find some of those.'

'What about the thump from downstairs?'

'You know the fridge makes a noise, don't you?'

'The fridge?'

'I noticed it when I was there. The motor runs and then when it stops for a bit it makes quite a loud juddering noise. I don't think you notice it in the daytime because of all the birds and the sea and the wind.'

She thinks about it. 'Yes – it could be that, I suppose.'

'Do you want me to come round tomorrow? I could be on the last ferry of the morning if I get a move on, leave early. I'll see if I can get some mousetraps on the way.'

'Are you sure? I mean, were you coming anyway?'

'Aye, I was. I said I was. I had things to do here, but I was planning to come back for the rest of the week. I can lend a hand. I know I'm a dealer and all that and you probably think I have ulterior motives...'

'It had crossed my mind.'

'Well, if I'm honest, it had more than crossed my mind too. I've been dying to get a look inside Auchenblae since I was a lad and we used to think your granny was a witch, God forgive us. But I'm happy to help.'

'We could venture into the tower.'

'Are you scared of it?'

'A bit. It seems so neglected. As though my grandmother didn't even go there. I don't know why I feel like that but I do. I'll feel better when I've explored it.'

'We'll brave it together then.'

'OK.'

To tell the truth, she wishes he were here right now. Preferably in bed with her. For a moment, she wonders how he would react if she came right out with it. He would run a mile probably. She has to remind herself that he's almost certainly more interested in her house and its contents than her body. For two years previously, she had been in an on-off relationship with a history lecturer, separated from his wife and wary of committing himself fully to anybody new – or so he said. Then she had seen him with one of the younger lecturers, sitting at a table in the Kelvingrove gallery, knee touching knee, hands entwined across the table.

'I didn't want to hurt you,' he had said.

That had been last year. She had promised herself there and then that she would take a break. Concentrate on taking her business to the next level, whatever that might be, until the unexpected news of her inheritance and her unknown grandmother had thrown everything into confusion. The last thing she needs now is another attractive but potentially unreliable man. All the same, in the early hours of the morning, in her crumbling castle, the prospect of his company seems very comforting.

'See you then,' he says. 'Oh, and by the way, I'll be bringing somebody with me.'

'Who?' She has a pang of disappointment. His girlfriend maybe?

He chuckles into the phone, intimate, very close to her ear. 'You'll see,' he says. 'And if you hear any more sinister noises, give me a ring. I don't know what I can do from the back of the Botanics, but I'll do what I can. Even if it means sending out the lifeboat.'

He rings off. She falls into a deep and dreamless sleep, and is woken only by the seabirds, screeching around the house in the early morning. It promises to be a very fine day.

ELEVEN

In the morning, Daisy finds a selection of cleaning materials and starts on the downstairs rooms, mopping the floors, opening windows and letting in air and sunshine. On the seaward side of the house she finds a couple of lines strung between clothes poles. She hauls some of the rugs outside and pegs them out for the breeze to freshen them. Just after her late breakfast or early lunch, a gallon of coffee and a slice of toast and marmalade, Daisy hears what she assumes is Cal's car on the quiet road outside. There is no other traffic. Auchenblae sits on a narrow lane between high gorse hedges, blooming more or less all year round, but beginning to be dazzling at this time of year. Beyond the house, the potholed lane bends away from the sea again and narrows into a muddy track, leading only to the wishing tree. She hears the creak of the iron gates as Cal swings them open before driving in and goes to open the door for him.

Her hair is pulled back with a rubber band and she is wearing a grubby blue and white striped apron that she found hanging on a peg in the kitchen. When she first put it on, she found a tissue in the pocket. It smelled faintly of lavender and she wondered if Viola had left it there. She wishes she could speak to her grandmother. There are so many questions she would want to ask. She has found the time to pick a big bunch of budding wild flowers, campion and bluebells and frothy ground elder, and she has stuck them in a cream stoneware jug on the oak table.

Cal gets out of the car and goes round to open the passenger door. To her surprise, a shaggy, biscuit-coloured dog of indeterminate breed leaps out and starts to cavort around her, wagging his tail, play-bowing in front of her. The animal searches frantically for something to give her, finds a stick, seizes it and drops it at her feet, his tongue lolling, his head on one side.

'Meet Hector,' says Cal. 'I told you I was bringing somebody with me.'

'I thought you meant a person!'

'Hector, she thinks you're not a person! I can assure you he is. In fact, he's got more personality than most people I know. He's a recycled dog. Very suitable.'

'Recycled from what?'

'From the dog rescue place at Cardonald. He'd been dumped as a puppy. He looked as if he had mange, but it was just a flea allergy. Chucked out on the A77 somewhere south of Glasgow. Don't you just love people, eh?' He looks very fierce all of a sudden.

Hector wags his tail frantically in agreement. He genuinely does love people. He comes to be petted, then rushes off in pursuit of his stick again. His sandy coat is rough and shaggy under her fingers.

'How are you with dogs? I should have asked you, but I figured he could stay in the car if you're not a fan. I usually bring him with me. He does love the island so much.'

'No, I'm fine with dogs. It's fine.' Last night, hearing the thud downstairs and the rustle and scurry above her head, it had occurred to her that it would be good to have a dog. The flat in Glasgow has always been too small to house anything but the most undemanding pets: the odd gerbil or goldfish, when she was much younger.

'You can borrow him if you like,' says Cal, suddenly. 'I mean temporarily. I wouldn't give him away for the world. But he can sleep here while you're on the island if you want.'

'I have to go home at the weekend anyway. I have a fair.'

'Ah yes. So you said.'

'But I'm planning to come back soon. Stay for a bit longer if I can. I needed to suss it out first. See if the place was habitable.'

'And it is, isn't it?'

'Yes. It is. So I thought I might come back for a few weeks. See how I get on. But I have to keep selling things. I don't have any other income. I have to make a living.'

'Well, if you want to borrow Hector for a while, you're very welcome. We can make some arrangement.'

'Would he be OK here?'

'He seems to like you. And he's a very discerning chap, our Hector.'

Hearing his name, the dog wags his tail, rushes over, licks Cal's hand briefly, and charges off to sniff the undergrowth.

'Actually,' says Cal, 'he's not so much discerning as easy. He'll go with anyone who feeds him. He's the most laid-back dog I've ever met. I have this town house at the back of the Botanics, in Glasgow, and he spends some of his time there, sleeping, or in the gardens when he can persuade somebody to take him for a walk, some of his time on the road with me, and the rest here on Garve, chasing rabbits whenever he can.'

'It sounds like a great life.'

'It is. He's happier than I am. But he's no guard dog. Although I think he'd be company for you. Just having him in the house.' He looks around. 'Seems to me that you have enough stock here to last you a lifetime.'

'Well yes. But I have to be careful. I don't want to let anything go that I might regret later.' She frowns at him, still suspicious.

'Oh, that's for sure,' he says, ingenuously. 'No dodgy house clearance guys in here!'

She finds herself laughing. She can't help it. He's the kind of man who makes you laugh. 'No. In fact, no dodgy guys at all.'

'I don't do house clearances, hen.'

The way he calls her 'hen' reminds her both of her father and her grandma Nancy. Hen, sweetheart, which is she?

'I don't suppose you do. Not with a shop like the one you have.'

'It's not mine, though. My mum and dad own the shop. I just have an interest in it and they pay me a retainer, for the buying, plus commission on sales. Quite a lot of commission sometimes. But it's their business really. Not mine.'

They go into the house. She makes a big pot of coffee and they sit at the oak table in the living room. The back door is open and Hector stretches himself out across the doorstep in the sunshine.

'You sound as though you don't much like the shop.'

'Have you ever worked in a shop?'

'No. Only fairs. My dad's a musician. I started off doing stalls when he had a gig. Now I do quite a bit of online stuff as well. I have a degree in history, but I worked for one of the west of Scotland auction houses for a while. It kind of gave me a taste for it.'

'My mum worked in an auction house too.'

'I don't think I was on quite the same level as your mum. I was a lowly porter. Packed things, unpacked them. Made sure the punters didn't smash them. Or pocket them. Took phone bids. They can be a grumpy bunch, dealers. Especially the old men. I expect your mum's an expert.'

'Have you been talking to Mrs Cameron?'

'She was telling me a bit about you. I asked her,' she says, apologetically.

'Mum's an art historian and conservator. She met my father at a private view.'

He frowns, drains his mug and holds it out for a refill. She wonders if his apparent hyperactivity is down to caffeine. 'Have you seen his work? Do you like it?' he asks, abruptly. The truth is that she has indeed seen some of the work and disliked it, but before she can think of anything tactful to say, he pre-empts her. 'I don't mind his early stuff. He used to do these strange little studies of the island. But that was before he got bitten by the urban bug. Now it's just moody, repetitive crap as far as I'm concerned.'

She shifts uncomfortably, not used to hearing somebody criticise a parent so forthrightly. She would never be so disloyal to her own father. Besides, she loves him too much.

'Sorry,' he says, noticing her discomfort. 'I get the bit between my teeth where Dad's concerned. We don't often see eye to eye. He's difficult. Thinks I should knuckle down and spend a lot more time in the shop.'

'What do you want to do then?'

'Me? I did a course in furniture restoration. I'd like to do a lot more of that.'

'I'd have thought your dad would approve of something like that.'

'You'd think so, wouldn't you? But he doesn't get the whole artisan thing. Despises what he calls crafts. Spent a fortune on our education, mine and Catriona's. That's my younger sister. And we both discovered that we wanted to go off and get our hands dirty. Catty more successfully than me. Very dirty indeed.'

'What does your sister do?' She doesn't like to admit that Elspeth Cameron has already told her.

'She escaped. Catty's married to a hill farmer, back on the mainland. Jake Brodie. Not all that far from the ferry, which means I get to see them all quite often. Sheep farmers. Hard graft. As far as I can see, sheep mainly want to get dead and they find a hundred ways of doing it. But she thrives on it. They both do. And they have three kids as well. I like their life. Not sure I'd want to live it myself, mind you. But I do like watching them living it.'

*

A little later, he finishes his coffee, stands up and says, 'It's now or never, sweetheart. We'd better go and have a look at this tower.'

Hector stands up too, yawns and shakes himself. He's ready for anything, wagging his tail enthusiastically, grinning at them.

'There's a door in the kitchen, isn't there?'

'Yes. And one outside as well, further along. The one in the kitchen will be easier.'

'Let's go in that way then.' He picks up the tray and heads for the kitchen, Hector scurrying after him, his nails clicking on the floor. She follows them more slowly.

'You've left the key in the door.'

'I had a look in and then locked it again. It's OK. It's not too stiff.'

She watches as he turns the key in the big lock and tugs at the door. It swings open, quite quietly. No horror movie creaks this time. Hector patters inside, stops, turns to face them, tail down. He doesn't like the look of the broad stairs, curving both up and down.

'So where does the outside door go in then?'

'Further along. Just before you get to the bit where the tower meets the garden wall. There must be another stair along there.'

'So there must. The levels are a bit different then.'

'How do you mean?'

'Well, you'd sort of expect the rooms in here to be on the same level as the house back there, but they aren't. Not quite anyway. I'm wondering which came first?'

'The tower, surely.'

'You'd think so, wouldn't you? But perhaps not. This tower could be an addition. The new wing.' He chuckles. 'Except not that new.'

She's intrigued, in spite of the almost constant tension in the pit of her stomach at the sheer magnitude of her inheritance.

'I wonder what's down there?' She peers down the curve of the spiral.

He grins. 'Maybe you have dungeons!'

'It isn't dark enough for dungeons. Old kitchens, maybe?'

Cal pushes Hector out of the way and heads down the first few stairs. She hangs back, her hand on the dog's wiry coat.

Cal calls up to her as he goes. 'It's OK. There's a doorway here. It isn't very far down at all. It's actually wired, Daisy. There are lights here. Bet the leccy's a bit dodgy, though.'

Hector gazes after him, whining.

'Go on,' she says, patting the dog on his bum. 'Go on down! You'll be fine.'

He still doesn't like it much, but when Cal calls to him, he gallops down the stairs and disappears. Daisy follows, reluctantly, but this section of stair is very much shorter and wider than she expected. There are metal light fittings with wires leading up to them, and dusty lightbulbs on the walls. Only a little way down, there is another massive oak door. It is standing open and she can just make out Cal inside, with Hector sitting next to him, panting. The room is gloomy, but not dark. She has imagined the tower to be empty and echoing, big, dark rooms, smelling of damp. Cobwebs everywhere. Large spiders, undisturbed for years. But it isn't like that at all.

'What is it?' she says. 'What's in there? Is it a kitchen?'

'Come in and see for yourself! I don't think this was the old kitchen. I think that's further down still. The stairs keep going. I'll bet the door you can see from the outside is on this level. In fact, I can see it. So the ground must slope a bit.'

She steps into a large room with stone walls and floor, incredibly dirty windows on opposite sides shedding some light: salty on the outside, dusty and cobwebby on the inside. This room is only a little way below the level of the rest of the house. Shrouded shapes, covered in dust sheets and grubby blankets, loom at her. Cal finds a light switch – an old circular affair that makes him draw in his breath and mutter 'not seen one of these for years' – and gingerly presses it. There are meagre lamps on one wall. They are surprised to find that the lightbulbs appear to be working. They don't exactly flood the room with light, but it becomes easier to make things out: tea chests, one piled precariously on top of another, old-fashioned wooden blanket boxes, a couple of metal trunks, a pile of elderly suitcases and larger pieces of furniture shrouded in dust sheets. There are a great many heaps of frames stacked face against the wall so that you can't see at first glance whether they are empty or still contain pictures.

'See what I mean,' Cal says, grinning at her through the gloom. Hector is skittering about sniffing at things. 'Hector! Don't you dare pee on anything,' he says, sharply. The dog, looking guilty as only dogs can, comes back, wagging his tail.

'Oh God!' Daisy shakes her head, between fascination and dismay. 'I thought this would be empty.'

'I was afraid it would be,' he says, giving her a sidelong glance.

'It's all right for you. I mean, everything is quite neat in the other part of the house, or half empty, like the servants' quarters.'

'You thought Viola or her parents might have had a big clearout.'

'I was kind of hoping that would be the case. I can't cope with all this.'

'You don't have to do it all at once. You don't have to do it at all if you don't want to! Shall we head on upstairs? I think this might have been a living space of some kind, if the old kitchen and storerooms are downstairs from here, anyway.'

He points across the room to the outer wall, the one adjoining the walled garden, where a huge stone fireplace stands, quite empty. Up above it, though, there is yet another armorial panel, much less worn than those outside. They can make out a boat with a furled sail and oars, two lions and, in the top right-hand quadrant, a fish and what might be a hand, although time has reduced it to an indeterminate blob.

'McNeill,' she says.

'How do you know?'

Daisy shrugs. 'I remember stuff like that. I'm a history geek.'

'You don't look very geeky to me.'

Before she can respond, he heads for the stair again and she follows him. There are two more floors above this one, but, mercifully, this is the most cluttered. In the room above, they find a few more boxes and chests, and a wooden bedstead, in solid oak.

'Wow,' he says. 'Would you look at this, Daisy!'

'Is it really as old as it looks?'

'I should say so.' He runs his fingers over it, over the multitude of carvings. She can see leaves with birds half hidden among them, flowers – roses and thistles – and foliate heads of some kind. 'God alone knows how they got it up here. Must have come up in bits. But why wouldn't you use something like this if you were lucky enough to possess it?'

'Maybe my grandmother found it intimidating. She was here on her own most of the time.'

'I suppose so. But it would take a normal mattress. It's big, but if you set it up it would be more chunky than anything else. A sturdy bed. Antique beds tend to be a bit smaller than our king-size things.'

'I'm not at all sure I'd want to sleep up here, though. Not the way it is now.'

'No. Well, there is that.'

There's not much more in the room, except for a low and unobtrusive doorway leading to a narrow back staircase, corkscrewing off into darkness.

'A secret stair. Maybe that leads down to the doorway at the seaward side of the house,' she ventures.

'Probably. I suppose they would need more than one way out in case of unwelcome visitors. You could cover this with tapestry or whatever and nobody would know it was here.'

They leave the bed behind and head upstairs again. Hector seems to have got used to the spiral stairs and happily gallops ahead of them. They find themselves in a high room, with more windows looking out onto land and sea. There's a small stone fireplace, an oak press and a high-backed oak chair, both with rudimentary carvings of stylised oak and ivy leaves, and an empty stone closet in one corner.

'A privy maybe. Renaissance en suite. Do you know that they used to keep their clothes in them because the smell of pee killed the bugs? Or so they thought.'

'What a mine of information you are, Daisy!'

'Mostly useless.'

A sudden breeze seems to have got up, a squall blowing in from the sea as it so often does. You can feel it buffeting walls and windows, finding a way into the room, the damp smell of salt and seaweed everywhere.

No, she thinks, *I wouldn't like to sleep up here at all. It would be a lonely place to be.* The word comes drifting into her mind and stays there. Lonely. Somebody was lonely up here. She doesn't know how she knows it, but it's true, nevertheless.

Beyond this room, the stairs go on only a little way until they stop at a wooden trapdoor, which no doubt emerges onto the battlements at the top of the tower.

'We'll save that for another day,' Cal says, to her relief. 'We'd need to get a ladder up here.'

Emboldened, they head downstairs and keep going, below the level of the rest of the tower, where they find what must once have been a kitchen. There's another enormous stone fireplace, and a little warren of other rooms branching off, storerooms probably. The whole place smells damp. It's a basement rather than a cellar. There are windows, but they are high up in the walls and only a little light filters in. It's a gloomy place and nobody would want to linger long here. The stone floor exudes coldness and in parts seems to be bedrock, part of the hillside upon which the tower is built, rather than any kind of flagstones.

'No dungeons,' she says. 'Thank God.'

'Do you want to look at some of the pictures?'

A sort of exhaustion seems to have possessed her. There's so much to take in. But she agrees. 'Why not? We have to start somewhere, don't we?'

They head upstairs, back into the main room, where Cal hauls one of the piles of pictures away from the wall. A large and leggy spider scuttles away, making both of them jump back.

'You too, eh?' he says.

'I never kill them if I can help it, but they scare me. They're a lot worse dead than alive, though.'

Hector is very interested in the spider. He pursues it across the floor but it scuttles behind one of the tea chests. He whines at it for a little while, but then gives up and comes back to look at the pictures.

'They only make you sick, Hector,' says Cal, rubbing his ears. 'Then you eat them again.'

The pictures are a mixed bunch: there are old prints, foxed landscape engravings mostly, in heavy black frames. There are a couple of Victorian woolwork pictures, cornucopias of flowers, that seem to have survived unscathed, very dusty but well framed and under glass.

'Not my thing, but maybe yours,' Cal remarks in passing.

'I like them a lot. People buy them to turn into cushions some-times. Or to cover stools and chair seats.'

There is an exceedingly ugly portrait of a military man, a print done in a beautiful and very detailed stipple engraving. It seems a waste of such an effective technique on such an ugly person. Cal has no hesitation in saying so. Daisy has been thinking exactly the same thing. 'All the same, it's probably worth quite a bit,' he says. 'Look – Bartolozzi. That's a very good name.'

'So it is. And I won't mind selling it.'

She waits for him to say, 'I could maybe sell it for you', but he doesn't.

There are several landscapes in oils, too grubby for it to be immediately obvious whether they are collectable or not. There are cows, drinking from a burn, and a stag on a high hill. There is a pair of pictures of Highland lochs in gilded frames. None of them seems very old or particularly interesting. But then, he slides out a smallish picture from the back of the pile. It is wrapped in black silk, from which it emerges in glorious colour.

Even in this low light, the picture is stunning.

The frame is almost bigger than the canvas, in carved and gilded wood, with scrolls and leaves and a riot of lily flowers, garlanded round it. It is clear that this has been a precious thing. It is a portrait of a very young woman, eighteen or nineteen years old perhaps, gazing straight out at the artist, pensively and with only the faintest smile. Nevertheless, she is not shy of him. There is a certain warmth in her gaze.

She has red hair, what you can see of it, because it is quite severely parted in the centre and then swept up and back into a head-dress that is floral in some way, perhaps with embroidered or ribboned flowers with jewelled centres, the edges ornamented with tiny pearls, freshwater pearls maybe, and a single pearl hanging down in the very centre of her parting. You can actually see the gentle frizz of hair that has escaped confinement, just a shadow of it on the sides of her forehead. The skill of this seems extraordinary to Daisy.

The girl has no earrings, but she does have a short necklace of larger pearls, just visible in the 'v' of her gown, the high white collar curving up and outwards, neatly pleated and with a tiny ornate lace trim, like tatting, along the edge, the whole thing framing her face, intensifying her prettiness. There is all the freshness of youth about her: a high forehead, wide-set, ingenuous brown eyes, straight nose, a firm rosebud mouth. Over that fresh, white, inner garment, she is wearing a vivid yellow bodice, startling in the intensity of its colour, some kind of textured silk, closely fitted, with the seams braided for emphasis and with – when you look more closely – tiny fleurs de lys embroidered onto the fabric. You can just see the way it buttons up the front, the round buttons constructed of the same braid, but this is not a full-length portrait, which is somehow tantalising. The skirt is almost certainly in the same gorgeous fabric. Her left hand is raised across her body, just below the full curve of her breast, and the hand has all the smoothness of youth about it. Beneath the edge of her sleeve, more pleated silk or satin trim peeps out, softening her wrist. She is holding a spray of white lilies, their yellow centres reflecting the colours of her gown. They are so glowing, so vibrant, that you can almost smell them.

She looks like a young woman of great character. No shrinking violet she.

It is one of the most beautiful pictures Daisy has ever seen.

'Oh my God,' she says. 'Look at her. Would you just look at her!'

Cal is examining the canvas but there seems to be no signature of any kind.

'Shall we take it down into the light?' he asks, tentatively.

'Oh yes. Of course. We can't leave her here, can we? Let's take her into the light.'

TWELVE

1588

He had almost forgotten what it was like to sleep in reasonable peace and security. First, the woman called Beathag had taken them outside to a place where a vigorous stream ran down from the slopes above the house and collected in an arrangement of stone cisterns. Here, she encouraged them – or perhaps briskly instructed might be a better description – to shed their clothes and immerse themselves fully in the cold water at the very bottom of the slope, before it drained away into the sea. Their clothes were so filthy that they had become moulded to their bodies, and in places, skin came away with fabric. She had rolled up her sleeves and pushed their heads brusquely below the surface, like a violent baptism. *Kill or cure*, Mateo thought, as he came up spluttering, worried about this renewed onslaught on Francisco's constitution. But at least if it killed them, they would go to their God in cleanliness. Francisco merely did as he was told. He seemed too weak to protest. Then as they emerged pink and shivering, Beathag, who seemed to be not at all disconcerted by the sight of two naked young men, had wrapped them in rough linen sheets and instructed them in words, and in mime, to rub themselves dry and warm.

Before she took their foul clothes away, however, Mateo managed to extract his last and most precious item from the inner folds of his linen undershirt. It was a gold ring, too small to fit over most of his fingers, but he managed to slide it onto his pinkie, where he stood a chance of hiding it, temporarily, and where it would be safe enough until he could find a way of secreting it elsewhere. When both men seemed reasonably clean and decent, Beathag took them back into the house, this time into the lower floor of the tower, where there was a warren of rooms: sculleries and storerooms for the use of such members of the household as could not be accommodated in the more comfortable family chambers on the upper floors of the tower, in the hall itself or outside in the stable lofts. It was some time before they would fully understand the layout of the house and, for now, they did only as they were bidden. It had occurred to Mateo that they would be banished to some distant and chilly garret above one of the stables, but then he thought that McNeill wouldn't trust them anywhere near his precious horses. No. They would be housed somewhere where he, or other members of the household, could keep an eye on them.

It was fully dark outside as Beathag took them to a small chamber with a fireplace where a peat fire gave off welcome heat, the whole faintly illuminated by a lamp that smelled strongly of fish. She gave them to understand that they were lucky, since very few rooms in this part of the house had such fires, and those were reserved mostly for extra cooking, when there were visitors. There was a rudimentary wooden bed with a heather-filled mattress and woollen blankets that smelled of last summer's lavender. She left the men to dry themselves properly, and came back in a little while with a heap of clothes: saffron shirts, woollen trews and plaids, well worn, patched and darned to be sure, but clean enough. Then she drew from her pocket a pair of wickedly sharp shears, at which Francisco backed away in alarm, but she only smiled, and mimed cutting his hair. When he still seemed reluctant, Mateo sat down on the only chair in the room, a very rickety driftwood affair that had clearly been relegated from one of the family bedchambers, and allowed her to chop away at the dark hair that had grown long and matted in the months of their voyage and subsequent pursuit. When she had also trimmed his beard to her satisfaction, she motioned to Francisco to take his place on the chair.

'There now, lads,' she said, in her curiously accented Scots, when she had finished. 'You look more like good Christian lads than *daoine borba* – than savages.'

She swept the matted locks into a heap with a heather broom that she had brought, and then left them in peace for a while with their clothes and with a fine toothcomb between them. 'You can have the pleasure of using that yourselves,' she said. 'See that you do. My Lady Lilias has a horror of the wee *mialan*. The headlice. Although the Good Lord knows most folk have them.' She told them to find their way back to the great hall once they were dried and decently dressed.

Once they were clothed – not without difficulty – in the strange foreign garb, Mateo found a convenient inner pocket for his precious ring. They surveyed each other in astonishment.

'What have we come to?'

'I don't know, Mateo. But it seems safer than anywhere else we've been for the past months.'

'That's true. Or I hope so. They are a rough and ready people, but they don't seem inclined to murder us in our beds. Not when they have clothed us. After a fashion.'

Francisco sighed. 'I'm glad to be here. Although I would be happier still to be at home.'

'You're not alone in that, Paco.'

'But how are we to get there?'

'I have no idea. And I don't suppose you have either.' The notion of all the miles of ocean that lay between this place and their own island was dizzying. It didn't bear thinking about.

Francisco yawned. 'I would like nothing more than to sleep for a week.' His eyelids were drooping, even as he mentioned the word, but his face was flushed, and Mateo noticed with some alarm that his breathing was laboured.

'Are you well?' he asked.

As always, Francisco nodded. 'Of course. Yes. I'm well.'

The truth was that they could both have slept where they sat, but it was hunger that drove them back to the great hall and the fireplace with its cooking pots. They attracted a good deal of unwelcome and occasionally downright hostile attention from those people who worked in and about the house and its surrounding land, and who had come in for a rudimentary supper before bed.

'This is but half the household,' explained Beathag, who seemed to be summoning more of the Scots tongue the more often she spoke to them. 'The cattle are not yet come back from the shielings on the higher pastures, but that will be happening soon and then we'll have a full house of it.'

The main meal was in the middle of the day, she explained, but she served the two strangers with bowls of fragrant pottage, decent food that they had not tasted for many a long day.

'McNeill tells me that you must be fed,' was all she said. 'And that nobody is to insult or attack you.' She raised her voice as she said this, so that some of the assembled company could hear. It was clear that McNeill's word was law here, which was reassuring.

Mateo thought he could taste barley, rabbit, vegetables of some sort. There were flat oatcakes to go with the stew, and a mild ale that had a faint scent of honey about it. So they were not to be starved, at least.

Mateo warned Francisco not to eat too much, just at first, since they had eaten so little for so long, but he need not have taken the trouble. The younger man ate only a few mouthfuls of the savoury stew, then handed the earthenware bowl back to his cousin. 'You finish it, Mateo. I'm afraid I can't.'

Ruaridh McNeill came down to greet them, although there was no sign of Lilias or her sister, who had presumably already retired to the upper rooms of the tower. He drank with them, and seemed more disposed to be friendly.

'Rest for a few days. Then we'll see if we can find some work for you,' he said. 'Although if you are who you claim to be, the sons of noblemen, I doubt if you have any skills that we can use.'

Mateo suppressed a momentary indignation. They were in no position to argue. 'When our strength returns, I'm sure there is plenty that we can do. But we don't know the customs of this country and you must instruct us, or find somebody who will.'

'Aye well, you might be more of a hindrance than a help. What did you do aboard your ship? Other than plot invasion?'

'I was navigator. My cousin assisted me.'

'A navigator eh? Who instructed you in those arts?'

'The same man who tutored me in English and philosophy. And mathematics.'

McNeill regarded them steadily. 'They are seen as dark arts in some quarters.'

'Mathematics?'

'Aye. Not so far removed from magic. Those who are adept in such things sometimes have an evil reputation.'

'There's nothing magical about mathematics. And nothing evil about me.'

'Perhaps not. But it may seem so. To the uninitiated. How are you with horses?'

'Competent. We have horses at home.'

'And can you build a drystane wall, or mend thatch?'

'I've never tried. But I can learn.'

McNeill smiled grimly. 'Good. Our winters can be very wild but the house must be made ready for the storms, the beasts too when they are brought back, and all their housing as well. I'm sure we can find plenty for you to do. But what of your cousin? He looks like thistledown, as though a strong wind might blow him over.'

'He isn't usually so weak.'

They both gazed at Francisco, who was seated beside the fire, unaware of their scrutiny, struggling with sleep, his eyelids drooping.

'Well, well. He may have other skills. My lads are away from home. Kenneth, the eldest, is in St Andrews and Malcolm is over the sea with his foster family. But my youngest lass might have need of a tutor, and he seems a kindly enough lad. I'll not have my lassies treated with anything but courtesy. Lilias does what she can, but she has her household duties to attend to. Lilias learned much from her mother. And I would have Ishbel learn how to read and write, how to draw. Music, even, although there are few instruments here save the pipes and the clarsach. But others might be procured. I have a mind that my girls should be schooled as if they were not the daughters of a rough-and-ready islandman. I would have them made fit for lowland society. Fit for good marriages. Perhaps your friend can oblige in the time that you spend here.'

It occurred to Mateo that Lilias would grace any society in which she found herself, but that seemed a dangerous thought and he repressed it. He refrained from asking how long their time on the island might be and instead merely nodded. 'I think that might be possible. Francisco is a fine draughtsman, an artist of great skill.'

'Then what was he doing on such a venture? Eh?'

Mateo sighed. 'I don't know, sir. It was folly. Folly from beginning to end.'

'Ah well. We have all been guilty of that. Take him to your room, if he can stand. If not, you'll just have to carry him, which should be no great hardship, since it seems that you have carried him for long before this.'

Mateo roused his cousin, and pulled him to his feet. 'I'll bid you good night sir, and thank you. Thank you for your help and your hospitality.'

'Thank me later. I fear you may be at the beginning of yet another long and hazardous road. Thank me when the way ahead becomes clearer.'

THIRTEEN

In the living room, after the gloom of the tower rooms, the picture seems even more vivid, more full of life. Cal holds it horizontally and blows gently along the surface, but it seems to have been protected by the silk and by the larger pictures that were standing in front of it and the years have been kind to it.

'I think this is its original frame,' he says, examining the back of the picture. 'Looking at the way it's constructed. I'm amazed it's so clean. Maybe it was hung somewhere in the house. Away from direct sunlight, that's for sure. I can't believe it was just stored in your old tower for all these years. It would be in much worse condition if it had been.'

'I suppose it depends when they stopped using the tower. Nobody's lived in it for a while from the look of it. Certainly not my grandmother.'

'No. It looks very much as though she used only this part of the house.'

'I don't think she even went up to the servants' quarters very much. One person would just rattle around this place.' She pulls a face, thinking of herself, trying to sleep in her mother's old bedroom. 'I suppose they must have just decided to move out of there completely. I honestly thought we'd find it empty. I thought maybe Viola or her parents had cleared it out. Instead it's a medi-aeval glory hole.'

'It isn't so easy to get rid of stuff on an island. It can be an expensive business just transporting things, even if you want to sell them.'

'I suppose so.'

He shifts his gaze from the portrait for a moment to smile at her, but keeps his own counsel. It occurs to her that he is being careful not to upset her. Perhaps he has an ulterior motive. She likes him a lot already, but she doesn't trust him. She still can't help feeling that he might be sizing up her possessions. After all, it's part of what he does. She's all too aware of the pitfalls because it's what she does as well.

He props the portrait on a side table. 'Look, there's a name on the frame.'

In the very centre of the heavily carved frame, almost obliterated by leaves and flowers, is a single word: Lilias.

'A bonnie name for a bonnie lass,' he says suddenly. ''Hence the lilies. In the picture and on the frame.'

'Is it as old as I think it is?' she asks. This is a find. And with it comes a certain responsibility.

'Sixteenth century, I'd say.'

'You mean, Elizabethan. Genuine Elizabethan?'

'Aye. The first, not the second.'

'Oh God.'

'Look, there's text on the picture. Bit faded, not surprisingly. Although maybe it's deliberately quite subtle.'

She peers more closely. Lilias, whoever she is, has been painted against a very dark background. That's another reason why her fresh face, her red hair and her golden gown stand out so vividly. There are small letters, painted onto the background.

'Un temps...' He squints at it, then fumbles in the pocket of his jacket and brings out a jeweller's loup, a small magnifier.

'*You* came prepared,' she says, and can't keep the faint note of accusation out of her voice.

'I always carry it. I'm always prepared, hen.' He grins, wickedly.

She has a sudden throb of inadvisable desire in the pit of her stomach. *Don't go there*, she thinks.

'*Un temps viendra*,' he says, dropping the lens back into his pocket.

'A time will come.' She translates automatically.

'Get you.'

'I'm not daft. Just don't know as much about pictures as you do. Is it French, then? Is *she* French?'

'I don't have a scoobie. I don't think Lilias is a particularly French name. And what's she doing here, anyway?' He gazes at her, thoughtfully. 'She has your hair.'

'It's a mixed blessing. It was my mum's hair too. You know the fishermen don't much like to have red-headed women on their boats?'

'So I'm told. Well, you can come on my boat any time you like.'

'Maybe she doesn't belong here at all,' she says. 'Maybe the Neilson family bought her. It. The picture. They were industrialists, weren't they? Wealthy. This was their rural bolt-hole.'

'I don't know. They're your family.'

'But that's the thing, Cal. I don't know either. I don't know the first thing about them except that my mother more or less eloped with my dad and cut herself off completely from her own mother. From Viola. You don't do that kind of thing lightly.'

He shrugs. 'Maybe you do. People have their reasons.'

'But I don't *know*, do I? My mum died when I was too young to be able to ask her and even my dad says she never properly explained it. She loved him to bits. I'm pretty sure of that. He certainly loved her. And I can just about understand why he never brought me here after Mum died.'

'Why?'

'He thought Viola would fight to get custody of me. Normally, she wouldn't have had a hope, but he says he was a bit of a mess after Mum died. I never noticed. He was never anything but a great dad to me, but he was afraid of Viola and maybe he was right.' She looks around. 'All this represents a certain power and influence, doesn't it?'

'If you're the laird it does anyway. This was a McNeill stronghold. And a string of McNeills would have had a hell of a lot of power and influence here. Don't you just feel it?'

She gazes at him. 'I do. It's overwhelming. Five hundred years of it. Maybe more. And now it's all mine, God help me.'

'Aye, poor you.' He grins at her. 'Anyway, the Neilsons were incomers. Even if there was some family connection somewhere. And I don't think they ever owned that much land. What do you have now?'

'Five acres, Mr McDowall said. Nothing useful. Woodland and willow scrub and moorland.'

'Even when the Neilsons bought the place, there would have been a few tenant farms at the most. Which they'd probably sold off before Viola inherited. But they must have been wealthy.'

'Probably the kind of industrial wealth folk made on the backs of other people in Glasgow or Paisley or somewhere. And then Viola's grandfather or great-grandfather or whoever decides to come over all paternal and exploit some islanders for a change.'

'I can see you're going to take to the role of lady laird in a big way.'

'You should hear my dad on the subject of land ownership. I think that's one of the reasons why he's keen for me to sell the place.'

'So what about Lilias? Who do you think she was? Don't you want to know?'

'Of course I want to know. I always want to know the history of everything.'

'Me too.'

'But maybe she was just one of their acquisitions. The Neilsons, I mean. She looks a bit too wealthy for a small island laird's wife. Or daughter. Especially back then. That's a pretty posh frock for starters. Not to mention the pearls.'

He frowns. 'But not impossible. They didn't just hang out on their islands all the time, you know. The McNeills. The MacDonalds. They went to Edinburgh. They acquired a few luxuries when they could. Auchenblae might have been quite comfortable back then. They were quite civilized.'

'But it's such a small island.'

'Good harbours. Strategically placed too. The Garve McNeills were dedicated fence-sitters, I believe. Liked to make as few enemies as possible. Imagine your old tower with fires burning, tapestries, floor coverings, that oak bed with proper hangings and hand-woven linen. I'd lay bets that carved bed belongs here. Maybe Lilias belongs here as well.'

They stare at the picture in silence for a moment. Lilias stares back at them, enigmatically.

'It's a lot to take in, Cal.'

'It is, isn't it?'

He sets the picture down flat, reverently. Wraps it up again in its silk. 'You'd better look after this.'

She makes more coffee. The day is wearing away but he is making no move to leave. Not that she is in a hurry for him to leave, but she's surprised. It feels as though they've known each other for years. She doesn't want to be left alone in the house. Not today. Not yet.

'I'll tell you what we could do,' he says.

'What?'

'We could do a bit of research. Lilias. It's a fairly unusual name. I mean, it's not like Anne or Mary. And if she does belong here, I think she would have been a McNeill or some variation on that name. They were lords of this particular isle for hundreds of years, even when they held it with the agreement of the proper Lords of the Isles, the MacDonalds. I'm sure some of the genealogy sites might be able to help.'

'I have a tablet but I don't have a broadband connection yet. I have to sort all that out.'

'I have a laptop in my cottage.' He stands up. Hector leaps to his feet in anticipation, runs to the door, wagging his skinny tail. 'Do you want to come and see my cottage? Well, I say see, but if you blink you'll miss it. Not like this place! Hector wants you to come as well. Don't you, Hector?'

It will be something of a relief to get out of the house for a while. She can't ignore her inheritance, but she needs some sort of perspective on it as well.

'Come on,' he says. 'We'll take my car. I'll bring you back later. You look as though you need a break from all this.'

'I do really.'

'Come on then. Grab your bag and let's go.'

FOURTEEN

They drive through the village and past the hotel, where people are sitting outside in the late afternoon sunshine. Briefly, she wishes they could do the same. Wishes they were a couple. But ever since that moment on the beach, he has been friendly but no more than that. And perhaps that's fine. Perhaps it's the situation in general she wants, rather than him in particular. Holding hands across the table. Drinking wine. Being in love with somebody. Any reasonably attractive man will do. Perhaps she's just feeling lonely and a bit tired.

They slow down for tourists on bicycles and on foot. He waves vaguely to the left where a wooden sign points to a 'Gallery'.

'That's Ardachy down there. Where the McNeills live. Well, one lot of them anyway. Donal and Alys and their kids. She makes jewellery. She uses a lot of antique beads.'

'I once signed up to a jewellery-making course and I thought that's what it was going to be. Found objects. Vintage and antique beads. I had all kinds of ideas. As soon as I got in the door I realised my mistake.'

'Why? What did you do?'

'We spent hours hammering a bit of copper into a ring shape. It was the most boring class in the history of the world. I hated it.'

'I suppose you have to start somewhere.'

'Yeah, but it wasn't what I expected. I was never going to be a silversmith. I never went again. I didn't really want a copper ring.'

'They turn your fingers black.'

'They do. I'm quite good at sticking at something but I was frantic with boredom.'

'Well, if you stay, Alys does classes. And I think it's much more your kind of thing. They opened the gallery a few years ago. I believe it does quite well, although she sells in Edinburgh too – and online of course.'

'They're the people who own the embroidered cabinet in the hotel, aren't they?'

'Yes. Fabulous thing. You seldom see them in that condition. But Donal's never going to sell it. He says it belongs here. Who's to say he isn't right?'

A mile or so beyond the turn-off to Ardachy, they come to another narrow junction and he swings the car sharply to the left. A straight stretch of track runs between high hedges, alight with gorse, towards the sea. It is so dazzling as to be disturbing and when she winds down the window the powerful scent of coconut invades the car.

'You can see why I have a four-wheel drive, can't you?' he says, as the vehicle bounces along.

The centre of the track already has a good growth of grass sprouting up between stones and dry earth. They pass a cream-painted farmhouse and then, just before the track ends at the seashore, he veers to the right along a short stretch of green lane and pulls up in front of a fence with a swing gate set into it. It's fastened shut with a bit of baler twine. Beyond, she can just make out a low stone cottage, white walls, grey roof, tucked in above the shoreline.

He opens the gate and Hector bounces ahead of them. The tiny cottage sits on a hillock, a risen circle of garden just above the sea. There is lush grass with grey-brown rocks poking through here and there, drifts of pink thrift, a natural rock garden. There is a bird feeder with blue tits balancing on it. Hector rushes at them, barking, but they don't seem too perturbed and return as soon as he turns his back.

'Does it have a name?' she asks. 'This place? Mrs Cameron mentioned it but I've forgotten.'

'Oh they all have names. Gaelic names of course. Every field and stone practically. This place is called Carraig.'

'Big stone?'

He smiles. 'And the house does sit on solid rock. Do you speak Gaelic?'

'No, but I did some Scottish history as part of my degree. Place names were a thing.'

'They're a big thing here too. The old maps show a significant building with chimneys here. But this cottage is only a couple of hundred years old.'

'I suppose most of the island houses had no proper chimneys at all back then.'

'No. The smoke just found its way out through the thatch or the turf or whatever. This place was probably thatched when it was first built.' He grins. 'Mind you, it's a bit like that here in winter even now. The chimney smokes. Depends what way the wind's blowing.'

'Do you often come in winter?'

'I come whenever I can, sweetheart. If the ferry isn't off.' He gestures towards another wooden gate in the far fence, against which a riot of fuchsias, just coming into bud, are scrambling. 'There's a causeway down to the sea. Bit like the one at Auchen-blae only smaller.'

She smiles. 'Everything's smaller. Don't knock it. I quite like it. Where do you keep your boat?'

'There's a harbour of sorts down there. It's nice. We walk down there a lot. Don't we, Hector?'

Hector hears the magic word 'walk' and bounds up, tail wagging, tongue lolling.

'Later,' says Cal. Hector looks disappointed. He has expressive eyebrows. He finds his water bowl outside the back door and laps enthusiastically. He's enthusiastic about everything but especially walks.

The house has white walls, battered by wind and weather and in need of a coat of paint. There are climbing roses, carefully pruned back, and a big ceanothus, just coming into bright blue bloom. Several hydrangeas have been planted against the wall on the seaward side, a mass of new leaves at this time of year.

'My mum does the garden when she comes,' he says. I cut the grass but that's about all. I don't know what's what. She does. But she doesn't get to come here very often. Not now.' He looks sad, but offers no other explanation.

The cottage is low and compact, a single storey with a shallow sloping roof. It has a tiny kitchen extension and a lean-to shed at one side. There's an open wood store with neatly stacked logs, and a dark green shed with a padlocked door. This looks newer and more watertight than any of the other buildings.

He nods at it. 'I do a lot of antique buying up the west coast and use this as a stopping off place on the way back to Glasgow, so I have to have somewhere secure to store things temporarily. I know it isn't really on the way to Glasgow, but it's worth the detour.'

He leads the way inside the house.

'We never open the door on the other side at all. Always use this one.'

'You don't lock it?'

'I do when I go away. Not so much when I'm on the island. Nobody comes down here. I keep the shed locked of course. There's almost nothing worth stealing in the house. The fiddle maybe. A couple of my father's pictures. But his style has changed so much that I don't think anyone would recognise them for what they are.'

If Auchenblae is dauntingly huge, this place is compact in every way. Daisy is reminded of a boat interior or a caravan. There are two tiny rooms: a living room at the side of the house facing the sea and a bedroom at the back. The door to the bedroom is ajar and she can see a double bed, unmade, with a heaped duvet and old-fashioned woollen blankets. A utility wardrobe in walnut almost fills the available space. The kitchen is very basic, with a Baby Belling cooker, the smallest possible washing machine and a mini fridge. There's an equally tiny shower room with a lavatory, all clean and fresh and smelling of bleach. No central heating, but oil radiators here and there. And a fireplace with a diminutive wood burner, a chipped blue enamel kettle sitting on the top. The place smells of the sea with an undertone of soot, and with the coconut of the gorse drifting in, like sun lotion. It smells of holidays.

'We used to spend a lot of time here when we were kids.' It's clear to Daisy that he loves this place.

'Where did you all sleep?'

'There were bunk beds in the lean-to. I use it as a workshop now but it was OK. In fact, when we were kids, it was magic. Like camping but more comfortable. We had hot water bottles and lots of blankets for chilly nights. It was before we had the shop. Dad was always going off painting and he'd given up on islands by that time. He would go off to various European cities, preferably without any encumbrances. Mum would bring us over at the start of the school holidays and that would be us for the whole time. Me and Catty. We just ran wild.'

'It sounds wonderful.'

'We set off down the shore every morning and explored. Walked into Keill to play with some of the kids there or cycled north and climbed *Meall Each*.'

'Is that the big hill you can see from just about everywhere?'

'That's the one. If you set off from your house and head inland, there's a track to the top. Fantastic views. Catty was fearless. We could have had a hard time as incomers, but mum belonged to the island and the other kids admired Catty.'

'She's younger than you?'

'A couple of years, yes. But it didn't matter. They'd tell me she was mad, and so she was, in a good way. There was nothing she wouldn't dare do. In fact, she was often the leader of the pack. Good with her fists and they couldn't hit back because she was a girl!'

His hazel eyes are shining. He's back in some treasured past time. He gestures to a couch with threadbare cushions and she sits down. He sits opposite in a battered old armchair. The scent and sound of the sea filters through the doorway but there can hardly be a house on Garve into which the powerful sense of the sea does not intrude. *It shifts your perspective on everything*, thinks Daisy. The island seems like a world within a world. Hector's bed is beside Cal's chair. He climbs into it, turns around three times, heaves a big sigh and settles down.

She looks around the room. There are pictures on the walls, many of them island scenes.

'Which are your dad's?' she asks.

He points them out: two small but detailed studies of rock pools. She wouldn't have guessed that they were by the same artist whose bleak cityscapes she had seen in Island Antiques and in the occasional magazine feature.

'Like I said, this is early stuff. He doesn't rate them any more. That's why they're still here. Most of the others are pictures my mum acquired over the years. A friend of hers did that one.' He points to a framed watercolour sketch over the mantelpiece. Two children are playing on a beach, a boy and a girl, the boy tall, slender, intent on digging with a long spade, with his brown hair flopping forward; the little girl turning a cartwheel, her polka-dot skirt hanging down, navy knickers showing, and a pair of skinny brown legs and bare feet waving in the air. There's a glass jar on the sand beside the boy. He's concentrating fiercely on the job in hand, but behind him, the younger child is all energy and movement and carelessness.

'Is that you and your sister?'

'Aye it is. Digging for bait. Except that Catty was always distracted. And she never liked the worms. She was always letting them go, setting them free, she called it. That's Mum's favourite picture. I like it a lot.'

'Did your dad never paint you and your sister?'

Cal seems to find her question quite funny. 'No way. You must be joking. Dad doesn't do people at all!'

She thinks about what little she knows of William Galbraith. There have been exhibitions in some of the big Glasgow galleries and elsewhere too. He has slowly but surely built up a fine reputation in Scotland and beyond. One or two US stars have acquired his work and that has helped things along. He seems to paint nothing but cheerless images, without people or even sunshine. They have always looked to her like the aftermath of some terrible holocaust, although she doesn't want to say as much to Cal.

The room is warm and bright and too full. Not like a man's room at all, but she senses the unseen presence of his mother everywhere. There's a table with a red and white gingham cloth and a shallow slipware fruit bowl in the middle, a couple of shrivelled apples and a lemon sitting in it. There's a dark wood spinning wheel, a well-stocked bookshelf, faded embroidered cushions, a threadbare rug covering most of the floor area, an ancient fiddle hanging on the wall. She can understand why he comes back again and again. She finds herself wishing that she had inherited a cottage like this. It wouldn't present quite so many problems as Auchenblae. She could keep it. No worries.

'My dad would love the fiddle,' she says.

'Of course. I'd forgotten your dad's a musician. It was made on the island. I can't play. My sister can, though. Not well, but she can coax a tune out of it.'

'Maybe when my dad comes he can give it a go.'

'I'd be honoured.'

*

After a while, he goes into the kitchen and investigates the fridge. 'I've got eggs and cheese,' he says. 'I can make us an omelette. Or

141

scrambled eggs. Actually, it amounts to the same thing with me cooking it.'

He beats the eggs and she grates the cheese, a big block of supermarket cheddar. They just about fit in there, but keep bumping into one another, saying 'sorry'. Hector is very interested in the cheese.

'His favourite thing. But then everything's his favourite thing. Except the vet's. He doesn't like the vet much. Which is a shame, because the vet likes him.'

Cal makes a big omelette on top of the stove, sprinkles the cheese on top and then finishes it under the grill. While Hector wolfs down a bowl of dog food, they eat fluffy omelette with crusty bread from the village shop, and a salad consisting mostly of tomatoes with some chopped basil from a plant on the window-sill, olive oil and lemon juice. He opens a bottle of Pinot Grigio. She thinks about the drive back to Auchenblae, but doesn't say anything.

After supper, they go through the gate in the back garden and head down towards the sea, accompanied by a deliriously happy Hector. Looking back the way they have come, she can see that the house does indeed seem to be sitting on a stony mound, with the path they have walked down a deliberate causeway leading to the sea. There is a small horseshoe of a bay and a low drystone jetty stretching out a few metres across the mouth. The tide is out and a blue painted wooden boat with an outboard propped up on the stern is sitting picturesquely on the white sand, tied up to a rock just above the shoreline.

'I'll take you out in it some time,' he says.

'That would be good.'

'You see all sorts out there. Seals. Dolphins and porpoises if you're lucky. There are lots of rocks and islets. It can be a bit dodgy, but I know it like the back of my hand.'

'Sounds good to me.'

'I put out a line for mackerel sometimes. Donal McNeill puts out creels for crabs and lobsters. From Ardachy, back along there. You can't make much of a living out of it, but he says he does OK alongside all his other work.'

The sun is setting, slipping into a bank of high clouds, making the sky look like a bolt of grey silk. A breeze has sprung up and it's chilly. She wishes she had brought something warmer to wear.

'I thought we were going to look up Lilias,' she says.

'Maybe we should. Come on then.'

*

Back in the house, he switches on a couple of lamps, sets a match to wood and paper, already laid in the wood burner, and finds her a sweater. It is a big navy blue gansey with holes here and there and too-long sleeves that practically cover her hands.

'Mum knitted it years ago. The sleeves are long on me as well. She's not the best knitter in the world, but it's nice and warm.'

She notices how it smells of him: faintly of some citrussy cologne mixed with the oily scent of the wool, and lavender from where it has been stored away.

As she's putting it on, she sees that he's watching her, his forehead creased in a frown.

'What?' she says.

'This may sound daft, but I keep thinking I know you from somewhere. Have we met before?'

'We have, as it happens.'

'Where? Why didn't you say?'

'It took me a while to figure it out myself. It was at a boot sale. You rescued me from a dealer. I was unpacking and he was muscling in, the way they do, bullying me. You did your knight-in-shining-armour bit.'

She can't keep the tinge of sarcasm from her voice but she's smiling and he starts to laugh. 'Christ! I remember. He's terrified of his wife, that one. Big Agnes. I still see her from time to time. To tell you the truth, I'm terrified of her as well!'

'I haven't done a boot sale in a long time.'

'They're hell on wheels. Especially if you're on your own. I'm glad that's cleared up, though. It's been bothering me. I thought I might have chatted you up or something.'

'No. You never did that.'

He sits down on the sofa and opens up his laptop. He's blushing slightly.

'I have to say, the signal's pretty crap here. Slow. But then it can be just as slow in Glasgow.'

She has to go and sit beside him so that she can look at the screen with him. She's mesmerised by his long fingers on the laptop keyboard, suntanned or maybe just wind burned, and has to wrap the sweater more closely round herself to keep the feelings in check. He signs on to a couple of specialist genealogy websites, using his mother's account details. 'She doesn't mind. She's quite keen on family history.'

It takes a while and they have to keep refining the search, but eventually they find one Lilias McNeill born on Garve in 1570. Her father is Ruaridh McNeill, at *Achadh nam Blàth*, which is surely Auchenblae. He is described as the Laird or Thane of *Eilean Garbh*. Her mother is Bláithín McGugan from Islay.

'Just like my mother's maiden name,' says Cal, surprised.

'Yes – you said!'

'Fiona McGugan.'

A further search reveals that Bláithín died in 1580, 'possibly in childbirth?' says Daisy, and Cal nods. Lilias had siblings: an elder brother called Kenneth, a younger brother called Malcolm and a younger sister, Ishbel, born in 1580, which seems to confirm the speculation.

'Looks as though we've struck gold. Could well be your Lilias,' he says.

'More likely than not.'

'I don't know about the inscription, though. *A time will come.* What time? When?'

The signal drops out and they drink more wine, finishing the bottle and opening another. Daisy feels the familiar excitement of research, exacerbated by the alcohol and his proximity. It occurs to her that she is entirely happy in this moment. She gets more of a kick out of this kind of hunt than almost anything else in her life. It's what she loves most about the kind of antique dealing she does: not the prospect of a bargain, not the prospect of making a find, although those things are important too. What she really loves is finding out about the history of things, about the life of these objects stretching back through time and passing through her hands for a little while only. She's wondering if Cal might be a kindred spirit, because she's never found one before. Not a man, anyway. Never one so attractive.

Hector is in his bed and dreaming. His legs twitch and he emits short, tinny barks.

'What do you suppose he's dreaming about?' Cal asks.

'Chasing rabbits maybe.'

'I think so too. There are lots of them in the dunes down the shore. He usually has a field day there.'

The broadband comes back on and they pursue Lilias down the remaining years of her life. She was married to one Matthew McNeill of *Dun Sithe* in 1589.

'I'll bet that's Dunshee,' says Cal. 'It's a small farmhouse at the south end of the island. I wonder why there? The laird's daughter as well. But maybe it was a more important place back then.'

The records state that Lilias gave birth to a daughter called Flora in that same year, followed by seven sons, the last born in 1605. She had died in 1620 at the age of 50.

'Eight kids in however many years? Sixteen?' says Cal. 'I'm surprised she didn't die of exhaustion.'

'It wasn't uncommon. If they survived the process of childbirth for long enough.'

'You're right, of course. There's a story from way back in my great-grandfather's day of thirteen kids in this cottage!'

'Thirteen? Where did they put them all?'

'God knows. But even when they moved, they kept the cottage in the family. There was some cousin or other renting it for a while but then they moved away and Mum and Dad came back when he was just starting out as a painter, when they were first married.'

Cal's voice suddenly manages to be cold and angry at the same time. 'The island was his brand for a while, before branding was even a thing. There were a few lifestyle pieces in the Sunday supplements. Mum kept them. Unrealistic nonsense about life on a Scottish island. It wore off quite quickly, though. As soon as he changed his style and began to make serious money.'

The bitterness in his tone makes her shiver. 'He stopped coming?' she asks.

'Mostly. Mum used to bring us. He would pay the occasional visit, but the lack of space bugged him.'

They are intrigued to discover that Lilias's firstborn, Flora, had married into the Galbraith family, at a place called Knockbaird. She nudges him. 'She might be one of your forebears!'

'Maybe. There are quite a lot of Galbraiths on the island.'

'Is Knockbaird still there?'

'It is. It's very small, though. Just a cottage, a bit like this one, not far from Dunshee.'

'So Lilias's daughter married the boy next door?'

'She must have done. We used to know the people who lived at Knockbaird, but they moved away. I think somebody who works at the distillery has it now. You should take a run down there some time.'

It is very dark by now, and they have both drunk a lot of wine. She yawns, widely. 'I should be getting back. But you've drunk as much as me.'

'I know. The police don't tend to frequent this place at night, but all the same, I don't feel very competent to drive. Do you want to stay the night?'

When she hesitates, although there seems to be no other

option, he says quite casually, 'This is a sofa bed. We often have visitors, or we used to, when Mum came. It's quite comfortable. I can easily make it up for you.'

She really doesn't want to go back to Auchenblae. Not now. Not in the dark. It's one thing to be there and settled, quite another to arrive there with the vast house in darkness and the thought of the tower with its accumulation of possessions, the mice in the servants' quarters, the monstrous fridge in the kitchen. She wants to stay in this small cottage with the warmth and the glow from the stove, with Hector sighing and snoring in his bed, with Cal in the bedroom next door. To tell the truth, she wouldn't mind being in bed with Cal. She wouldn't mind it at all. She can feel the warmth of him beside her. His energy. But she thinks it's much too soon. She hardly knows him. She has had too many disasters or near-disasters to be anything less than wary. And besides, he seems to be as careful as she is. Or perhaps she's reading too much into it. Perhaps he doesn't find her attractive at all.

'OK,' she finds herself saying. 'Why not? I don't much want to go back there in the dark anyway.'

'No. I can understand that.'

He finds a new toothbrush for her, still in its cellophane packet, in the bathroom cupboard. There's a blue towelling dressing gown and a pair of pyjamas that he says belonged to his sister, although she isn't entirely sure he's telling the truth about that one. They are rather elegant, with fine lace trim, and don't fit in with his description of Catty at all. She wonders how many women he has brought back here, taken down to the beach, made omelettes for, charmed with his energy and his openness. Plenty, she supposes.

While she gets undressed in the shower room, he opens up the sofa bed, gets out the spare duvet, a soft wool blanket and a couple of pillows stored beneath it. The pyjamas are too tight across the top, and much too long in the leg. She hadn't pictured Catty as being this tall and slender either, but maybe time will tell. Hector wakes up, sniffs at the sofa, wags his tail and gets back into his own bed again, quite happy to have some company.

She lies, wakeful, for a long time, listening to the wind moaning around the cottage, to Hector's rhythmic doggy snores, to the settling of logs in the stove. Cal's bedroom door lies permanently ajar. He apologises for it. 'It just won't stay shut and if I try to close it, it will bang in the draught all night.'

'Don't worry about it. It's quite comforting, really.'

Later, she wonders why she said that. He must think her pathetic. Especially after his sister who is allegedly afraid of nothing. He has his bedside light on for a while, presumably reading, and then he switches it off and the house is in darkness, except for the subtle glow from the expiring logs through the glass door of the burner. It surprises her that she trusts him so completely. She's attracted to him, but there is no sense in which she feels anxious here. He seems absolutely trustworthy. In this at least. She's not so sure about him where her new possessions are concerned. It crosses her mind that he may quite deliberately be trying to gain access to those new possessions. That's what Mr Cameron seemed to be implying, in the hotel. Well, he'll be disappointed. She's no fool. No pushover.

On the verge of sleep, she again hears the piercing note of a seabird passing over the house, an impossibly lonely sound, at once enchanting and saddening. She hears his voice from the next room, very low, in case she's asleep. 'Oystercatcher,' he says. 'St Bride's bird.' She doesn't respond. The image of Lilias comes into her head, a young woman gazing out of the picture, gazing enigmatically at the artist, looking into an exhausting future, but with hope in her eyes.

She's woken in the morning by Hector, gently licking her nose. There's a smell of coffee in the room. Cal, wearing shorts and a baggy white T-shirt, is prowling about the kitchen, trying to be quiet. He comes through with a couple of mugs of coffee. He has remembered how she likes it: milk and one sugar.

'Did you sleep well?'

'Like a log. I hadn't realised how badly I've been sleeping since I got here. This is the best night I've had on the island.'

'Well that's good to hear.' He smiles at her. 'I don't have much in for breakfast I'm afraid, but there's toast.'

'Toast is fine.'

The shower room is warm and still scented with his shower gel. He must have crept in there and had a shower without waking her. By the time she has showered and dressed, he has already taken Hector down to the beach for a quick run and is back, slicing the bread.

'You're very domesticated,' she remarks.

'Comes of living alone for a while.'

'You don't have a partner?'

'Not right now. I lived with somebody who works in the shop for almost a year but it didn't work out.'

'Does she still work in the shop?'

'Annabel? Yes. It was all very amicable. And let's face it, I'm not in the shop all that often. She sees more of my mum and dad. She was never going to leave a well-paid job just because she'd had enough of me. But that was a couple of years ago. Nothing serious since. What about you?'

'I was in a fairly serious relationship for a while but it ended last summer.'

'Puts you off, doesn't it?'

She finds herself laughing. 'Well, yes. In a way it does. You kind of need breathing space from all the angst.'

They drink coffee, eat toast and home-made marmalade from the shop at Scoull. Then he drives her back to Auchenblae. To what they have begun to call her 'crumbling castle'.

'Do you want to borrow Hector?' he asks. 'I'm serious. I'm quite happy to lend him to you. And I'm sure he'd be happy to stay with you till you get used to it.'

'Will you be here next week?'

'Should be. I'm away this weekend. There's a big house sale

near Oban. But I'll be back on Monday or Tuesday. I'm working on a bit of restoration. It's a nice old Scottish dresser. I should have shown you. I never thought.'

'Well, I'll maybe take you up on the offer of Hector as house guest for a little while. But I think I might just head for home today. My dad's going off on tour for a few weeks and I want to see him before he goes, make sure he's organised. And I have things to sort out in Glasgow. I could come back on Tuesday, though, and stay for as long as it takes.'

As long as what takes? she thinks. But she doesn't know the answer to that one, not yet, and he doesn't seem prepared to ask the question either.

'Well, I'll see you next week, Daisy.' He pauses, just before she gets out of the car.

'What are you going to do about the picture? The portrait? Lilias.'

'I don't know. Why? Should I be doing anything about it?'

He frowns. 'I know you think I have ulterior motives in all this. I know you don't really trust me. But it's potentially a valuable piece of work, you know. It's been safe because it's been so hidden away. Now we've brought it out into the light. Don't just leave it sitting on a table. I know this is a low crime area, but it does kind of leap out at you as soon as you see it.'

'Would anybody else think that? I mean, it doesn't seem to be signed.'

'No, it doesn't. And if you decide you want somebody to look at it with an expert eye, then my mother would be the person. I don't know half enough. She does. But I'm not twisting your arm. Just – make sure you put her away, eh? Lilias? While you're not here. Hide her somewhere. Just in case.'

'You're making me nervous.'

'I don't mean to. I'm certain it'll all be fine. But there's something about her. I don't know what it is. And it may have nothing to do with value at all. Or not monetary value.'

'I know what you mean.'

She gets out of the car, waits by the door to wave him off. Hector jumps into the passenger seat and pokes his head through the open window. He is grinning, his tongue lolling. Cal has wound down the window on his own side too and, as he pulls away, he blows her a kiss. She returns it. She can't help herself.

FIFTEEN

1588

Mateo recovered his physical strength quite quickly. He was, however, beset by persistent nightmares and an occasional sense of disorientation. Sometimes he would wake up in the night with a feeling of panic, an apprehension of danger so intense that he would sit bolt upright, staring into the grey light of early morning, filtering into the room from the single high window, his heart pounding. Once or twice it happened in the dead of night, and the suffocating darkness made it much worse. At such times, he would find it hard even to catch his breath, his whole chest feeling tight and constricted, his head buzzing with a peculiar sound, like insects dancing in there. He would have a dreadful sense of unreality, as though the whole world had changed, magically, becoming altered in some terrible and threatening way. Then his eyes would find the glowing remnants of the fire, banked up with ashes to keep it smouldering for morning, and gradually the feelings would subside.

The first time this happened, he realised at last that in his panic, he had filled his chest with air and was holding his breath, rigid with fright. He managed to persuade himself to force the air out and, slowly but surely, the feelings subsided and he became properly aware of his surroundings, leaving only a sort of general anxiety, with very little obvious cause. The house was quiet enough at night, with only distant snoring from the other inhabitants, the bark and whine of a dog, and the occasional footstep as somebody passed by to relieve himself. He was aware too that a couple of men always stayed on watch in the great hall, taking it in turns to sleep, making sure that the big fire was stoked and the house was safe from unwanted intrusion, although such things were rare in this enclosed world of the island.

Mateo had been a vigorous man and his strength returned with good food, activity and a certain amount of personal security. He was aware that the people living and working in and around the house were deeply suspicious of both of them, but they obeyed McNeill unquestioningly. It was their custom and their habit and though they might occasionally look askance at the Spaniards, or make remarks in their own tongue that he knew were less than complimentary, they would not translate any of that suspicion into physical abuse. Not yet, anyway. McNeill had spoken. They dared not go against his wishes.

Francisco took longer to recover. During the weeks following their arrival on the island, he became very ill. Beathag came to their small chamber, felt his forehead and said that, although her inclination was to give him one of the higher rooms with more light and air, he had better stay where he was. If it was some sort of contagion he should be kept well away from the rest of the household. He burned like a torch in the night, and Mateo, sleeping beside him, would have to move away from him as his poor body radiated heat. He feared greatly for his cousin, believed that one morning he might wake to find that Francisco had not survived the night. But the lad lingered on.

One day, not long after their arrival, Lilias came to their room with Beathag. The women consulted together about the young man's condition and then left for a while. When the two of them came back, some time later, it was with a little three-footed pipkin of some fragrant liquid and a stone jug of plain water.

Mateo sniffed at the medicine. 'I didn't know physic could be so palatable!' he said. It had a faint scent of honey, along with green and growing things. A grassy scent with something of springtime in it.

Beathag glanced at Lilias, expecting her to explain. Her own Scots, although growing in confidence, was still hesitant.

'It's made with water from a holy well called Tobar Moire, Mary's well, on the other side of the island,' said Lilias. 'I suppose you might call it a spring. It is something of a catholicon for all diseases, or so the people here believe, and we always keep some in the house. It's fresh and cool and none takes ill from drinking it. But all the water here is good.'

'How do you make the physic?' he asked.

'Beathag makes a tincture from the blessed thistle. And a few other herbs for good measure. Self-heal, marigolds. And honey, of course.'

'I didn't know you had the knowledge of such things.'

'Oh we are not quite savages! We cultivate a small physic garden among the kale, in the shelter of the wall beyond the tower. Not everything will grow here, but some things will. It may do your friend good, if you can encourage him to drink. And...' she glanced sidelong at Mateo, 'it might do you some good as well. At least it will do no harm.'

'But I'm not ill.'

'No. But Beathag tells me your spirit is troubled and your sleep likewise, and we must not neglect you in trying to treat your friend.'

Mateo had another shameful desire to weep. He had been beset by these sensations too often of late. Her sympathy struck him to the heart. And for a foreigner, and an enemy at that. He could feel the constriction in his throat, and tears forming behind his eyes. It would be terrible to weep in the presence of these two women. He clenched his fists, trying to banish the misery that had descended on him like clouds on *Meall Each*.

To his surprise, Lilias reached out and caught hold of his hand. Her fingers were cool and dry.

'Sir — there's no shame in sorrow. You've seen unimaginable

horrors. You and your cousin both. You must take time. This is a peaceful place, for now.'

'So it seems.'

'It hasn't always been, for sure. There have been turbulent times for us, many of them. And it will not always be peaceful. Who knows what the future may bring? Those who can foresee such things have no great comfort to give. These are troubled times as you well know, and there are troubles to come. We are small people, caught up in the grand dreams of others. But for the present, my father takes good care of all who rely on him. You have washed up on a tranquil shore. Let it soothe you for now. Be like the lilies of the field. Be like my namesake, in the words of yours.'

'Mine?'

'Mateo. Mata in my tongue. Matthew in the Scots tongue, I think. Or Matha, sometimes.'

He found himself eager for her fingers to remain on his, and he clung to her, briefly. She smiled and her smile lit up the gloomy room.

'Be not careful for your life, what ye shall eat or what ye shall drink, nor yet for your body, what raiment ye shall wear.' She quoted the words almost merrily as though they were deeply ingrained in her. As though they were favourites with her. 'Behold the fowls of the air; for they sow not, neither reap, nor yet carry into the barns and yet your heavenly father feedeth them. Are ye not better than they?'

She paused, retrieved her hand suddenly as though reminded of the unsuitability of the contact by Beathag's frown, even though the older woman had understood only some of the conversation.

'Beathag,' she turned to her companion, full of mischief. 'I'm quoting Matthew's own gospel. These are my verses. My mother always said so, at any rate. I still have the holy book she brought with her. She taught me my letters from it, and taught me to read in the English tongue at the same time.'

'Aye,' said Beathag, dourly in her own language. 'Quoting the

New Testament and holding hands with a foreigner!'

Lilias laughed even more, but keeping her hands neatly folded, resumed her instruction.

'And why care ye then for raiment? Behold the lilies of the field how they grow. They labour not, neither spin. And yet for all that, I say unto you, that even Solomon in all his royalty was not arrayed like unto one of these.'

Confused as much by his own feelings as by the words, Mateo bowed to her. 'My lady, your name is fitting for I think even Solomon was not as wise as Lilias.'

'How charming you are! And you must know how seldom I ever receive fine compliments even here in my father's house. It is not the habit of our people. But we must leave you to tend to your friend.' She was suddenly serious. 'Make him drink the physic if you can. He has such a fever, but if it will only break, he may survive. Beathag has brought clean linen and more of this blessed water. Bathe his forehead, his arms, his feet even in the plain water and all may yet be well.'

The room seemed cooler and sweeter when she left. It was as though for a brief moment her presence had illuminated and freshened it. He could and did follow her instructions, bathing his cousin's poor attenuated body, and encouraging him to drink, wetting his lips with the physic constantly when it seemed that he could not swallow.

Whether it was the physic itself, the water from the holy well, Mateo's constant ministrations or Francisco's own spirit rejecting an early death, he couldn't say. But the young man recovered. One night the fever left him. The bedcovers were wringing wet and Mateo feared that the end had come, but in the morning, Francisco sat up, weak as a kitten, but cool, wide awake and able to eat a piece of oat bread and drink a cup of Beathag's heather ale. When he slept again, it was peacefully, his breathing gentle, and Mateo was able to leave him alone and report on the improvement to those responsible for the physic.

SIXTEEN

Daisy takes the small car ferry to the mainland in the early afternoon and drives the long road home through Inveraray, crossing the Firth of Clyde to Gourock at Dunoon and heading for Glasgow. Loch Lomond might be quicker, but the road there is busy and always seems too narrow for the traffic. Instead, she drives down the side of Loch Eck and hardly sees another car all afternoon. The road is fringed with birchwoods and vivid bluebells. It's a long drive and she finds herself wishing she had Hector in the car beside her. Cal too, but it seems safer to be missing the dog than his master. She stops once for tea and a sandwich at a small lochside café, then drives on. She has been on Garve for only a few days, but already she finds the city overwhelming, the constant noise of traffic, the looming buildings. Heaven knows what it will be like if she stays on the island for a few months. She manages to find a parking space not too far from the flat and hauls her bag past the pretty art nouveau tiles with their stylised lilies, and up the stone stairs. The residents take turns to keep the stair clean and she realises that she has probably missed her turn. If her dad hasn't done it – and he may be too excited about his road trip to remember – she'll have to do it tomorrow, otherwise there will be complaints.

Her father is in his room, sorting out his instruments: a fiddle, a mandolin, a selection of whistles. He has got out a couple of old kitbags and his precious army sleeping bag but he hasn't begun packing yet. He looks happier than she's seen him in a while.

He gives her a hug. 'I've been worried about you. How was it?'

'Fine,' she says. 'It was fine. But I'm really glad to see you all the same.'

'Is it a wreck?'

'No. Not at all. Things need doing. But it doesn't seem particularly damp or derelict. There's a lot of stuff. Especially in the tower. I thought it would be more or less empty, but it isn't.'

'I shouldn't be going anywhere,' he says, anxiously. His hands go to his pockets. She suspects he sometimes smokes when she's not looking, when he's under stress, but he pretends he doesn't. 'I should be going back over there, helping you to sort all this out.'

'Don't be daft, Dad,' she tells him. It used to be him telling her not to be daft, telling her that she could do anything she wanted. 'Of course you have to go. You'll love it. I'd feel bad if you didn't do it. When are you leaving?'

'Monday. I'll help you with your fair, though. Are you sure you have enough stuff?'

She begins to laugh, helplessly. He seems quite bemused. She's on the verge of tears. He hands her a tissue and she dries her eyes, then starts to laugh again, stuffing the tissue into her mouth. Her laughter is infectious and he laughs too. He can't help himself, even though he's not sure what they are laughing about.

'Are you OK?' he asks eventually, when the hysteria has subsided. 'I didn't think I'd said anything very funny.'

She takes a deep, shuddering breath. 'It isn't funny at all, really. It's just that you asked me if I had enough stuff. Oh, Dad, I've got enough stuff to last me a whole lifetime. The place is literally stuffed. I don't even know what's valuable and what's not. There are boxes, chests, tea chests, cupboards. And she left it all to me.'

'Well she *was* your grandmother.'

'I know. But it still seems bizarre.'

'What about probate and all that? Inheritance tax. Won't you have to pay a fortune? Have they done a proper inventory?'

'They've done one. That's what Mr McDowall said, anyway. And to be honest, at first glance, it looks like a hoard, a load of junk. I mean, it's just lived in. And a lot of the stuff in the main house is pretty scruffy. Brown furniture and you know how little that fetches.'

'There's brown furniture and then there's...'

'Brown furniture. I know. And there are a few good pieces of old oak. A big carved press, a couple of chests. A fabulous table. And a bed. But the kitchen was probably last done in the 1970s. It's like...' she hesitates. She has taken some photographs on her phone, but even they don't give a proper impression. 'Dad, imagine a weekly sale at some small-town auction house. You know, the ones where they say it's a sale of household goods and the whole place is full of trays and boxes of miscellaneous junk and damaged furniture and foxed pictures. Some of it is going to be really good, but you wouldn't know from a casual glance. That's what it's like. The main room in the house is OK. I think my grandmother spent most of her time there when she wasn't in her bedroom. But the main room's comfortable enough and the kitchen's functional.'

'Where did you sleep?'

She hesitates again. 'In my mum's old room.' She thinks it's probably better not to mention, at this stage, that she also slept on a sofa bed in a cottage with a comparative stranger and his dog. Her father, a hippy at heart, has a blind spot where his daughter is concerned. He worries about her all the time.

He's silent for a moment. 'I never saw it properly, you know. Or only from a distance. Jess never took me to the house. Said her mother wouldn't approve. I stayed on after the gig. Camped out in the van. Couldn't leave her but we met elsewhere. In one of the villages, in a quiet corner of the pub. Or down on the beach.'

Daisy has heard this story many times, and seen the old photographs, but it still seems impossibly romantic to her: her tall, skinny father with his long dark hair and his beloved fiddle, performing at a folk festival on the island, falling for her red-headed mother, Jessica May, in the middle of the music and song, camping in the old van that was to become their home, her home too for a large part of her early childhood, although her mother had made plenty of modifications to it.

'But you met Viola, surely?'

'I met Viola once. It was a folk festival and it wasn't her kind of thing at all. But she agreed to come to a supper in the hotel at Scoull, afterwards. They'd laid on this big buffet – everyone brought something – and somebody had persuaded her to come. She sat there like the lady of the manor. Like the Queen Mother without the sense of humour. She seemed quite old to me, but she can't have been more than sixty. Your mother was a late baby. Viola must have been forty or so when she had her.'

'And unmarried? Wouldn't that have been a big scandal?'

'I suppose it must have been. There was certainly no sign of a father. No father named on your mum's birth certificate either.'

'Didn't she ask?'

'Of course she asked. But she told me she had never got a satisfactory answer. Your mother always said she thought it must have been a visitor. Nobody from the island. Otherwise, word would have got about. It's that kind of place. They keep secrets from outsiders, but they talk among themselves.'

'It must have bothered her. Mum, I mean. It would bother me.'

'I'm not sure that it did, all that much. It meant that she could fantasise about some glamorous stranger! You never know, there might be some clues in the house still.'

'I suppose there might. I don't think Viola threw very much away. It'll take months to go through all the old paperwork. I wish I'd met her.'

'You might have been disappointed. I don't think you'd have got much out of her. She was a formidable woman. You didn't cross Viola. Not unless you were very brave. Or so your mother told me.'

'What did you think about her? Did she talk to you? When you met her?'

'She shook hands with me and patronised me like hell. Jess thought it was hilarious. I didn't. But she didn't know there was anything going on between us. I think we managed to hide it well. Or maybe she just couldn't imagine that anyone would fall for me, let alone that it might be her beloved daughter.'

'But she did love her?'

'Yes. I think she genuinely loved her. But it was a repressive kind of love. It must have been, or your mum wouldn't have done what she did. Wouldn't have run away. What was Jess's room like?'

'Like Mum, I suppose. Colourful. Nice. You can come and see it some time. It's full of her things, still. But quite clean so Viola must have looked after it all these years since Mum left. I slept there and it was OK. It's the only bedroom in the house that seems genuinely comfortable.'

She can see that he's upset. Even after all these years, the thought of Jessica can both move and sadden him. His eyes glisten. 'Ach, it'll be sold soon enough. Why don't you just get rid of it, contents and all, Daisy?'

'I'm not sure about that, yet.'

He looks aghast. 'What on earth do you mean? I thought you were just going over there to have a poke about and then let the place go. Take the money and run.'

'Is that what you want me to do?'

He looks aghast in a different way. 'No, no. Don't misunderstand me, Daisy. I don't want any money! I just think it's such a huge undertaking. Wouldn't it be better to sell everything? There's all kinds of things you could do with the money.' He looks confused, sheepish again.

She hugs him. 'I know, Dad. I know. I don't for a minute think you're after my money, although you'd be very welcome to it. God knows you've earned it. It's just – I can't explain it. I like the island.'

'It's a lovely place, right enough.'

'I feel comfortable there. You can see the sea from the windows.

There's a walled garden. I've hardly seen the half of it. I need time. Time to get to know it or for it to get to know me.'

'But do you have time? What about probate, taxes, things like that?' Money has never been his strong suit.

'It's paid, Dad. There was enough money in the estate to pay everything. Quite a bit of money, really, since Viola hardly spent anything at all and inherited quite a lot. There were farms and land that were sold off years ago. All that's left now is the house and gardens and a few acres of not very productive land. But you're right. It was a fairly large sum, but there won't be much left to do anything at all with the house.'

'How was it valued?'

'I don't know, to be honest. I think somebody from the firm of solicitors went in with some... expert.'

She stops quite suddenly.

'What's the matter?'

'Nothing. I was just wondering about experts. Local experts. Who they were. It's nothing. I'll ask Mr McDowall. He must have made the arrangements.'

'But surely, if there are valuable antiques...'

'It would be very hard to be certain. It's not a museum. I doubt if there'd be any dispute if somebody with the right credentials just went in and did a reasonable valuation without really going into too much detail. The tower is quite gloomy. You can hardly see what's in there. It took me a few days to pluck up the courage to go in myself, and even then I had help.'

She thinks of Cal, leaping confidently up and down those spiral stairs. As though he had been in there before. The local antiques and art expert. With credentials. Exactly the kind of person a city solicitor, perhaps knowing his mother and father and their classy shop, not far from his office, might call upon to do some kind of valuation of the contents of Auchenblae.

She feels slightly sick.

'What *is* in the old tower then?'

'The main room in there is one big junk room. You know, these small island lairds weren't exactly rolling in it. And even though Viola's family were pretty well off, I think for most of her forebears Auchenblae was just their summer house.'

'Some holiday home!'

'I know. Mr McDowall told me it wasn't until her parents that the family actually lived there properly, and I get the feeling they didn't do much to it. But maybe it's not all junk. There's an amazing carved bed. And pictures. It would be worth taking a good look at the pictures. There's a very beautiful portrait of a young woman. It looks like an Elizabethan portrait but the name on it is Lilias, and the laird at the time had a daughter called Lilias. We – I – looked her up.'

'You're getting sucked into all this, aren't you?'

'Would that be such a bad thing? I'm in a rut, Dad. You have a more exciting time of it than me these days. My thirties are marching on. There's no man in my life and I'm fed up to the back teeth of fairs and boot sales. I need a change.'

The fairs are no picnic. Bad enough setting up, hauling a dozen or more boxes of objects into some draughty hall and then building a decent display, but the breaking down at the end is arguably worse, with everyone trying to park as close as possible to the venue and falling over each other to get away. Somebody will always mind a stall for you while you go to the loo or fetch a coffee, and Daisy has friends who can sometimes be persuaded to help. Her father volunteers as often as he can. But too often, she does it all by herself and by the end of the day she's exhausted.

'You need a shop.'

'I can't afford to rent a shop.'

'You could easily afford it if you sold Auchenblae.'

'I could *buy* a shop if I sold Auchenblae. I could buy a shop and a house of my own.'

'Exactly. And wouldn't that be better than camping out in a

crumbling mansion? Wouldn't that be the sensible option? Why do anything different?'

'Because I'm my mother's daughter,' she says, before she can stop herself.

He sighs. 'There's no arguing with that. I just worry about you.'

She's not even sure that she wants a shop. It's the kind of thing that sounds wonderful in prospect, but she's worked with the general public before, and they can be a sore trial, day in and day out. Especially when you're on your own.

'Listen. The house isn't going anywhere. Nor the contents. What I'm thinking is that I'll spend the summer on Garve. I'll have a good look at what I've got. Get proper broadband and carry on with the online business. Explore. Research things. Sell things from the house, but on my terms. It just seems wrong to let it go, to abandon it without documenting it all in some way. I don't think I could bear to just invite some auction house in and have them clear it all out.'

She has been thinking about this for the whole drive from the island. Working out the possibilities. Now she realises that she can't bear to let Cal take what he wants either. Has he earmarked things? Did he do the inventory? Did he find the picture of Lilias on that first visit? Hide it? People do hide things. She's done it herself, burying desirable objects in the bottom of boxes of rubbish on viewing days so that a casual browser might not find them.

'Wouldn't that be easier, though? It's one hell of a job for you. And you said yourself, it's mostly junk.'

'It would be easier. But think of what I might be missing?'

'You wouldn't miss things. They'd value things for you. Sort them out for you. Sell them.'

'I don't just mean that. It's something to do with my history. My heritage. We lost Mum when I was too young to have asked her anything.'

'But the family were just incomers to that place.'

'Yes. They were. In a way. But they were Neilsons and they lived there for a hundred years. Maybe there was some connection with the island already. The names are so similar. Neilson and McNeill. I just don't know. Maybe there are family papers, letters, photographs. The kind of thing I've never had. Or only on your side. Never on Mum's. I'm curious. And I won't know until I've looked at what's really there.'

He shakes his head but she can see that he's half resigned to her plans already.

'I suppose so. I suppose it would do no harm.'

'There's this portrait. It was in the tower. Stacked in a pile of pictures on the floor. Not hung on the wall or anything.'

'You said.'

'Lilias McNeill. It's absolutely stunning.'

'Worth a bob or two then.'

'Yes. I'm sure it is. But it made me think. Who was she? Who painted it? Why? There's an inscription on it. It says, "A time will come". *Un temps viendra*. I began to think, maybe this is my time. Maybe I need to spend some time there. Give a bit of time to the house. It feels so neglected. I could go. Just for the summer.'

'You've got too much imagination for your own good, Daisy,' he says. 'But I suppose that makes you your mother's daughter as well.'

'Well, I'm being practical too. There's enough cash for me to live there for a few months, do some online selling. It needs a massive declutter and since I'm in this business, I might as well do it myself. Otherwise I'm just handing it over to somebody who might know even less than I do about it!'

'That's true. And you can always keep your options open.'

'I can. And when you've finished touring, you can come and see for yourself.'

'Aye. I will. I'll do that. Maybe visit a few old haunts.'

'We could see if the Clootie Tree's still there.'

'Didn't you go?'

'No. I didn't. I thought about it. I thought about going to see where Viola's buried as well, down at Keill, but I didn't do that either. Maybe next week.'

'Do you remember the tree?'

'All too well. The road past the house doesn't go anywhere else.'

'I wonder if people still tie their wishes onto it.'

She catches herself thinking that maybe she could walk up there with Cal and Hector. And then she thinks about the inventory and her suspicions. Of course she could be imagining it. It might have been somebody else entirely who valued the contents of Auchenblae. She'll have to phone Mr McDowall tomorrow and ask him. But perhaps she shouldn't be going anywhere with Cal and Hector. Perhaps she shouldn't trust Cal at all.

SEVENTEEN

It's a relief to stop thinking about Auchenblae for a while. On Saturday morning she and her father go to the antique fair as planned. They stuff as many boxes and cartons as possible into Daisy's car, most of it from the small storage unit they hired a few years ago. This involves getting up so early – a bleeding ungodly hour, says her father – that Rob can hardly keep his eyes open and Daisy drives while he leans back in the passenger seat and tries to doze. They would have packed everything the night before, but it never seems wise to leave it in the car overnight, in the city.

'This place wouldn't hold a fraction of the things from Auchenblae,' she remarks as they lock up the unit. 'If I wanted to keep some of it. And I'd have to clear the house before I sold it. Or let somebody else do it.'

'So you're still thinking of selling it, are you?' Rob yawns widely.

She had woken up in the middle of the previous night and couldn't get back to sleep with the worry of it all. But then everything seems so much worse at three or four in the morning. She switches constantly between excitement and panic.

'I don't know.'

Half an hour later, they manage to find a parking space not too far from the entrance to the suburban hall where this monthly fair is held, and then lug and trundle everything into the foyer.

'If I don't get a coffee soon, I'm going to kill somebody,' Rob remarks, mildly.

The organisers are late, an accident on the motorway causing a mega traffic jam, and the exhibitors have to wait among
the assorted trolleys and boxes until the keyholder arrives. The
stallholders are an eclectic mix of young hopefuls, middle-aged
and some elderly dealers who are either winding down to full
retirement or desperately trying to supplement their pensions.
They will cheerfully tell her that they have 'done quite well',
when they've only made the price of the stall, but they're a kindly
bunch on the whole. She and her father have nicknames for some
of them: Mr Desperate, Mrs Grumpy, the Hippy Sisters, Green
Welly Man. She sometimes wonders what they call her.

The sale is held in a familiar draughty hall that smells of frying
bacon from the pop-up cafeteria tucked into a small kitchen at
the far end. The smell is appetising at first, but by the end of the
afternoon, it always becomes sickening. She's made up a picnic:
sandwiches and fruit and a flask of black coffee that her father falls
on as though it is nectar. Around lunchtime Rob will invariably
wander off and come back with trays of chips and more coffee in
paper cups, because they will have drunk the whole flask before
mid-day but never seem to get round to buying a spare flask. Fairs
invariably make Daisy hungry. She once managed to secure a stall
at a mixed crafts and collectables fair opposite a couple selling
home-made chocolates. They were very liberal with free samples
for their fellow stall-holders and by the end of the day Daisy felt
faintly sick.

She has a feeling that as soon as Rob is off on his trip, any of his
healthy eating will be abandoned with a fair amount of enthusiasm.
She has to remind herself that it isn't her job to police his behaviour,
just as it isn't really his job to police hers any more. Not that he ever
did. She must decide for herself what she wants to do. The inheritance, and everything that comes with it, is hers and hers alone. He
doesn't want her money and won't accept it, even though she'd be
happy to give him some of it. Until now, they've been sporadically
comfortable, with periods of borderline hardship. Daisy has grown

up with it and doesn't mind it. She knows that money doesn't necessarily buy happiness, but it certainly makes the occasional misery a whole lot easier to bear.

The hall has rows of folding tables, carefully arranged, with exhibitor names on printouts taped to them. If people encroach on somebody else's space, disputes can break out. She covers her two ugly tables with a white linen cloth with shamrocks and roses woven into it, and tries to make the stall look enticing. Rob follows her about, tweaking this and that. Occasionally people ask if they can buy the cloth, but it's so useful that she always hangs onto it, even though it's difficult to wash and almost impossible to iron. *I have a whole trunk full of these now,* she thinks. *Perhaps more.*

Footfall is poor. May is generally a bad month for customers, and she finds this surprising, because she loves May and June better than any other time of year. But the so-so sales must have something to do with the bank holidays at either end of the month. Maybe people have other things to spend their money on. Some of the early customers are fellow dealers who are looking for a bargain. Rob stands his ground about prices and she's irritated to note, as she always is, that they'll offer him slightly more than they offer her. They think they can bully her. They never try to bully him. Sometimes they even recognise him.

'Aren't you Rob Graham? You play the fiddle, don't you?'

Once or twice somebody has asked for his autograph. He pretends to be surprised but he's tickled pink, she can tell. He isn't exactly famous, so any recognition is a bonus. Still, Glasgow always likes to celebrate its own.

Mid-morning is busier; then there's the lunchtime slump. A shower in the early afternoon brings more people in. Finally, there's a very quiet time before the last-minute rush of those who think they'll get a bargain during the free-for-all at the end. She sometimes makes most of her money in the last half-hour. People see something, think they might want it and then make up their minds at the last minute.

Fairs pass by a lot faster when they're busy, and this one is just busy enough, but she's still feeling uncharacteristically jaded and bored with the whole procedure. She sells a black Chantilly lace shawl that she wouldn't have minded keeping for herself, a small model yacht, a not very good oil painting of a Clyde coast sunset, an exceedingly battered set of the poetry and letters of Robert Burns in four volumes, a milking stool, a carved spinning chair, a bundle of ancient gardening tools – she can't remember where she acquired these, but it was probably at some country house sale, a house very much like Auchenblae – a couple of pieces of costume jewellery and a miscellaneous collection of bric a brac from her bargain basket. It's a pretty good day. While her father is packing up, she tells the organisers that she won't be needing her stall for a few months.

'I'm going away for the summer.'

'Anywhere nice?'

She can't even begin to explain. 'I've had the offer of some work on one of the islands,' she says. 'On Garve.'

'I've never been, but I hear it's lovely there.'

'I don't know it well, but it is lovely. My grandmother used to live there.'

She's not sure why she says this. She hasn't mentioned her grandmother like this at all before. Not to somebody who didn't know her. Even as the words are coming out of her mouth they seem quite alien to her.

Her father is already loading things onto a folding trolley. As a musician, he's used to this kind of thing, struggling with cumbersome equipment in problematic parking situations. Most people don't realise just how tiring these one-day fairs are, but he does. And then everything will have to be unpacked and stored away at the other end. A thin drizzle is falling outside to add to their troubles, and it's chilly for May.

'Christ on a bike,' he says, laconically. 'Why do we do this, Daisy?'

'I don't know. To make a living. But I need a change. Which is why I'm going to Garve for a few months.'

'For what it's worth, I think you're probably doing the right thing.'

'Do you?'

'Aye, I do. I've been thinking about it while we've been standing here. You can still decide to sell when you want to. But maybe you *should* go and stay there for a while. See how you feel about the island, about the house. It's part of your heritage as well as your inheritance and the only way you can get to know about it is to experience it. It'll tell you something about your mum, as well.' He stuffs the last box into the car and slams the tailgate.

'I know quite a lot about Mum from you. I hardly know anything about Viola.'

'Me neither. Have we got beers in the house?' he asks.

'I don't know. I could do with a very large glass of wine. Or three.'

'Let's stop at a supermarket on the way home.'

*

She doesn't mention Cal to her dad at all. On Sunday, he packs up his own gear but he's used to travelling light. They go for a friendly father and daughter walk in the Botanics, since the weather has turned fine again, but they hardly mention the house or the island. She badly wants to tell him about Cal, to ask his advice, but she doesn't want to worry him, doesn't want to spoil his trip.

On Monday morning, a woman of about his own age, with short grey hair and a sweet face, arrives to pick him up in a Transit. Daisy wonders if this is the latest fling. Her father introduces the driver as Fran, Frances. She leans out of the window and shakes hands with Daisy. 'I'll take good care of him,' she says. Very English. Daisy has a vague memory of seeing and hearing her sing somewhere: Òran Mór or some other Glasgow venue. Rob stows his musical instruments away with great care – more care than he ever takes with her stock, she notices – gives her a hug and a kiss and clambers in beside Fran.

'Have you got your phone?' she asks.

He's not good with phones, forgets how to work them, tends to lose them. He pats his pockets. 'Somewhere.'

'Phone me. Keep in touch.'

'I will, yes. I'll probably stay with Fran between gigs.'

'Where would that be?'

'I'll text you the address. Near Glastonbury.'

'Oh, very suitable.'

He grins. 'And you do the same, Daisy. Let me know how it goes.'

'I will.'

She waves him off cheerfully enough, but when he's gone, she feels faintly bereft.

*

She plans to go back to Garve the following day. She has some sorting out to do in the storage unit first, but at some point during the day, she passes Mr McDowall's office and climbs the stairs on the off-chance that he's in. He is between clients and sits her down with a cup of Earl Grey tea.

'So you've seen the house?' he says. 'What do you think? Do you want me to organise the sale?'

'Not yet. I'm going to spend the summer there.'

'Are you really?' He peers at her over the top of his glasses. He's a precise man, intelligent and cautious.

'Yes. Really. I want to spend a bit of time there and summer seems as good a time as any. I can carry on with my online business from Garve. In fact, I can sell some of the contents myself.'

'Of course. I always forget what you do for a living, Miss Graham.'

Some living, she thinks.

'How did you get into it?' he asks. 'I mean, it doesn't run in your family, does it?'

'Oh, I don't know so much. My mother's family seem to have known a bit about antiques and collecting, don't you think?'

'That's very true. I hadn't thought about that.' He steeples his fingers, gazing at her with frank interest. 'I believe Viola's father was fond of art and other *objets de vertu*. But you didn't know that.'

'Then it's in the genes. Besides – I used to go to the saleroom with my other granny, my dad's mum, down in Ayr, when I was a wee girl.'

'Was she a collector?'

Daisy smiles, thinking of her gran. 'Not really. I think she started going to the auctions after my grandfather died. She enjoyed the company. She was there every week, come rain or shine. She'd buy trays and boxes full of God knows what and put most of the things back into the sale the following week.'

'So you went down to Ayr in the summer?'

'I did. Dad was often working so I spent summers with my gran. I miss her a lot.'

She thinks about their saleroom days, the anticipation of wondering what they might find, and then the crowds on auction day with gran worming her way into a good position, pushing Daisy ahead of her. 'On you go, hen. Use your elbows,' she would whisper. They always went to the same café at lunchtime. Then gran would pack her purchases into a tartan shopping trolley and trundle them home.

'And that was where it all began for you?'

Daisy nods. 'You learn a lot just by being there. Watching the real dealers. Working out why they're bidding on something but not on something else. And because I was a chatty wee thing and they all knew my gran, they were nice to me. I enjoyed it. Started doing a bit of bidding on my own behalf when I was old enough.'

'But you went to university between times?'

'I did a history degree. Probably should have been fine art, but I didn't fancy it. I still stayed with gran during the holidays and they gave me a temporary job in the saleroom. Then I moved onto one of the Glasgow houses. I don't think I was ever going to make a career of it, though. The auction houses, I mean. But I quite liked the buying and selling.'

'This explains a lot,' he says. 'I did find myself feeling a little curious about you. One watches, er, *Bargain Hunt*, you know – my wife is very fond of that programme – and one wonders how they get into something like that.'

She suddenly remembers the real purpose of this visit. Mr McDowall is an engaging man and very good at getting information out of people, but he owes her some information in return.

'The valuation,' she says suddenly. 'Of the house contents. For probate.'

'Yes?' He sits up very straight. 'My dear, it had to be as fair and as accurate as possible, but we didn't want to over-value things either. You can surely understand that. As it is, most of your grandmother's money has gone to the Inland Revenue.'

'No, no, I'm not complaining. And I'm not unhappy with the valuation. I've been there, remember? I know what a mixed hoard it is. I'm just curious. I was just wondering who...'

'Ah, who assessed it? Well, it had to be somebody with the right credentials of course. There's a shop called Island Antiques, on Byres Road.'

She nods. 'I know it.'

'It's run by William Galbraith, the artist, and his wife Fiona, of course. Between you and me, I think Fiona does most of the work.'

'It's a bit out of my league.'

'My wife prefers a more contemporary look. But I've met them socially. Well, Fiona Galbraith and my wife are on a couple of committees together. William keeps himself very much to himself these days.'

'So who...?' But she already knows. She just needs confirmation.

'Their son is in your line of business, I believe. Fine art and antiques.'

'Yeah. Well, I think he's out of my league as well.'

'I never knew there was such a hierarchy.' He looks faintly disappointed.

'In everything, isn't there?'

'I suppose so. Anyway, Calum Galbraith spends a lot of time on Garve. William has a cottage there that he hardly ever uses, but Calum does. I asked him if he would do a general valuation of the contents, one that would satisfy the Revenue, and he did it for a very reasonable fee.'

'Reasonable?'

'A lot more reasonable than if I'd had to bring somebody over from the mainland.'

'I expect it was. I met him.'

I slept on his sofa bed, she thinks.

'Ah, that's good. I've always found him to be a very engaging young man. I used to see him when he was just a lad. When Fiona used to take him and his sister to the island for the summer and I would pay the occasional visit to Viola.'

'Engaging. Yes.'

Mr McDowall chuckles. 'He confessed to me that he had always wanted to get a look at the contents of Auchenblae, but Viola didn't exactly welcome visitors, especially young antique dealers. He knows his stuff. It's just occurred to me that you could do worse than get him to take a much closer look at whatever is in your house. I'm sure he'd be able to advise you about getting the best price for the more desirable pieces, such as they are.'

'I'm sure he would. I'll think about it, Mr McDowall. I'll certainly think about it.'

EIGHTEEN

Later that day, she finds herself on Byres Road, on the way back to the flat, hauling two hessian bags of shopping with her. On impulse, she heads towards the corner where Island Antiques sits. It's in a prime position with big shop windows on two sides, the door positioned diagonally on the corner with a shallow marble step. It's a shop that she has always found daunting, and she can remember venturing into it only once before. Softly lit, the space is arranged into three rooms, with vastly expensive pieces of furniture and equally expensive artworks on the walls. Through the window, she notices a miniature bureau, with a detailed floral inlay, so desirable that it practically makes her salivate, an elegant chaise longue with a paisley shawl draped over the back, a proper straw Orkney chair with a drawer underneath the seat, and a very dark oak chest with naïve carving and the patina of five hundred years.

On her first and only previous visit, the briefest glance had told her that she wouldn't be able to afford anything in the shop and now – even with her unexpected inheritance – another glance tells her that nothing has changed. It is all very beautiful, but it is way out of her league. She remembers when she was working in the big auction house, watching the price of a Gillows desk climb higher and higher until it reached £50,000. She remembers that it sold to 'Island'. Everyone else seemed to know who that was, but she was too shy to ask at the time. She supposes that it finished up in this shop where presumably it was marked up even higher and sold on. Glasgow isn't an obviously wealthy city, but there are certainly a great many rich people here, often living cheek by jowl with the extremely deprived. There are streets, especially here in the West End, where million-pound Georgian and Victorian houses at one end, built by those who made their money during the industrial revolution, give place to down-at-heel council estates at the other. It is not as pronounced as in London, but it is there, a fact of city life.

She takes a deep breath and goes in. The bell tinkles musically. The shop is very quiet, an oasis in this busy part of the city, although she can hear Mozart playing in the background. Everything seems perfect. There are glass cases with fine china and porcelain. On one wall, several stunning silk rugs are faultlessly displayed. The floor is polished wood. A cabinet, beside the mahogany counter, has a selection of jewellery and pretty silver items: a card case, a chatelaine, an art nouveau mirror. There are a couple of easels with subtle lighting above, displaying large canvases that she recognises as being by Cal's father: bleak urban exteriors with not a single living soul to be seen. The shop smells sweet, of pot-pourri, lavender and roses.

A tall woman of about her own age sits at a desk, sleek head bent over a tablet. Everything about her matches the shop itself. She's impossibly slender and glossy, from the tips of her designer shoes to the very top of her immaculate blonde head. It's as though some fairy godmother has touched her with a magic wand and transformed everything about her, instantaneously. Her nails are long and palest pink. Her make-up is faultless. How does she do it, wonders Daisy, smiling at her, fighting the urge to ingratiate herself in some way. She just knows that beneath the devastatingly simple black dress – looks like linen, but with not a crease and how does she do that, too? – her underwear will be equally perfect. Minuscule but perfect. She probably wears a thong.

The woman looks up, briefly, from her tablet. Daisy would lay bets she is reading a novel, but she makes it look as though she is being interrupted in the middle of some vital piece of work.

'Can I help you?' she asks, only just disguising her boredom.

'May I have a look around?'

'Oh. Feel free.' She spreads her hands, giving a very Gallic shrug, although she sounds posh Scottish. Kelvinside. She looks astonished at the very idea of somebody wanting to browse. 'Are you looking for anything in particular?'

'Not really. I'd just like to ... *look*.' *For God's sake*, she thinks. *It's a shop, isn't it?*

The woman goes back to her reading. Daisy could swear that there is a barely audible 'tut'. She feels trapped. What on earth is she doing in here? She thought she might be able to see Cal's mother and father, satisfy a certain curiosity about them. But the repellent assistant seems to be in charge and now she'll have to stay for a few minutes at least, save face, look around, uneasily aware of the blue eyes boring into the back of her head. Surely this can't be Annabel, can it? The woman Cal talked about down at Carraig. Time will tell. *I may have tried to squeeze into your pyjamas*, she thinks. The idea makes her giggle, but she turns away to hide it.

She is making a good show of examining a Scottish lowland grandfather clock, brightly painted with female figures representing the four seasons, when the door opens and somebody positively erupts into the shop.

'Jesus!' says a husky voice. 'I've spent half the fucking morning on the fucking phone to the fucking parcel company about that fucking pig, and I'm getting fucking nowhere!'

The paragon at the desk says nothing to this tirade of profanities, only opens her lovely eyes a little wider and looks from the incomer to Daisy and back again, with a meaningful gaze. The newcomer is an attractive if disorganised older woman, wearing a crumpled green linen dress, layered over a bright turquoise top. She has an embroidered bag slung over her shoulder and comfortable sandals on her feet but she looks hot and extremely bothered. Daisy, who is suppressing another overwhelming desire to laugh at the notion of the fucking pig, instinctively feels that here is somebody appealing. Also, she thinks, beautiful. When she was younger, this woman must have been absolutely stunning, but not in any glossy or artificial way. Not like Annabel. Even now, the newcomer has the uncompromising beauty of something slightly worn but no less precious. She has white hair coiled up on her head, but it is tumbling down, high cheekbones, porcelain pink and white cheeks with small lines. *Craquelure*, thinks Daisy: the network of fine cracks on an old painting. Over the years, her father's friends have always included warm, slightly dishevelled women like this: musicians, artists, poets, occasionally prone to outbursts of swearing. The older woman's hand flies to her mouth at the sight of Daisy.

'Oh,' she says. 'I do apologise for my appalling language, but I'm at the end of my tether.'

Daisy smiles at her. 'Don't mind me. I've heard a lot worse. And I know all about some parcel companies, believe me. What did they do to the pig?'

'They broke its fucking ear and glued it back on – with super-glue, no less – and tried to pretend that it had been that way to begin with. I mean, do I look like I have the word mug tattooed across my forehead? Or pig for that matter? Don't answer that, Annabel,' she adds, glancing at the blonde, confirming Daisy's suspicions. *Cal, how could you?* she thinks. All too easily, of course. What man wouldn't? She and her father call glossy young women like this 'wedding cakes'. But most men seem to appreciate them.

'Was it a particularly good pig?' Daisy asks.

She notices a scornful expression crossing Annabel's face, but the newcomer understands and answers the question immediately. 'Oh Lord, yes. A large Wemyss pig. Huge. Shamrocks. Fabulous.'

'What a shame.'

'I know. I always take these things quite personally. I shouldn't but I do. My poor pig.'

'They'll pay up, Fi,' says Annabel. She sounds bored with the whole thing. 'They always do, you know. Get William to call them.'

Daisy realises that the dishevelled woman must be Cal's mother. Her son doesn't look very much like her, except for something about the clear hazel eyes, the floppy hair caught back from her face with an ornate leather clip. Cal is taller and more wiry.

She says, 'Excuse me, but are you Fiona Galbraith?'

'Yes, I am.' She looks momentarily confused. 'Should I know you?' She seems genuinely worried that she might have met Daisy somewhere and forgotten her.

'No. No, we've never met, I don't think. But I met your son, briefly, last week, on Garve. He was... he was asked to value the contents of my house. Well, my grandmother's house.'

'Ah, yes!' She breaks into a broad grin, shakes Daisy by the hand. 'He mentioned it. You must be Viola Neilson's long-lost granddaughter.'

'That's me. Daisy Graham.'

'Good to meet you. We knew nothing about you. Viola was a clam. You could never prise anything out of her that she didn't want you to know. Even my husband didn't know that there was a granddaughter, although he knew about the daughter, Jessica. Everyone did. The elopement was a nine days' wonder. With a travelling musician, no less!' She stops, suddenly. 'Oh my goodness, but that was your mother.'

'And my father. They did marry, you know. But Mum died when she was very young. Dad took good care of me.'

'I'm so sorry about your mother. And now you've got the house. Do you know what you're going to do with it?'

'I don't have the foggiest notion. But I'm going to spend the summer there.'

'How lovely!' She looks momentarily elated, then sad. Daisy thinks that she has one of the most transparent faces she has ever seen. Fiona is clearly a woman who can't disguise her emotions. Which must make life difficult for her at times. Daisy sees the scornful expression flit across Amanda's pretty features again, quickly hidden.

'Sea and sand,' says the younger woman. 'That sounds so exciting.'

'Oh, but it's so much more than that!' Fiona shakes her head. 'You must ask Cal to show you the sights while you're there, Daisy. And our cottage. I used to love going there. My husband tired of it but I never did.'

'Can't you still go there? Even on your own?' Daisy blurts it out before she can stop herself. She can't imagine not being able to do something just because your husband objects, but that seems to be what this woman is saying.

'I could, but I never seem to have the time these days. Too many broken pigs!'

'Anyway,' says Daisy, suddenly embarrassed. She doesn't want to get into a conversation about the cottage, or the contents of her house. 'Anyway, I should go. I have packing to do. I'm off to Garve tomorrow, in fact.'

'Oh, I do envy you. Give my love to Cal if you see him. And Hector. Did you meet the dog? We all love Hector.'

Annabel shrugs minutely. She doesn't love Hector at all, thinks Daisy.

'Yes. I met Hector.'

'And you will see Cal again while you're there, I expect. It's not such a huge place and Carraig isn't all that far from Auchenblae.'

'I thought he was meant to be on a buying trip in Argyll,' says Annabel.

'He is. He has been. And he's good. You know that. He works hard. He can always ferret out a bargain.'

Indeed he can, thinks Daisy, but says nothing, fixing her smile to her face.

'Oh yes. I suppose he is.' Annabel yawns widely, showing sharp white teeth, like a cat.

'But you're right. He'll always take a detour to Garve when he can. Cal and Hector both! And why not?'

'Why not indeed? That's what I'm about to do.'

She heads for the door. She has the distinct impression that Annabel isn't as kindly disposed towards Cal as Cal seems to think. Perhaps the break-up wasn't amicable at all. Men can be very obtuse about such things. Although it could be that she has a chronic grudge against anyone who doesn't quite live up to her own high expectations. Fiona seems blissfully unaware of it or so used to it that she can safely ignore it. Daisy wouldn't trust Annabel as far as she could throw her, as her granny used to say. 'Fur coat and nae knickers,' she would have said. Daisy smiles at the memory. Except that, of course, there will be expensive knickers as well. She's a pretty woman, no doubt about it.

There's a weird dynamic going on in the shop. Daisy finds herself wondering, with a certain amount of relish, what happens when Cal and his father are added to the mix. Then it occurs to her that it may be something as simple as jealousy. Perhaps Annabel would like to get back together with Cal and doesn't like the fact that he seems to spend so much time away from Glasgow, in a tiny cottage with a dog. She has to admit they'd make a very handsome couple. Besides which, she gets the feeling they'd deserve each other.

'I hope you sort out your pig,' she says to Fiona, at the door. 'It's been nice meeting you.'

As she heads off down Byres Road, she realises that she meant it. It has been nice meeting Fiona Galbraith. She'd like to know her better. Which, given her son's ability to be economical with the truth, doesn't seem very likely now.

NINETEEN

1588

Lilias, along with her young sister Ishbel, seemed to have taken it upon herself to be chief translator and educator of Mateo and his cousin. Mateo felt happier about this than seemed wise. She told them a little about the landscape of the island, for they had seen almost nothing of it beyond the house and its immediate surroundings, and had no idea of the extent or nature of the island to which they had come. McNeill had intimated that they were free to go where they pleased on *Eilean Garbh*, as long as they did not attempt to leave it, but they had had no inclination to venture very far away from the immediate vicinity of the house. For one thing, they didn't trust the islanders to be friendly. They confessed themselves quite ignorant about the place that had offered them shelter. Ishbel seemed surprised, with an eight-year-old's assumption that her home was the very centre of the world, and must therefore be famous, even to strangers such as Mateo and Francisco. Lilias smiled indulgently at her sister.

'I don't suppose you know very much about the place where they come from either,' she said. 'Although it's an island as well, isn't it?'

'Like this one?' asked Ishbel.

'Not so much like this one. Or at least I don't think so, for I am almost as ignorant,' Lilias replied.

'The sun shines nearly all the time,' said Mateo. 'And all kinds of things grow there that I think do not grow here. Flowers and fruits of all kinds.'

He said it so sadly that Ishbel left off petting the dogs, her chief occupation on this wet afternoon, and came over to hug him. 'Oh, but we have flowers here!'

'I have seen very few.'

'You have seen only those few that survive into the winter months,' said Lilias. 'In springtime it will be quite different.'

'You must wait till springtime and then, if you are still here, you will see flowers in plenty,' added Ishbel.

'I think we may still be here.'

'Then I'm glad of it.' The child, with a strong sense of what was fair, went over and hugged Francisco as well.

'Leave them alone,' said Lilias.

'I don't mind!' Francisco looked up. 'She reminds me of my little sister.'

'What's her name?' asked Ishbel.

'Sofia Isabella.'

'But that's your name, Ishbel,' said Lilias. 'Ishbel and Isabella are the same.'

Ishbel put her arm through his. 'I can be your sister while you're staying here. And when spring comes, we can show you some more of the island.'

'I don't even know how big this place is,' Francisco ventured.

'Neither do I,' said Ishbel, giggling, looking to her sister for enlightenment.

The island was some seventeen miles long and seven miles wide, although a Scots mile was, so Lilias told them, somewhat longer than its English equivalent. She didn't know at all how one would count it in English miles.

Eilean Garbh was home to a great many people, all of whom owed their allegiance to her father. There were tacksmen, those who held their land from Ruaridh McNeill, often relatives, however remote, and their dependent tenants and servants in turn. All of them were as closely interwoven as a piece of fine cloth, all relying upon each other, especially during times of hardship when their chief could and frequently did remit the rent in part or in whole. The islanders relied on the laird to oversee their troubles and their quarrels and to administer justice whenever necessary. As for the laird, he was beholden only to his clan chief, far away on the island of Barra, so *Eilean Garbh* was entirely his own responsibility. In any one year, there would be beasts to care for – horses, cattle and sheep in the main – as well as justice to administer and rents to collect, sometimes in cash and more often in kind. Most of all, perhaps, it was important for the chief to have a number of men whom he could 'call out' at need, during times of strife. But the life of the island and those living here relied on Ruaridh McNeill and his immediate family, to a greater or lesser extent, and Lilias seemed well aware of the responsibility that entailed.

'Not an easy task,' said Mateo, thinking of the quarrels, the troubles, the problems that so often arose for his own father with a smaller estate, a smaller area of land to oversee. He thought that his father brought some of his troubles on himself, being a harsh and autocratic leader. He knew little of McNeill, but the man seemed both firm and fair. Slow to anger, anyway.

'No indeed. And one that certainly demands the wisdom of Solomon in all his glory,' she said, smiling at him.

It had occurred to him that she could not resist flirting with him. They were always supervised, and since she had a certain freedom here, he had begun to realise that she prudently arranged it that she would be chaperoned. This meant that she was able to talk to him without raising the suspicions of those who might be observing them. It emphasised the innocence of their conversations. If Beathag could not be with her, or one of the younger women who helped about the house, then Ishbel was always beside her. Today, they were seated in the hall. Francisco was still given a certain amount of leeway because of his illness, and because

Beathag had taken a fancy to him and seemed happy to treat him like a younger member of her family. He was sitting huddled before the fire, with one of the few precious books the house possessed lying open on his lap, although he was dozing and waking, alternately. Mateo, anxious for work, had been given the task of repairing various pieces of household equipment that had suffered in the course of the summer: a salt box whose lid had fallen off, a new pestle that needed to be whittled for the mortar – the old one having been chewed to fragments by one of the hounds that now lay contentedly at his feet. Finn and Bran had accepted him as one of the household, sooner than their human companions perhaps. It struck him that dogs would make up their minds quickly, and then seldom change allegiance.

A few days ago, a party of young people and children had climbed one of the hills behind the house where a group of fir trees stood, and had gathered splinters of resinous wood for making fir candles to see them through the winter. A good portion of these had to be hung over the fire so that they were completely dry before they could be used, and Mateo was engaged in bundling them and sticking them into the heavy links of the chain that held the big cooking cauldron.

'There's always work to be done,' McNeill had told him, 'but after the turn of the year, there will be more physical tasks, if you are so minded. You had best make the most of this quiet time.'

Today, Lilias was spinning reddish-brown wool, harvested and dyed earlier that year from the flock of four-horned sheep with their strange dark and silvery-grey fleeces, kept quite close to the house and sometimes even along the shore where they were happy to eat what Ishbel, taking Mateo confidently by the hand to show him, had called 'sea ware'. They were brought in and housed in stone sheep cotes by night. These sheep were, Mateo had observed, rather timid creatures and McNeill himself had confirmed that they sometimes behaved as though they 'would rather be dead than otherwise', although the weather didn't seem to bother them much at all, so perhaps they were hardier than they looked. They gave a very fine fleece, albeit not much of it, but it could be spun into good yarn and ultimately woven into cloth that was both light and warm.

'May I see your spindle and the ... what is this thing?' he asked. 'A whorl.'

The spindle whorl was made of stone with a curious curved design.

'It is very old, I think. My brother Kenneth found it in the old tower by the seashore. We were always playing down there when we were younger. Nobody goes there much now.'

'Where does the colour of the wool come from?' he asked, idly rearranging his fir strips in an effort to prolong the work and the moment in her company, rather than from any great necessity. 'The bright yellow of your wrap and the red such as you have there.'

'This? This wool is combed to make it finer. I didn't do it. I have small patience with it, although my friend Morag does. And this is dyed red with the crotal, the yellow that you see on the rocks by the shore.'

'So the yellow crotal does not give yellow dye?'

'No. It is very mysterious. The yellow crotal gives this reddish brown and when we comb it, it will make for a very fine cloth.'

'And the yellow? The bright yellow such as you were wearing the day I first saw you?'

He caught her blushing, as red as the wool she was spinning.

'Ah, that was a gift, from my young brother's foster family, the Darrochs, the last time they came to this island. A very fine gift. That wrap was dyed with the purple heather, when it is in full flower. And you would not expect that either. I'm told it needs some skill on the part of those who do the dyeing. I am rather poor at it, and too many of my colours turn into mud as you will no doubt see in time.'

'I saw you the day McAllister put us ashore. It was beautiful.'

But he meant that she was beautiful. He knew it and she knew it. She gazed at him with her bright hazel eyes.

'To be honest,' she remarked determinedly changing the subject, 'I have not seen the whole of *Eilean Garbh* myself, although my father has walked or ridden every last mile of it, as has my elder brother, Kenneth. When we were young, before he went away to college, I would ride or walk with him, and we would go for many miles in a day. There is some safety on an island, and my father was quite happy for me to go. That is how I know about the great well of *Moire*, whose water helped to heal you, Francisco. And the *Sgurran Fithich*, the Raven's Peak at the top of *Meall Each*, not too far from here, from which you can see far out to the west, and *Port Na Currich* to the south. I have only been further than that a few times in my life so far. In spring, in May, they take the cattle north to the slopes of *Dun Tarbh* and round by *Loch an Tarbh Uisge*, where there is tolerably good grazing. There are houses up there and the folk who go seem to have a happy time of it.'

'I wanted to go with them this year,' piped up Ishbel. 'But Father said no.'

'Aye, well, Father and Mother said no when I asked them years ago. But I still regret that I can't go with them, for they tell stories and sing songs and folk play the pipes for the dancing, and they seem to enjoy themselves very much.'

'Yet they seem glad enough to come home,' added Ishbel thoughtfully. 'I wonder if they saw the water bull this year?'

'What is the water bull?' asked Mateo, intrigued.

'The loch takes its name from the water bull, and the hill is named after the bull as well.' Lilias shrugged. 'I haven't the faintest notion whether the creature is real or not, but they say it is a magical being that lives in the depths of the loch and comes out at night to mate with the cattle. It is a mild enough creature, though. Not like the *Each Uisge*. My grandfather had sight of one in his youth, or so they say.'

'And what is the … *Each Uisge*?' He said the word carefully.

She smiled. 'Ah now, that is a more fearsome proposition altogether and you would not want to encounter one of those. A water horse. They call him a kelpie in the lowlands. He will change shape. On land he can become a handsome young man. But if he catches you, he will drag you down to the bottom of the loch and you will never be seen again. So you see, you have to be very careful of handsome young men in these parts.'

'Of course. Handsome strangers. You never can tell.'

'There is a tale told here that a young woman very like myself once met with a fine young man, black-haired and very beautiful, on the shore of the dark loch, near *Meall Each* in the middle of this island. Only he was an interlowper, a water horse in human form. They sat down beside the loch, and he laid his head in her lap, and fell fast asleep. She began to stroke his hair, his dark curls were so bonnie, much like your own, Mateo, only she found that there was sand and seaweed among the curls. Which alarmed her very much indeed for she knew what that meant.'

'What did it mean?'

'It meant that she knew his true nature at last.'

'And that was?'

'Oh, not good. The *Each Uisge* can't help himself. He is what he is. He does what he must.'

'What did she do?'

'She leaped up and ran for home, they say. The story doesn't say where she lived. But the creature was immediately changing into his true shape of a fierce water horse, and went chasing after her. They are very fleet of foot, the water horses, and if once he had caught hold of her, even her foot or a single toe, into the loch she would have gone and she would have been lost for ever.'

'So how was she saved?'

'Her father had a captive water bull in his stable. A *cailleach*, a wise old woman who worked upon the farm, called to him to set the water bull free if he wished to save his daughter. So he did. The bull ran after the water horse, and the horse was distracted enough to give up the chase. Then horse and bull fought into and out of the water, something terrible to behold, but at last they sank beneath the waves and were never seen again.'

'Is this a true tale?' he asked, smiling.

'As true as I'm sitting here. My mother told me and she never lied. Although I'm bound to admit that she was a great storyteller!' She smiled too and glanced over at a captivated Ishbel. 'Let that be a warning to you, sister. Do not be persuaded by dark-haired strangers, however handsome, for they may turn out to be monsters in disguise.'

'And if he was not such a monster after all? If he was truly in love?' added Mateo. 'If he had elected to stay on land? To abandon his evil ways and become a man.'

'The stories don't tell of such things. But I suppose it might be possible. Everyone can change. Even wicked strangers.'

'And some strangers aren't wicked at all,' piped up Ishbel. 'Look at Paco. And Mateo.'

'Well.' Lilias raised her head from her work, and gazed into his eyes. 'Perhaps not like Mateo. Or Paco. Perhaps we can make an exception for them.'

TWENTY

On Tuesday, the sun shines more or less all the way as Daisy drives north and west to Garve and when she opens the door to Auchenblae, the big room is very warm. Already there's a certain familiarity about it, and that surprises and pleases her. Maybe it'll be easier to spend the night in the house now. It smells of beeswax, as though the sunlight has woken the scent of polish from the oldest pieces of furniture. It's been a long drive and she's glad to be here. She's not sure how Cal can go back and forth to Glasgow so regularly, let alone trek across Scotland – so much bigger than it looks on the BBC's weather map – in search of antiques every week. But then he has a much more comfortable car. It would be nice if there was a dog like Hector to greet her. *Maybe I'll get a dog of my own*, she thinks. *A dog that needs a home. After all, I've got plenty of space. But what if I go back to Glasgow?* She has to keep reminding herself that if she sells Auchenblae, she will be able to buy a bigger flat or even a town house, like the one Cal lives in, at the back of the Botanics. They look neat and well-kept and comfortable. Not only do they have gardens of their own, but they have the whole of the city's botanical gardens beyond. And in that case, a dog would be no problem at all.

She takes the portrait of Lilias out of the cupboard where she hid it away, wrapped in silk. As she props it up, she notices that the back is firmly corded for hanging. Somebody had loved it enough to want to see it all the time. She scans the wall and finds a large portrait photograph of a solemn man with a huge moustache, perhaps Viola's father or grandfather. She's curious about him, but he isn't immediately engaging. She takes him down and hangs Lilias in his place, well out of direct sunlight. Cal might not approve. He thinks the portrait is a treasure, too valuable to risk. But what's the point of a treasure if you can't enjoy it? Why should it be hidden away, or worse, kept out of sight in a bank vault. She faces the portrait while she eats a sandwich for lunch. Lilias gazes out at her. A sunny girl. Warm and golden, she inhabits the room and brings it to life.

She's finishing a mug of tea when her smartphone vibrates in her pocket. It's a message from Cal. 'Are you back? Do you want to borrow the dog?'

She grimaces at the phone and ignores it. Instead she hauls her suitcase up to her mother's old bedroom (*I'll have to stop calling it that*, she thinks) and starts to unpack her clothes. Then she opens the wardrobe door and finds to her consternation that it is already full. She had been too overwhelmed to investigate properly last time. The thought of a cell, without possessions or ties to the world, is beginning to seem very attractive. She's weighed down with things. She never imagined it would be possible to feel this way, but she can understand how people walk out on their world in the desperate desire to be somewhere else, to become someone else. Perhaps that's what her mother felt. Perhaps the snug van and the good-looking man, who had played the fiddle like the devil, had been all she wanted in her life at that moment. The house had been too much for her to bear, with an ageing and possessive mother. Rob must have seemed like an unlikely knight in shining armour, coming to her rescue, but she had surely known that Viola would never approve of him. It had come down to a straight choice and against all the odds, Rob had won.

She drags out an armful of things and dumps them on the bed. They're on a mixture of wood and wire hangers, tangled together, a few of them empty. Had these once contained the handful of clothes Jessica had packed in a holdall and taken with her when she fled house and island together? The old carpet bag, musty-smelling and threadbare, had lain under one of the seats in the van for years, and after that was stored in a cupboard at the top of the wardrobe in her father's bedroom. He never used it, but could never bring himself to get rid of it either.

The clothes smell faintly of some sweet but slightly astringent scent. She recognises ylang-ylang, which she has always liked. She puts the fabrics to her face and sniffs, making herself sneeze. They're dusty, of course. But the scent catches her throat, so evocative is it of her mother. The van used to smell of it all the time, her mother's scent and the joss sticks she burned as well. She sets the clothes down and crosses over to the dressing table that must have seemed old-fashioned even when Jessica was young, kidney-shaped with a triple mirror, chintz skirts around the bottom and a matching stool. There it is, a half-bottle of White Musk perfume oil, in the familiar early 1980s Body Shop bottle: simple, no frills. She rubs a little into her wrist. Initially it seems to have gone off, but within minutes, it is surrounding her with the evocative and powerful fragrance of Jessica May. Rob and Daisy used to buy the scent for her at Christmas time, going into the shop together, trying things out, laughing. The silk scarf they had tied to the wishing tree had been faintly scented with it as well. Back when Jess was young, though, the summer when she met Rob, it must have been new and fashionable. Something girls talked about. Something they could afford, that was nevertheless exotic.

Daisy sits down among the heap of clothes, determined not to cry. There are the usual worn jeans, shirts and T-shirts. There's a traditional navy blue winter coat in heavy wool, and a green waterproof. But then she uncovers several pretty dresses: one is high-waisted with pink flowers on a turquoise background and there's a madly romantic maxi dress with puff sleeves. It's closely fitted on the bodice, with a long flared skirt, in a blue and white print like a china teacup. The dresses remind her of the Indian cotton gowns from the late 1700s she has seen in museums, which was surely the intention of the designer. Once, there had been a consignment of six antique gowns and associated trims in the sale-room and if Daisy had been able to afford them, she would have bid on them, but her wages didn't stretch to such luxuries, and her father wasn't in funds at the time. They might well have fitted her too, back then, although she has put on a bit of weight since. Not so much that she won't get into these dresses, though. Jessica had been quite voluptuous until illness made her lose weight. These look as though they will fit.

She finds the labels, and sees that they are Laura Ashley dresses. Further along, a gorgeous sky-blue smock dress with a low neck has the Finnish designer label Marimekko. So for all they were living on a fairly remote island, Viola was prepared to spoil her daughter with fashionable dresses. Did they go to Glasgow or Edinburgh to buy them? She holds the maxi dress against her and looks down at the lovely length of it. It is in perfect condition and worth quite a lot of money. True vintage but how can she ever bear to sell it? No. She'll wear it, and the others, if only for her own satisfaction. Surely there will be island events, the odd ceilidh in one or other of the village halls, functions in the hotels at Scoull or Keill. If she stays here for the summer, perhaps some kind of social life will emerge. Perhaps she can get to know Alys, the jeweller, and her husband. Perhaps, says an insistent voice at the back of her head, perhaps you can get to know Cal better. Or perhaps not. The thought of his long body, almost vibrating with energy, comes into her head. What would be the harm? Can she trust him?

As if on cue, her phone trembles again. Another message. 'Are you there yet? How are things?'

He's nothing if not persistent, although now she's fairly certain this has more to do with the attractions of Auchenblae and its contents than with herself.

She sighs and texts back, 'Yes, just got here.'

'Do you want to borrow Hector?'

'I think I'll be OK, don't you?' she writes.

'Your choice.' He signs off abruptly. She senses that he's miffed. *Tough*, she thinks, and puts the phone away.

*

Later that afternoon, she drives through the village, waving to Mr Cameron, who is pruning roses at the front of the hotel, and turns left towards the sea at the Ardachy Gallery signpost. The cottage is bigger than Cal's tiny cottage at Carraig, a sturdy white building with dormer windows standing above the broad expanse of Scoull Bay that stretches from the village itself, past Port Manus below the hotel, past Ardachy and beyond. It might be possible to walk across when the tide is very low. Maybe, too, you could keep going round the small headland to the north of Scoull Bay, back to Auchenblae. She'll try it some time.

Beyond the house, a lane curves down towards the sea and she suspects there will be another tiny harbour there, like the ones at Auchenblae and Carraig. Near the house, there is a neat vegetable garden with a row of early potatoes in sandy soil, and a fenced-off piece of grass, with chickens clucking quietly to themselves. At the gate she can see that they are different colours, and presumably different breeds, though she knows very little about such things. They look exotic and old-fashioned, like hens in a children's story-book. There's another well-made wooden sign beside the gate, saying 'Gallery Open. Please come in and browse.'

The gallery is in a low, separate building, clad in larch, with a slate roof. It is set to one side of the house and at right angles to it, with an open door on this side, and wide windows on the seaward side. The walls are white, the roof grey slate. In the sheltered triangle between the house and gallery, somebody has already planted up a wealth of tubs and pots that will be a blaze of colour in a few weeks. There are bicycles propped against the wall, one of them with a child's seat on the back, and a ginger cat sitting sunning itself on a Lloyd Loom chair. It gazes at her disdainfully as she comes through the gate, but doesn't move.

'Come in, come in,' says a friendly voice as she hesitates at the door. The enticing smell of coffee filters out. 'Come in and have a look around.' A woman is working at a table, with a magnifier and a bright lamp, although the room is already full of light. In one corner, there's a play house, a box of toys, a row of dolls and teddies seated on plastic chairs, with a little girl, perhaps four years old, holding court. She has soft dark curls tied back with a red ribbon, and she's dressed in bright blue dungarees. She glances up briefly when Daisy comes in, but doesn't leave her self-imposed task of instructing her toys.

'Are you Alys?'

The woman smiles, gets up, extends a hand. 'I am.'

'Mrs Cameron at the hotel said I should come and speak to you.'

'Ah – you must be Daisy. From Auchenblae. Flowerfield.'

'That's right. What a lovely set-up you've got here!' She looks around, taking in the display cabinets, the shelves, the work that seems to be a mixture of old and new, found things, fragments of sea glass and pottery, crystal and amber beads, silverwork and enamelling. There's a leaping hare on a chain, a cluster of island flowers in silver and beadwork, earrings with delicate flying birds. 'And what lovely work!'

'Thank you. It's taken us a while to get to this stage, but it's doing OK now.'

'But you're not from here originally?'

'No. I'm from Edinburgh. But my husband is an islander born and bred, which helps. I moved here – let me see – five years ago now. It was a big step to take, for me and my son both. But the right one, as it turns out.'

As if on cue, the gate swings open and somebody calls, 'Hi, Mum!'

Daisy sees a gangly teenager coming through the gate. He's in school uniform: a blazer and grey trousers, tie askew, a ridiculously heavy bag slung on his shoulder. He comes over to the gallery, pokes his head through the door, waves at the little girl, who waves back.

'Is Donal about?'

'No. He's taken a fishing party out.'

'Wish he'd waited for me.'

'Well, I don't think they could do that, could they?'

'Where's Malky?'

'On the boat. Go and get yourself something to eat and do your homework. They'll be back soon. He might take you out for a bit before tea.'

'Cool.' He turns to go.

'There are scones in the tin. Don't drink all the milk.'

He wanders off. 'I'll go and get changed.'

'Don't forget the homework.'

'I won't.'

He heads towards the cottage. 'I'll go too,' says the little girl, suddenly abandoning her dolls.

'No you won't, Grace,' says Alys firmly. 'Ben's doing his homework. And he doesn't want you interrupting him. I'll get you some juice in a minute.'

The child pouts but goes back to her toys obediently enough.

'My husband takes fishing parties out from the hotel,' Alys offers by way of explanation. 'Malky's the dog. I can't keep Ben away from the sea.'

'I suppose living on an island...'

'Oh I know. But you'd never believe he was born in Edinburgh, would you? And spent the first eight years of his life there. He's taken to island life like the proverbial duck to water.'

'But your husband's from the island?'

Alys nods, gets up and goes over to a side table where there's a push-button coffee machine, biscuits, a selection of pretty teacups and mugs. She pours orange juice into a plastic cup and hands it to the little girl, makes two mugs of coffee and hands one to Daisy.

'I moved here to be with Donal. I was divorced. My ex is

in Canada. It's all worked out fine. Donal and Ben are thick as thieves. They have this mutual admiration society. And they both love the sea.'

'So island life is OK, is it?'

'It depends what you want. What you expect, I suppose. It doesn't suit everyone. It didn't suit Donal's first wife. There isn't a lot of nightlife here. The young can get very bored. It worries me a bit. But we're OK so far.' She gestures to Daisy to sit down in another Lloyd Loom chair. 'Make yourself comfortable. Don't suppose I'll have any more visitors today.'

'What about your own work. I don't want to interrupt.'

'I don't do that much once Ben's home from school. The secondary school kids travel to the mainland every day. There's a primary school on the island at Keill. Grace goes to nursery but she'll be off to proper school this year, which will give us a bit more time to ourselves. I often come back through to work once Grace is asleep, though. Are you thinking of staying on the island for a while?'

'I don't know. Maybe. Everyone seems to think I'd be mad not to sell Auchenblae, and maintaining it might be a problem if I want to keep it.'

'What do you do for a living?'

'I deal in antiques and collectables. Mostly online.'

Alys raises an eyebrow. 'You could do that here, couldn't you?'

'I probably could. I've got so much stuff in the house, I wouldn't need to buy anything for years.'

'Donal says Cal Galbraith was asking about Auchenblae, in the hotel. Wondering what would happen to the contents.'

'Was he?' Daisy finds herself blushing. 'Actually, he's been in touch.'

'Has he been pestering you?'

'He seems to want to be helpful. He hasn't exactly been harassing me. What's he like? Really?'

'I don't know him well. My husband knew him when they were

kids. Cal and his sister and his mum. He's very friendly. His dog and Malky get on well if we meet them down on the beach. They say his mother adores the island, but she hardly ever comes here now. I think there's a fair bit of money in the family and in their business.'

'There is. I've been in the shop in Glasgow. Met his mum. She seems very nice.'

'His father doesn't come highly recommended round here, but I've never met him, so I can't really speak ill of him. Cal? Who knows? He's incredibly charming. Donal can't see it, but I can. He used to bring some gorgeous blonde over here for a while, all legs and teeth and glossy locks, like a hair advert.'

Daisy thinks this must have been Annabel, but she can't be sure. There are plenty of leggy, glossy blondes in the world and she can imagine that they might well appeal to Cal, or he to them. He's attractive, that's for sure.

'But anyway, that seemed to stop quite suddenly. I used to see them driving about together and it was clear they fancied themselves no end, as well as each other. Well, I suppose she did, more than Cal. He can't help being quite fanciable, can he? And then winter came and it was just him and the dog, who didn't seem to mind the wind and the rain. But perhaps I'm being unfair. He's the complete opposite of my husband and maybe that's influenced the way I feel about him.'

She pauses to drink her coffee and then giggles suddenly. 'Oh God, you must think my husband is a miserable git, but he isn't. He's just quieter and a lot more thoughtful. Cal's so instantly charming and full of energy that you catch yourself wondering what's underneath. If there is anything underneath. But don't let me put you off! He's good-looking, rich, so we're led to believe. Although he doesn't often go in for conspicuous consumption, I'll say that for him. What more do you want?'

'A lot more.' Daisy laughs. 'And I wasn't...'

'Looking for a character reference. I know. I can't help myself.

This place can be such a wee hothouse at times. It makes you absolutely fascinated about what makes people tick. Anyway, he knows his stuff where antiques are concerned. Or so I believe. I think he'd love to get his hands on Donal's embroidered casket.'

'The one in the hotel?'

'Yes. But it's going nowhere. We pay a fortune for insurance for it every year because the hotel shouldn't really have to foot the bill, and we have to have a special cabinet for it with an alarm system. But Donal says it has to stay on the island. And who am I to argue with him?'

'I can understand his thinking.' The portrait of Lilias comes into her mind, vivid and potentially valuable. 'Cal did a valuation of the contents of my house. For the solicitor.'

'That would be right up his street. Did he pocket something on the way round?' Alys puts her hand to her mouth. 'I shouldn't have said that, should I? I'll be had up for libel. Or is it slander when you say it?'

'I don't think he did, but how would I know?' She thinks about the portrait of Lilias, so carefully hidden at the bottom of the pile. But then Cal had been the one to retrieve her, to unwrap her and show her off.

Alys slides her chair back. 'You know, the very first time Donal took me out on his boat, he showed me your house. We used to come here on holiday when we were kids but I'd never seen Auchenblae. It's so hidden, so private, and we had only a couple of weeks at a time.'

'I'd only ever been here once before. When I was very young. For a flying visit.'

'I came back here all by myself after the divorce and met Donal. I remembered him from when we were both kids and it turns out he remembered me. That was six years ago, when Viola was still alive. I've never actually seen the house from the landward side. Only from the sea.' She laughs. 'Do you know, the first time Donal took me out on his boat he told me the place was empty. It was only later that he confessed he'd been fibbing about it. He did odd jobs for Viola and she was determined not to be bothered by visitors. He just got into the habit of telling everyone it was empty.'

'Would visitors have bothered her?'

'They might. We get a lot of tourists in the summer months. I shouldn't complain, because they're my bread and butter down here. But they can be a bit entitled. We've even had people picnicking in Donal's boat and leaving their rubbish behind.'

'I haven't seen anyone at Auchenblae so far. Other than Cal.'

'You wait. There'll be people knocking on your door and asking for conducted tours. It looks quite magical. Like some place out of a story. Sunk in time.'

'That's what it's like.'

'Isn't it a bit spooky? Staying there on your own?'

'Cal offered to lend me his dog!'

'Hector? He'd lick intruders to death.'

'I got that impression.'

'Although the chance of actual burglars on this island is fairly negligible.'

'That's what people keep telling me. And my grandmother lived there all by herself for years, didn't she?'

As she says it, it strikes her that it's one reason why she has hesitated to come here, to take possession of the house fully. Is she afraid of turning into her grandmother? Is that the problem? Seeing herself growing old and reclusive? But of course it won't happen. Her father for one would never allow it to happen. But what if he was no longer here?

'It's a bit of a challenge, isn't it?' says Alys. 'I mean, I can perfectly understand why you don't want to let it go without finding out exactly what you have there.'

'That's it.'

'Especially in your line of business. But at the same time, you need help and you can't be certain that the help on offer at the moment is entirely selfless.'

'Exactly.'

Alys pauses, gazing out of the window at the back of the gallery.

'Well, if you've nothing better to do, and nowhere better to be, I think staying for the summer is a very good idea. It's just gorgeous here in the summer. From now onwards, although every season has its pleasures. The white sand gets into your shoes, you know. You go away and there it is, and you want to be back here.'

'You fell in love with the place, didn't you?'

'I fell in love with the place and the man both. And here he is.'

A sturdy man of about forty is coming in the gate, carrying a pair of long wooden oars, and a plastic carrier bag. There's a black and white collie frisking around his feet. He's attractive in a shabby, understated way, dark hair sprinkled with grey, a weather-beaten fisherman's face and a weather-beaten fisherman's blue jersey over faded jeans. Daisy notices enviously how Alys's face lights up when she sees him and how the feeling is reciprocated, Donal's rather solemn face breaking into a broad grin. The child, Grace, rushes up to him and he picks her up and birls her round, her red sandals swinging. 'Gracie, my Gracie!' he says. The dog barks happily and jumps up at them both, desperate to be included.

'I told Ben you might take him out for a bit once he's finished his homework.'

Donal sighs momentarily, but nods. 'Yeah. Why not? It's a fine night.'

'This is Daisy, from Auchenblae.'

'Is it indeed?' He shakes her hand, gravely. 'Good to meet you. How are you getting on at the big house?'

'It's a big undertaking.'

'She's thinking of staying here for the summer. While she sorts it all out.'

'While I *attempt* to sort it out.'

'My dad used to help Viola with odd jobs and he would take me along. I used to get juice and biscuits from her in that big kitchen.

Then I took over and did a few bits and pieces of work for her myself. Her bark was always a lot worse than her bite. Bit like Malky here.'

'I never knew her.'

'That's sad.'

'She didn't even know I existed till just before her death.'

'Even sadder. We need family, don't we?'

'They tell me Auchenblae was probably once your family home.'

He grins again, blushes, the crimson spreading across his face. 'Oh now,' he says. 'Maybe, but that was so long ago that who would know? Or care? There was a Manus McNeill who was Laird of Garve in the late 1600s and early 1700s. He had two marriages, both to lowlanders, one in mysterious circumstances.'

He looks mischievous, exchanging a glance with his wife.

'Not that mysterious,' she says. 'You just like keeping secrets.'

'Of course we do. We're Celts. We are people who could keep a secret for a thousand years. Anyway, there would have been family before that. My McNeill forebears. Then slowly but surely everything went to hell for them.'

'Until the Neilsons came.'

'Aye – until the Neilsons came. And who knows, maybe they were a different branch of the same family. But by then it was all lost, all changed. And we were down here at Ardachy. With the wee box and all. The curiosity cabinet. And the things that were in it.'

'I think you've lost very little by that.' She looks around, realising how much she envies them both: their marriage, their children, this whitewashed house, the larch gallery, the days spent doing something worthwhile in each other's company. She's not foolish enough to think that it won't have its challenges, but it seems so much more desirable, right now, than whatever she has. So much more desirable than the challenge of coping with Auchenblae and everything in it, and not knowing who to trust. A curse as well as a blessing.

'Anyway,' he says, shouldering the oars again, 'I'll give Ben a shout and we'll be gone for an hour, no more. I'll leave Malky here, though. Think he's had enough sea for one day. If you need any help, Daisy, just let me know. I'm pretty good at lifting heavy things, as my wife will tell you.'

Alys grins. 'You're good at a lot more than that. I'll give Grace her tea and you can give her her bath when you come in.'

Again, Daisy finds herself envying the warm domesticity of this, even though she's not at all sure about living on the island. Maybe it's something to do with her age. Maybe it's the increasingly loud ticking of the biological clock, especially when she lies awake at four o'clock in the morning, as she so often does these days. She wants the kind of life that Alys seems to be leading, although she's not at all sure who she might want to lead that life with.

'You'll need to come for a meal very soon,' says Alys, just as she's leaving. 'Don't be a stranger. I don't have half enough female friends of my own age here. Or not friends with the same interests, anyway. I'm not really WRI material.'

They exchange phone numbers.

'If you need any odd jobs doing, just give us a ring. Donal might be available. Being a handyman on this island is like painting the Forth Road Bridge. He tends to work his way from one end to another, but by the time he's finished the last job at the north end there's another job at the south end all over again.'

'Does he do gardening?'

'He does. But I should imagine the garden at Auchenblae will be a huge job for somebody.'

'That's what worries me. Are there any other gardeners on the island?'

'One or two. All more expensive than Donal. I keep telling him he needs to put up his prices. There's a lot to do here to keep the gallery going as well. And the boat trips. Which he enjoys and they pay quite well.'

'He's a man of many talents.'

Alys grins. 'He is. He fits in odds and ends of gardening between the building jobs, and people are happy to wait for him. You know what they say? Mañana is a concept with just too much urgency about it over here. But the truth is, when you have a portfolio of work, you probably work three times as hard as somebody with a nine-to-five job!'

TWENTY-ONE

She has a quiet night at Auchenblae. She leaves the hall light on, and her bedroom window open and the dawn chorus wakes her. The mice seem to have calmed down, the fridge makes no noise at all. Maybe she was just too exhausted to hear anything, as she fell fast asleep, surrounded by her own and her mother's clothes. In the morning, a telephone engineer comes over from the mainland to set up her broadband and the landline. He gets lost on the way and has to telephone her to ask where the turning for the house is.

'God, you're in the back of beyond here, aren't you?' he says when he finally turns in at the gate. It would be costing her a fortune, except that he's been called to do some work on a couple of farms at the south of the island as well. Cal has warned her about the additional expenses of living on an island, even one with such good ferry connections as Garve; how delivery expenses can rocket, how some companies won't even deliver to anywhere north of the central belt of Scotland, and have a very restricted notion of where that central belt ends.

'Hell's bells,' the engineer says, looking at the box where the phone line from the road comes into the house. She hasn't noticed before but it could be made of Bakelite. 'Haven't seen one of these since 1970. It's a good job they sent me. Some of the younger engineers wouldn't know what they were looking at. I'll need to replace it. I'm surprised the phones worked at all.'

'The line's been disconnected, so I wouldn't know.'

She makes him tea and biscuits to speed up the work, leaves him to it and goes upstairs to sort out her bedroom, laying claim to it, making it her own. But she can't resist putting the Laura Ashley and the Marimekko dresses back in the wardrobe.

*

Later that afternoon, she's down on the beach, contemplating the sea and wondering how many relics of wrecked ships might be lurking down there under the sand. She still can't quite get used to the idea that the beach is hers, and in her heart of hearts she doesn't approve of anyone owning a beach. Her father would be outraged. Not that she could fence it off or prevent people from walking along it or would even want to. She hears joyful barking and looks up towards the house to see Hector careering down the path in her direction, leaping up and down through the vegetation. He thunders over the sand, puts both front paws on her knee and grins at her, panting, his tongue lolling.

'Where did you spring from?' she asks him, scratching him behind the ears. He sits down, thumps his tail on the sand, stands up again, grabs a piece of seaweed and shakes it vigorously.

'Hector!' His master is following at a more leisurely pace, picking his way down the track. He's grinning too, but not quite so ingratiatingly. 'He clearly loves you!' he says, nodding at the dog.

'I suspect he's anybody's, really.'

'Yeah. That's true. How was your trip?'

'Fine. The fair was OK.'

'Busy?'

'So so. I decided to come back here, begin to sort things out, make up my mind about the house.'

'You saw my mum. You went into the shop.'

'Did she tell you?'

'I phone her quite a bit. Just to make sure she's OK.'

Afterwards she wonders about this rather strange admission, asking herself why Fiona wouldn't be OK. She seems to be the kind of person who can look after herself. Also, she remembers the expression on his face when he said it. He's smiling, as ever, but just for a moment, his eyes are curiously at odds with the rest of him. She has a brief, incredible impression that he's completely exhausted, but hiding it well. Or perhaps she's reading too much into it altogether.

He throws a piece of driftwood for Hector. 'She said she was swearing like the proverbial trooper.'

'She was. Over a broken Wemyss pig.'

'She was mortified but she says you're nice. She thinks you look like your mother. As she remembers her.'

'I was only in there for five minutes. To be honest, if your mum hadn't come in, I'd probably have left sooner.'

'Ah.' He pulls a face. 'Annabel. She's OK when you get to know her.'

'She isn't exactly welcoming to the customers. Well, customers like me.'

'No. We have Mum for that. But you should see her get to work on the guys with money to burn.'

'That's a bit unscrupulous. And inadvisable. I might have been rich beyond the dreams of avarice.'

'Well, you're certainly worth a bob or two!' He laughs.

'Only if I sell up. But what happened to the customer always being right?'

'Annabel thinks that doesn't apply to her.' He looks sheepish.

'You're right there. I didn't see your father, though.'

'No. You wouldn't. He hardly ever comes into the shop.' He's silent for a moment, scratching behind Hector's ear. 'Is there something wrong, Daisy? Have I done something?'

'I don't know. Have you?'

He sighs. 'You've been talking to your solicitor, haven't you?'

'It's fairly usual.'

'I don't know why I didn't let on from the beginning. But it seemed such a cheek. To say I'd been in the house before you.

Seen some of the things. I mean, it isn't something I do very often. Probate valuations. In fact, I don't really do them at all. It's just that I was available.'

'I'd rather have found it out from you than from Mr McDowall.'

'Well, it felt embarrassing. And then because I didn't say it right out, it got really difficult to admit it. The moment never came.'

She can understand this. It's like when you forget somebody's name and then the moment passes and you can never actually ask them.

'You should have just told me. God, Cal, I slept on your sofa and you still didn't say.'

'I didn't think it was a big deal. Well, I kind of hoped it wouldn't matter.'

'It wouldn't have been such a big deal if you weren't actually a...'

'A dealer. I know. And so are you. But I'm not that sort of dealer, Daisy. I'm not like that.'

'You're still at the top end of the market and I'm closer to the boot sale bottom.'

'Not sure about that. I don't think the distinctions are so marked.'

'Oh I do. Believe me, when I go into shops like yours, I know my place.'

She's inclined to believe him, but she's been caught out like this before, giving men the benefit of the doubt. We want to trust people if we like them. Even more so if we're physically attracted to them.

He sits down on the rock beside her. She's acutely aware of him, warm and full of potential energy. He smells of soap and coconut shampoo.

'Plenty of people are that sort, though,' she says. 'I've met them. They'll go into some old lady's house to give her a valuation on her furniture, and they'll find something precious and slip it into the drawer of some piece of old pine, and make a cheeky offer

209

for it. I've heard them talking about it in the saleroom.'

'Yeah. Me too,' he says, ruefully.

'And the younger they are and the more charming, the worse it gets. They have this sense of entitlement. It's strange how when you've got something to sell it's always the wrong time, but when you're buying, everything is suddenly very popular and hard to get.'

He can't help smiling at this. 'Well, I've been guilty of that one myself.'

'Haven't we all? So did you actually *hide* the picture of Lilias? Given how valuable it is?'

He looks embarrassed. 'I cannot tell a lie. I did.'

She has picked up a piece of bladderwrack and is popping the dry pods between her fingers, compulsively, as satisfying as popping bubble wrap.

'Why, Cal? I mean, what were you planning to do? Get to know me and then make me some dodgy offer for it?'

He shakes his head vehemently. 'Oh, sweetheart, I told you. I'm not that sort of person. I pointed it out to you! I told you it was potentially valuable.'

After you saw me, says the subversive voice in her head. *After you realised I was no fool. No pushover.* She wishes he would stop calling her sweetheart, even though she can see that it's just a habit with him.

'I've hung it up in the big room.'

'Have you?'

'I wanted to see her. Lilias. She brightens up the whole room.'

'See, when McDowall asked me to do the valuation, I'll admit I was chuffed. I'd wanted a look inside for years.'

'But you undervalued it all a bit, didn't you?'

'Are you sorry about that? Did you want to pay even more to the Revenue? I made an informed assessment, Daisy, and I stand by it. Hell, it would take months to go through it all. *Will* take months. They didn't question it. I'd have been happy for them to go in and look at it and prove me wrong. There's a hell of a lot of junk in there, you know there is.'

'Don't I just!'

'Those boxes and chests of bric a brac, linens and things, they may well have a market value once you've sorted them out and cleaned them and worked on them. But looked at cold, just like that... their value is minimal. There are a few good pieces of furniture, old oak and so on, and I listed those individually. The odd piece of good porcelain. Some interesting books that you probably haven't seen yet. They're stowed away in one of the cupboards. I came across Old and New Testaments from the late 1700s. Gilt herringbone bindings. They'll be worth a bob or two, although the really interesting thing is the McNeill family names and birthdates in the back. I had a wee glance at them, that's all. You'll want to take a good look at those.'

'I will. I want to take a good look at all of it.'

'I know. And here's hoping we,' he hesitated, 'you, make a few more significant finds. The embroidered cabinet, what do they call it here? The curiosity cabinet. That was the real prize, but that's long gone.'

'Not from the island.'

'No. But it's gone from this house with the McNeills, and Donal will never sell it.'

'And the portrait? You said that's potentially valuable.'

'Maybe aye, maybe no. I only know it's beautiful and it's very old and for some reason it seemed to be nobody's business but yours. And mine for a while. It has a continental look to it. I'd like to get my mum to have a look at it. But I was never going to cheat you out of anything and I'm only sorry you got that impression. I should have told you right from the start that I'd done the valuation of the contents. My bad.'

He stands up, holds out his hand to her. She takes it, partly as the peace offering it's intended to be, and partly so that he can haul her to her feet.

'Tell you what,' he says. 'Do you want to walk along and have a look at the broch? The tide's pretty low and it makes it easier to get there. Look, Hector's up for it.'

'Hector's up for anything. Why not? It isn't far, is it?'

'No. It's on your land. Over there. You can just see the mound. There isn't much of the structure left, but it must have been quite impressive at one time.'

'As if I don't have enough heaps of old stones already!'

'An embarrassment of ancient monuments.'

*

They walk along the beach, over clean white sand, as far as the narrow promontory and then there's a scramble through shallow dunes, bent grasses, the spikes of flag irises just starting to open, and beyond that a stretch of short turf with blue self-heal and yellow trefoil.

She follows him and pauses, panting. 'I'm not as fit as I should be.'

'Too much city living. But a few weeks here will remedy that.'

Hector has been racing ahead – perhaps he has scented a rabbit – but now his sandy head peers over a hillock, encouragingly.

'It's well named, this place, isn't it?' she says.

'What?'

'Flowerfield. Auchenblae.'

'Of course. Yes. Field of Flowers. The island is full of flowers but there are more here than anywhere.'

She can see the broch, Dun Faire, more closely now. It's a circular structure, built of massive grey stones, with smaller stones scattered and tumbled around it. It stands on a low, rocky knoll, at the tip of this thin arm of land, stretching protectively out to sea. Following the outer ditch, they come upon a single doorway on the north side, with an impressive lintel over the top. This seems to be in a reasonably good state of repair. But beyond the doorway, there is little of the wall left; just enough to show its circular shape.

'Yet another heap of old stones for you,' Cal says, happily. 'Not the biggest broch in the world, but that seems to have been what it was.'

He heads for the door, ducks down and disappears inside. She follows more slowly, with Hector weaving anxiously around her, his herding instincts kicking in. She hesitates on the threshold. It's quiet inside and she thinks 'what if?' What if he has disappeared? Swallowed by the past. What if she is about to be swallowed by the past as well? Even as she tells herself not to be so daft, the thought occurs to her that she is about to be swallowed by the past anyway, if she's not careful. Isn't that what this house and all the land around her, all the heaps of stones, each with its own history, will do to her if she stays here? Absorb her into itself as it absorbed Viola, as her mother feared that she too might lose herself in the endless demands of the house and the land around it. And so, when the opportunity arose, Jessica escaped.

The dog has gone inside in search of Cal. She follows them, dismissing the fantasy. There is a sense of darkness beyond the door, even though the walls are only a little higher than the lintel, but as she passes through, she can understand why. There's a double layer of stones, with a passageway running between the two walls. Peering along to her left, she can just make out the remains of a ruined stair that must once have given access to the upper floors and galleries. She dredges up her knowledge of Scottish history and prehistory. These were Iron Age buildings, two thousand years old, although the experts couldn't seem to agree on whether they were defensive or simply grand houses for wealthy chieftains and their extended families. Perhaps both. It would make sense, especially with the siting of this one, as so many others, with an extensive view of the sea. You would always know if someone was coming.

She passes into the interior, already filling up with new bracken and heather, although there are flat flagstones here and there amid mysterious lumps and bumps. Perhaps stones have fallen down from the upper galleries at some point in its long history. Because of the thickness of the walls, the inner room seems quite small.

There is no sign of Cal or Hector, but then Cal whistles to her and she turns around to see that he's standing six feet above her, having scrambled up to the flat top of the wall and gallery floor, with Hector beside him. He holds out his hand to her. The inner wall has tumbled down here and formed a series of heathery ledges, uneven steps, and it's an easy climb. He hauls her up beside him. They sit together in companionable silence for a while, dangling their legs over the interior edge, while Hector rushes easily down the same steps, to sniff among the bracken and heather below. Cal pulls a bottle of water out of his pocket and passes it to her.

'Thirsty work,' he says.

'I wonder what Hector's after.'

'Wee beasties of all sorts. Maybe even foxes. He never finds them. Or at least whenever he rouses something, he'll chase it, but when he's on the verge of catching it, he'll stop and look vacant. Like, "What do I do now?" I've seen it happen. No kind of killer instinct at all. Bit like me, really.'

'Aye right,' she says, using the sceptical Scottish double positive. She drinks, hands him back the bottle and he slips it into his jacket pocket.

She closes her eyes for a moment or two and the silence that is really no silence at all presses in on her. She can hear a skylark, its song impossibly high and distant, tumbling through the blue above them. She can hear the trickle of the nearby burn – did they deliberately build near a source of fresh water, those ancient people? – and further off the soft incoming swish of waves on the beach. She can hear the rustle of the dog, ferreting about among last year's heather stalks. And she can hear Cal's breathing, feel the warmth of his body next to hers. She opens her eyes, turns and finds that he is looking at her as though trying to puzzle something out. His own feelings, maybe. Or hers. And then he's kissing her.

Or perhaps she kisses him first. Hard to tell. His lips are firm and dry. It's been a while since anyone kissed her but her instant response to him is almost frightening in its intensity. It takes her by surprise. He tastes of water and desire and he smells of peppermint and heather. They topple over onto the flat top of the wall. There's a familiarity about him. The ground is dry up here and the stones are cushioned with turf. Years of sand have formed a kind of mulch in which small sea-friendly plants have grown and spread, carpeting the stones. This would once have been a first-floor gallery with others above it when the tower rose to its full height. His face hovers above hers, questioning, intent, and they kiss again, awkwardly, as he tries to cushion her head against the stone.

His tongue is in her mouth. Her right hand is on the back of his neck where the hair is soft and fine, pulling him closer, but her left hand is on the stone, her fingers digging into turf, as though to anchor herself there, to ground herself in the real world. It's so fast, so sudden, this overwhelming desire that can so easily be mistaken for love.

But may not be.

'Cal!' she says, breathlessly.

At the same moment, Hector bounces up to them, and licks their faces.

'Oh, fuck off, Hector!' says Cal.

But they sit up, the moment broken, however temporarily.

Cal gets up, hauls her to her feet with Hector frolicking around them. 'Bloody dog,' he says.

'We should go back, anyway,' she says. There is no particular reason why they should go back, but she can sense herself dragging her feet to slow things down. He's a comparative stranger. However well recommended he comes on the island, she doesn't know very much about him, and doesn't fully trust him. They scramble down from the promontory and head back to the beach below the house.

Hector has rushed ahead of them onto the beach. He tugs at a piece of seaweed, shakes it, kills it satisfactorily, tearing it apart. They follow more slowly, their bodies inclining inexorably together. She wants to take his hand again, but wonders if she should. The dog has abandoned his seaweed and is now digging furiously in the sand beside a little group of rocks, scrabbling with his front paws, spraying damp sand out behind him. He seems to have made quite a big hole. They walk over to see what he has found.

'What are you like, Hector?' says Cal, cheerfully. Then he halts, peers down, grabs the dog by his collar and pulls him, protesting slightly, away.

'What has he found?' Daisy asks, coming up behind them. 'Is it something dead? They do seem to like dead seagulls.'

'No. I don't know. It looks like... Hang on a minute.'

Cal squats down in the damp sand, and reaches into the hole, the little pit that the dog has created, scraping away some of the sand just beneath the shelving rock, seawater already seeping in.

He tugs at something and out it comes. 'Look,' he says. 'Look what he's found. There, between the stones.' He's looking down at Hector in astonishment. The dog is sitting panting on the sand, oblivious and happy.

Cal brushes the sand away from the object and holds it out to her on the palm of his hand. There's the unmistakable gleam of pure gold.

TWENTY-TWO

1588

Before the candles were lit and the evening meal was served, and when Ishbel had wandered off, Lilias explained a little more about the forthcoming festival. *Samhain*, at the end of October, was the feast to mark the time when the cattle were finally brought down from the summer pastures, to the north and west of *Achadh nam Blàth*. Some would be slain and their meat salted, as much as might last through the worst of the winter, but most would be overwintered as far as possible, although feed for them was scarce and like to get scarcer the more the season progressed.

'Some of the other chieftains are sending cattle to the mainland, to be taken along the drove roads and sold at market, but on an island such as this one, it means shipping them and it's an uncertain and dangerous business,' she said. 'If we were just a little closer to the shore, the cattle could be made to swim.'

'Are they strong swimmers?'

'They are. But not strong enough to get all the way from *Garbh*. Nevertheless, father has been considering sending the best of the beasts off in boats if it can be managed.'

'Do people stay up in the hills all summer?'

'Many of the folk come down in July to help with all the summertime work, the harvest and so on. But the remainder bring the cattle back round about now, at *Samhain*. You'll see the bonfire lit upon the Dun there, and upon *Meall Each* as well. It's a time of great celebration.'

'But you have never been allowed to go?'

'No. For when I tell you that marriages are frequently celebrated afterwards, very soon afterwards, and babies born within a scant nine and sometimes eight or even seven months – plump and healthy babies I might add – you'll know why.'

She gazed at him, her eyes full of good humour, daring him to disapprove. Her openness about such things would have embarrassed him at home. Here, he was beginning to understand it. She was reserved and dignified when she needed to be, and cautious in her dealings with the strangers. He sensed that if they ever overstepped the mark with her, she would retreat. All the same, she seemed to expect frankness about these matters of life, death and courtship, both in herself and in others. She was full of a sense of fun and sometimes it bubbled to the surface in spite of anything she could do to contain it. Nobody complained or reproached her for it. Perhaps this was because of her position in the community. Her mother was dead. She had no elder sister and it was clear that she was the apple of her father's eye. McNeill relied on her and had given her a large measure of freedom and responsibility. She was a young woman of consequence in this small world of the island, and being quite outspoken seemed to be part and parcel of her authority. It discomforted and attracted him in equal measure. He thought that here was a young woman who knew her own mind. His own father would certainly have quelled any such behaviour with a glance and a harsh word, but Mateo found himself admiring her. He supposed it to be unusual, even here. He liked her. He had never been so openly friendly with any woman before.

*

The Spaniards had never seen anything quite like the celebrations at *Samhain*. To Mateo's eyes, they seemed to be savage and unchristian: nothing like the autumn festival in La Laguna for the statue of Christ that had been brought to the island by the Archangel Michael himself. Well, Mateo was sceptical about that aspect of the story, but the statue of the crucified Jesus of Nazareth, in wood, both venerable and disturbing, was so extraordinary that it might as well have been made by angels, an image of suffering so profound that it was impossible to see it and remain unmoved. Now, he had witnessed so much of the real thing that he could attest to its accuracy, even while thinking that he wouldn't be unhappy if he never saw it again.

At the end of October, the wind and rain that had been constant throughout the month abated, just in time for the return of the cattle from the shielings: compact and sturdy beasts in black and dun, very like the horses, the garrons, which were compact and very sturdy too. The climate and the terrain seemed to demand a measure of toughness if beasts were to survive. Beasts and people both. Bonfires were lit on the high hills, and those returning brought flaming brands down with them, and carried them sunwise around the houses, although carrying any torch around *Achadh nam Blàth* was quite an undertaking since the house was so big, the land around it so uneven. There were, besides, windy corners where the torches were in danger of being blown out, which was thought to be unlucky. When Mateo asked why they did this, he was told that it was 'for protection'. They sang as they walked and Lilias translated for him.

'May God give blessing to the house that is here,
May Jesus give blessing to the house that is here,
May Mary give blessing to the house that is here,
May Bride give blessing to the house that is here,
May Michael give blessing to the house that is here.'

So the Archangel Michael was known here too.

'Everything must go with the sun, not against it,' said Lilias. 'Did you not notice? When we women are waulking the cloth, we pass

219

it sunwise as we sing. Even the boats when they are brought onto the shore or when they are launched must never be turned against the sun. Our houses are blessed by fire in the name of God and his angels, but it must be sunwise. The very stones on the querns must be turned with the sun, otherwise the grain will go bad.'

'And you believe this?'

'Why would I not, when it is the God's truth?'

There seemed no answer to this strange combination of Christianity and something older, so Mateo simply assented. This was a powerful invocation and who was he to quarrel with it? He had been at sea for long enough to know that all voyages were mired in superstitions and heresies. If, on the island, these extended to everyday life, then perhaps it was necessary.

Later, there was feasting in the great hall, to which he and Francisco were invited as guests, along with a great many islanders. Lilias told them that the empty places set at the table were for the souls of the dead who might visit on this night. After the meal, there was singing and dancing. Stories were told of which Mateo understood not a word, but the sounds washed over him and it seemed to him that they brought their own strange and vivid images to his mind, of ancient battles and long-ago quarrels and loves lost and won. It seemed to him that the songs were sadder than those of his island, and it occurred to him to wonder if it had something to do with the dark time of year, the absence of the sun, which was such a constant on his island. The long dark nights were difficult to bear and he'd been told that the days would grow shorter still. No wonder so many prayers and songs were invocations to the sun for its return.

'But the days are much longer in summer,' Ishbel told them. 'You wait. There's hardly any darkness at all in the middle of summer!'

He found it hard to believe, but he knew that it must be so. It was different from the world he had left and lost, although it didn't make it any more comfortable to endure.

Late in the evening there were games of which, again, he understood almost nothing. Francisco had taken himself off to bed, well fed and as happy as Mateo had seen him since they left home.

'I think I might sleep soundly for the first time in months,' he said.

For himself, Mateo felt wide awake and animated. He had been sitting at some distance from her, but once the meal was cleared away, he had slowly but surely edged closer to Lilias, who was looking very lovely, in a yellow gown with creamy lace at the throat and cuffs.

'Is this heather-dyed too?' he asked, during a break in the music.

'This? Why no, Mateo. This is a silken gown from my brother in St Andrews. He brought it for me the last time he came home. It's the finest thing I own. Or have ever owned for that matter. I've never had a gown like it.'

'It becomes you very well.'

'Thank you, kind sir. Whatever did I do for compliments before you washed ashore? And have you enjoyed these celebrations that are so new and strange for you?'

'More than anything for a very long time.'

'Then I'm glad. I've never seen Francisco so happy.'

'Nor me, since we left home.'

'Is he sick for his home? Does he long for it as I would?'

'I think he is.'

'And you?'

'A little. Not just so much.'

How could he say that he was sick only for her company? That the thought of her filled his mind, all day, and half the night. Whatever work he was asked to perform, he did it with her in mind. It would not do. Her father would never permit it. She had told him quite freely and cheerfully that there was a man called Seoras Darroch, who held a considerable acreage of land on a nearby island, and who could command many followers. It was the same family where her brother was fostered. Seoras had lost his wife two years previously, and there had been some talk of a betrothal, but nothing had been formally arranged as yet. She thought that perhaps her father was not so anxious to be rid of her and so he kept putting it off.

'Do you want to be married?' asked Mateo, even though it pained him to ask the question.

She pulled a face. 'Not yet a while. He seems like quite an old man to me!'

At last, when people were leaving, to go home to their own cottages, to the rooms above the stables, to the chambers in and around the house and wherever they could find a bed, one of the lassies threw a handful of hazelnuts onto a flat-iron griddle and thrust it onto the fire. She called out her name, Cairistiona, and the name of one of the lads, Seamus, pushing the nuts side by side with a pair of tongs, trying not to burn her fingers. A group of girls gathered round, laughing, jostling, naming the little brown nuts, seizing the tongs and pushing them into pairs. Lilias was urged forward and chose the cobnut she fancied for herself, and then Cairistiona was pushing another nut alongside it, and whispering 'Mateo' and all the girls burst out laughing, so much so that the elders, huddled over their drinks at the other end of the hall, looked around in disapproval.

'Daft lassies,' said McNeill, and carried on with his discourse on the finer points of cattle-raising.

The nuts roasted and the smell of burning nutshell rose from the fire. Most leaped apart, many of them right off the metal plate and into the fire where they flamed up and disappeared. There were shrieks of mirth and disappointment. Love, like the nuts, would not last. One or two lay quietly side by side. Mateo stared at those named for himself and Lilias. The fire crackled and spluttered and the two nuts jumped up and leaped apart. He swallowed his disappointment. *How foolish*, he thought. *What a silly game.* But then there came another burst of flame from the fire and the two nuts rolled together again, and there they stayed, small, round, brown, and indisputably as close as it was possible to be.

Lilias got to her feet. Her cheeks were flushed, although whether from the heat of the fire or from embarrassment it was hard to say.

'I must take my leave of you!' she said to the group of young women around the fire, embracing her closest friends among them. 'Goodnight my friends. Sleep well.' She caught his gaze. 'Mateo de Tegueste, my partner amid the flames, may you sleep soundly too. May the good Archangel Michael, bonnie fighter that he is, protect and keep you, now and always.'

She dropped him a curtsey, the yellow dress swirling about her, her vivid hair escaping from its confinement after the activity of the day, and left. He joined a sleeping Francisco in their small room, and he lay down on the bed, his hands pillowing the back of his head. But he barely slept the whole night. He was wearing a crumpled linen undershirt, and he found his fingers compulsively searching for the inner pocket, where he had concealed his sole precious possession: a small, golden ring.

TWENTY-THREE

It's a ring, a gold band, slightly misshapen, with tiny fragments of sand still clinging to it here and there. Cal blows on it gently to clear the sand away, then peers at it more closely. She does the same, and their heads almost collide. But it's irresistible.

'Jesus!' he says. 'Where did this spring from? Did you know this was here, Hector? You couldn't have, could you?'

'Don't let him swallow it!' she says, momentarily panicked.

Hector sniffs at the ring, sneezes, backs away. Cal closes his hand protectively round it until the dog has lost interest.

'Bog off, Hector,' says Cal and surprisingly the dog does, looking hurt. 'I don't fancy having to retrieve it from the other end!'

She takes the ring from him, feeling the weight of it, and they bend over the extraordinary find again, intrigued.

'Gold?' she asks.

'Oh I think so, don't you? Nothing else feels so heavy and comes out of the sand and out of the sea still shining like this after...' He stops suddenly.

'Well, go on. After how long?'

He shakes his head, distracted. 'I don't know.'

'But it looks old, doesn't it?'

He stares at her for a moment or two. 'I know what I think, but it's better to be sceptical to begin with. May I?'

Carefully she transfers the ring back to his outstretched palm. He feels in another pocket and fishes out his jeweller's loup. He looks closely at the ring, tipping it this way and that, but always carefully, holding it between finger and thumb. He has nice hands, slender and sensitive. As she watches him, she shivers at the memory of his kiss, but she also has a sudden unreasonable desire to wrest the ring from him. *Mine*, she thinks. *It's mine. He found it here. On my land. My beach. I'm like Gollum*, she thinks, which makes her laugh. He takes the loup away from his eye and gazes at the ring for a moment or two without it, then holds it out to her again. He seems both puzzled and intrigued. She takes it back, relieved, and sits it on the palm of her hand. It already feels warm from his fingers. She can see that there is a design on the outside, and lettering of some sort inside.

He breathes out, bemused. 'I keep wondering what next? What are we going to find next?'

'Tell me what you think it is!'

'Well, I'm not a hundred per cent sure, but it looks to me like a posy ring.'

She frowns. 'Wasn't that poesy, originally? As in poem.'

'I think so.'

She's peering more closely at it. 'Is that a hare on the outside? A running hare and flowers. There are flowers.'

He offers her the lens and she squints at the ring through it. Suddenly, the design springs to life in vivid detail, only slightly blunted by time, the yellow metal impossibly warm and bright for something that might have lain hidden for many years. It makes her think of the brightness and warmth of the portrait of Lilias. The pattern is in shallow relief, the hare bounding around the ring's circumference through a border of flowers. Inside, there is an inscription, in tiny, precise lettering.

'*Vous et nul … autre?*' she says.

'That's what I think it says as well.'

'You and no other.'

'That's right.' He's looking at her solemnly, his face shadowed, his brown eyes huge. The sun has gone behind the wall and there's a chill in the air.

'It's a love token then.'

'I think so,' he says, carefully.

'Weren't they given as love tokens between courting couples? Or perhaps to mark a marriage.'

'But it was a time when marriages were often political or convenient, so sometimes they were secret gifts. This is a real love token, I think. A talisman.'

'How old is it?'

'Old. I think so anyway.'

'You mean very old? Like the picture?'

'Well, there are plenty of modern copies. Lots of jewellers started making them and they still do. We've had them in the shop occasionally. But never anything really old. They can be fifteenth or sixteenth century. Sometimes even older.'

'And this one?'

'Could be.' He shrugs. 'You'd need to get a jewellery specialist to have a look at it. We could take some pictures. I can give you some contacts. You don't need to let it go.'

It's as though he can sense her anxiety.

'Right,' she says, still holding the ring, peering at it. 'I think it might have been enamelled.'

'I think you're right. But the enamel will wear off with time, dissolve, leaving just the gold. When you look at it through the magnifier, there's just a tiny bit of colour, microscopic really, here and there.'

'I can see. And there seem to be two phrases, not just one. You and no other, and then another one. Even smaller. *Un temps viendra.*'

'That's what I thought it said. But that was...'

'On the picture of Lilias.' She almost whispers it. 'Is this for real?'

He shudders suddenly. 'I think it's fucking spooky,' he mutters.

'Does it bother you?' She's surprised. He doesn't seem the type to be spooked.

'A wee bit, it does. I don't know why. I don't like this kind of thing much. Coincidence. It's just coincidence, isn't it?' He seems to need reassurance, so she nods.

'I suppose so. Why would it be in French? It must mean that the ring is French, mustn't it?'

'I don't know. I mean they may have been imported. People may have had them made and perhaps the goldsmiths were foreign. I'm not sure. I know you tend to find them in England rather than here. The Ashmolean in Oxford has a collection.'

He's thinking aloud, as puzzled as she is, but feeling that he ought to know more. It strikes her how much men like to be seen as experts.

'How would it finish up here?'

'I have no notion. It would almost make more sense if it was in Spanish.'

'You mean the Armada?'

'Aye, I do, Daisy, but it's a mystery.'

He reaches over, takes up the ring and slides it onto the third finger of her left hand. 'I had a feeling it would fit,' he says dreamily, and it does.

She looks at it for a moment, seeing the ring on her finger, the hare leaping forever round and round, leaping with the sun, clockwise, endlessly circling the ring of gold.

'Clockwise,' he says. 'You know they won't turn their boats against the sun here, don't you?'

'How do you mean?'

'You ask Donal McNeill. If you're putting a boat in the water or taking it out, you have to make sure you turn it with the sun. Otherwise ill luck began to follow the unfortunate man – as somebody here once said to me. So I always turn with the sun too.'

She slides the ring off her finger. 'I don't think I should wear it,' she says. 'What if it really is four or five hundred years old? But I don't know what to do with it!'

'Let's take it back to the house at least. Find a safe place for it. Maybe it's a ring whose time has come.'

*

They both seem to find the ring disquieting, albeit for different reasons. For Daisy, it's one more responsibility. She can't quite fathom why wearing it made her feel so strange, nor why Cal is so apparently discomfited by it. Inside the house, she looks around the big room and finds a carved wooden trinket box on top of the oak press. Inside there is the usual guddle of receipts, a coil of string, elastic bands, some paperclips, an old hayfever spray and a half-used book of stamps from several Christmases ago. She tips them out, although they make her think of Viola all over again, puts a tissue in the box and sits the ring on top of it, covering it with another layer of paper.

'Don't forget where you've put it,' he says.

'I'm hardly likely to do that! If I had a safe, I'd be locking it away.'

'You should maybe just wear it.'

'I can't risk losing it.'

'The way somebody once did?'

'Do you think it was lost or hidden? Don't you have to report finds like this?'

'I'm not sure. Mum would know, if you don't mind me telling her about it. You're supposed to report treasure trove, but I don't know if a single ring like this would count. If you're not going to wear it, you should probably sell it.'

'I might not want to sell it. And I certainly don't want some government official to carry it off to a museum.'

'You could always pretend you found it in the house. I won't tell if you won't. Besides, we found it on your beach. Hell mend them. It's yours to keep.'

'I can't make my mind up about any of this right now, Cal. It's all too much.'

228

'Are you thinking of trying to keep the house as well?'

'It had crossed my mind. Yes.'

'It's an expensive business. The upkeep of a place like this.'

'And I don't have that sort of cash. But maybe I can sell some of this stuff. I don't want to become a hoarder.'

'All antique dealers have the potential to be hoarders. It's in our DNA, I think.'

'Isn't that the truth? You have to learn to live with things and let them go. But I've never had to deal with something as huge as this before, and so personal as well.'

'You don't have to make any immediate decisions, do you?' He looks at his watch. 'Listen, I have to go. I have work to do.'

'What are you working on?'

'I'm renovating a piece of furniture. It's an old Scots dresser with spice drawers along the top. Bit like the one in your kitchen. I've got it down at Carraig. But there's a customer for it and Mum promised it would be ready in a week and I'm nowhere near finished.'

'I'd love to see it.'

'Come down, any time.' He hesitates. She's suddenly shy of him, not sure how to pick up where they left off, or even if she should try.

'I'm going to leave Hector with you for a few days. Just till you settle in properly.'

The dog, who has been lying comfortably in the middle of the biggest rug, pricks up his ears at the sound of his name and sits up, thumping his tail on the floor.

'You're going to stay here,' Cal says. Hector wags his tail obligingly. 'I've brought his bed and some food.'

'There's no need, honestly,' she says, but he can see that she's half-hearted in her rejection of the plan. The truth is that it would be nice to have the dog in the house at night. It crosses her mind that it would be even nicer to have Cal in the house at night, but he doesn't seem willing to take things further at the moment, or even to resume whatever they had begun. Still, he's willing to leave his beloved dog with her.

'No. I'd feel happier about it. Humour me, Daisy. I know it's fine in the daytime, when the sun's shining and the birds are singing, but it's different at night. Even at Carraig, it's different at night, and I know every stone and blade of grass down there. But this is a big place.'

'I've been leaving the television or the radio on. Or singing loudly.'

'Do you sing?' He's intrigued.

'A bit. My mum was the songbird in our family, but Dad says I'm not half bad. Which is a compliment coming from him.'

'What do you sing?'

'Oh traditional stuff. What else, with my background? "The Lea Rig", "Will Ye Go, Lassie, Go", "A Red, Red Rose". But I don't sing in public. Or very seldom and only when I've had a few glasses of wine!'

He fetches Hector's essentials, his tartan lead, dishes, bed, blanket and a ravaged toy that he says is a favourite. She puts the bed at the bottom of the stairs, the dog food and water dishes in the kitchen. Hector gets into his bed, turns around three times and lies down, but gets up again anxiously when Cal heads for the door.

'You're staying here for a wee while, pal,' he says.

He turns before he opens the door, and as though on a sudden impulse, pulls Daisy into his arms and embraces her, quite brusquely. He kisses her, his hand on the back of her neck.

'Come down and see me at Carraig,' he says. 'I really have to get this thing finished but come down soon. Tomorrow if you like. Hector's fine in the car. He'll just sit beneath the passenger seat. You won't need to put him in the back.'

After he leaves, Hector whines and sniffs deeply under the door, but when she goes through to the kitchen to make something to eat for both of them, he seems to resign himself to his new circumstances and patters after her obediently enough. She has never seen a more amenable dog. She wonders if his owner is quite so amenable and still finds herself doubting it, although whenever her thoughts touch on him now, she feels a little tingle of dangerous desire.

Later that night, Hector lies at her feet as she watches the television. She finds his presence reassuring, until she sees him sit bolt upright, watching something across the room, his eyes following some movement or other. She comforts herself with the thought that it must be an insect, a spider or moth perhaps. When she peers at the wall, in the direction of his gaze, she can see nothing except the portrait of Lilias, but although he is staring vaguely in that direction, he doesn't seem to be especially fixated on it. He doesn't seem distressed by whatever he's watching either, just interested.

'What is it, Hector?' she asks him. 'What are you watching?'

He looks round at her and wags his tail, putting his ears back in acknowledgement of her question, then cocks them again and carries on watching whatever is absorbing him. He wags his tail, fractionally, now and then, and once or twice lifts and stamps his front paws impatiently, but at last, and greatly to her relief, he settles down and falls asleep, waking only when she lets him out for a late-night pee. She has a momentary worry that he might head off home, but he comes indoors when she calls and settles down in his bed at the foot of the stairs. When she goes up to her own bed, she realises that Cal was right. It is a great comfort knowing that Hector is on guard down below. She falls asleep with no trouble at all, closing her door and switching off the light. In the early hours of the morning, she hears the clicking of his nails down the hallway outside, interspersed with the occasional sniff as he investigates the various doors. Then there's a thud and a heavy sigh as he locates her room and throws himself down against the door. There's silence. She drifts off to sleep again and when she goes down to make her morning tea, she sees that he has gone back to bed and is ensconced there, wagging his tail to greet her, and grinning at her, his tongue lolling. He has clearly decided that his change of home is no bad thing. She doesn't know whether to be glad of his easygoing nature or appalled by his disloyalty. Most dog owners fondly assume that their pets will pine away without them. Not Cal and certainly not Hector.

*

In the morning, she suppresses her almost overwhelming desire to phone Cal and decides that she must at least make a start on sorting things out. If she's not careful, she will simply be overwhelmed by the magnitude of the task and do nothing at all. Grasping her courage in both hands, she goes into Viola's bedroom. She brings a couple of big cardboard boxes from the car, sturdy saleroom boxes, and a roll of bin bags, and she works diligently for some hours, chanting 'keep, chuck, sell, donate' like a mantra.

It is only moderately successful, mainly because she keeps finding interesting things: not just the old scents and the costume jewellery and scarves, which all seem very personal, but other more childish and nostalgic keepsakes. In particular, there's a framed photograph of a leggy, freckled child in shorts and a T-shirt, down on the beach, her hair pulled back into a long ponytail. This reminds her uncannily of herself. There are similar photographs of Daisy, aged eight or nine, on the beach at Ayr, but she quickly realises that she is looking at her mother as a little girl, on Garve. There are old birthday cards with 'To my lovely mum who is always kind to me, with love from your Jess' written on them in a careful, childish hand and heartrendingly treasured down all these years. In a drawer, she comes across a trove of precious drawings, again done by a child, presumably her mother. She turns over the pages one by one and sees that her eight- or nine-year-old mother has drawn a series of 'rabbit tea parties' in pencil and coloured crayon, with bunnies gathered around a picnic cloth, some on a beach and some on the terrace, with a sketchy approximation of Auchenblae, complete with tower, in the background.

The drawings are unsigned, but they trigger a remembrance – at once happy and sad – of Jess drawing similar tea parties for her own small daughter, complete with lop-eared rabbits. Jess had obviously loved her mother dearly, so when had that love turned sour? Or was it only that the house and its situation and perhaps even the island itself had begun to suffocate the girl as she grew to adulthood? Back then, it was much harder to leave. Cars had to be winched on and off the ferry. Now even the bin lorry comes over from the mainland. Daisy knows from her own experience with her father that, although he had set boundaries and protections in place, he had always encouraged her to fly.

'You have to make your own choices, Daisy,' he would say frequently. 'You have to decide what's right for you. I can only advise you. But I can't make those choices for you. You have to make your own mistakes. I'll always be here to support you. Always be here to pick you up and try to make it better.'

He had been as good as his word. When she had been bullied by a group of older girls at secondary school he had visited the head teacher and, although she never knew what he had said, the bullying stopped. He had comforted her and raised her spirits when her university course seemed too difficult, when money was tight, when jobs were hard to come by and when the work in the saleroom seemed exhausting and thankless. Most of all, he had been there when whatever relationship she had embarked on – and there had been plenty of them – had come tumbling down. She and her female friends, women she had been at university with and latterly a close friend called Victoria, a trainee auctioneer from the saleroom, joked that they were the Bridget Joneses of Glasgow. But one by one, as they approached their mid-thirties, they had found partners, while she, Daisy, never seemed to meet the right person. But Rob had always been there, with tissues, wine and sympathy. Bitter experience tells her that Cal probably won't be the right person either.

Now, sitting on the soft green eiderdown, sorting through

Viola's things, she wonders if her grandmother had been too quick and keen to make choices for Jessica May, too afraid of losing her. She doesn't know and has no way of telling. The story of their mother and daughter relationship is all here, but it is almost impossible to pin down the truth of it. It is much too late to ask her mother, and she suspects that her father never really knew, but that – easygoing as ever and very much in love – he simply acquiesced in whatever Jess thought was best.

All this time, Hector has been sitting patiently on a dusty sheepskin rug beside Viola's bed.

'What do you think, Hector?' she asks him. 'Do you think I should just give up and resign myself to becoming a recluse in my crumbling castle? There's enough space here for a whole hoard of cats anyway!'

Hector stands up and barks.

'You know that word?' she asks. 'Cats? You wouldn't approve of that, would you? But you could always go home to Cal.'

He barks again, goes into down dog, front legs on the rug, back raised, tail wagging. Doggy yoga.

'God,' she says. 'I'm having a conversation with a dog.'

By early afternoon, though, she has filled her boxes and bags to overflowing. She thinks there may be a charity shop along the coast at Keill, so she hauls the 'donate' bags down the stairs and puts them in the boot of her car. She leaves the neatly packed 'sell' boxes in the most empty of the other bedrooms on this floor, and takes a couple of sturdy bin bags full of old but not vintage underwear, dresses that even the poor wouldn't want, miscellaneous papers, tattered and torn paperbacks and a selection of old and uninteresting cosmetics, dried face creams and empty toothpaste tubes down to the bins, one for recycling and one for general waste. She drags the vacuum cleaner up the stairs and runs it around the carpet; finds furniture polish and dusts the newly emptied surfaces. She has sorted out the shoes, Viola's elegant and surely not very practical shoes, into those that can be sold and those that need to be disposed of. She herself hasn't worn such small shoes since she was about ten and she's certain her feet have never been this narrow. She has tackled all but the rack of stylish vintage clothes in the wardrobe, but thinks those can mostly be photographed and sold from the island. She strips the bed and throws most of the old bedding and even the stained feather pillows away, although she keeps the eiderdown, and a good linen top sheet. The mattress is surprisingly good too. Perhaps Viola had replaced it quite recently. Two of the pillows look new as well, and she keeps those.

After this, she thinks that she will reward Hector and herself with a trip to Scoull for a late lunch at the hotel. Maybe they will go as far as Keill with the charity bags. This will mean passing the turn-off to Carraig. She checks her phone, but there has been no message from Cal. All the same, she says to Hector, 'Do you think we should go and see your master? Do you think we should go and say hello to Cal?' To which suggestion Hector responds with his usual and predictable enthusiasm. Before they go out, she can't help checking that the posy ring is still safely in its box, and she makes sure she bolts the back door and locks the front door behind her.

TWENTY-FOUR

1588

Time passed. People rose early to tend to the animals and Mateo went with them to do whatever he could, especially with the horses, since he was not ignorant of their care. Francisco offered, but Mateo could see that they thought him weak and clumsy. Eventually, he suggested that his cousin should take on the instruction of little Ishbel and a couple of other children of the house deemed old enough to learn: Beathag's granddaughter Annag and a promising young lad called Alan, the son of one of the nearby tacksmen and a close cousin of McNeill. Francisco was charged with teaching them their letters and instructing them from an old Latin breviary that Lilias had found tucked away among her mother's possessions. It contained brief lives of the saints, including Scottish saints such as Margaret and Kentigern. Francisco occupied himself during some of the daylight hours by trying to render these lives into his version of English and writing them out on the pages at the front and back of the book, as an aid to instruction. He thought, accurately, that the lives of these saints were less dry and a good deal more interesting than the bulk of the breviary. His command of the spoken language was much improved, although his writing of it proved to be a difficult and laborious business, and he was forever asking his more learned cousin for help. Ishbel too was never backward in telling him where she thought he might have made a mistake. Consequently, the pages were full of crossings-out and blots, but they all learned from each other and afforded each other a good deal of harmless amusement during the winter months.

The wind blew constantly around the old house, wailing and howling for admittance, rattling on the glass where it was to be found, confounded by the shutters. One short winter day blended into another. Mateo had never felt so tired. It seemed as though the lack of light affected him as it affected all of them, so that they became impossibly drowsy. The rush lights and the fir candles that he had dried in the autumn might be lit, bringing some welcome light to the Great Hall, but it made little difference. When darkness fell, they needed sleep and would be yawning constantly. One person had only to begin and a positive storm of yawns would afflict the entire company.

'We are like the swallows that sleep away the winter at the bottom of the loch,' remarked Lilias. She and Ishbel, Mateo and Francisco had taken the opportunity of a fine, sharp day, without rain or even a cloud in the sky, to walk down to the shore below the house, ostensibly searching for driftwood to make or repair small pieces of household furniture or simply to add to the fuel stores. The two dogs, Bran and Finn, had followed them or perhaps had been sent by McNeill or one of his henchmen as tactful overseers, and were fossicking about along the tideline, picking up pieces of seaweed and squabbling good-naturedly over them. The sea was calm for a change. The sand was white, flat and washed clean, with the occasional piece of salt-bleached wood, a few shells and shiny pebbles deposited here and there. Ishbel ran about, gathering up her treasures.

'Where did you say these swallows go?' Mateo asked. Francisco was absorbed in the landscape, breathing in the fresh air gratefully. Mateo was absorbed only in Lilias and in pretending to himself and to her that he wasn't. It was becoming increasingly difficult to dissemble.

'*Gobhlan-gaoithe*. They sleep in our lochs for the whole of the winter and rouse themselves only in the spring.'

Mateo raised his eyebrows. 'Do they? I don't know these birds.'

'Do you not have them on your island? Maybe they are not fond of the hot days, although they seem to like the sun. They fly constantly and build their nests of mud upon our houses, very cunningly. You must have seen the nests. They come back to them each year and repair them if they are broken down, much like men and women. But they disappear in the winter. They must sleep, surely.'

'I think I know what birds you mean. We have them too. But I don't know that they sleep beneath the inland water, for we don't have quite so much of it!' He turned to Francisco and explained in Spanish. Paco took up a sharp piece of driftwood and drew a passable pair of swallows on the sand.

'That's it!' said Lilias. 'Come here, Ishbel. See what Paco has drawn! I didn't know he was an artist.'

'He's a fine artist.' Mateo clapped his cousin on the back. Francisco only smiled, blushed a little but didn't deny the compliment.

'Why did you not say?'

'It didn't seem a very useful occupation,' said Francisco, quietly. 'Everyone here is so busy and so hard pressed.'

Lilias pursed her lips. 'What kind of things do you paint?'

'All kinds of things. But my teacher at home was a painter of portraits and that was my first love.'

She regarded him steadily, shaking her head a little. 'Francisco, what brought you to our shores? Why are you not at home, painting? Mateo here I can understand, perhaps. He's fierce enough to be a soldier. But you seem to be such a man of peace.'

'I thought I wanted an adventure.'

She turned to his cousin. 'You should not have let him embark on such an enterprise!' she said, forthright as ever. 'You may be a bonnie fighter, but you should have had more wisdom where your cousin was concerned. I think you *do* have more wisdom.'

'Aye, well. Some of it acquired along the way. And a hard lesson it has been for both of us,' Mateo replied.

'I'm sorry. I shouldn't be scolding you like this, but if God has seen fit to give somebody a skill that few have, then he should make the best of it.'

'I know it. And if ever we win back to our own island, I'll make sure he does precisely that.'

She was silent for a moment or two. 'I wonder,' she said, 'if it would be possible for you to paint portraits of myself and Ishbel, Francisco.'

Ishbel came dancing up with shells and sticks held in her petticoat that she had kilted up to make an impromptu bag. 'Will you make my picture, Paco?' she asked. 'It would be very fine to have a picture of myself painted like a great lady. Like McNeill of Barra's wife.'

'Could you sit still for long enough?' asked Francisco, smiling at her, tugging at her plaits affectionately.

'She cannot sit at peace for more than five minutes together!' said Lilias.

'I could try, Lily. I could try.'

'Maybe so. But I certainly could. My father has often spoken of this, you know.'

'Has he?' said Mateo. It didn't seem the kind of thing that McNeill would have cared about.

'Oh yes. He used to travel more often than he does now, and once or twice he stayed in a fine big house, or so he told us, and he was very taken with the family portraits that were hanging on the walls there. There was a portrait of our poor Queen Mary that took his fancy. He was her admirer ever after. He said she was as beautiful and perilous as one of the fairy women.'

'I'm told she was a handsome woman. But I've seen some who would compare with her.'

She chose to ignore this very obvious piece of gallantry. 'We have no portraits, not even of the family. There are a few gloomy old woodcuts of I know not what, that have been here for ever, and a picture of the Virgin Mary and the baby Jesus that my mother brought with her and used to use for her devotions. But I think my father would like it fine if there could be portraits of the two of us.'

'It's not so easy. Where would we find the canvas, the pigments, the brushes?' asked Mateo, seeing his cousin's sudden enthusiasm. 'Francisco has some skill at mixing his own colours, but at home we acquired whatever we needed from the peninsula and sometimes from Italy. Even then, it was expensive and difficult. It is a long way from Scotland.'

'I think it could be done. Messages could be sent. Scotland still trades with many other countries and such things are to be found in Edinburgh. We are not the savages you think us, Mateo. My brother will be coming home from St Andrews for a visit when the season and the weather allow, but I know he has friends in Edinburgh, and if I can write a letter for my father, it could be sent to the mainland and might reach him. There are people who travel back and forth. And then he could bring whatever you need when he returns. It wouldn't be an impossibility, believe me, if we were prepared to wait a while. And you're not going away very soon, are you?'

'No.' Mateo shook his head. 'We're not going away, Lady.'

'Well,' said Francisco, 'perhaps I could make a list and perhaps we could try to get something. I had thought of trying to find and mix what I could from plants. But it is all so unfamiliar and difficult. I wouldn't know where to start.'

'Like the dyes that we use for the wool? But that is a different matter and nothing turns out as you expect. There is a kind of magic in it! I'll speak to my father. Portraits are very good ways of finding husbands, you know. Especially if they are flattering enough and can be shown to prospective bridegrooms.'

Mateo felt a pang of disappointment at the thought of prospective bridegrooms for Lilias, but said nothing.

Ishbel danced off and the dogs raced after her. 'More shells!' she called. 'We need more shells.'

'There are more in the next bay,' said Lilias to Mateo, preparing to follow her sister. 'Its name is *Sligeachan*, which means the shell place and so it is.'

'Why does she gather them? These...'

'*Creachainn*. Clam shells. Mostly because she likes to collect things, likes to squirrel things away. She hangs them in our bedchamber where they make a pleasant noise in the breezes that find their way inside. But they have other uses, especially for skimming the milk.'

Ishbel was already running towards the narrow headland that sheltered the bay and they followed her, climbing across the promontory at its lowest point.

Francisco was striding after the child, but Lilias lingered and Mateo hung back with her. 'This was where I first saw you. You were standing near this tower. What is it? Was it a part of your house? A watch tower?'

'Maybe. I don't know for sure. It's said to be very old. We call it *Dun Faire*, which certainly means the watch hill or fort. But we don't build such round towers now, nor do folk even know how to build them, or so I'm told. They were made by people who were here before us. Long, long ago. A strange and monstrous people who came from the sea. Well, some say they were monstrous and some say they were beautiful beyond compare. Our threats have always come from the sea, you know. For hundreds of years. Long before you came in your big ships.'

'In our big, bold and not very adequate ships.'

'That's a brave admission, Mateo de Tegueste. Who am I, a mere woman, to say whether it's true or not?' She was laughing at him again, he saw, even flirting with him, and he began to laugh with her.

'But all the same, there have been so many enemies. Interlowpers in the lowland tongue. The *Gall-Ghaidheil*, the foreign Gaels from the outer islands, and the fierce Norsemen before that. Pirates. Men from Ireland, or from the Scottish mainland too.

That's why we have our own big tower, back there, and why there are guards set on top of it during times of trouble. Looking out for the enemy.' She smiled at him enigmatically. 'But this tower was already a ruin when my father was a boy, and when his father before him was a boy too. It's a curious place, though. Come with me and I'll show you!'

All unexpectedly, she took his hand and pulled him along until they reached the tower. The short afternoon was almost done, the wintry sun sinking behind the island hills. Soon this coast would be in twilight. A mist was rising from the sea and starting to drift across the sand, making ghosts of the rocks. He had never been so close to the tower before. He could see that it must once have been very tall, a monumental structure, its stones fitting together beautifully without benefit of mortar or clay or any other means of fixing them.

'Quickly, quickly, before they notice we're missing!'

She took his hand and pulled him into the shadow of the building. He saw that there was a doorway in the stone, also well-constructed, and once through it, he realised that the walls inside were double, with a dark passageway between them. Peering along, he could just make out a stair. Still holding his hand, she kilted up her skirts and clambered up the precarious stones so that he couldn't help but follow. The place smelled of damp and cold stone and the sea. There was a cell built into the thickness of the double wall – a guard room perhaps – and then they were in a completely circular upper chamber. The place was quite open to the darkening sky but he could see that there had once been more floors, joined by a string of galleries and stairs. Now they led nowhere. In this room, there were flagstones set upright, forming an enclosure of some kind, and others in the shape of a rudimentary flat-topped table or cupboard.

He stood still, intrigued and surprised. 'Did people live here then?' he asked.

'We don't know. Maybe. Maybe they lived here before *Achadh*

242

nam Blàth was ever built. Although my father tells me that our Great Hall is very old indeed. Older than the tower at the end of the hall. And this is older still. But if they did live here, they must have been quite cramped. Maybe they kept the beasts down below. Who knows? I sometimes wonder if that was a bed. You could fill it with heather, and sleep there. Like Diarmuid and Grania.'

'Who were they?'

'They were lovers. They ran away together. She was meant to marry somebody else. He made her a bed of heather. Perhaps they used this as a lookout, the people who lived here, and if they saw the enemy approaching, they might assemble in here. It would be hard to breach this and a few fighting men could defend it.'

'But wouldn't the enemy have come from the west?'

'Not always. And besides, there was once another tower just like this on the west side of the island. I've seen it with my own two eyes, back when my brother and I used to roam the moors beyond *Dun Tarbh*.'

'Thank you for showing it to me.'

'It's a very private place,' she said. 'Nobody comes here. Even from our house. They say that the fairy washerwoman can be seen washing the shirts of those who are about to die, down there beside the shore where the water from the burn gathers in pools. But I don't think so. I think it's just a little sad. Like you, my friend.'

She was standing so close to him that he could feel her breath on his neck, and she hadn't relinquished his hand. All of a sudden, she stood on tiptoe and planted a lingering kiss on his cheek.

Then, before he could respond, she had turned and was pulling him after her, out of the tower. She let go of his hand. The space between them seemed vast. The dogs came rushing up from the beach, their coats sandy where they had been rolling on pieces of seaweed and other fouler things. They were followed by Ishbel with Francisco, the child still holding up her skirts, full of shells and small sticks, although Francisco had taken his share of the burden, as many as he could hold in his arms.

'Where were you?' Ishbel asked. 'You didn't come.'

'No. It'll be getting dark soon, and I wanted to show Mateo the old tower. But we'd best be going home. Beathag will be fretting and wondering where you are, Ishbel. Here. Give me some of your sticks as well. Mateo can take some too. That way, we'll go more quickly. Time for supper and then for bed.'

TWENTY-FIVE

At the Scoull Hotel, Daisy sits outside at one of the picnic tables with Hector's lead tied to the wrought-iron table leg so that he won't bother the other customers. Mrs Cameron is behind the bar, chatting to her daughter-in-law, who is serving a bevy of visiting yachtsmen and visitors to the campsite in the field behind the hotel.

'Go back and sit down. I'll bring a tray out to you,' Elspeth Cameron says. She's looking slightly flushed with excitement and she clearly has news of some kind.

When she brings out Daisy's late lunch, Hector greets her like a long-lost relative.

'I see you've borrowed Cal's dog!'

'I had no choice. He was foisted on me. But to be honest, I'm very glad of the company.'

'You can bring him into the bar, you know. We're dog-friendly here. Just not into the restaurant.'

'It's nice to sit out while the weather's good.'

Daisy realises that she's ravenous and falls on the prawn salad sandwich and coffee with enthusiasm. Elspeth Cameron has brought out her own drink as well, a tall spritzer. 'Do you mind if I join you?'

'Please do. I've only had the dog for company since yesterday. He's lovely but it's nice to talk to a human being. I've started sorting things out.'

'Well, if you need help, just say.'

'Don't you have enough to do?'

'Yes, but your place is more interesting. You could have a garage sale.'

'I could have several and I probably will when I get things organised. I could do it in the old sheds at the front of the house.'

'So where's Cal? Has he gone back to Glasgow?'

'No, I don't think so. He said he had a restoration job to do down at Carraig. He's working on a piece of furniture. An old Scots dresser.'

'He's a talented lad, that one.'

'Is he? I wouldn't know.'

'He did a couple of pieces of nice old furniture for us. Made a good job of them and didn't overcharge. Not like some.' She glances around and lowers her voice. 'Did he say anything about his father coming over?'

'His father? No. Not at all.'

'Have you ever met him, William Galbraith?'

'Not to my knowledge. I've seen pictures of him online and occasionally in the press. Why?'

'It's just – he's here. Arrived on the first ferry of the afternoon. He's upstairs.' Her voice sinks almost to a whisper.

'In the hotel? Why is he staying in the hotel and not down at the cottage?'

'He always does. Well, he never comes here at all now. Or almost never. But on the few occasions when he does, he books a room here.'

'Maybe he thinks the cottage is too small.'

'He used to come over when Cal and Catty were young. But even then not very much. It was Fiona who brought the kids to Garve for the summer. I'm told he came when they were court-ing, though. That was before we had the hotel. He did quite a bit of painting here back then.'

'Cal doesn't seem to rate his new work.'

'Cal doesn't rate his father at all. Or his work. But I liked those early pictures. Now he's changed his style completely. Forgive me, my dear, I know very little about art, but they seem very bleak. Very heavy and grim.'

'I'd agree with you. But Cal never said his dad was coming. I mean, he was out at Auchenblae yesterday. That was when he brought the dog. To keep me company.'

She thinks about the posy ring, but decides to keep quiet about it for the time being. The fewer people who know about it and the portrait of Lilias the better.

'He didn't mention William then?'

'He never said anything about his father at all.'

'I don't think he knows he's over here then. Oh dear.'

'I don't understand. Do they really not get on?'

She can't imagine Rob arriving anywhere and not wanting to see her. Nothing would be more important. From time to time it occurs to her how lucky she has been to take for granted something that so many other people don't have. Such unconditional love.

Elspeth leans closer. The windows in the upstairs bedrooms are propped open. Daisy wonders which one Cal's father has checked into. But surely he can't possibly hear from up there.

'They don't. I probably shouldn't be saying this, but they don't get on at all. That's one of the reasons why Cal spends so much time away from Glasgow. Fiona more or less runs the shop, or at least she does all the dogsbody stuff. She does as she's told. I've occasionally seen them together, and my dear husband always remarks that if he ever spoke to me like William speaks to Fiona, he would find a saucepan fitted over his head, and it would probably be made of cast iron. And he's right.' Little Elspeth Cameron looks very fierce all of a sudden, her cheeks very pink.

'I had no idea. He never said anything about it.'

'He never does. Too concerned for his mum.'

'He did say something about the restoration work. How he preferred doing that, but his dad said it was just craftwork and not worth bothering with.'

'That's the long and the short of it. But I wondered if he knew that William was coming over and now you tell me he doesn't.'

'He may know. He doesn't tell me everything. In fact, I hardly know him.' Why does she feel the need to stress this? Is she protesting too much?

'He doesn't lend Hector to just anyone.'

'Doesn't he?'

'No. But I'm in a quandary. I don't know whether to phone Carraig and tell him that his dad's here, or whether I shouldn't be sticking my nose into things that don't concern me. That's what my husband says anyway. That's his advice. Leave well alone, Elspeth.'

'Maybe he's right.'

'He's not such a big fan of Cal, that's the trouble. William's booked in for an evening meal. I keep wondering what he's going to do in between times. And why he's here.' She gestures towards the car park. 'That's his car. You're parked alongside it.'

'The big white Jag?'

'That's the one.'

'Good grief. I was wondering who owned that. I don't know whether you should tell Cal or not. I mean, he'll know soon enough, if his dad turns up on his doorstep, won't he?'

'That's what my husband says as well. Messengers have a habit of getting shot, though.'

'They do.'

'You wouldn't like to tell him? Text him or something?'

'No!' She's appalled at the very idea. Hector gets up, startled by her tone. She scratches him behind the ear and he sits down again. 'No, I can't. Mrs Cameron, Elspeth, I don't know his dad from Adam, do I? If I text him, he'll know we've been talking about him. And that's awful.'

Elspeth Cameron finishes her spritzer with a sigh. 'You're right, of course. But I can't help thinking it's not going to be good news. He's a...' She hesitates, searching for the right description and finding something unexpectedly poetic. 'He's a vortex of negativity that man.' Then she splutters with laugher. 'God, will you listen to me?'

'William?'

'Yes, of course. Not Cal. Cal's an angel by comparison. Well, perhaps not an angel, but he wouldn't do you a bad turn. William could start a fight at a meeting of Quakers. And it's worse than that. He can be incredibly charming when it suits him. But he also rubs people up the wrong way. He has this unerring instinct for their weak spots. He makes it seem all harmless and coincidental, but afterwards you realise he meant it, meant to be rude. Unless he thinks he can get something out of you. It's calculated to make you feel small and insignificant. And he does that to Fiona all the time.'

'I went out with somebody like that once. Just for a couple of months. Found myself thinking I was in the wrong all the time but I couldn't figure out what I'd done. I kept finding myself apologising to him and then *for* him as well. He was rude to all my friends.'

'Exactly.'

'My dad told me to kick him into touch and after I stopped being angry I could see that he was right.'

'Even when he stays here, there'll be complaints. He'll say nice things and then there'll be a sting in the tail. The only person I've ever known get the better of him was Donal, one time anyway. Donal from Ardachy. William said something quite unpleasant about his wife's jewellery, damning it with faint praise, you know, and Donal spoke to him in Gaelic. He has some of the language. From his father, Iain. It was Iain's mother tongue, of course. I think William didn't know whether it was an insult or a curse but suspected it was a curse, and it unsettled him. He always likes to be in control, that one.'

Now she's intrigued. 'I was going to go down and see Cal later on. Take Hector down to say hello. Do you think that would be a good idea? I don't want to walk in on a row of any kind.'

'Yes. Maybe you could do that. Galbraith is booked in for an early dinner at six o'clock. He said he didn't want any lunch so he'd eat dinner early. You could go down then. That way you'd be sure of missing him.'

'I was going to take some stuff to the charity shop at Keill anyway. So it would be fine. I'll have a cup of tea if there's a café or a pub there and wait till almost six.'

'There's a pub. The Ferryman's. They'll do you some tea.'

'But I still don't quite understand the problem.'

'I can't explain. I've just got a bad feeling about all this and I don't know why. But I'll feel a whole lot better if somebody goes down to make sure that everything's OK. Cal loves the bones of that dog. You and Hector ought to go down and make sure he's all right.'

*

Mrs Cameron leaves Daisy alone to finish her sandwich in peace. Before she sets off to drive to Keill with the charity shop donations, she puts Hector in the car and heads indoors to the lavatory.

She's passing through reception when she almost bumps into a tall man who looks vaguely familiar. She realises it's only because there's the faintest resemblance to Cal. He's in his sixties, tall, very slender, with floppy grey hair receding at the temples. Unlike Cal, though, he has pale grey eyes. He has a handsome, hawkish face: lined, distinguished, full of a certain confidence, the kind of man who always walks with his head held high, ignoring anyone he deems to be unworthy of his attention. But perhaps she's been too easily swayed by Elspeth's prejudices. Maybe she should give him the benefit of the doubt.

'Sorry,' she says, smiling at him. Why do women apologise all the time when there's nothing to be sorry for? Should she introduce herself?

He doesn't give her the chance.

'Oh, excuse me!' he says, with a brief, chilly glance at her.

She's nobody of note. Keys in hand, he's heading for his beautiful car, the most expensive in the car park. Her muddy Polo seems remarkably shoddy by comparison. He seems intent on something and very much in a hurry, in his smart leather jacket, a man bag over his shoulder, shiny brown brogues on his feet. There's an atmosphere of money and sophistication about him that she suspects his son will never quite possess, or even want to possess, no matter how apparently successful he becomes. Cal is good-looking and charming, but charmingly ordinary. This man, striding along with his head in the air, has an elegance about him that seems the epitome of success. Doors will slide open for him. Life will be easy on him. And even if it isn't easy, he won't care. He won't even notice the hurdles, because he'll walk straight over them, mowing them down in the process, as well as anyone who has the misfortune to get in his way. The door to the car park is open, and she sees and hears Hector making a racket as William passes her car. He is up at the window of the car, barking but wagging his tail at the same time. William casts a look of immense irritation and perhaps puzzled recognition in the dog's direction. It's only when he's gone, folding his long limbs gracefully into the sleek car, that she realises something else about him. Where Cal is all warmth and energy, with a certain vulnerability, there is nothing remotely warm about his father at all.

As soon as he has gone, Elspeth Cameron emerges from the office at the back of the desk like a rotund cuckoo from a clock, to hiss, 'See what I mean?'

'He's a bit...'

'He's absolutely full of himself. You go and see Cal. Find out what's going on. Lend him some moral support. Because nobody else will. Or nobody who can make a difference, anyway.'

All the way along the meandering coast road to Keill, she thinks about this and wonders what kind of difference she can possibly make, what is it that is worrying Mrs Cameron so much? After all, Cal's a grown man, a significant part of his parents' antique and fine art business, with talents of his own. William Galbraith is ridiculously successful as an artist, but surely that means that he can do without his son. And surely that would suit Cal himself. He seems to be a gifted dealer with the knack of finding a bargain, but he's also a clever restorer. If the worst-case scenario involves closing the Glasgow shop – and she can see that Fiona might be finding it a bit of a trial, having to work with the appalling Annabel, day in and day out – then surely she could retire from the shop and do her own thing: research or teaching. Cal could set up his own business, buy and sell online, do restoration and upcycling in Argyll, sell in Glasgow and Edinburgh and further afield. It wouldn't be the end of the world. But it's really none of her business, is it?

'What am I like?' she asks Hector, who is on the floor beside her.

Everything is easier when there's a lot of cash floating about, she thinks, and has to remind herself that if she sells Auchenblae there will be quite a lot of cash floating about in her life as well.

In Keill, she leaves the dog in the car with the window open and drops off several bin bags full of clothes and bric a brac to a pair of delighted charity shop volunteers, retired ladies, and asks the way to the church of St Columba and the adjacent cemetery. When she tells them whose grave she's looking for, she can see that they're curious, but politeness prevents them from enquiring too closely.

'It's my grandmother,' she says, taking pity on them.

Now they will be able to place her. They obviously know all about Auchenblae and Viola and everything that has gone before. They direct her to a narrow road at the back of the village. 'Follow the signs to the distillery,' they say, which amuses her, but the distillery is apparently a couple of miles beyond the church. She has picked a bunch of wild flowers from the garden and she takes them out of the back of the car.

The headstone is easy to find, because the charity shop ladies have described it to her, one of those ostentatious Victorian affairs, with Viola's name the last one on it: Viola Neilson, born in 1920 to Hugh Neilson and Lily Galbraith. Lily's surname startles her for a moment. Could her great-grandmother have been related to Cal's family in some way? But Galbraith is a common enough island name and like the McNeills there would have been plenty of them. There are other names on the stone: Hugh's parents, Alexander and Mary Neilson, who both seem to have lived well into old age in the 1950s, with Mary outliving Alexander. Hugh Neilson 'fought for his country' but the year of his death is 1921 at the age of thirty, not long after his daughter, Viola, was born. There is no date of death given for Lily on this big, ornate stone, but glancing to one side, she sees a plain granite headstone, very much smaller than the Neilson edifice: 'Sacred to the memory of Lily Galbraith, beloved daughter of Islay and Iain, who passed away on the 24th December 1930. Sweet flower transplanted to a clime where never comes the blight of time.'

How odd, she thinks. *This separation*. She senses a story here. Were Lily and Hugh engaged to be married? Had the war intervened? Had Hugh been injured, but not too badly to father a child? Presumably, after his early death, Viola had been brought up by her mother and her Neilson grandparents, who had assumed guardianship after Lily herself died. She notes that after Lily's death, Viola had clearly remained at Auchenblae, rather than being brought up by her other grandparents, Islay and Iain Galbraith. She thinks, with a little frisson, of her father saying, 'Viola would have wanted you, and back then she might have got you.' The Neilson family had clearly been wealthy and powerful. The Galbraiths, possibly tenants, would have fallen in with their wishes. That was the world into which Viola would have been born, even though things were already changing.

Then she notices that, already almost obliterated by yellow crotal, the name Jessica May Neilson has been carved into the big stone between Mary and Viola Neilson. Jessica May, 'Sadly missed, never forgotten' without any date at all.

How could she?

How could Viola ignore Jessica's marriage?

It occurs to her that for a long time, Viola couldn't have known where her daughter had gone, and had probably found out about her early death only long after the event. Her father had been so worried about Viola claiming custody that he had kept everything as quiet as possible. There had been no newspaper intimations, only a small, sad mention in one or two of the folk magazines; but Viola wouldn't even have been aware of those. And back then, social media hadn't got going. It would have been good to have got to know her grandmother. Good to have found out more about her mother and her Neilson forebears, about Hugh and Lily. And why Lily Galbraith, who outlived her husband by only ten years, was buried in a separate grave. It occurs to her that perhaps the answers to some of these questions might lie in Auchenblae. There must be papers somewhere: letters, birth and death certificates perhaps. She'll have to hunt for them.

There's an empty stone vase with a metal flower holder, misshapen with age, fitted into it, at the foot of the larger grave. Nothing for Lily. She has brought a plastic bottle from the car. She finds a tap, fills the vase with water and arranges the flowers, but she makes up a separate posy and puts it on Lily's grave, drenching it with water to keep it fresh.

There's a church, lower down the hill, dedicated to St Columba, with a stained-glass window of the saint, standing up precariously in a small boat with an island behind him. It makes her think of the islet, *Eilean a Cleirich*, she can just see from the upstairs windows at Auchenblae. Cal told her that one of Columba's monks built a cell there and spent his time praying for the souls of the islanders who converted to Christianity. There's an ancient graveyard there too, where the old lairds and their ladies were traditionally buried. Here, at Keill, she sees the ruins of an older church, a shell only,

254

with more tombstones round about: a mouthful of grey teeth, yellow with crotal. It's a peaceful place, but sad too.

She'll come back here again. Where is Lilias buried, she wonders? On the islet maybe? But there are other ancient graveyards on Garve. She has left Hector tied up to the gate and he is delighted to see her all over again. For now, it's time to find somewhere to get a cup of tea and then she'd better drive down to Carraig and see what has been happening to Cal.

TWENTY-SIX

She parks the car outside the swing gate and holds it open to let Hector through. He disappears round the side of the house, delirious with delight at being home again. The world would be a nicer place if people could be as open to joy as most dogs. She hears a couple of barks of recognition and then silence, except for the usual chorus of birdsong and the sound of sea on shore. She ventures round the house more slowly. The back door is standing open, but there's no sign of Cal. She becomes aware of a distant banging sound, like somebody hammering in nails. It stops and starts again. Perhaps he's working on something. She pokes her head in at the cottage door and is alarmed to see pieces of smashed porcelain on the floor but it's only a broken mug, a splatter of coffee beside it.

Hector rushes in, laps at the coffee, sneezes and rushes out again. She follows him as he trots into the lean-to at the side of the house. She hasn't been in here before, but it's more spacious than she realised: a room tagged onto the house, where Cal and his sister had once slept during their island visits. Now, there's a long bench, tools, the usual clutter of a working craftsman. Cal is sitting on a high stool, leaning on the bench. There's a heap of wooden drawers, large and small, in front of him. He's been working on them, or trying to, but he's not working now. He's sitting there, staring into space. Hector jumps up and paws at him, but he pushes the dog away, not violently but more brusquely than usual. Hector decides he's not wanted and disappears into the garden. To her considerable alarm, Daisy sees that Cal is holding a hammer. He seems to have been bouncing it, rhythmically and persistently, against the hard wooden bench, making little dents all along the edge of it. As she watches him, he starts up again.

'Cal!' she says, but he doesn't seem to hear her. She's unwilling to go any closer. It strikes her that she doesn't know him well at all, and they are surrounded by potentially dangerous implements: knives, files, chisels, saws and hammers. 'Cal,' she says again, more loudly.

He stops hammering, gives himself a shake and looks at her. 'Daisy!' he says, dully. 'What are you doing here?'

He looks absolutely furious. Not with her, but furious all the same. His dark brows are gathered together in a frown and his eyes are gleaming with suppressed rage.

'Just visiting. I've been to Keill. To the charity shop and the cemetery.' She finds herself trying to distract him. 'I took some flowers to Viola's grave. We passed your road end on the way back. I thought you might like to see Hector. Maybe not, though.'

He follows her gaze, looks at the hammer in his hand, says, 'Oh, sorry. What am I thinking?' and sets it down, carefully. His face clears.

'Are you OK?' she asks, although it's clear that he's far from OK.

He runs his hand through his hair, shakes himself again, like Hector. 'Not really,' he says, but he's smiling at her and looking more like himself. 'But all the better for seeing you.'

'Come inside. I'll make tea or something.'

'Yeah. Or something.' He gets off the stool and heads for the back door. She wonders how long he's been sitting there, hammering viciously at his bench.

'Be careful where you walk. I broke a mug.'

They pick up the pieces and put them in the bin. She mops up the spilled coffee with some kitchen towel.

'My father was here.'

'Cal, I was in the hotel. I saw him there. Elspeth Cameron was worried about you.'

'Did she send you down to rescue me?'

'I was going to come anyway. But did you not know he was coming?'

'He never says. Just turns up and expects everyone to fit in with his plans. Which they usually do.'

He goes over to a cupboard and fetches out a bottle of *Eilean Garbh* malt and two glasses. He pours himself a large measure and holds up the bottle to her, raising his eyebrows.

She shakes her head. 'I'm driving.'

'You could stay again.'

'OK. Just a small one.' She could stay for a while, drive later.

The spirit is extraordinarily peaty with a definite tang of iodine. It catches in her throat but she can feel the wonderful warmth of it spreading through her. She could get used to it. He downs his own drink in one and pours himself another. 'That's better.'

'What's happened, Cal? Is there something wrong in Glasgow?'

'The only thing that's wrong in Glasgow is my fucking father.'

The raw viciousness of this alarms her all over again, but she waits quietly for him to calm down and explain. He's practically trembling with rage. Vibrating with it.

He sighs, shakes his head. 'He wants to put this place on the market.' He drinks again, gazes at the floor. 'A holiday cottage by the sea with potential for development. It'll sell in no time at all.'

'This place?' She looks around. This is only her second visit but even she can see how much Cal treasures it. What a sanctuary it seems to be for him. 'Why would he do that? Do they need the money?'

Cal bursts out laughing but it's obviously not very funny. 'No. Of course he doesn't need the fucking money, hen. He's rolling in it. You should see his personal VAT bill, the one for his art sales. And that's nothing to do with the shop. A separate business altogether.'

'Then I don't understand. Doesn't he know how you feel about it? How much you love it?'

'Of course he knows. That's one of his reasons for doing it. He likes to be in control and this is just another way of making sure everyone including me is under his thumb.'

She's speechless for a moment or two. The thought of her dad, of Rob, doing something similar, is so far beyond her imagination that it's hard to understand why any father would contemplate doing it to a child, unless in desperate circumstances.

'Why?' she says again. 'I mean, what's in it for him?'

'What's in it for him is that he thinks I'll have to go back to Glasgow and take over running the shop. He sees this as my bolthole. My sanctuary. Which it is, of course. He thinks I make excuses to be here all the time, working on my fancy bits of furniture. Upcycling. You should have heard the way he spat that word out!'

Maybe he does make excuses to be here all the time. The thought had certainly crossed her mind, although she can't say that to him now.

'Can he do it?' she asks instead.

'Of course he can do it.'

'But what about your mother?'

'Well, yes. Her name is on the deeds right enough.'

'I thought the house was in her family originally.'

'It was. But she added his name when they got married. She once told me she wanted to share everything with him, and he was painting over here back then.'

'So it's in both their names?'

He looks exasperated, as though she's being obtuse. 'Yes, of course. She would have a say in it. As his wife. But you know, Mum tends to do as she's told. And if he wants to sell, that's what he'll do.'

'Does she? Do as she's told, I mean?' This is more or less what Mrs Cameron said too. But Fiona hadn't struck her as being particularly meek.

'Oh, Daisy, you don't know the half of it. Years of living with my dad.' He shakes his head. 'What do they call it now? Coercive control? Gaslighting.'

'Surely not!'

'It's hard to prove. Impossible really. It's so well hidden and he's so bloody charming in public. Or he can be, when it suits him.'

She remembers Mrs Cameron talking about a 'vortex of negativity'. She had thought her overly dramatic, but perhaps not.

She hesitates, drinks some more of the whisky, almost whispers, 'Is he violent?'

He shakes his head again but seems unperturbed by the question. 'No. That's not the way he operates. It's all words, all to do with control. He's a very strong character and a very attractive character, Daisy, and when you pair that with the kind of success he's had, everyone thinking how wonderful he is, telling mum how lucky she is... God, he's the most selfish individual I've ever known. It took us years and years to understand it. How afraid she'd become of crossing him. As though the sky might fall if she challenged him. I don't know what she was like before she met him, but people have told me everything was different.'

It strikes her again that she has met people like that in the past, people who seem able to exert an unreasonable pressure. Often deeply attractive men. It's how they do it. One or two of her friends have been involved with men like this and she has seen how they work, finding fault, quarrelling with friends and family, gradually detaching their partner from their circle of support, and all for their own good. Allegedly.

'I think it was here that we first noticed it, though. Me and Catty, I mean. We used to get off the ferry and come here for the whole summer. The three of us. I always remember, the first thing we did, after we'd opened the door and put the bags inside, we'd go straight down to the beach. We'd be running about, making sure everything was as it should be: the rocks, the dunes. One year there'd been a terrible spring gale and a high tide and the sea had eaten into the sand hills. As though a giant had taken big bites out of it. And the salt had burned all the young leaves in the garden. We hated that. We liked everything to be the same.'

'I used to feel like that whenever I went to stay with my gran in Ayr. I hated it if she'd redecorated, or moved furniture around.'

'Anyway, Mum would be sitting on a rock and just breathing. We didn't notice so much when we were little kids, but when we hit our teens we did. I remember Catty saying to me, "Isn't she different? Isn't Mum different on Garve?" And she was. All the tension just drained out of her. It was as though she could be herself here. Until there was the occasional short visit from Dad, and then she'd change again. He was forever telling her she was doing things wrong: her driving, the garden, the cooking, the way things were here in the house, the fact that we'd go down to the beach in our pyjamas if we wanted to. The only saving grace was that he never stayed. He'd go and we'd all breathe a sigh of relief and get back to the way we were.'

'Is that why she doesn't come here much now? He doesn't want her to?'

'That's about it. When we were kids, he wanted the peace and quiet, so he was quite happy for her to bring us here. Now he needs her in the shop and for making sure the house runs the way he likes it. So she doesn't come. She always says she can't get away. But she could. Annabel could manage the shop perfectly well. Even Catty comes here sometimes, with the kids. They make do, bring camp beds.'

'So he wants you to run the shop?'

'He wants me there. I think even he realises it's getting a bit too much for my mum. They're not getting any younger, and he doesn't want to do it full time, or even part time, but he doesn't want to let it go either. He could, you know. He could sell up. Just paint.'

'But wouldn't you miss the income from it? I mean you, your-self.'

'I'd manage. You trade online, don't you? I have a big fat book of contacts now. I could do some buying and selling, but concentrate on the restoration side of it. It's Dad who likes having a shop window for his pictures. But I think, most of all, he likes us to be there, under his thumb. He's like Hector, only without the good nature. He gets uneasy when he doesn't know where we all are and what we're doing.'

Hector hears his name, pokes his head briefly round the door in case there's any dinner in evidence and wanders off again.

'But your sister must have got away.'

'She did and he's never quite forgiven her for it. Or Garve for that matter. She met Jake at a ceilidh in the Keill village hall. He was over here on farm business. At some level, I think Dad blames the whole island!'

'It sounds almost pathological. I mean, it could have been worse. She could have run off, like my mum.'

He smiles, grimly. 'It is pathological.'

'Can't you – I don't know? Buy this place yourself?'

'You mean sell my heavily mortgaged house in Glasgow?'

'I suppose so.'

'Besides, I have to be there sometimes, and I can't live under the same roof as him when I am. And even if I could sell, I'd never get a mortgage on this place – it needs too much modernisation – and it would be long gone. He'd never let me buy it. He'd take a cut in the price before he'd let me do that.'

'Does your sister know about all this yet?'

'No. She'll be horrified. But there's nothing she can do either. They don't exactly make a fortune and what they do have goes back into the farm or they spend it on the kids.'

He looks around in desperation. 'Christ, Daisy, I love this place. The best bits of my childhood were spent here. I can't bear it. If I can't come over to the island, I don't know what I'll do.'

She can't help herself. She feels so much pity for him that she goes over to him and embraces him. Then he's pulling her into his arms and kissing her fiercely, desperately. She can hardly remember how they find themselves in the bedroom, but she knows he closes the door and jams a chair against it. 'Hector,' he says, succinctly.

The bed is unmade but the bed linen is clean. It all smells of Fiona's lavender, like everything in the house. They struggle to get their clothes off, reluctant to part even for a moment. His lips are warm and dry. They taste of whisky, but so do hers. He fumbles around in the bedside drawer and emerges with a condom.

'Jesus,' he says. 'I didn't think I had any. I don't do this all the time. I really don't do this all the time.'

She stops his words with another kiss, desperate for him, for his long, strong, whip-thin body. It's ridiculously quick, this first time. They want each other too much and come quickly, together, laughing at themselves, at their sudden undeniable craving for each other, lying back on the pillows and on the crumpled sheet, the duvet a tangle at the foot of the bed.

'God, that was good!' he says. 'Almost worth...' He hesitates.

'Worth what?'

'I was going to say, almost worth having to suffer my pitiful father.'

'I didn't ... it wasn't...'

'Out of pity. I know that, sweetheart. You're going to stay the night, right?'

She nods. 'But have you...'

'Any more of these things? I don't know. I'll have to have a hunt around. Let's hope so, eh? Otherwise I'll have to get myself to the hotel.'

'The hotel?'

'There's a machine.'

'Ah, of course!'

'Can you imagine it?' he says, and there's genuine laughter in his voice this time, laughter that bubbles up and infects her. 'Can you fucking well imagine it? I might meet my father in there. Just as I'm putting a coin in the slot.'

She spends the night in his bed. He finds another condom at the back of the drawer and they wake at first light to make love again, this time more slowly, just as enjoyably. He's considerate, a kindly but passionate lover. Unselfish. She can see that she will have to be careful with this one. Never before has it occurred to her so soon and so swiftly in a relationship that here is a man she might love. He's immensely loveable. And they fit well together. She feels comfortable with him, but given his troubles with his father, given his background, she can see that he might not be a straightforward man to love. The physical side is one thing, but he clearly has, to use the cod psychology term, baggage. And she's mature enough to see that unpacking those bags might just be beyond her capabilities, no matter how much her overwhelming desire for him is currently clouding her judgement.

'Is your dad coming back?' she ventures to ask, as they are eating breakfast together, her bare feet resting on his, under the table.

'Lord, no.' He looks bleaker than he has since last night. 'No. He gave me his ultimatum. He'll be putting this place on the market at the end of June, so I'm to clear out my stuff before then. But it isn't all my stuff. A lot of it belongs to my mum's family. He's going off on the first ferry. Doesn't want to hang about. Tell you what, though. He took his two lousy pictures with him!' He gestures at the wall, where she sees two blank spaces where the small rock pool studies were hung.

'What a plonker!'

He starts to laugh, genuine laughter again. At least he's seeing the funny side of it all. He can't help himself. 'Exactly. He is. He's a plonker. But sadly, he's a plonker with power. And an unimpeachable reputation.'

'What are you going to do?'

'I'm going to phone Catty later on, once she's got the kids off to school. We'll have a chat about it. You're going to have to meet her, you know. Otherwise you'll think my entire family is crazy, and she's reasonably sane and sensible now. Well, compared to the rest of us she is.'

'I'd love to meet her.'

'I think you'll get on.'

'Am I sane and sensible too?'

'You know what I mean. In one way she's as mad as a box of frogs. I'm sure that's what my father thinks.'

'I do know what you mean. Listen, why don't you come to the house later? To Auchenblae? You can let me know what she says. You're going to have to think about all this, aren't you?'

'I am.'

'Don't make any hasty moves.'

'You mean like last night.'

'No. You can make those hasty moves as often as you like. I mean with this house. Don't let yourself be bullied.'

'It's kind of hard not to when he has all the best cards in his hand.'

'But he doesn't. You only think that. He's made you think that. You're a grown man with all kinds of talents. When push comes to shove, he can't dictate to you any more. He just thinks he can and he's got you thinking he can as well.'

'You're right of course. It's just...' He looks around, sadly. 'Here. Garve. I can't bear to lose this.'

'Where there's a will there's a way.'

'Aye right,' he says. 'Talking of wills, I suppose I could just bump him off. That would be one way out of it.' She thinks he might almost be serious. But then he grins at her again. 'I don't mean it. If he crashes his car on the way down the side of Loch Lomond, it wisnae me, hen. I didn't tamper with his brakes.'

'We'll work something out between us. And until then, hell mend him.'

'Hell mend him,' he says, raising his coffee cup in a salute.

TWENTY-SEVEN

She heads back to Auchenblae, taking Hector with her. He seems to have accepted the sudden imposition of dual ownership, and hops into the car happily enough.

'What an obliging dog you are,' she says to him. He wags his tail.

On the way, she drops in at the hotel, relieved to see that the Jaguar has already gone. So William must have got the first ferry, as planned. She explains things, as far as she can without breaking too many confidences, to Elspeth Cameron.

'He's selling Carraig?' says the older woman, horrified. 'But that will break Cal's heart. He loves the place and he loves the island too. What will he do?'

'I honestly don't know. He's going to phone his sister for a chat. Maybe she'll have some ideas.'

Too late, she realises that Mrs Cameron will almost certainly make assumptions about where she has spent the night. Should she fib, say she has just driven in for milk and bread? But then she might be caught out in the lie. And it isn't really any of Mrs Cameron's business. They're both grown-up people. As it is, Elspeth is too shocked about Carraig to enquire, although she may well speculate later on.

'Can he just do that? Up and sell it, just like that? I thought it was Fiona's cottage, originally.'

'Cal says it's William's property as well now. I suppose once they were married he had joint ownership. He can presumably do what he likes with it if Fiona doesn't object. It isn't Cal's main home, or William's for that matter. It's a holiday cottage, although I don't think that's how Cal sees it.'

'But that's appalling. And I don't suppose Catty will be able to do anything about it either.'

'He says not.'

'Well, hill farming, three kids, there's no spare cash in that branch of the family, that's for sure.'

*

She has coffee with Elspeth Cameron while they chew over the sins of William Galbraith, *sotto voce* in a corner of the hotel lounge. Then she heads back to Auchenblae. Hector seems just as enthusiastic about being back here as he does about Carraig, rushing about happily, finding his water bowl and his bed.

'We might need to get you another bed,' she tells him, aware that she is planning for the relationship with Cal to continue, wondering if that's wise. If Carraig is sold, he might never come back here again.

You can see him in Glasgow, whispers the voice inside her head. *And besides, there are other possibilities, aren't there?*

'Don't go there!' she says aloud. Hector looks up at her and wags his tail obligingly. Don't go where, he wonders, more or less understanding the phrase, not aware that he had been doing anything amiss.

The thought has occurred to her that she could ask Cal to come here, to Auchenblae. It isn't as if she doesn't have plenty of room. Plenty of rooms, as well, although she can't see that being an issue. And outbuildings where it would be perfectly possible to conduct a furniture renovation and upcycling business. But it seems much too early in their relationship to suggest such a thing. It's one of those convenient fantasies, and if it all goes pear-shaped, as these things seem to have a habit of doing, what then? How could she, not to put too fine a point on it, get rid of him, once he was settled in? She needs more time. Perhaps by the end of June things will be clearer, if William carries out his threat to put Carraig on the market. Perhaps he will think better of it. Perhaps something will happen to stop him.

She goes upstairs and starts to sort out the things from Viola's room that she has considered selling, dividing them all over again into items that might go online and others that might be better sold at an antique fair in the city. She remembers passing a signpost to an antique centre on the way to the island and it strikes her that she might be better to rent space closer to the island for the present, or find more local antique markets or fairs. It's all very well for Cal to try to work between the countryside and the city, but in view of the magnitude of the task in front of her – reducing the contents of the house to more manageable proportions and attempting to make some money out of them at the same time – it might be better to focus on that and whatever income she can make from it over the summer.

Later, she opens the box containing the posy ring, just to be sure it's still there. She takes it out, puts it on the oak table, examines it, slips it on her finger. When she lifts her eyes it's to find the portrait of Lilias watching her – but of course in this kind of portrait the gaze often does follow the viewer. Nevertheless, it's almost as though there is a certain reproachful quality to it. The ring is warm and comfortable on her finger. *A time will come. You and no other*, she thinks. Quite suddenly, she is assailed by a sense of ... what? It's like being dowsed in a shower of emotions, so powerful that they make her catch her breath. She wonders if it is sadness, but there's more energy about it than that. It's positive. She realises that what she is feeling is desire: overwhelming, uncomfortable, physical desire. She tries to pull the ring off but her finger must have swollen because it catches on her knuckle and she can't get it off. She panics, tugging at it, but the more she pulls, the more firmly it seems to be lodged.

She hears a car in the lane, followed by the gate opening. Hector barks and then wags his tail furiously. It's Cal. She's still sitting at the table, frowning at her finger that is now red and swollen. She calls to him to come in, the door's open. She waves her hand at him.

'Look. I can't seem to get it off.'

'Let me see.'

She tries to laugh, but it's becoming increasingly painful: like a band of barbed wire around her finger.

'It's ridiculous. It was quite loose yesterday!' she says.

'I know it was. I put it on the same finger.'

He takes her other hand and pulls her to her feet. 'Come into the scullery, quickly, before it gets any more swollen.'

In the scullery he seizes a bottle of washing-up liquid from behind one of the sinks, and dowses her finger in it. To her relief, the ring slides off and into his hand.

'Well, that was weird,' she says, massaging her finger. The swelling is already diminishing, although the pain remains.

'But it was loose, yesterday, wasn't it?'

'It definitely was.'

'What made you put it on again?'

'I don't know. I was just interested in it. Wanted to see if it really did fit me.'

'Which it doesn't seem to, now.'

'It's getting better, though. Look.' Her finger is almost back to normal. 'Did you phone your sister?'

'I did.'

'And what did she say?'

'It was unrepeatable, what she actually said. But we both think there's not much we can do. I'm going to finish this restoration job as soon as I can, and cart it down to Glasgow next week. Mum's customer will be ready for it. And I'll see my father then as well. See if I can talk some sense – or generosity – into him. But I'm not holding my breath. And my mum always does as she's told. Do you fancy taking Hector for a walk?'

269

'Why not? Why don't we go up the hill there? I don't even know if the tree is still there. Do you know it?'

'The Clootie Tree. Aye, it's still there. Although nobody publicises it and folk don't go there so much now. Load of nonsense if you ask me.'

'Not necessarily.'

'Have you been up there?'

'Once, years ago. The only other time I visited the island. When my mother was very ill.'

'I'm sorry.' He understands immediately. 'It didn't work, I take it?'

'Well, it worked after a fashion. According to my dad. There was our wish, but he had another one. And since that was much less specific, much more down to him to accomplish, that one came true.'

'Which is typical, isn't it?'

'What do you mean?'

'Fairies, otherworldly creatures, weavers of magic spells. There's always a get-out clause, always the gold turning into dried leaves in the light of day, always the trick question, the instruction they neglect to give you!'

'Humour me. I want to see it again and I'd rather you were with me.'

He gives her a small sidelong glance. Smiling. 'OK. Do you want to make a wish?'

'No, but you do.'

'It's a piece of nonsense, hen. It really is.' Whenever he becomes exasperated like this, his accent turns into pure Glasgow. She finds it very attractive.

'Nevertheless. Do you have anything that belongs in the cottage? Something we could tie to the tree.'

'Oh for God's sake, Daisy!'

'Humour me,' she repeats.

He sighs, spreads his hands wide in capitulation. 'As it happens, there's an old tea towel in my car. I use it to wipe the windows. Will that do?'

'Go and fetch it.'

The tea towel is faded almost beyond recognition and thread-bare too, but it once had a pictorial map of Garve on it with yachts and fishing boats, oystercatchers and dolphins, and the outline of churches and houses including Auchenblae. All washed out and ghostly now.

'We got it for my mum, years ago. They had them in the iron-mongers shop in Keill for a while.'

'Perfect,' she says. She doesn't tell him that they should write the wish on it. It would be a step too far for him. It will just have to do. He folds it up and tucks it into his pocket. They head out of the gate and turn left up the hill. The narrow lane is warm and damp and sweet-smelling. It is so sheltered that the fuchsias in the hedge are beginning to flower remarkably early here. A blackbird is singing in the thicket, and here and there they hear rustles and squawks as small birds squabble and jostle for place.

The lane narrows even more, until the grass growing down the centre begins to take over, and it becomes little more than a muddy track, winding up to the top of the hill. The lane ascends slowly through a mixture of willow scrub, taller hawthorn and beautiful birches, their leaves like dazzling coins of light at this time of year. The track takes a final twist and they find themselves in a shallow saucer of land at the top of the hill. It isn't a very high hill, only a few hundred feet, but the rise from sea level makes it seem higher.

'There's your Clootie Tree!' says Cal.

Oddly, Hector, who has been lolloping ahead of them, lies down suddenly on the very rim of the saucer, panting and whin-ing. No matter how much they coax him, he will go no further.

Almost at the centre of the saucer of land stands an ancient hawthorn. It is massive, grey and hoary as a venerable old man, and the prevailing winds have twisted its shape and canted it over to one side, although not without difficulty. The tree seems to have fought a constant battle with the wind for much of its life. The many branches are covered in beards of lichen and moss, but the topmost branches have, against all the odds, blossomed, and there is a crown of sweet-scented white flowers up there. A great many of the leafless lower branches are festooned with fabric – scraps of cloth, scarves that remind Daisy of herself and her father, tying her mother's pale silk scarf on a branch, all those years ago: old-fashioned handkerchiefs, cuttings of this or that textile, rags of all kinds, from ancient linen sheets to pieces of pillowslip and more garish bits and pieces from garments associated in some way with the wish. There are even the sad and tattered remnants of a baby dress, hanging high up, just below the crown of flowers. She had forgotten almost all of this over the years. But perhaps she and her father had been too intent on what they were doing to notice their surroundings, and her father had been desperate to get back down the hill and away from the island without encountering his mother-in-law or without Viola seeing her, Daisy, at all.

'Wow,' she says. 'It looks like a person.'

The fluttering rags do have the effect of making the branches look like arms, as though the movement in the fabric is giving the illusion of the tree itself moving.

'Where's your tea towel?'

'Here.' He fishes it out of his pocket. 'But where will we put it?'

The lower branches have split and fallen or are already full of decaying cloth. She can't see anything resembling her mother's silk scarf and can't remember where they put it; the elements must have done their work and it is long gone, shredded by wind and rain. The place has a very strange feeling. Daisy doubts if she will come back up here, or certainly not on her own. The tree is not promoted in any way to outsiders. There is nothing about it in the island tourist leaflets and nothing on the website. She doubts if many casual visitors to the island even know of its existence, although some of the offerings festooning the lower branches look quite new, so at least some of the islanders are still indulging in a little paganism now and again.

'See,' he says. 'Even Hector thinks it's weird here.' The dog is still crouching on the lip of land, looking across at them and whining, but coming no further.

'Lift me up, and I'll tie it onto a branch,' she says.

He puts his arms around her, jiggles her upwards until he is holding her under her bottom ('this is nice,' he says, his nose against her breast, breathing her scent), and then he hoists her high into the air, like a weight-lifter, staggering slightly.

'Ooof,' he says.

'Are you implying I'm heavy?' she asks. For someone so slender, he's surprisingly strong. He's all muscle. It strikes her that this is very far removed from the last tragic time she was here, and yet in its own way, it seems equally important.

'Get a move on for God's sake!' he says, but he's laughing too. She balances in his arms, finds an empty branch, reaches up and ties the worn tea towel round it, thinking of Fiona swearing over the Wemyss pig, thinking of Cal, sitting on the bench, hammering angrily at the wood. Thinking of his lovemaking and how much she enjoys the sensation of his long body welded to hers.

She could wish for all kinds of things for herself: for the wisdom to know what to do with the house, for her father's happiness, for a nice faithful man in her own life and even, as has lately crossed her mind, for the possibility of a child. Tick-tock says the biological clock. She has been deaf to it until now but it has been there all along and now she can hear it. Soon it will become insistent. But she doesn't wish for any of those things at this moment. Instead, she whispers, so quietly that the wind carries the words away and he can't hear them, 'I wish it would be all right for Cal. Let him keep Carraig. Let things sort themselves out in the right way.'

Then, she braces herself on his shoulders. 'Right,' she says. 'You can put me down now!'

'Thank Christ for that,' he says. 'I don't need a hernia right now.'

She slides down his body, but he keeps his arms around her and pulls her close, kissing her deeply, his tongue in her mouth. She's dizzy with desire for him. There's a big boulder on top of the hill, not far from the tree. It could be the remains of a standing stone, or just a huge piece of granite. It has a smooth, vertical surface. He lifts her again and staggers towards the stone.

'What are you doing?' she asks, but he just shakes his head.

He sets her back gently against the stone, running his hands down her body, tugging at her jeans.

Breathless, she asks, 'Have you got anything? Cal?'

'It doesn't matter,' he says, 'not for this,' and then he's on his knees, pulling down her jeans and pants. She's resting on the stone, which feels curiously warm against her back, threading her fingers through his hair, feeling his tongue, warm and insistent. Momentarily, she wonders what would happen if somebody climbed the hill, saw them, but Hector would bark, wouldn't he? She can hear him snuffling about among the willows. And then she can think only of Cal. She leans against the stone and sees green leaves, white flowers, a pale blue sky and at last a wave of the most intense, helpless pleasure scythes through her.

Then he's looking up at her, grinning wickedly. 'Was that good?'

'Do you need to ask? It was good! But what about you?'

'Don't worry about me,' he says. 'It was good for me too. We'd best go back down to the house before the dog decides we've gone missing.'

'Where is the dog?'

'Over there. I can just see his ears.'

'Why won't he come into this circle?'

'Why indeed. He's spooked, I think. I'm spooked too.'

'It didn't seem to stop you.'

'No. But maybe that's part of the ritual.'

'Do you mean that?'

'No. I'm joking. But we can pretend it is.'

All the same, she wonders. This is a primitive place and with him, all her impulses seem primitive too.

'Are you staying the night?' she asks.

'Do you want me to?'

'Yes, I want you to.'

TWENTY-EIGHT

1589

The winter seemed impossibly long. *How do they bear it?*, thought Mateo, when he woke yet again to a day of thin rain, mist on the hills and grey skies. Francisco carried on teaching the three children as best he could, although Ishbel was by far the most amenable. McNeill had managed to obtain some precious paper and charcoal from the priest, whose small church lay in the south of the island, while Lilias, with her father's permission, had written a letter to her brother to be carried to the mainland by the next visiting vessel. It listed the various pigments, canvases, brushes and other essentials the Spaniard needed to enable him to paint two small portraits. Any more would be prohibitively expensive.

In February there was a brief respite when the young women of *Achadh nam Blàth* and the nearby clachan celebrated St Bride's day. They took a sheaf of oats from the previous year's precious harvest, formed it into a rudimentary figure, dressed it in some scraps of wool and linen, and trimmed it with whatever decorative items they could find: a handful of glass beads from broken jewellery, small shells from the seashore, a garland of daisies, snowdrops, coltsfoot as well as hazel catkins, culled from sheltered parts of the island. The figure was supplied with a slender white wand formed from a piece of birchwood with the bark scraped off. Ishbel had made a bed of rushes covered by a baby blanket close to the house door. There, Bride was welcomed in and laid down comfortably for the night with a couple of candles burning to keep her company.

'She was the foster mother of Christ,' explained Lilias. 'And so we honour her in this way. But she brings the springtime with her as well. Soon, soon it will come.'

'It can't come too soon for me,' said Mateo.

In the morning, the cousins found some of the household looking at the cooling ashes of the fire. 'There they are,' said Ishbel. 'The marks of her wand. She has been wandering about in the night, and there will be a good crop!'

'And a prosperous year,' added Lilias.

Mateo peered into the ashes. There were patterns and spirals there for sure, although nothing that might not have been created by the wind blowing down the chimney. But who was he to quarrel with or to quell their joy?

When it became apparent that the days were lengthening, Mateo learned how to use a *cas chrom*, the long foot plough called the 'crooked foot', which enabled one man, working all alone, to plough several acres of inhospitable and rocky ground so that oats and bere could be planted there. The implement was simple enough, an iron foot over a long wooden shaft with a peg sticking out to one side. The shaft was the slender trunk of a birch tree. It was a long, hard and tedious job, working backwards, slowly and carefully, along a trench, pushing and rocking and turning, pushing and rocking and turning and then starting over again. Once he got into the rhythm of it, there was a certain pleasure to be had from the sheer repetitiveness of it, the physical effort, the chik-chik, chik-chik as the implement sliced into the sod. It took his mind off Lilias and that single thoughtless kiss, hardly a kiss at all. Had it been friendship or love? How could he tell? It took his mind off his home and the weather, the bloody events of the past year, and the uncertain and possibly ruinous future for himself and his cousin. Nobody helped him, although sometimes the islandmen eyed him, in passing, hardly acknowledging his presence.

In March, while Mateo was still working away at his task, dog-gedly, sodden with mud, washing himself in the painfully cold burn afterwards, like a form of penance, Lilias's brother sent a heavy wooden kist, locked and bound all around with iron, to the island. The key to this precious cargo was in the possession of McAllister, whose birlinn had ferried it to *Eilean Garbh*. They opened it to find all that Francisco had asked for in terms of paints and pigments, brushes and canvases and more. Kenneth had postponed his own visit home until the summer, but had sent the things to Islay with a friend, who had engaged McAllister to bring them on to *Garbh* during a reasonably calm spell. Lilias confessed to Mateo that she had no notion how her brother had got the money, the 'siller' she called it, to pay for these things, since her father had sent nothing save the letter requesting them, and Kenneth was always without resources. But he must either have won the money by gambling, or borrowed it, both of which seemed alarming to her. They seemed faintly alarming to Mateo as well, but he was pleased on his cousin's behalf. Ishbel was wildly excited at the thought of having her portrait painted. Lilias was less exuberant, but he could tell from the sparkle in her eyes that her vanity, such as it was, was flattered. He hoped his cousin could do her justice.

McAllister seemed surprised to find the Spaniards still on the island. Perhaps he had expected them to escape. Perhaps he had expected them to be killed. He seemed more surprised still at the nature of his burden as they hauled it up the track to the house.

'Pictures?' he said and spat on the ground outside the house. 'Pictures? He wants *pictures*? Ach, what is McNeill thinking of? What next?'

Iain Og McNeill, a house servant and a remote cousin of the family, who had been sent to help with the kist, sniggered.

Ruaridh McNeill, standing just behind the door, overheard them. 'Aye,' he said. 'And do you know what I'm thinking, McAllister? I'm thinking that I will most certainly be paying you far too much for fetching a wee kist such as this one from one island to another. As for you, Iain Og, have you no work to do?'

Iain Og slunk off, while McAllister had the good grace to look embarrassed. But he and McNeill were soon chuckling over a silver *cuach* of whisky shared between them, the best spirit, redolent of peat and honey, and the best *cuach* too, normally kept locked away for the most important visitors. The truth was that McNeill saw the portraits as giving a certain status to his daughters. Only the wealthy had their portraits painted. He was not wealthy, at least not in terms of gold and silver, but he had a significant number of men at his beck and call and a significant number of cattle, so why shouldn't his daughters have their likenesses done by a real artist. He never doubted that the foreigner was a real artist, and indeed it quickly became obvious that Francisco was very skilled.

Ishbel's portrait came first. They knew that the child wouldn't be able to sit still for very long. Francisco sketched her with charcoal, and then bribed her with sweet cakes, made by Beathag with her precious stores of summer honey. They were at the bitter end of the year and supplies of everything were dwindling, although it had been a mild enough winter and the cattle had done well. McNeill would come in and peer over Paco's shoulder for a while, making him very nervous, but the laird said nothing, only grunted in a noncommittal way. He seemed happy enough with what he saw.

Lilias would sometimes come out to watch Mateo working in the field, the rhythmic push and rock, cut and turn of the *cas chrom*, following every movement, as though following the melody of a song.

'Stop,' she would say, sometimes. 'Just stop and talk to me.'

'I have to finish this stretch of land. I promised.'

'Who did you promise?'

'Your father.'

'If you don't do it, somebody else will.'

'That isn't the point. I gave my word.'

She sighed. 'Ah God,' she said suddenly, 'I do wish the *cailleach* would go to sleep. Can you not feel her, nodding and yawning. Like a child who resists with every wee piece of her. Can you not feel her?'

He came over to where she was perched upon a rock, laid the *cas chrom* down, and sat down beside her, brushing the sour earth off his hands.

'What are you saying? I have no idea what you are saying? Who is the *cailleach* and why must she sleep?'

'I am always forgetting how very little you know. The *cailleach* is the wise old woman. Such as I will become in time, God willing. She walks the fields, bringing winter in her wake. A good thing too. The land needs to sleep and we need to rest for a time, while she walks and renews, walks and renews. Only now, she's growing weary. It's her turn to lie down and sleep. Then the springtime will come. You can feel her clinging on. Soon, she'll not be able to resist. She will lie down and take her rest, and the blessed Bride will come and bring the springtime with her all over again.'

She took his hand, dusty from the *cas chrom*, the nails chipped and stained and dirty, and laid it at her breast. He felt her heart beating strongly beneath his fingers. The stretch of land where he was working, while not remote, was at least hidden from prying eyes. Or so he thought. He held her at arm's length for a moment, afraid of muddying her gown, her wrap, and then unable to resist the desire in her eyes, bent and kissed her full on the lips. Heedless, she pulled him closer. 'Oh my darling,' she said. 'What are we to do?'

'What are we to do? What *can* we do?' he echoed.

'I'm sure I don't know. We have a saying here: what's for you won't go by you. Perhaps we should wait and see what the springtime brings.'

*

They must have been watched. Not closely, perhaps, otherwise the consequences would have been even worse, for Lilias as well as for himself. But from a distance, Iain Og McNeill, returning from some errand for his master, had perhaps lurked and watched and seen what amounted to an unwise intimacy between the incomer and the daughter of the house. Maybe the kiss had been observed. Afterwards, Mateo found himself wondering why the man had not gone straight to Ruaridh McNeill with his suspicions, but then it occurred to him that Lilias would have denied it. Of course she would. She would have described it merely as a friendly encounter, because she was in the habit of bringing the stranger some refreshment when he was working out in the fields like this, as she brought bere bannocks and a flask of ale to the other men and women from time to time. She would have expressed outrage and indignation and Ruaridh would have believed his daughter. Whatever he may have suspected, he would have trusted her. Besides, he was well aware that the presence of the two young Spaniards on the island was causing a certain amount of discontent and even downright hostility among some of the islandmen, who saw them as a threat, as unwelcome strangers, possibly even as enemy spies. They could not go against McNeill's wishes, but the feeling persisted all the same and McNeill knew it.

Mateo had finished his day's work and was trudging home, carrying the cumbersome *cas chrom* as best he could. He was so tired that he could think of nothing except the warmth of the fire, food of some kind and a long sleep. Darkness was coming on. He was passing the walls of a long-abandoned cottage when some never-quite-quiescent sixth sense kicked in, the tingle of danger, and he suddenly became aware of movement out of the corner of his eye. All his old instincts of self-preservation surfaced. Three men were slinking out from behind the remains of a turf wall where they had been lying in wait for him, far enough from the house for them to attack him without anyone coming to his assistance. Three against one. *Bad*, he thought, *but not insurmountable*.

He saw even in the gathering gloom that they had no weapons. So they planned to give him a beating, but would stop short of killing him, knowing that their chief had guaranteed his safety, would be forced to investigate and punish a murder. They circled him warily. They had been hoping to take him completely by surprise but now they had to rely on their greater numbers. He recognised Iain Og, and two more of McNeill's followers, herdsmen. He didn't know their names but they had been among the young men who came down from the shielings in the autumn. They spoke to each other in their own tongue, but he didn't need to translate what they were saying. He had fought enough men, sometimes to the death, to be able to read them. The fight was brief and brutal. They relied on fists and strength but he had the *cas chrom*, which – he immediately realised – was a pretty good defensive weapon if needed. He had been exhausted, but the energy of battle suddenly surged through him and he swung it like a great sword, catching Iain Og on the side and throwing him off balance. The other two rushed forward, but he swung the heavy metal foot back again, sweeping it low to the ground and knocking a second man down. As Iain regained his balance, Mateo carried on swinging in a wide arc, hearing the satisfactory crack of metal colliding with bone. Iain gave a great cry of pain, and hopped away backwards, groaning. One of the attackers had circled behind him, and jumped on his back, throttling him, but Mateo instinctively crouched down low as he had been taught by his father, and used the man's own forward momentum and body weight to throw him to the ground. Sending a little prayer of thanks home to his father, fierce and uncompromising as the man had been throughout his childhood, he stood back, panting, reversing the *cas chrom* and holding it by the weighty metal foot. One of his attackers was winded, one disabled. The third made a last attempt to seize the improvised weapon, but Mateo had the advantage and thrust it forward into the man's belly, knocking him to the ground.

'Enough?' He held the plough ready for another bout.

The three men cursed him and backed off. He couldn't tell

exactly what they were saying, but the general tenor of their words was obvious.

'Leave the lassie alane,' growled Iain Og. 'Do you hear me, interlowper? Leave the lassie alane. You've been warned. Next time we'll bring swords.'

They left him then, the two bruised men helping Iain along, walking on either side of him so that he could take the weight off his leg. Mateo wondered what story they would tell Ruaridh, or Beathag, who would have to tend to their injuries. Not the truth, surely. Reaction set in, and he had to sit down on a stone for a while, to recover himself. He was torn between laughter at the nature of his weapon and fear that somebody really had seen the kiss and would tell tales to McNeill. But when he arrived back at the house, Beathag and the other women were gossiping about the kicking and subsequent broken bone that Iain Og had had from one of the beasts. Lilias was nowhere to be seen.

'It was a clean break, and should heal well enough. But you should never get between a cow and her calf,' said Beathag wisely. 'Let that be a warning to you too, Mateo.'

Relieved and weary, Mateo thought that he and Lilias had had a narrow escape. They would have to be more careful in future. Or perhaps, for her sake as much as his own, he should follow the advice of the three men and 'leave the lassie alane'.

*

For the first time in his life, Mateo envied his cousin. They had been as close as brothers, even though he was so much older, but perhaps for that very reason, he had always been the leader, always giving instructions while Francisco had been content to follow. It occurred to him now that his cousin may have resented this, even though he had never spoken of it. Now, Francisco was spending days, as long as the light lasted, painting the portrait of Lilias. He had already finished a charming study of Ishbel, in her best gown, a basket of clam shells in her hand, like a little pilgrim, and the two dogs at her feet. She looked half young woman, half sprite, 'a changeling for sure,' her father said, but Mateo could see that he was very pleased, and was glad of it. As soon as Francisco began his portrait of Lilias in her yellow gown, with her pearls and her lace, Mateo went back moodily to his ploughing, and stayed there, although he kept a close eye out for angry islandmen and kept his plough at the ready when he was walking to and from the fields. Nobody approached him. With every chik-chik, chik-chik of the blade, he thought about the kiss. Thought about her closeness. The scent of her, the warmth of her. He thought too about all the lines and planes of her, the mathematics of her, the right, perfect proportions of her. He could travel to the ends of the earth and he would never find her like again. The earth was loose beneath the foot plough, so the work could have been worse. The island was damp and windy, but seldom troubled by frosts. His first sight of snow here had been on the distant peaks of another island, but it was a rare winter indeed when snow came to *Garbh*. It was not entirely unknown to him either, since Teide, the sleeping dragon of his island, was occasionally snowy, even while the uneasy earth below the peak was beset by fumaroles.

McNeill followed the progress of the portrait: Lilias in her yellow dress, lace at her breast, pearls at her throat and a spray of entirely imaginary lilies in her hand, for such things were unknown on this island, but not unknown to Francisco, who could paint them from memory. Lilies for a lily. McNeill had plans for the portrait. He had had word that Seoras Darroch of Jura, who had fostered Lilias's younger brother, was still interested in making a match with his daughter. He was a gentleman of superior quality, a man of means, with herds of cattle and plenty of fighting men at his call. A good husband, a good provider too. If Lilias thought that he was also an old husband, she was a girl who could put off till tomorrow anything that she didn't need to worry about today. Independent in so many ways, she was in the habit of obeying her father without question. He had never given her bad advice in her life. Never gone against her wishes. Until now. And even now, she had to admit that he might be right. A marriage to Darroch might be a good thing. He was a prosperous man and, by reputation at least, shrewd.

She spoke to Mateo about it one evening when they were sitting by the fire, in full view of whoever might pass through the Great Hall. He was grateful that she could confide in him, but it was a confidence that was not much inclined to raise his spirits. Her proximity was a peculiar kind of torment to him. It felt as though there was a fine mesh of threads between the two of them, pulling them closer together. With every breath he had to resist the impulse to reach out and touch her. He wondered if she felt the same.

'The truth is that whenever I think about leaving this island, about going elsewhere, going to live among strangers on a bigger, bleaker island altogether, my heart quails. I can't lie about that. I would have to make a new life for myself as the wife of an older man and the mother of his surviving children. It's a daunting prospect. I can't even begin to picture it.'

Having failed to picture it, she dismissed it from her mind until it seemed impossible to choose otherwise. Impossible to quarrel with the plans that were already being drawn up for the marriage.

'I feel,' she said in an undertone, 'much like the poor woman who was enticed to touch the water horse. I'm being dragged along to my doom, and there is nothing I can do to remedy it.'

'Can you not tell your father how you feel?'

'How can I?'

'I don't mean about me. I don't mean for you to tell him that you have any feelings for me. If you have.'

She gazed at him for a moment. 'Do you doubt me?'

'I don't know what to think. But perhaps you could tell him that you have changed your mind. That you don't wish to marry this Darroch after all.'

'The truth is that I never wished to marry him. I was given

no choice in the matter. Assumptions were made. And I didn't contradict them. If I had, I think my father wouldn't have taken it so far, even though it's a good match. Now it's too late. I need the water bull to rescue me.'

'I'd gladly sacrifice myself to save you.'

'But it would do you no good, Mateo. For they would be outraged and they would still make me marry him. Your fate would be very uncertain. My father is a good man, but he is also a hot-tempered man.'

The plan was that Darroch would visit in the spring. There would be a betrothal ceremony. The portrait would be a wedding gift to Ruaridh McNeill's new son-in-law, although McNeill had been heard to say that he would prefer to keep the likeness here on *Garbh*, to remind himself of the much-loved daughter he was about to lose. Francisco, hearing this, relayed it to Mateo.

'I suspect,' he said, 'that McNeill is in no great hurry for the marriage to take place. I think he would be happier if both portrait and girl stayed here on the island. Or at least that's what Beathag told me.'

Difficult as communication was between them, Beathag had grown very fond of the young man. His vulnerability seemed to have struck some chord in her and she mothered him.

'But what use is this to me? Or to Lilias?' Mateo asked, morosely. 'McNeill may not want to lose her, but that doesn't mean he'll consider me a fitting husband, does it?'

'Why not? If she loves you? It seems to me that he indulges her in everything. Besides, we are men of good family.'

'We are penniless foreigners here, Paco. Nothing more. If it comes to a choice between an alliance with a wealthy chieftain and an unwise marriage to an enemy stranger, which one do you think he would prefer? I have nothing to offer her. Nothing.'

The days grew longer, and the Spaniards began to see what Ishbel had meant, last year, when she said that the island would be full of flowers. The house was well named. The stretch of land above the shoreline was a natural tapestry, woven, as Lilias would have it, by 'blessed Bride herself' striding openly through the fields now while the *cailleach* slept: great drifts of early primroses and violets, marsh mallow, self-heal and trefoil, clover, pink campion, bluebells and frothy cow parsley. Across the hills behind the house, the early white of blackthorn soon gave place to golden whin and creamy, sweet-scented may. Mateo thought about the almond trees at home, in all their beauty, but saw that the flowers of this island were just as lovely. Lilias told him of the yellow flag irises and the purple foxgloves that were to come. Clumps of sea pinks would rustle in the breeze along the seashore. There would be roses, delicate pink and white roses scrambling among the rocks and a froth of heady meadowsweet. Lilias told him the names whenever they could snatch a moment together and he repeated them after her. He was dizzy with the beauty of this landscape and dizzy with a desire for her that he could do nothing to remedy or assuage.

Darroch postponed his visit. He sent word, via McAllister, that he had much to occupy him at home. He would come later in the summer. He could not spare the time for a betrothal and a wedding right now. Lilias didn't know whether to be glad or offended. McNeill was offended but tried hard not to show it. Darroch was something of a catch and proud men must be given some leeway. He was a proud man himself and understood this well enough, but his daughter was such a prize. Why did the man not treasure her as he, her father, did? Why did he seem unaware of his own good fortune?

*

The portrait was finished, the spring sowing was done and the cattle had left for the shielings and the higher pastures, taking half the *Achadh nam Blàth* household and the inhabitants of the nearby clachans with them. Mateo noticed with some relief that two of his attackers were among those departing. Iain Og's leg was not yet mended, but as soon as it was sound, he would be joining them. The *cailleach* was asleep, and Bride still danced through the fields, strewing flowers in her wake. While Francisco taught Ishbel the rudiments of drawing and painting, and while McNeill was away on business of his own to the settlements in the south and west of the island, Lilias and Mateo slipped away separately and unnoticed, and met in the privacy of *Dun Faire*. They climbed the crumbling stairs to the higher floors, sitting up there watching the sea, the distant islands, the occasional fishing coble or galley, the patches of wind and the cloud reflections moving across the changing face of the water.

They contrived to meet like this on several occasions, becoming adept at dissembling, leaving the house individually on this or that pretext. It was easier for Mateo, who had the excuse of outdoor work. Lilias was always having to invent excuses for leaving her little sister behind, but since Francisco was complicit in their arrangements, they managed it somehow or other. It helped that so many people had left for the higher pastures, and that McNeill himself was often away from home at this time of year.

For a while, they were happy simply to be in each other's company, but inevitably the desire that had plagued them both could be satisfied only by kissing and soon enough kissing turned to touching. One day Mateo came early to the Dun, bringing his knife that had been returned to him by McNeill, for practical rather than warlike purposes, and cut enough young heather to make a soft bed among the stones. Even as he worked, feeling the rough stems and the soft shoots against his fingers, he knew what his intentions were and how unwise they might be, but the strength of his feelings and the recognition that she felt the same overrode all prudence and propriety. There, on a heather bed, like many young men and women before them, they lay close and made love, lip against lip, breast against breast, arms and legs and at last bodies intertwined, neither knowing nor minding where one person ended and the other began.

After that, passion would not be denied and they met often, becoming careless in their desire. But whatever goddess oversees such things, Bride herself perhaps, was disposed to be kind to them, and their secret remained safe within the ancient walls of *Dun Faire*. Longing to make some gesture of good faith, he took his precious golden ring from its hiding place, next to his heart, and placed it on her finger. She admired it on her hand for a moment or two, kissed him, and then slipped it off to examine it more closely.

'This is the most beautiful gift anyone has ever given me. The hare. The lilies. And have you seen that the hare is leaping sunwise?'

'I noticed it when you spoke about the boats going with the sun. Lilias, it's the only thing of any value I possess. Well, that and my honour. It has been with me for many miles and through many trials. Whatever happens, I want you to keep it.'

She peered inside it. 'What does this say? *Vouz et nul autre*. Is that Spanish?'

'No.' He smiled at her pronunciation. 'It's French. It means you and no other. The ring is from France and it's very old. Perhaps a hundred years. See – there's another inscription too. *Un temps viendra*. A time will come. Maybe our time will come at last.'

'Maybe so, but I don't see how. Maybe this is all the time we have,' she said sadly. 'How did you come to have it?'

'It belonged to my mother. But her great-grandmother came from France, or so the story goes. The ring has been in our family for many years. It's a poesy ring: a love token. The words are words of love but they are worn in secret, next to the skin.'

'Oh my darling, this is a family treasure! Are you sure you want me to have it?'

'You and no other!'

'I'll have to wear it in secret too. I shall put it on a chain, next to my heart. Oh Mateo, how can I bear to leave you? I think my heart will break with the pain of it.'

'How can I ever bear to let you go?'

TWENTY-NINE

Cal stays the night and the one after that as well. Her mother's old bed is much too small, so they make up the bigger bed in Viola's room and move in there. She's glad she cleared this room out first, since it isn't half as odd being in here as she thought it might be. And the bed turns out to be very comfortable. It hardly creaks at all. She's not used to sleeping – actually sleeping – with somebody else. It's been a good long while since she did it. Cal seems equally unsettled by it at first. They toss and turn, feel too hot; he's all bones and muscle and sharp angles, a foreign body in her bed. He manages to open the difficult window and the fresh air from the sea improves things. At last, they find a position that suits them, his chest to her back, their bodies neatly fitting together like two spoons. They fall fast asleep and wake to broad daylight, birdsong and the sound of rain.

He says, into the back of her head, 'Do you suppose she died in here? Your granny?'

She sits up, plumping the pillow. 'What a thing to say, Cal!'

'Does it bother you?'

She thinks about it. 'Actually no, it doesn't. But I think she died in hospital. The room overwhelmed me when I first came into it, and I'm glad I cleared a lot of it out, but I don't mind sleeping in here. Well, I don't mind it with you.'

'And not just sleeping.'

'And not just sleeping. But I often find myself thinking about the things that pass through my hands. Professionally, I mean.' He's grinning, wickedly, and she slaps him. 'Stop it. But don't you wonder about all these things? Who owned them? How did they live and die? What were they like? Who did they love and who did they hate?'

'All the time,' he says thoughtfully. 'I do that all the time. But not everyone in our line of business does, you know. What are your favourites?'

'Textiles. Clothes. Lace, although that's hard to come by. Embroidery. I love embroidery. Women's things most of all. Jewellery too, like the ring. But I know very little about the really precious pieces. Only costume jewellery.'

'I've been thinking about that ring.'

'Me too,' she says. 'Whose was it? What does the inscription mean? *You and no other* is plain enough, but *a time will come*? What time?'

'I don't know. But I've been thinking about the picture too. I think the ring predates the picture. I think it's even older. It has a mediaeval look to it.'

'I wondered that myself. But both of them seem...' she hesitates. 'I mean, OK, the ring inscription is in Old French. The portrait of Lilias is sixteenth century possibly?'

'Yes. But it looks kind of foreign too. There's something about it. It doesn't look Scottish at all. And yet it seems Lilias was Scottish, if it's the same girl, Lilias McNeill. It's a mystery.'

'I love a good mystery. The research is half the pleasure, isn't it?' she says.

'It is. Do you want coffee?'

'Are you offering?'

'I am.' He slides out of bed, finds a towel on the floor where he dropped it last night after his shower. He wraps it round his waist. *He has a nice bum*, she thinks. She can see his tan line. Even this early in the year, he has brown arms and shoulders. If it's warm he must work outside, take off his shirt. She thinks of his arms and hands, working away at some piece of furniture or other. She has a little tremor of renewed desire.

'Back in a minute,' he says.

She hears him pad down the stairs, with the clicketty-click of Hector's nails on the floor beside him. He's chatting amiably to the dog in the kitchen below, letting him out for a pee in the rain, calling him in again. She has a sudden intimation of joy, so intense and overwhelming that she has to close her eyes for a moment, clutching the bedcovers. *How dangerous is this?* she thinks. She can hardly bear his absence. It won't get any better, will it? The 'L' word comes unbidden into her mind. Can this be love? If it is, she suspects she has never felt it before. Certainly never felt such intense and unexpected passion for and empathy with another human being.

She has a sudden insight into her mother, into the reasons why Jess left home, her mother, the island, everything she had once held dear, and never looked back. Perhaps it was very little to do with Viola being an overbearing mother. Or the island seeming too small, too stifling. Perhaps none of that mattered. Maybe it was something at once as simple and as complex as love. The lightning strike of love at first sight. You and no other. If Jessica had felt like this about her father, but realised that Viola would never approve of a wandering musician, why wouldn't she simply pack her bags and go if the opportunity arose, if the feeling was as mutual as it so clearly seemed to have been?

'Whither thou goest, I will go.' She surprises herself by saying the words aloud, as though somebody has put them in her head. 'Thy people shall be my people.'

'What?' He's back, bearing a tray of coffee, closing the door firmly against a disgruntled Hector, who promptly throws himself against it with a bump and a sigh.

'Fuck off, Hector, there's a good lad!' he calls. They hear the dog patter away down the stairs.

'Poor Hector. He'll be feeling neglected.'

'He's spoiled rotten.' Cal pours coffee for them both, climbs back into bed. They sit companionably for a while, drinking. He makes a very good cup of coffee: another of his virtues.

'I've been thinking,' he says and then hesitates.

'What?'

'I've been thinking about the portrait of Lilias.'

'And?'

'How would you feel if I took some photographs of it and sent them to my mum? I know she'd want to see the real thing, but you can tell a lot from a good photograph. She'd be able to – I don't know. Give us a ballpark figure, for the date I mean. She's good. Knows her stuff.'

'OK. Yes, why not?'

'You wouldn't mind?'

'Why would I mind?'

'I thought you didn't trust me.'

'I don't make a habit of going to bed with people I don't trust.'

'Well, I thought that as well. Hoped that. But I can't pretend I'm not intrigued.' He looks around. 'I just love all your stuff, hen!'

'All of my stuff?'

He takes her mug, puts it down alongside his own on the bedside table. Pulls her into his arms and slides down the bed with her. '*All* your stuff,' he says. 'All of it. Every last little bit of it.'

*

A day or two later, he goes back to Carraig. 'I have to finish that dresser!' he says. 'I promised it to Mum's customer, and I'm going to be late with it as it is and it's all your fault.' But he's punctuating the words with kisses. She has work to do as well, not just clearing and cleaning, but her internet shop is badly in need of attention. The broadband is up and running, so she has no excuse now not to do some online selling. She has to take some photographs, measurements, examine things, describe them: all the time-consuming minutiae of online selling. Besides which she should be investigating the possibilities of taking space at a market. Cal has made one or two recommendations and she really ought to chase them up if only by phone or email. Before he leaves, he takes a series of detailed pictures of the portrait of Lilias, and a few close-ups of the ring as well.

'I've promised to send Mum some pics of the dresser, how it's progressing, so I might as well send these at the same time. I know you don't want a valuation.'

'I do want a valuation. Or at least, I wouldn't mind one. It's just that I'm not absolutely certain that I want to sell.'

'What is it with you McNeills and Neilsons?' he teases. 'You never want to sell things. Well, you never want to sell the really valuable things.'

'How can you bear to lose something so precious?'

'My father always says everything has its price,' he says with an undertone of bitterness.

'And do you agree with him?'

He stares at her, candidly. 'For him, it's true. Not for me. Not really. There are some things I could never bear to sell.'

'You mean Carraig?'

'Aye I do. And everything in it. But it looks as though it's going to happen anyway. The bugger is just cruel enough to sell it, contents and all.'

'Don't give up hope.'

'That Clootie Tree had better be getting to work,' he says, as he drives off.

*

Listings ended last week in her online store, and she has put nothing new on for weeks. Here she is, sitting in a house choc-full of collectables and some fine antiques and she really needs to get rid of some of them. So she spends the day taking photographs of the kind of things it's reasonably easy to send through the post: some of Viola's handbags and fancy shoes that look as though they have hardly been worn, a selection of costume jewellery, a wool coat with a distinct look of the 1940s about it, and a crepe de chine slip with lace trim. She hesitates over that, thinking that she might well wear it herself, but she knows that there are more where that came from. She keeps her mother's Laura Ashley dresses and the Marimekko too, but finds a couple of 1970s pant suits lurking in Viola's wardrobe and lists them as well. *True vintage*, she thinks. In one of the drawers, she comes across several hand-stitched cotton nightdresses, stored away for years. But like the linen sheets and tablecloths and napkins, the starch on them has turned sour and they smell peculiar. They'll all need to be washed and ironed. A mammoth task.

She's becoming aware of just how difficult it is to sell personal items. Dealing is easy when you buy at auction or at a boot sale. You can appreciate things, cherish them for a time, and let them go with reasonable ease. She always thinks of it as rehoming. But when they are an intrinsic part of your own past, a past with which you are only just becoming familiar, then it's so much harder. The impulse is to hoard, especially when, like Daisy, you have a great fondness for the past and a desire to know more about it. Again she thinks about Cal losing Carraig and its contents, wonders how he will ever be able to let it go, and feels a wave of resentment against William, whom she hardly knows. How can he do such a thing to his son?

She works assiduously for most of the day, taking pictures, editing them, drafting out enticing descriptions, uploading information. She stops only to take Hector down to the beach in the pouring rain at lunchtime, throwing stalks of seaweed for him, which he brings back and kills, shaking them savagely and then depositing them at her feet.

Later, Cal phones her to say that he has sent the photographs to his mother and has been working diligently on his dresser. He wants to see her soon, but he needs to finish the work, get it out of the way. 'If you don't mind, I'll work on. How about we meet up in the hotel for lunch tomorrow? We've never been on a date, have we? I've never yet bought you a meal!'

'That would be very nice,' she says, disappointed at not seeing him, but equally certain that he's right to slow things down. 'Let's hope it's not pissing down like today.' The rain has come down in a steady stream all day, never once letting up. 'Dreich' is the Scots word for it.

'I get a lot more done when the weather's like this. There's a leak in the corner of the workshop, but if it's going to be sold I'm buggered if I'm going to fix it. Hell mend him. I've put a bucket under it.'

Before he rings off, he sighs, his mouth close to the phone. 'I should never have phoned you,' he says. 'I should just have texted.'

'Why?'

'Because when I hear your voice, I want to fuck you.' He whispers it, as though half ashamed to be saying it. 'And go to sleep with you and wake up with you and do it all again. What have you done to me?'

'I'll see you tomorrow,' she says, firmly. 'Get back to work. I've got a lot more to do as well.'

'OK, OK, I'm going. Tomorrow, about one? In the hotel. I'll book us a table.'

THIRTY

That night, feeling conflicted, Daisy goes back to sleeping in her mother's old room rather than Viola's. It would be too strange, and although they have slept together in this house for only two nights (and not just slept, she can hear him saying), she doesn't want to be in there without Cal. But she sleeps well enough and in the morning the sun is shining on an island washed clean by yesterday's downpour. She checks her online store and notes that there are lots of watchers and even a couple of bids, which bodes well for being able to run a business from the island.

She takes Hector down to the beach, but this time they climb back up to the house along another path at the south end of the garden, closer to Scoull. It is beginning to be very overgrown already here and her trainers are soaked by the time they get back. It means traversing a wilderness of willow scrub, bracken, rampant brambles, small self-seeded elders and wild roses. By the time high summer comes along, it will be a jungle. She can't see any way of taming it, although she can imagine Cal with a scythe might be able to make some inroads into the grassier parts. She's momentarily distracted by the idea of Cal with a scythe, but practically speaking, perhaps she should turn her attention to the areas closer to the house first: the walled garden, for instance. Who knows what treasures might be hidden inside? Specimen plants, perhaps, brought here by the Neilsons. Possibly even older plants, surviving from the McNeill years. She wonders who first decided to establish a flower garden here, and when.

She dries Hector with an old towel – rushing through damp undergrowth has soaked him – and remembers Cal's instructions to check him for ticks, but is relieved to find none. They find his wiry coat hard to negotiate, but still every year Cal has to deal with a few. He has even left her with the appropriate tweezers.

'Watch yourself in the undergrowth as well,' he said. 'They can carry very nasty illnesses.'

It strikes her that for all its urban stresses and strains, you don't have to worry about ticks and adders in Glasgow. Although there are a few bloodsuckers and snakes of the human kind. Especially at car boot sales.

She leaves Hector in the house with biscuits and water and drives to the Scoull Hotel where Cal is waiting for her. He envelopes her in a bear hug, kisses her, pulls her closer, lets her go with some reluctance.

'Lunch,' he says.

They are sitting facing each other, finishing pudding and drinking coffee, when a vision in layers of printed cottons, chunky jewellery, a bizarre knitted cardigan and bright blue sandals comes rushing into the restaurant.

'Cal!' she says. 'Oh and Daisy. How nice to meet you again!'

Cal has leaped to his feet in surprise. He embraces his mother, pulls out a chair for her. 'What on earth are you doing here? Why didn't you tell me you were coming?'

Fiona sits down. 'I got the first ferry of the afternoon. I brought the hatchback. I can take the dresser back if it's finished, Cal. But I had to drive like a maniac to get here in time. I put my foot down on that last long stretch and kept thinking I'd meet a fucking police car round the next corner!'

Daisy can't resist looking round to see if anyone is upset by the profanity, but the restaurant has emptied, and there's only a Latvian waiter, sorting out cutlery and napkins in the corner. Seeing the newcomer, he politely approaches their table.

'Have you eaten?' asks Cal.

'Yes, I had something on the way. Stopped off in Inveraray. And then started looking in shops. Which is why I almost missed the ferry. It was so liberating. Such a novelty. I can't remember when I last came away on my own. I thought I'd hate it, but I didn't. I'll have a coffee, though. And a pudding maybe? Could I have a pudding? Your dad doesn't do puddings.'

She says this so ingenuously that Daisy warms to her even more.

'Mum, you can have anything you want. But what's going on? Why are you here?'

Cal orders a helping of sticky toffee pudding with ice cream for his mother. It is brought to the table by Elspeth Cameron – an unusually large portion, Daisy notices – and the two women embrace enthusiastically.

'I haven't seen you on the island for years!' says Mrs Cameron. 'I've missed you. We all have.'

'I've missed you too. I'm on ... what did they used to call it in the olden days? Furlough. Or maybe not even that. French leave? An unauthorised absence?'

'How long are you here for?'

'Just one night. Probably.' She looks momentarily sad. 'Can I stay at Carraig, Cal? Is that all right? I know I could get a room here, but I'd really like to sleep in the cottage.'

'Of course it's all right. Why wouldn't it be?'

Fiona hesitates, looks from her son to Daisy and back again.

'Mum, you've met Daisy, haven't you?'

'Yes. We met in the shop. Daisy Graham. You're Viola's granddaughter. From Auchenblae.'

'That's right. My completely unexpected inheritance.'

'I can't believe that you didn't even know your grandmother.'

'She was quite lonely towards the end,' says Mrs Cameron, with just the faintest hint of reproach. Before she can elaborate, she's summoned to the kitchen and leaves them to the remains of their lunch with some reluctance.

'Well, from what I knew of Viola,' says Fiona, when she has gone, 'she was something of a loner all her life, so perhaps it was her own doing. She was a great one for repelling boarders. "Don't you get sick of people, Fiona?" she used to say to me. Have you decided what to do with the house, Daisy?'

Cal groans. 'Don't go there, Mum. Poor Daisy's thought of nothing else.'

'He's right. And I still don't know. But I'm not in any hurry. The taxes are paid. Viola had been a great saver. Just that there's no more cash to spend on the house and I certainly don't have any.'

'And old houses can be money pits of the worst kind.'

'They can.'

'Maybe Cal will help you?' she says brightly. 'To sort it all out, I mean. He told me about your picture. Lilias. A time will come. And the ring. A real posy ring. It's so romantic. I'd love to see them, Daisy, if you wouldn't mind. What William wouldn't give to have them in the shop!'

Cal looks alarmed. 'You haven't told him?'

'No. I haven't told him. And I won't. Don't worry. You're not wanting to sell, are you, Daisy?'

'I don't think so. I have a lot of other things I do want to sell, but not those.'

'Donal never sold the embroidered cabinet, did he? I was worried after I heard he'd got married, but I see it's still here, in the hotel.'

'Yes, Mum. It's still here.'

'It's such a piece of island history. And I think so are your ring and your picture, Daisy. I just hate the idea of dismantling something. Of destroying a story. The story of this island. There *will* be a story, even if we never know it or know it only in fragments, like a crazy patchwork quilt. And it's the same at Carraig, in a small way. The fiddle. The garden. They're part of my family's story. Our story. My great-grandfather, seemingly, made violins and that old fiddle is the last one.'

She's silent for a moment, then she eats toffee pudding and ice cream with gusto. 'Oh you don't know how much I'm enjoying this! To hell with the waistline.'

'Cal has been a big help already,' says Daisy.

'I'm very glad to hear it.' She looks from one to the other. A certain shrewd perception crosses her open features, but then she smiles at them both. 'Very glad.'

Her phone buzzes in her bag. She takes it out, glances at it, frowns, then mutes it altogether and puts it back in her bag. Daisy would lay bets the call was from William.

'Problem is,' says Cal, pouring more coffee for the three of them, 'that I don't know how much longer I'll be here. You know Dad's been here. He's planning to sell Carraig. I think he wants me back in Glasgow all the time, working in the shop. Maybe he wants to get rid of Annabel. Who knows? She's not exactly customer-friendly.'

'No she isn't. I could never understand why you went out with that lassie for so long!'

Cal glances at Daisy. She can see, with a certain amount of satisfaction, that he's blushing.

'I thought you liked her, Mum.'

'Your dad likes her. She irritates the life out of me, if I'm honest.'

'I wish you'd told me.'

'Would it have made any difference?'

'Well, no,' he concedes. 'It wouldn't. Not at the time.'

'And is that what you want? I can see you don't want Annabel. Not now. I mean, do you want to be in Glasgow all the time?'

'No. I don't want to be in the shop at all. But I worry about you.'

'I can't have you changing your whole life to suit me.' She looks sad, suddenly. But then she pats his hand. 'Anyway, it's all right. I've told him.'

'Told him what?'

'That I won't sell.'

Cal looks utterly fazed. Daisy realises that this is a very big deal.

'I went to see Mr McDowall. He's your solicitor too, isn't he, Daisy?'

'That's right. He's been incredibly helpful.'

'And to me too. Carraig was mine. OK, your dad has a half share, a significant interest in it. But he can't sell it without my agreement, and I've told him I'll never agree.'

'Christ, Mum!' says Cal.

'I know, I know. It was a bit scary.'

'Did he go ballistic?'

'No. He went very quiet and, well, you know how he is.'

'I know how he is.'

'We all have lines in the sand, Cal. Your dad thinks everything has its price. I don't. Although if it didn't involve you, I'd probably have given in. I always do give in. I know my limitations. But in this case, I'm transferring my interest in the cottage to you. Well, it's already done. I've brought papers for you to sign. He can't sell without your say-so and even if you both agree that you want to sell, he has to give you first refusal to buy him out.'

'I'm gobsmacked,' says Cal.

'I'm kind of surprised myself. You don't think Catty will mind, do you? But I know you'll see her right.'

'No. I don't think she'll mind at all. But what did you say to him? To Dad?'

'I said, he'd better agree, or I'd take early retirement, and then he'd have to find somebody else to work in the shop. I told him I'd been offered a bit of part-time art history teaching. Which is true. But it's only a couple of hours a week. For once, he believed me. He's not very happy.'

'He's never very happy, Mum. And now he'll be very angry as well.'

Daisy has been listening quietly. They both focus their attention on her.

'Oh Daisy. I'm so sorry to take up your lovely lunch with all this boring family stuff.'

'No, it's fine,' she says. 'I was just thinking...'

'What were you thinking?' Cal asks.

'About the Clootie Tree.'

'Is that still there?' asks Fiona. 'I remember going up there when I was very young.'

'Me too. Did your wishes come true, Fiona?'

'Only after a fashion. Although I thought they had. I remember saying exactly that. All my dreams are coming true, I said. I went there with William. Be careful what you wish for, isn't that what they say?'

*

They take a detour to Auchenblae so that they can pick up Hector, who is delirious with delight at seeing Fiona.

'I think he always sees me as the bringer of cake,' she says while he winds around her skirts, wagging his whole body rather than just his tail.

Fiona makes suitably impressed and admiring and sympathetic noises about the house and gardens.

'What a gift. But what a grave responsibility,' she says.

Daisy shows her both the posy ring and the portrait of Lilias with her golden gown, her lace collar, her jewelled head-dress and her red hair.

'How young she looks!' exclaims Fiona. 'And how innocent.'

Daisy is deeply impressed by how this woman, who seemed so whimsical, so Bohemian, suddenly turns solemn and professional when confronted with the portrait, examining it carefully, turning it this way and that in the light, clearly entranced by it.

'Well?' asks Cal impatiently. 'What do you think, Mum?'

'I can't be absolutely certain, you know that. And it would be helpful to take it out of its frame, but I don't want to do that. It's so precious and so fragile. But...'

303

'But what?'

'I think the ring is older than the portrait. I think it *is* French, you're right. And that's not just the inscription. I mean that's a no-brainer. But it could have been inscribed in French and made elsewhere. Except that the style, the enamelling, looks French too. I think it was enamelled. You can just see some remaining fragments. It's very hard to date such things. They were popular for such a long time. But if pushed, I'd say it's fifteenth-century French.'

'So how on earth did it end up here?'

She shrugs. 'Your guess is as good as mine. Washed ashore? All sorts of ships went down off this coast.'

'Yes. We found an old oak block down at the beach, didn't we, Cal?'

'And yet I'm told there's almost nothing of them left. Folk have gone diving down there and seen very little. Bits and pieces wash up from time to time. Maybe the ring too. Where did you find it? Was it in this house?'

'Even stranger than that,' Cal says. 'We found it down there on the beach as well. Hector was digging under a rock, the way he does. Madly.'

'How odd!'

'It was down between two stones,' says Daisy. 'Honestly, if we'd been down there with a metal detector, we'd probably have found nothing. But Hector was digging a big hole and suddenly there it was.'

'Bizarre. But I wonder how it came to these shores. Maybe with some foreign visitor? Do you think that's a possibility?'

'Would they have had visitors like that?'

'Oh, it was far from being as uncivilised as people like to think. Garve – *Eilean Garbh* back then – was a strategically important place for all that it's a small island. Or so I was always led to believe. The Laird of Garve would have been a man of some consequence, even then.'

'When?'

'That's the problem. This may have been an old ring even when it came to the island. People would have treasured such things, just as we do. So, your ring may have been made in the 1400s, but come here in the 1500s. With some merchant. Some trader. Even with the Armada.'

'You mean the Spanish Armada?'

'That's the one. There were shipwrecks. It's a dangerous coast.'

'But didn't people murder them when they came ashore?'

'Not necessarily. Not in Scotland anyway. I think it was much more complicated than that.'

'Things usually are.'

Fiona smiles. 'Aren't they just? This was a Catholic island. They would have been supporters of Mary, not Elizabeth. We forget how divided the place was, back then. How shifting people's loyalties were. How much tension there would have been between the domestic, the requirements of day-to-day living, and the political. Dangerous, dangerous waters. Even now. How much more so back then? We tend to see everything from an English point of view because that's the way it's presented to us. But it would have been a lot more equivocal than that. Here in Scotland. Especially here, on the islands.'

Daisy has known the bare facts, for sure, but Fiona has helped to shift her perspective.

'What a good teacher you must be!' she exclaims, involuntarily. Fiona looks a little embarrassed. It's clear that she's not used to receiving praise.

'All the same, I've never heard of any Spanish ships being wrecked off Garve,' she says regretfully. 'Tobermory yes. But not Garve.'

'And the picture?' asks Cal, practical as ever.

'Later, I think. I would say late sixteenth century. From the costume alone as well as the style. Was there a Lilias then? On Garve? It shouldn't be impossible to find out.'

'There was. There was Lilias McNeill. Her father was Ruaridh McNeill, Laird of Garve.'

'So a fond father had his daughter's portrait painted.'

'We wondered if that was the case,' says Daisy. 'Lovely Lilias, in her posh frock.'

'A very posh frock. But you'd be surprised how much finery might have come from Edinburgh, if you were one of the favoured few. The thing is,' Fiona hesitates, 'it has a continental look, just like the ring. If I didn't know better, didn't know its provenance, I would have placed it somewhere in southern Europe. A piece of Spanish or Italian art. I wonder who the artist was. It isn't signed, is it?'

'Not that we can see.'

'Which together with the ring makes it even more of a mystery, doesn't it? Don't be selling it, will you?' she says to Daisy, impulsively. 'I mean, not unless you have to.'

'No. I don't need to, not right now, anyway, and I'm not planning to. I'm like those people on the *Antiques Roadshow* who go on about something being in the family, so they can't sell it. I was always a bit sceptical, but I understand them now.'

Cal shakes his head. 'What are you two like?'

'He feels the same, really,' says Fiona, confidingly. 'You know that, don't you, but he's far too macho to admit it.'

THIRTY-ONE

1589

In June, word came to *Eilean Garbh* that a number of Spaniards who had taken refuge in various parts of Scotland were to be mustered in Edinburgh and transported home to Spain, via France, from the port of Leith. They had escaped the killing that had ended their ill-starred enterprise only through the good offices of those Scots who were far from well disposed towards the English Queen. This was by no means all of them, and depending upon where they had washed ashore, their position as foreign enemies was still precarious. Besides, some of them were men of means in their own country, and money might be paid for the release of people who were now seen, to some extent at least, as hostages. How far do you go to accommodate the stranger? So said some of the clan chiefs, although others disagreed and said that you went as far as necessary, especially where enemies of the English throne were concerned.

Elizabeth had agreed to a request to grant the ships safe passage, although even those who were less than friendly to the Spaniards saw very little reason to trust her word where Scotland was concerned. But it might be a risk worth taking for those who wanted only to win home again. This news was brought to the island by McAllister, who had been told to relay it to 'all those who had some knowledge of the Spaniards' since their whereabouts had been kept a secret by those who had sheltered them.

McNeill summoned Mateo and Francisco to his bedchamber where they could speak in private and told them of these developments.

'I'm minded to let you go or stay as you choose,' he said. 'You've been no trouble to me. Quite the contrary. You've both worked hard, each man in his own way. I'm aware that there are some who are suspicious of you, but they'll change, in time. They'll accept you and if they won't they'll have me to answer to. If you decide that you want to stay, I propose to rent you some land here. There's decent-enough land in the south that nobody is cultivating. I'm thinking especially of a place called *Dun Sithe*, above the seashore near the high cliffs at the south end. It's not far from Knockbaird, which is the place dedicated to our poets. A bard and his family still live there, although he does little enough in the way of poetry these days and little enough in the way of tilling either. Perhaps the days of heroic deeds are all over. But *Dun Sithe* has been neglected these many years past. The name means the fort of the fairies, the good people. Do you understand what I'm talking about?'

'I think so,' said Mateo. 'Beathag explained that they are somewhere between angels and men. They were cast out of heaven. And they are perilous beings.'

'They are perilous beings if you offend them. Or so folk believe. Which explains why the people are hesitant to plough and sow down there. And those who do plough find the ground full of elf shot, wee arrowheads and the like, and so they are afraid. But there is nothing that cold iron will not drive away. And I hear that you are a good man with a *cas chrom*, Mateo.' He grinned suddenly. 'In more ways than one.'

So he had heard. Did nothing happen on this island that he didn't, sooner or later, hear about? God help them if that was the case.

Mateo smiled uncertainly. 'I am. And I could stay and make a life for myself here. But all the same, and grateful as I am for all that you have done for us, I am minded to go. What about you, Paco?'

Francisco seemed very surprised. 'I thought you would surely want to stay,' he said, colouring up. 'For myself, I'm very thankful for all your hospitality and your generosity, sir. But if there is a chance, however remote, of finding our way home again, then I should like to take it.'

'Should you now?' said McNeill. He seemed disappointed, but quick to disguise it. 'I had hoped that at least one of you would want to stay.'

'Are you sure, Paco?' asked Mateo. He had been certain that Francisco would stay on the island. He would have stayed himself, if he had been able to bear the thought of *Eilean Garbh* without Lilias. He wondered if, yet again, Paco was being carried along against his will.

'Yes, Mateo,' said Francisco very firmly. 'Cousin, even if you were not going to attempt the voyage, I would. I miss my home. I've never stopped missing my home. I'm grateful for all you've done, sir' – this to McNeill – 'but I should dearly like to see my own island again.'

'Ah well, who am I to force you into a course of action that is against your better judgement?' McNeill sighed. 'My lassies will be disappointed. But when Lilias is married and away from here, later in the summer, perhaps Ishbel can go along with her for a while and the experience of new sights and sounds will be enough to cheer them both. My elder son will soon be coming home and searching for a wife of his own. Perhaps a whole crop of grandchildren will raise my spirits.'

'I hope so, sir.'

'You'll sail with McAllister, initially. There are one or two more of you from nearby islands. A scant handful. Our people can keep secrets when there is need, you see. When you come to the main-land, you'll be met, and you should follow the drove roads across to Leith. It's a long journey, but this is the best time of year for it. And you'll be travelling light.'

When they were in their own room again, Francisco gazed at his cousin in some perplexity. 'I don't understand!' he said. 'I was sure that you would wish to stay here.'

'Why would you think that?'

'Lilias,' he said simply. 'You love her and she loves you. I know that you two have been meeting in secret. There have been times when I have smelled the very scent of her on you, at night. Don't lie to me, of all people.'

'But she is to marry another man. Her father wishes it. Her brother wishes it. The plans are made. There's nothing to be done.'

Francisco shook his head. 'Nothing is certain until it happens. You've taught me that, cousin.'

'I have nothing to offer her. It would be folly. And she dare not disobey her father.'

'But she has no feelings for this other man. This Darroch.'

'How could she, when she's met him only a few times? Love may grow. Few of her status ever marry for love. Few of ours either, Paco. It's a dream some of us have. Few ever attain anything but the cold shadow of it. I've heard nothing bad about him.'

'Nothing good, either, I'll be bound.'

'Well, he's considerably older and he has children from his first wife. But he has men and cattle and horses in plenty and a fine house. As big as *Achadh nam Blàth*. Bigger. It will be a good match. She'll be comfortable there. And who could not love her?'

Francisco was silent for a moment or two. Then he repeated, 'But she loves you. I've seen it with my own two eyes. When I was painting the portrait of her, whenever she was sitting and you came into the room, I saw her eyes light up for you. I know I saw it, because I tried to catch it with my brush. And I think perhaps I did. If I'm honest, Mateo, I was envious. I half wished that she would look at me like that. But she never did. Look at the portrait and you'll see that she has eyes only for you!'

'Don't! Don't torment me.'

'You gave her the poesy ring, didn't you?'

310

'How do you know? She wears no ring.'

'She wears it next to her heart, on a golden chain. I've seen the chain and guessed what it held. I see everything. It's what I do. I use my eyes and paint what I see and what I feel. Oh, Mateo, can you do nothing? Will she not tell her father how she feels?'

'I don't think she can. And I can't betray her trust. If I did, her good name would be gone for ever. And we would still be banished. Or slain. We're still the enemy, even here.'

'Have we not won some respect?'

'Our position is equivocal at best. No. It's better to let things take their course. We'll go, as we came, with McAllister. And soon it will be as though we had never been here, and life will resume its old pattern for them, as it should. It's the best I can do for her now.'

*

Heartbreak is not instantaneous. It takes time, like a lingering malaise. Mateo thought he might die of the pain of it, but he didn't. He worked hard by day and was glad of the oblivion of sleep, but as soon as he woke up, he was instantly swamped with more pain. He and Lilias managed one more meeting before the day of their planned departure, slipping out of the house independently, very late one night. She was quieter than usual but when they made love on the heather bed in the old round tower she clung to him in sudden desperation.

'I shall die,' she said simply. 'I shall die. How can I live without you?'

'Don't say that.' He was helpless in the face of her love.

'It's the truth. I can't do without you. I'll have to tell my father.'

'You mustn't. If I thought it would do any good I would have told him myself. Asked him for your hand. But I have nothing to offer you. Nothing that would suffice for the laird's daughter. I don't much care what happens to me, but you would be shamed in the eyes of your people.'

It was a warm night. The dim twilight of midsummer hung over the island. It would never quite get dark. The air was soft and sweet. They heard the sudden sharp piping of an oystercatcher, passing overhead, seeking its mate perhaps.

'Bride's bird,' she said. 'That's St Bride's bird. Perhaps it's an omen.'

But of what, she didn't say.

They rose, dressed, climbed down the stone steps and walked along the shore below the Dun. She kilted up her skirts and paddled out into the water a little way. Her hair was loose, the heavy red length of it, and when she bent down and lifted water in her cupped hands, he saw that the droplets glowed and shone with their own inner light as they fell. He caught his breath.

'Is this magic?'

She laughed, close to tears. 'No. It's no magic. Or only in the way that all beautiful things are magical. It's usual, on fine summer nights like this one. Our fishermen speak of it often.'

'How can I leave this place?'

'Don't go!'

'How can I stay when you're marrying somebody else?'

They walked back to the house, but separated before they reached the door. He let her go first, heard her greet the man who was on watch in friendly fashion. 'The night is so fine that I thought I would walk along the shore!' she said. She went inside by a private stair that led up to her and Ishbel's chamber, high up in the tower. He lurked outside for a while and then went round by a circuitous route, and in by another door, where Francisco was waiting for him.

'Come and see,' he said. 'Come and see what I have done!'

In the room they had shared for so many months, the portrait of Lilias was propped up against the wall. The little crusie lamp was burning. By its uncertain light, Mateo saw that Francisco had inscribed, across the background to the portrait, the words *Un temps viendra*. A time will come.

'My work,' he said. 'I thought it a fitting inscription.'

'What will they say when they see it?'

'I doubt if they'll even notice it. Not McNeill, anyway. He doesn't have his letters, does he? It will mean nothing to him. But it may mean something to Lilias.'

A few days later, McAllister sailed into the bay. The birlinn anchored offshore, and the light tender was rowed ashore and hauled onto the sand. The two Spaniards were carrying packs made of hide, containing a few spare clothes for the journey and enough food to last them for some days: oatmeal for mixing with spring water to sustain them along the way, oat bread and cheese, flasks of ale and a little whisky. More than they had arrived with, anyway. Beathag had hugged them, and then run off, weeping, her face buried in her apron. Ishbel had done the same. Lilias was nowhere to be seen, and McNeill, who was resolved on walking down to the shore to wish them a safe voyage, seemed annoyed. The dogs were frolicking around him, uncaring. All comings and goings were alike exciting to them, as long as McNeill himself or his daughters did not leave.

'The least the lass could do is show herself to wish you God speed and a safe journey,' McNeill said, irritably.

'Perhaps she dislikes goodbyes as much as we do!' said Mateo, bleakly. 'Don't scold her on our account, sir. We saw her earlier. Give her our good wishes for her wedding.'

'Hmm.' McNeill persisted in his ill temper, although whether it was at the disturbance of their departure, or at the thought of the forthcoming wedding, they could not say. He was a man who liked things to be the same, day by day, week by week. To everything there was a season.

The tender was floated, the Spaniards stepped in, being careful to step into the middle, so as not to overturn the little craft. Then one of the oarsmen pushed it off the sand, and stepped deftly aboard, picking up the oars as he did so, making sure that the boat turned with the sun. As they began to pull away from the white shore,

Mateo looked up and saw Lilias standing – as she had stood on the day of their arrival, last autumn – on the very tip of the promontory, close to the Dun. She was wearing her yellow gown, and her hair was streaming out in the sudden breeze that seemed determined to push the coracle back towards the island. The oarsmen cursed and struggled to keep her right. Slowly but surely they began to make way. Looking down, Mateo could see an underwater garden through clear water, another world, like a mirror of this one, where anything might be possible. Out on the skerries, seals were singing, sounding curiously human. No wonder the islanders told stories about seal men and women, strangers who came ashore and stole the hearts of humans. Did all such tales end in disaster? Need it always happen?

He looked up again and was lost.

She was calling to him, frantically, her arms extended and wide open to him. He didn't think twice. He left bag and baggage, half stood up, and then, almost upsetting the tender and risking throwing the other men into the sea, he went head first into the water. The intense cold was a shock. He had forgotten that the waters here never really grew warm. For a moment or two he was under the surface. Time slowed. He opened his eyes, saw the reddish sea ware waving sinuously below him, like a woman's hair. Saw crabs walking sideways along the bottom. Saw tiny silver fishes swarming and scattering in front of his gaze. Then he broke the surface like a seal himself, the droplets cascading down his face and his hair. He was gasping for breath, his heart pounding with the shock of the sudden immersion. But he was floating. He saw the surprised faces of the men in the boat, saw Francisco break into a smile. Already the tender was moving away in the direction of the birlinn. Leaving him behind.

His cousin cupped his hands. 'Go!' he shouted. 'Go back! God go with you!'

Mateo raised a hand in acknowledgement, almost sank again, and then turned towards the shore. It was further than he thought, and before he reached shallow waters, he was struggling. Suddenly, there was a flurry of activity, and he saw that Lilias had pulled up her skirts and was wading through the water, heedless of her fine gown, heedless of her father who, quite unable to swim and thoroughly bemused by the turn of events, was wringing his hands on the shoreline – 'Come back!' he called. She paid no attention to him at all, but stretched out her two hands to Mateo again, and hauled him ashore. She toppled backwards and he fell forwards and they lay for a moment, quite winded, laughing and crying simultaneously. The dogs thought it was some wonderful game. They gambolled about, licking faces, tugging at clothes, delirious with delight.

It was Mateo who got to his feet first, pulling her with him. He had captured her hand in his and was vowing that nobody would ever prise them apart again, even if her father killed him for it. But he spoke in Spanish, lest McNeill should suit the action to the words.

McNeill stood in front of them, frowning, shaking his head in astonishment. The tender had reached the galley, and Mateo saw them unfurling the sail, preparing to leave.

'What is the meaning of all this?' McNeill asked. 'Daughter? Mateo?'

Mateo shook himself and the drops scattered onto the sand. 'Sir, I should like to marry your daughter. I love her. I have loved her from the moment I first set eyes upon her, and I will go on loving her until death and beyond.'

Lilias looked, clear-eyed and defiant, at her father. 'He's my husband,' she said. 'Do you understand me, Father? The man I want to share my life with. He wants to stay here with me. I want to be his wife.' She moved her hand to her stomach, damp with seawater. 'I think I *need* to be his wife. Do you understand what I'm telling you? Will you agree to this match? You'll not shame me, will you, you who have always been so kind to me?'

McNeill was speechless for a moment or two. It was not a

315

condition in which he ever found himself. He puffed out his cheeks and blew a breath out, slowly, buying time perhaps.

'Darroch will be angry,' he said at last, as much to himself as anyone else. He shook his head. 'I think I shall just have to pay him. Siller settles most matters, does it not?' He turned to Mateo, frowning. 'But it must come out of your wife's dowry, Spaniard. I take it...' he halted, anxious to regain his dignity. 'I take it you've changed your mind about the offer of *Dun Sithe*? I take it you want to stay here, on *Eilean Garbh*, and become my tacksman as well as my son-in-law?'

Mateo found himself bowing and nodding, still holding Lilias by the hand. The water dripping steadily from both of them somewhat undermined this attempt at dignity. He realised that McNeill was trying hard not to laugh. 'I do, sir.'

'Then so be it. Although I wonder that you had to half drown yourself and my daughter besides, to achieve what you could have had for the asking.'

*

It was much later when Lilias realised that, in the struggle to save Mateo from the sea, her chain had broken and the poesy ring had gone missing. They spent time down on the seashore, hunting for it, but they never found it again. Mateo realised that it did not worry him unduly. It seemed a fair exchange: a sacrifice of sorts, a ring, however prized, for a much-loved wife. In due course, somewhat earlier than might have been expected, there came a much-loved daughter, too, the first of many children. Perhaps the sea had taken what it needed in exchange for the gift of a future. Perhaps St Bride, whom he discovered was also responsible for boats and boatmen, had taken it for herself. Seoras Darroch professed to be angry at the loss of a bride, but it soon became apparent that the delay on his side had been the result of his sudden fondness for one of his house guests, a lady of more mature years, whom he married very soon after.

They never heard from Francisco again.

Stories were told that Elizabeth had betrayed the Scots yet again in her hatred of Spain, that although she had granted the ships safe passage, she had managed to get word to the so-called Dutch Sea Beggars, seamen of fearsome repute, who had waylaid the Scottish ships, and that many sailors had died in their attacks. Still, some had managed to win home. Perhaps Francisco was one of them. They liked to think so.

The portrait of Lilias remained at *Achadh nam Blàth*, to remind McNeill of his elder daughter, although truth be told, he was always finding or making excuses to ride to the south of the island to see her and her husband in their hilltop house, where Mateo was always turning up elf shot with the *cas chrom*. But perhaps the cold iron was effective against the wrath of the fairy folk, for no harm befell them. If McNeill noticed the inscription on the picture, he did not remark upon it, but then, he could not read.

Mateo de Tegueste fulfilled the single request that McNeill made of him, beyond the relinquishing of some of his daughter's dowry to placate Seoras Darroch. Truth to tell, he would have taken her without a *tocher*. He would have taken her even if she had come to him in her shift. But he did not say as much to Ruaridh McNeill. That would have been beyond his pride and besides, Lilias had forbidden him from saying it, and he had fallen quickly into the habit of doing exactly as he was told, where she was concerned at least. Thus, they began how they meant to go on.

He did, however, change his name.

Records show that in the year of Our Lord 1589, one Matthew McNeill, a visitor to the island and a gentleman, was lawfully married to Lilias, eldest daughter of Ruaridh McNeill, Laird of *Eilean Garbh*, of whom he subsequently became tacksman, holding lands at *Dun Sithe*, for himself and his many heirs in perpetuity.

THIRTY-TWO

Much later, they are all four of them, Cal, Daisy, Fiona and Hector, at Carraig. The humans have eaten cheese and biscuits and are still drinking an inadvisable amount of wine, while Hector has been salivating over the occasional piece of cheese that has come his way like manna from heaven. The weather seems to have settled for the time being. The house is warm, bathed in late evening sunlight that is slanting in through the bedroom window at the back of the house. The sunset is colouring the western sky from deep crimson to palest pink but the living room is falling into shadow. Fiona has shed her cardigan and sandals and has her feet up on the sofa, with Hector leaning against her to have his ears scratched. Daisy is in the big armchair and Cal is sitting at her feet, leaning back against her. The temptation to stroke his hair is becoming too much for her but she is slightly distracted by Fiona's presence. She is also worried about going back to Auchenblae. They have all drunk so much. Given that Fiona will either be taking Cal's bed or the sofa bed, she wonders where on earth she will sleep. Then she realises that Cal is stroking her feet. Surreptitiously, she reaches down and runs her hand across the back of his neck, where the hair grows softly over his collar.

'Right,' says Fiona briskly. 'Sleeping arrangements. I don't mind the sofa bed. It's very comfortable. I take it Daisy's staying. And there's more room through there, Cal.'

Daisy finds herself blushing. But she sees that Cal has gone rather pink as well. The back of his neck has, anyway.

'Oh for goodness sake,' says Fiona. 'Anyone with an ounce of awareness could see that you two are an item, so why pretend otherwise?'

'It's kind of new for us,' confesses Daisy.

'Is it? You look as though you've known each other for years.'

This is true, and also disturbing.

They set up the sofa bed for Fiona while she commandeers the shower room. She comes through wearing scarlet tartan pyjamas and clambers into bed. She seems to fall asleep almost instantly, snoring gently, with Hector lying contentedly at her feet, but then, as Cal says, it has been a very long day for her. And for the dog too.

They go to bed in the next room, the door jammed shut, and conduct a conversation in whispers, so as not to wake her.

'What do you think of it all?' he says.

'Aren't you happy about Carraig?'

'I'm delighted. And she's presented me with a fait accompli. But I worry about her all the same.'

'Your father?'

'Aye. It sometimes feels as though the sky will fall if she crosses him. As though all hell will break out but I don't know why. I sometimes feel that way too, although I've fought against it, and him, all my life. Catty was the bravest of all of us and she's supported me through thick and thin. But we can't make Mum's choices for her. And in some strange way, I think she still loves him. Always has done, always will.'

'He won't be happy about it, will he?'

'No. He won't.'

'What will he do?'

'I don't know. Nothing right away. That's not the way he works. He's a great believer in the revenge served cold theory. So he'll bide his time and get his own back. He never forgets an injury. Never forgets and never forgives.'

'You make him sound like a monster.'

'He's a narcissist, that's for sure. Why does the world excuse men with talent for behaving badly?'

'Because they're men? With talent? It's outrageous, but they seem to get away with it. Can't you persuade your mum to stay on? Even for a little while?'

'I've tried. She's set on going back. She'll take the dresser, so that's one less trip for me to make. I have other projects I want to work on.'

'There are things in my house you could work on too. The bed. But I'd quite like to keep that. I was wondering if the carved oak bed would fit in Viola's bedroom.'

'The oak bed? Really? Something else you don't want to sell?'

'I know. But it would be fun, wouldn't it? To sleep in that bed. Not in the tower, though.'

'Lots of room to move,' he says, sliding his arm around her. 'Talking of which.'

They make love silently, which is something of a feat and also surprisingly stimulating and intense.

In the morning, they have breakfast together, and then Cal and Daisy haul the heavy dresser out of the workshop and manage, with a great deal of huffing and puffing and a good deal of hindrance from Hector, to install it in Fiona's hatchback.

Fiona hugs Daisy and kisses her on both cheeks before getting into the car. 'Look after him!' she says. 'I worry about him, you know.'

'He worries about you too.'

'I'll survive. Good luck with the house.'

'You'll have to come back and see it properly. You haven't seen the half of it yet.'

'I will,' she says.

'Promise?'

'I promise.'

Hector sits sadly watching her go. The car – laden with the dresser – labours up towards the lane where she gives a cheery double hoot, and then drives off towards the ferry terminal. The cottage seems emptier without her. She's such a large, vibrant presence that it's hard to imagine her being cowed by anyone, let alone her own husband.

Cal and Daisy sit outside in the sunshine, watching Hector, who is eyeing the birds squabbling over the feeder, his ears semaphoring his intense interest.

'Do you think she'll be all right?'

He shrugs. 'Oh, sweetheart, your guess is as good as mine. I worry about her a lot. I have to keep reminding myself that she's a grown woman and she can probably cope. But she's my mum and I love her.'

'She's a very lovable person.'

'She's not the only one.' He turns to her and kisses her very tenderly. '*Vous et nul autre*,' he says.

'*Un temps viendra*.'

'My flower girl. From Flowerfield. What do you want to do today?'

'We should be working.'

'I know we should. But there's always tomorrow. It isn't every day you meet the love of your life, is it?'

She takes a deep breath. 'Let's walk from here to Auchenblae. Is the tide out?'

'I think so.'

'Then let's walk along the sand. Let's walk home along the shore and see what the sea has brought in for us today.'

ACKNOWLEDGEMENTS

Thanks are due to the many good friends, including my Scottish island friends, who have motivated me to create Garve and Flower-field. I'm indebted to Oenone Grant for a great many fascinating conversations about art and antiques and to Alison Bell for all our 'Dobbies days' that have kept me on track and inspired. I don't think I could have done it without you. Thanks must also go to Gary Skilling for information about inheritance and taxation, to all at Thomas R Callan, the friendly saleroom in which I learned so much about antiques and collectables over many years. Huge thanks to my best ever editor, Ali Moore, to Sara Hunt, Robbie Guillory and all at Saraband, and to Joe de Pass for the perfect and perfectly beautiful map of Garve. Finally, love as always to my artist husband Alan Lees, who first painted the island for me to my somewhat demanding specification, and to our son Charles. I couldn't have done it without you either.

THE ANNALS OF FLOWERFIELD

WILL CONTINUE WITH

THE MARIGOLD CHILD

When Daisy Graham and Cal Galbraith are renovating Auchenblae, they make a distressing but intriguing discovery hidden behind 16th-century panelling in the ancient stone tower. It is an uncanny find that will herald a family crisis – and lead to momentous changes for all of them, not least Cal's much-loved mother, Fiona.

Meanwhile, on 17th-century Garve, Ruaridh McNeill's grandson Kenneth, an uncompromising and pugnacious man and now the laird, desperately wants an heir. His Irish wife, Róisín, is pregnant, but she has twice given birth to stillborn girls and feels trapped in a situation she is powerless to control. Can travelling poet Alasdair Galbraith and his sister Catriona do anything to help the unhappy young woman?

And in the present, why does the island legend of Lus-Màiri, the changeling child, seem so relevant to the history of Auchenblae – and to Daisy herself?

ABOUT THE AUTHOR

Catherine Czerkawska is a Scottish-based novelist and playwright. She has written many plays for the stage and for BBC radio and television, and has published eight novels, historical and contemporary, including *The Physic Garden*, *The Jewel*, and *The Curiosity Cabinet* (with the same Scottish island setting as *The Posy Ring*) for Saraband. Her short stories have been published in many magazines and anthologies. She has also written non-fiction in the form of articles and books and has reviewed professionally for newspapers and magazines. *Wormwood*, her play about the Chernobyl disaster, was produced at Edinburgh's Traverse Theatre to critical acclaim in 1997, while *The Curiosity Cabinet* was shortlisted for the Dundee Book Prize in 2005. Catherine has taught creative writing for the Arvon Foundation and spent four years as Royal Literary Fund Writing Fellow at the University of the West of Scotland. When not writing, she collects and deals in the antique textiles that often find their way into her fiction.

ALSO BY
CATHERINE CZERKAWSKA

   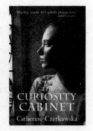